SECRETS REVEALED

Jacqueline Miller

Secrets Revealed
Author: Jacqueline Miller
Editor: Brenda E. Cortez
Proofreader: Jean Sime
Layout: Michael Nicloy
Cover Design: Michelle Fairbanks

ISBN: 979-8-9907205-6-5

Published by BC Books, LLC, Franklin, Wisconsin
Quantity order requests may be emailed to the Publisher:
info@bcbooksllc.com

Printed in the United States of America

Dedicated to Jack, for his enduring support
through all the "twists and turns of the river."

CONTENTS

PROLOGUE

The trailer was silent, except for the distant sound of a boat motoring on the river. Carrie sat on the deck, one hand cradling a cup of beer, the other gently probing the bruise under her eye. It throbbed faintly—a painful souvenir from a night that spiraled out of control.

Across the deck, Tori leaned against the railing, holding an ice pack to her swollen and purple eye. Her split lip oozed tiny droplets of blood as she stared at the floor, her exhaustion palpable.

"We need to start going somewhere else for next summer," Tori said in an emotionless flat voice.

Jen stood aside, looked at her friends, and let out a tired, unintentionally humorous laugh. "Yeah," she murmured, "We really do."

Outside, the river glistened in the sunlight, a picture-perfect contrast to the chaos that had unfolded within the group. But the scars, both visible and hidden, told a different story. One of fractured friendships, buried secrets, and the kind of drama that seemed to follow them like a storm cloud every summer.

Yet, Carrie couldn't shake the feeling that this place—their summers here—was more than just a backdrop to the turmoil. It was a mirror, reflecting truths about themselves they weren't ready to face.

PART ONE

2002

CHAPTER 1

"You and Tom should come to Riverbanks for the Fourth of July," Jen suggested. "My parents have a trailer up there, but since they moved to Colorado, we can stay there anytime. We could ask Dylan to come too. He has been out of control lately with drugs and hanging out with the wrong crowd. It would be good for him to get away from all that. I also invited Drew and Tori. You met Tori. She shoots darts with us on Terri's team."

Carrie contemplated Jen's invitation and then responded. "Sure, that sounds like a fun time!"

The plans were set to go to Riverbanks on the Friday before the Fourth of July, and Jen and Carrie were determined to bring Dylan along. It was Tuesday, wing night at the Pub, and no doubt he would be there. Since his divorce, he rarely missed a night at the Pub, and a foul-mouthed, drug-induced male or female companion usually accompanied him.

"Hey loser, we knew we'd find you here," Jen announced.

Jen's deep, sultry voice often turned heads, so Dylan slowly turned around to see who it was. Her voice always sounded raspy as a result of her extreme smoking habit, and part of how she earned the nickname Whiskey Jen.

"Heyyy," Dylan stooped down to hug Jen and looked behind her shoulder at Carrie.

"Hey, you, long time no see." Dylan winked at Carrie. He had the appearance of being slightly buzzed, which made him even more charming to Carrie.

"We came to rescue you," Jen exclaimed.

"Nah, I don't need rescuing," he replied.

"Of course you do! You're not back with that booze hag, are you?" Jen's loud voice turned heads again, and Carrie and Dylan pulled her away from the bar.

"Shhh… no, that girl is crazy." Dyan looked around to ensure no one could hear. "She came here last night all wigged out and was looking for me, but I was gone already."

He stumbled over a little. Carrie thought maybe he was high since his eyes seemed a little glassy. She knew that look.

"Well, alright then. Perfect. You are coming with us to Riverbanks! I have a trailer up there, and we're going for the Fourth of July." Jen took a drag of her cigarette. "You need to get away," Jen said as she looked at him with apparent disdain for how he had been carrying on.

The rumor was that some friends took in Dylan

after Ally left him and moved out of state. They had heard he was hanging out in "drug houses" and surrounding himself with pill poppers and coke heads, which is not the path they wanted to see him go. Jen and Carrie decided early in their 20s that they did not want anything to do with drugs and that they would not associate themselves with users. They considered alcohol and occasional pot smoking the only acceptable vices.

"Wait, wait, wait, what's the setup? I mean, where would I sleep?" Dylan slid over to Carrie and put his arm around her. "Can I sleep with you?"

Carrie knew Dylan had a thing for her. It developed more recently, as she had lost weight and was married. Unattainable attracted Dylan. She had a crush on him, too, but more in a playful way. She liked to flirt with him, but would never take it further. Still, the attention from any man always enticed her to be a bit naughty. The margaritas she had with Jen earlier didn't hurt.

"My husband wouldn't like that, but then again, he'll probably be passed out somewhere," Carrie replied as she pulled him close to her. She could smell the booze and sweat on him, but somehow, it smelled exciting, unlike Tom. Dylan was a tall, fit guy, much more appealing than her increasingly tubby husband.

"He won't care," smirked Dylan.

"Now, you two, no funny business! You have the couch, and you, my friend, are in the bedroom with your husband."

Jen had a way of being the one to rein Carrie in when she got carried away. She pulled her away from Dylan and gave him a shove, so he stumbled back, laughing the whole time. "We're leaving on Wednesday. Tom is going up early to fish. You can ride with me and Carrie. We'll pick you up after work. What time do you get off?"

Dylan looked at both of them with a smirk. "Whenever."

"We are going to have the time of our lives!" exclaimed Carrie, and they all toasted their beers.

~ ~ ~

As planned, the girls picked up Dylan at the shop where he worked. He had his duffel bag packed and was ready to go. It was a hot, sunny day, and they were both so excited that they practically skipped to the car once he came out. The friends have always felt so free and wild together, without their significant others.

"Grab me a Smirnoff, Dylan."

Carrie sat in the front seat while Jen drove. Dylan sat in the back seat, relaxed with his long legs stretched out and bare feet on the console. He reached into the portable plug-in mini fridge and pulled out Carrie's favorite pre-game drink.

"Keep that bottle down!" Jen demanded.

"I've got your lipstick painted on my dipstick," Dylan sang between gulps of his beer.

"Wait, that's not the lyrics." Carrie interrupted as they all laughed hysterically because of the play on the actual lyrics of The Cult song.

Carrie faced back towards Dylan with her cold bottle of Smirnoff. She wore her favorite tan linen shorts, which fit loosely since she had started slimming down. She had a new exercise obsession along with a habit of drinking more and eating less. There was a feeling in the air, as the hot breezes messed up their hair, that this summer in Riverbanks would be one hot, fun time. Carrie envisioned the endless margaritas and felt both anxious and excited in anticipation. They sang along to The Cult's "Painted on My Heart," using Dylan's more sexy lyrics, praying this feeling of fun and freedom would never end.

"I wonder if Tom caught any fish or if he's just catching a buzz," Jen commented. "I mean, the fishing isn't that great without a boat, and there are plenty of bars to visit if he is bored."

"I don't know. It depends on what Tom is drinking." And just like that, the mood in the car came down a notch." If he's drinking brandy, there's no telling." Carrie turned herself to face forward and slumped down in her seat a little. "I wish he weren't even coming, but I don't know how I could have gotten away with that. I want to have a good time and not have to deal with him."

"What do you mean? I thought you guys had fun together. I mean, it always looks like it." Jen looked at Carrie more closely, as if trying to read her.

Dylan was digging around in the cooler to find a beer for himself. He also grabbed a Smirnoff for Carrie and leaned forward to offer it to her. She accepted it as she looked up at him with sad brown eyes.

"What's going on, girl?" Dylan asked with his warm smile, as if to make her feel like she should have no cares in the world. He was comforting that way.

"Oh, Tom's just an asshole." Carrie pulled her knees up to her chest and lit a cigarette. "And he can be dangerous when he's drinking."

Jen turned around and looked at Dylan and then back at Carrie. Everyone in their group liked to drink, as did she. But this was different. Carrie's tone and body language gave off a sense that his drinking was something more profound and darker.

"Well, nothing's gonna change if you don't make it happen," Jen replied. They could all sense her stern yet loving tone.

CHAPTER 2

The car hugged the curves of the winding road, the tires humming against the pavement. Cornfields stretched endlessly, their green stalks swaying in the breeze. The river teased them, flickering in and out of view between the rows of crops, its surface sparkling under the midday sun.

"There it is!" Jen pointed ahead, her voice rising with excitement.

The billboard loomed large against the empty sky, its weathered letters proudly announcing Riverbanks Resort in bold, faded colors. An arrow directed them to a narrow turnoff, and Jen gripped the wheel as the energy in the car shifted.

The road curved sharply, and then, as if on cue, the river came into full view, winding lazily through the landscape. The sight of the shimmering flowage left the friends breathless.

"Look at that," Carrie murmured, leaning forward for a better view.

Rows of cozy cabins and trailers were nestled along the riverbanks, each bursting with life. Kids darted between makeshift volleyball nets while adults cast fishing lines from weathered docks. Smoke rose from the grills, carrying the mouthwatering scent of burgers and hot dogs.

Red, white, and blue banners hung from decks and porches, fluttering in the breeze. Boats of every size and color dotted the water, their passengers waving and laughing as they passed.

Jen slowed the car, taking it all in. The familiar buzz of the resort filled the air, and she couldn't help but smile as the excitement spilled over from the back seat.

"Alright," Dylan said with a grin, breaking the moment. "Let's get this weekend started."

"Wow, this place is rockin'," Dylan exclaimed while his head poked out the window. "I hope there are some single chicks here."

"Dude, we're your girlfriends this weekend," said Jen.

Dylan smirked, shaking his head as he glanced between the two girls, his voice steady. "I'm not sleeping with either of you, so that's a load of crap."

His eyes drifted across the crowd, scanning the couples scattered around the resort. But then, something caught his attention—groups of young women on a deck outside one of the bars, laughing and chatting in the sunshine. They wore shorts and baseball caps without a care in the world—his kind of crowd.

Dylan tugged at the brim of his cap, a habit more than a need, and surveyed the scene. His Adidas shirt and cargo shorts were practically a uniform around here. He'd blend right in.

They turned down a narrow road and headed to the back of the bar and restaurant, where the trailers lined up in a patchwork of old and new. The newer models were farther down, their sleek exteriors a sharp contrast to the weathered ones that had been here for years.

Jen's trailer sat at the far end, tucked behind River's Edge bar, standing alone like a relic. It was one of the oldest in the park. Creeping rust accompanied the black-and-white peeling paint, and its faded charm gave it the appearance of having been untouched since the '70s, if not earlier. Despite its rundown appearance, the trailer offered a surprising amount of privacy, nestled far enough from the row of rentals across the lot.

The deck out front was large enough for a grill and a few chairs, perfect for lazy afternoons spent with cocktails in hand. Beyond that, a wide patch of grass stretched out, dotted with a few worn grills—ones you'd find at a beach. A group of young people tossed a Frisbee around and sipped beers, their laughter cutting through the summer air.

Jen pulled up in front of the trailer, and the car door flew open before she could even come to a complete stop. They scrambled out, eager to see what lay inside, forgetting their bags in the backseat. Jen grabbed the key and twisted it into the rusted lock.

"Voila!" she declared with a grin, as though unveiling something grand, though the words didn't quite match the reality of what awaited them.

The door creaked open to reveal a blast from the past: shag carpeting in an unfortunate shade of yellow and orange, like a relic from a '70s sitcom. Floral curtains draped the windows, faded and threadbare, while a couch, covered in a floral fabric, sat in the corner. Dusty fake flowers cluttered every available surface, and a small, old-fashioned tube TV sat in the corner, its screen somehow managing to look even more outdated in the time capsule-like space.

Carrie couldn't shake the feeling that spiders had long since taken refuge in the corners, waiting for the unwelcome disturbance of new guests. The air smelled thick with mildew, like an old cabin or a grandma's house that hadn't been aired out in years.

The rugged charm felt oddly comforting despite the dated decor and musty scent. It was the kind of place that could withstand whatever chaos their group could throw at it over the weekend.

Carrie and Dylan exchanged glances, both grinning as they wandered through the trailer, taking in their temporary home. Carrie moved toward the kitchen, curious to see what it had to offer. She opened the cabinets, scanning the shelves. Salt and pepper shakers, bottles of oil, mismatched plates and cups—it was all there, simple but sufficient.

"Perfect," she murmured to herself. They had all

chipped in and brought food for the weekend, and Carrie's task was to get the sandwich fixings for the swimming pond. Her fingers brushed over the stack of sandwich bags neatly tucked in one of the cabinets. Jen must keep it stocked for weekends like these, Carrie thought, smiling at the thought of the little details that made it feel like home.

Dylan was busy checking out his sleeping quarters—the pull-out bed in the main living room area. He patted the old couch, knowing it had to be uncomfortable.

"This will be mighty comfy later when I am passed out."

"Remember, there is no room for girls in here, Dylan," Jen said with her arms crossed across her ample chest.

He looked at her with a sly expression. "There are always the bathrooms in the bar."

"Ewww," exclaimed Jen and Carrie at the same time.

"Keep your pecker in this weekend," replied Jen while opening up windows to freshen up the place.

"I've got your lipstick painted on my dipstick." Dylan sang with a cigarette dangling out of his mouth.

"We need music!" yelled Carrie.

Jen opened a cabinet and pulled out a small radio. Based on its appearance, it had to be from the fifties, Carrie thought.

"This little thing can get some stations in." It crackled with static at each turn until she finally reached a clear station. Third Eye Blind belted out of the radio, "How's it gonna be?"

Carrie jumped up and clapped her hands. "Yay, let's get this party started!"

"You and Tom are in the back bedroom," Jen yelled to Carrie as she was bringing her bags in.

Carrie wandered to the back of the trailer, finding a surprisingly intact bedroom. The bed had a faded but neatly folded quilt, which looked handmade with love decades ago. An end table sat beside it, and a modest dresser stood against the wall, its surface nicked with years of use. She unpacked her toiletries, setting them neatly on the dresser. Finally, she placed her favorite perfume bottle, Tommy Girl, in the center.

Unscrewing the cap, she inhaled its crisp, familiar scent. It brought a fleeting moment of happiness, but the thought of Tom arriving and sharing this small room with him quickly wiped the smile from her face. Shaking off the thought, she pivoted, deciding she'd feel better unloading the bags of food and booze. A strong drink was suddenly in order.

Jen was already unpacking in the kitchen, her bags strewn across the counter as she organized supplies. In the living area, Dylan claimed the couch as his spot for the weekend, spreading out a blanket and tossing his duffel bag into the corner. From the bag, he pulled out his contributions: a mid-sized bottle of Jack Daniels and a case of Coca-Cola, which he added to the growing stash of alcohol on the table.

"Alright, you brought the margarita mix. I brought mine, too!" Carrie looked back at Jen. "You brought your t-shirt, right?"

"Of Course!" Jen was already sipping from a glass filled with a pretty green liquid. They had recently discovered their love of margaritas, specifically the Jose Cuervo premix. Carrie found cute, matching powder blue t-shirts with a stick-figure girl drinking a green drink that said, "margarita girl."

Carrie hurried outside, eager to unload the car and start mixing drinks. She and Tom had come fully stocked for the weekend: a large bottle of vodka, lemonade, margarita mix, and a cooler packed with Smirnoff Ice and beer. She figured Tom had a bottle of Korbel stashed in his truck, and she wouldn't have been surprised if he was already taking a swig from it.

Back in the kitchen, Carrie grabbed a rocks glass from the cabinet and opened the freezer in search of ice—better to save the cooler stash for later. Her hand paused when she spotted a half-empty bottle of Mezcal tequila tucked in the corner, the kind with the worm floating at the bottom. She hesitated, her fingers brushing the frosted glass before deciding against it. Pulling out a handful of ice cubes instead, she dropped them into her glass with a clink, shutting the freezer door firmly behind her.

There was a knock on the front door, and through the screen, they saw a short, blonde woman. She was smiling and waving.

"Knock, knock," she yelled into the door.

"Hey, Marcy," Jen said as she walked to the door. Carrie noticed Jen opened the door but did not welcome her in.

"I see you made it," she said, peeking inside to see who else was in the trailer.

Carrie took her drink and sat very close to Dylan on the couch. They each had a cigarette and a drink, not paying too much attention to the strange lady at the door.

"Yeah, we just pulled in." Jen lit a cigarette and practically blew the smoke in Marcy's face. Marcy, in turn, moved the smoke away with her hand.

"Bobby just stumbled in, fuckin drunk as usual. He was supposed to take Brandon out on the boat, but now that's not gonna happen. He said he saw a guy at Brett's who claims to know you. He was on one of the machines." Marcy stated in an agitated tone.

"The other guy is my husband," Carrie said. She stood up and walked over to the door to get more information. Just great, she thought. She wondered how much money Tom was blowing on the gambling machine.

"Oh, I didn't know." Marcy looked Carrie up and down, staring at her shoes —a cheap pair of flip-flops —and eying the cute, bright pink pedicure Jen had forced her to get.

"Are you coming by us tomorrow for the party?" Marcy inquired.

Carrie looked at Jen with a questioning look. "What party?" She waited for an answer and an introduction to this woman.

"Carrie, this is Marcy, by the way. She has a trailer in the back. Dylan and I went to high school with her. She's having a party tomorrow for the Fourth of July and has invited us. Marcy, this is my friend Carrie."

Marcy looked suspiciously at Dylan and Carrie, having just mentioned her husband. Dylan walked over to her, his bottle of beer and cigarette in hand, and held out his hand to shake. "Nice to see you, Marcy." He smiled his big, charming smile, and her eyes lit up. She even blushed a little.

"Can I get you anything? A beer, or?" Dylan motioned towards all their booze on the counter.

"Oh no, I have to get back. I'm prepping for the party, and Brandon will be back at the trailer. I don't want to leave him too long. He can get into a lot of trouble!"

Carrie wondered what this woman was doing leaving her young son alone, but who was she to judge?

A black BMW pulled up as Marcy walked towards her trailer. "Heyyy," the girl yelled out the window.

"Oh, cool, Tori's here," Jen said, walking towards her car.

Carrie rummaged through her purse until her fingers closed around a crumpled pack of cigarettes.

She pulled one out, lit it, and inhaled deeply before stepping outside, her cocktail in her other hand. The nicotine hit, paired with the burn of vodka, eased her nerves as she tried to figure out how to connect with Tori. The cigarette gave her an excuse to linger, something to do with her hands while she found her footing.

"You made good time," Carrie said, blowing smoke into the warm evening air. Her tone casual, but the words carried a hint of surprise. They weren't expecting Tori until well after dinner.

"Yeah, since Drew decided not to come, I headed out earlier."

Jen looked puzzled. "Why didn't Drew come?"

Tori started pulling her bags out of the car, and Carrie and Jen helped her. "He has a new project for his company and wants to work on it."

Everyone in the group knew Drew and Tori as the well-off couple. Drew was a pilot for a major airline, and Tori ran a thriving esthetics business. They fit the classic "DINKs" label—double income, no kids—but Tori managed to blend her casual vibe with an air of understated luxury.

She wore her honey-blonde hair swept into a sleek ponytail, neatly tucked under an Audi baseball cap. A pair of Ray-Bans perched effortlessly on her nose, their glossy frames catching the sunlight. She kept it simple—a fitted black T-shirt and crisp cargo shorts that somehow looked more designer than practical. Even dressed down, Tori had a way of making everything she wore feel high-class.

"More girl time!" Jen nodded in agreement, "Yeah, yeah, and we brought Dylan, you know, from darts."

Dylan came walking out just then and sauntered towards them with his beer in hand. "Tori! Another lovely lady!" he exclaimed, holding his hand out to Tori. Her real name was Victoria, but she went by Tori to those she knew well.

She peered at Dylan over the top of her sunglasses. "You're nice and strong. Can you help me with my cooler?" She looked at Jen and Carrie, raising her eyebrows a couple of times, while Dylan went to grab the cooler.

"Why don't you put that stuff away when we get back? We were just about to check out The Edge and look for Tom." Jen said to Tori, who was already unpacking.

Jen and Carrie freshened up their margaritas, and Dylan made a Jack and Coke. Tori looked at all of them preparing drinks, opened her cooler, and retrieved a cold Heineken. She opened the bottle and took a quick swig. "Ahh," she exaggerated, "let's go!" They poured their drinks into plastic cups and headed out to explore the bars and find Tom.

CHAPTER 3

Jen's trailer was tucked just a few yards behind River's Edge—better known to everyone as The Edge—a sprawling bar and grill perched on the west side of the river. The Edge was a weekend hotspot, drawing crowds for its live bands, frozen pizzas crisped up in a pizza oven, and the well-worn pool table and dartboard in the corner. Upstairs, a handful of modest rooms catered mostly to fishermen looking for a place to crash.

Across the dusty parking lot sat Brett's Boat Dock Inn, a bar and banquet hall that served as a central hub for boaters and trailer renters alike. While it wasn't as close to the water as The Edge, Brett's was famous for their Bloody Marys, a hearty breakfast buffet, and a row of ever-enticing gambling machines. The boaters appreciated the laid-back vibe, especially the unspoken rule at both bars: you could walk in with a drink from elsewhere as long as you bought the next round there.

"Let's start at The Edge," Jen said, stepping off the deck and motioning for the others to follow. "I want to give you guys the full tour."

The late afternoon air was warm and carried the faint scent of the river, mingling with the distant sounds of laughter and music drifting from the bars. It was just after 3 p.m. Early enough to avoid the dinner rush, though the thought of food would creep in soon enough.

They all felt the light buzz of afternoon drinks, just enough to loosen up. No one had gone full party mode yet, so the margarita-themed T-shirts stayed in the closet. Carrie adjusted her black tank top, patterned with subtle floral designs, feeling confident in how it hugged her curves. Jen, ever practical yet effortlessly cool, had swapped her earlier outfit for tan shorts, a simple T-shirt, and her signature cowboy hat, tipped at just the right angle.

Dylan strolled between them, flicking his lighter to ignite a cigarette. Jen and Carrie followed suit, the glow of their smokes bright against the fading daylight. Tori trailed a few steps behind, carefully avoiding their haze of smoke.

Jen led the group through a path that felt like a forgotten junkyard. Rusted metal scraps and old machinery were scattered haphazardly, and an unexpected chicken strutted around a makeshift coop, clucking indignantly as they passed.

They reached the bar's rear entrance, a heavy metal door that creaked as Jen pushed it open. The Edge was nearly empty this time of day—most people were still out on the water or hadn't yet arrived for the holiday weekend.

Carrie's eyes landed on a Photo Hunt game in the corner as they stepped inside, and she grinned. She'd played a few rounds on smaller tabletop versions before, but this standing model looked like it was begging for her attention.

"Photo Hunt! No way!" Carrie shouted, darting toward the machine with an excited bounce in her step. Jen, Tori, and Dylan trailed after her as she fished a quarter from her pocket and dropped it into the slot.

The screen blinked to life, revealing two almost identical photos of shirtless men. The challenge: spot the difference before time runs out. Everyone leaned in, eyes darting across the images as they pointed and shouted over one another.

"There! His tattoo is missing!"

"No, the hat's different!"

The frantic pace and ridiculous images sent them into fits of laughter, the countdown clock adding to the chaos.

When Carrie finally stepped back, her cheeks flushed from laughing too hard, Jen and Dylan slid into her spot, determined to beat her score. Tori wandered off, exploring the bar, which was dark and blissfully cool compared to the heavy summer heat outside.

Digging into her tiny purse, Carrie pulled out a disposable camera, gleefully snapping candid shots of her friends. She giggled as she snapped one aimed squarely at Dylan's backside.

Meanwhile, Tori reappeared, rolling herself into view in a dusty wheelchair she'd found in one of the corridors. "You guys! I'm upgrading my ride!" she called, spinning in a circle as if testing the wheels.

"Weeee!" she yelled, one hand holding her beer and the other working the wheel. Carrie snapped a photo, and Tori gave her a crazy look.

"You should get a digital camera, Carrie, and get with the times," Tori said as she butted her in the leg. Carrie laughed and said, "Nah, I love developing pictures. I don't want that digital crap!"

Jen kept yelling "fucker, fucker" at the game, so Carrie returned to the machine, squeezing herself between Jen and Dylan, touching spots on the screen that were different. Each would slap the other's hands away, and soon, they were on the third game. They scored pretty high, so when they had to enter their name as the top score, Jen punched in F-U-C- and Carrie stopped her. "You can't put that in!" So she backspaced and punched in 4-P-A-C-K. Pleased with the entry, Jen told them it was time to go.

Their eyes squinted from the sharp sunlight as they pushed open the back door. They all quickly reached for their sunglasses, shielding themselves from the bright glare. Jen started toward Brett's Place, but a sudden burst of noise caught their attention. From behind the chicken coop, they could hear music blaring from Jen's trailer. Tom's truck was out front, its engine still running as the stereo blasted some upbeat tune.

"Looks like Tom found my trailer," Jen said, so they headed that way.

Brandy, Tom's German Shepard, came trotting towards the group with her tail wagging, happy to see them.

Dylan was the first one to greet the dog, extending his hand.

"Hi, girl." He said and petted her head.

Brandy was a good dog—well-behaved and friendly enough, but Carrie wasn't exactly a dog person. Growing up, she'd had a handful of dogs, all mutts, and none of them were ever properly trained. They'd jump up on anyone who came by, and the male dogs were particularly fond of humping people's legs. The dogs never stuck around for long. Her mom would get fed up with their antics and give them away. When Carrie met Tom, he already had Brandy as a puppy, so she had always thought of her as his dog, not hers.

The door opened, and Tom came out carrying a large dish full of water for Brandy. He put it down and yelled towards them, "I was just about to come look for you. Where've you been?"

"We found Photo Hunt in The Edge," Carrie answered as she walked towards him. "I heard you found the gambling machines."

Tom looked down at her with dark, stormy eyes. He grinned slyly and replied, "Yeah, but I didn't lose any money." He swayed a bit and poked her arm.

"What the hell is a Photo Hunt anyway?" She ignored him and walked into the trailer to pour herself a drink.

"How did you know where to find my trailer"? Jen asked

"Some guy from the bar told me. Bobby, I think, was his name?" Tom bellowed, almost too loudly.

"Dylan, how's it going?" he stumbled over and held out his hand. He shook it aggressively, and Dylan backed away.

"Hey man, you know me. I'm just chillin' with the ladies."

Inside the trailer, Jen joined Carrie. They both pulled out the bottle of vodka and made a mixed drink with some Diet Seven-Up.

"Time for Happy Hour!" Carrie smiled at Jen, and they both toasted their glasses.

They grabbed their drinks and stepped onto the deck, the scorching heat lingering in the air. The sun would be relentless for another hour, casting a harsh glare over everything. On the deck, Tom and Dylan were deep into a heated argument about fishing, with Tom stubbornly asserting his opinion like he always did. Dylan, slightly buzzed, was in no mood to back down. Sensing the brewing tension, Carrie quickly stepped in, grabbing Dylan's arm. "Come on, let's sit over here," she said, pulling him away. She gestured toward the plastic patio table, which had four seats. They were the collapsible chairs that always seemed in short supply, but there was usually one to go around.

Tori, starting to get irritated by the argument, said, "I'm going to put my stuff away." She motioned her arms in the fashion of "walk like an Egyptian" and went inside.

Carrie sat down heavily and sighed. "So, has anyone started watching American Idol? The auditions so far are hilarious! I like that Justin guy, but Simon Cowell is something else!"

"Oh yeah, that's right. I forgot it's on. Hopefully, we can get it here on the TV," said Jen.

"I don't know, I've been watching it too, but it's not as good as I thought it would be," replied Dylan.

"I do like seeing Paula Abdul, though," he smiled. "That video Straight Up...mmmm!"

"The new season of Sex and The City is premiering July 21st. I have to watch that! Carrie, don't you watch it? That seems right up your alley." Jen asked. She, of course, had HBO and was a big fan of television and movies. Carrie envied that Jen had just about every channel available.

"Why would I want to watch a show about beautiful women running around New York having tons of great sex? I would be jealous." Carrie and Tom did not have HBO (or good sex). Not that they couldn't afford it, but Carrie and her sister grew up without cable, so she never even considered it.

At that moment, it wasn't clear where Tom had gone. After the argument with Dylan, he stormed off toward the pond, as he often did when the conversation turned to things he wasn't interested in.

He seemed to disappear whenever the girls got into their girly talk. But just then, Carrie spotted him—Tom was walking back toward them from the pond, Brandy trotting along beside him. He climbed the stairs to the deck, his eyes locking with Carrie's as he reached the top.

"So, who's going to get dinner started? I'm hungry."

Of course, he was hungry—Tom was always hungry. On the other hand, Carrie rarely felt like eating after a few drinks, so she wasn't concerned. She glanced at him and said, "I thought you were. You brought all the fixings for a cookout, after all." She chuckled, realizing she had no clue how to start the grill, and Tom knew that all too well.

"Figures," he muttered. "Just sit there and drink your cocktail." He headed inside the trailer, rummaging through the bags for the brats and hamburgers.

From inside, Tori's voice drifted out as she finished unpacking. "I brought some pasta salad," she called out, her words carrying across the deck.

"Have my lazy wife bring it out," he yelled.

CHAPTER 4

After the food was ready, everyone headed inside to make themselves a plate and top off their drinks. Laughter and casual chatter filled the air as they gathered around the table on the deck, plates piled high. But Carrie barely touched her food, pushing it around absentmindedly, while Tom devoured his burger in large, aggressive bites, his eyes never leaving her.

When Carrie took the bun off her burger and started to eat the filling with a fork, Tom's patience snapped. Without warning, he stood up, snatched the bun from her plate, and crumpled it in his fist. Bits of bread spilled onto her plate like a harsh reminder of the tension in the air.

"What the fuck, dude?" yelled Dylan from across the table.

"Don't start with me. Carrie doesn't eat anything. She thinks she's a beauty queen or something." Tom hollered back in his loud, angry voice, scaring all of them. He stormed off the deck, grabbed his wallet, and started walking towards his truck to get a drag of his pipe and a pull of Korbel. "Come on, Brandy." She followed him obediently.

Carrie looked at Jen, Dylan, and Tori. All three stared in disbelief. Carrie felt more embarrassed than mad, so she took some bites of her food to cover it up.

Jen was the first to speak. "What the fuck?"

"Oh, don't worry about it. Tom gets like that when he's drinking, especially brandy," Carrie covered for him.

"You better not let him treat you like that. What a bastard!" Tori replied as she squeezed her eyes together.

Dylan walked over to her and rubbed her shoulders as he stood behind her. "You okay, Carrie?" he asked tenderly.

"Yeah, I'm fine." She smiled at him. "He's gone now, so let's just have fun."

Carrie stood there as Dylan's warm hands gently massaged her, and her thoughts drifted back to 1995 when she met him and Jen.

Dylan was engaged to Ally, her co-worker, and they all frequented The Pub—a Reagle Beagle for the young 90s crowd, full of angst and "smells like teen spirit." They brought her into their group of friends, and she quickly became a regular.

Jen had attended high school with Dylan, and Carrie met Jen at Ally's bachelorette party. They quickly became friends. Carrie admired Jen because she had her life together as a single woman and managed her father's jewelry business downtown. Carrie felt inadequate compared to her because she was working for a small construction company, going nowhere, and settling into a dysfunctional marriage, to say the least. They had hung out a lot after work, but then she and Jen lost touch once Carrie married Tom. They reconnected when Jen reached out and asked her to join a dart league with Dylan, Ally, and Tori. Carrie gladly accepted, not realizing she would meet the friends who would change her life.

The party continued, with drinks flowing and their laughter mingling with the sound of the music. Tori had brought out her old boombox, cranking up the volume on their favorite stations. When U2's One started playing, Carrie and Dylan belted the lyrics at the top of their lungs, their voices blending with the beat.

Carrie made her way to the trailer several times to fix new drinks. Her movements were slower with each new drink. Jen watched her closely, a furrow of suspicion creeping across her face. Carrie's thoughts began to blur as the night continued, her speech slurring with each pass. Finally, Jen couldn't hold back.

"You don't have to give 'er the first night," she said, her tone sharp but with an underlying concern. Jen always knew when to stop, when enough was enough—something Carrie never seemed to learn.

"Yeah, I hear you," Carrie said. "Maybe we should start winding down. We have a long day tomorrow. Dylan, you want to go for a little walk with me before we call it a night?"

Dylan was quite drunk from Jack and Cokes, but was having a good time. "Yeah, let's walk and see what this pond is all about."

"You kids go right ahead. I'm going to call it a night." Tori said as she headed inside. Jen followed behind her.

Dylan grabbed Carrie's hand, and they started walking towards the pond. They were both teetering back and forth, trying to walk straight.

"So, are you happy, Carrie? It doesn't seem like it to me," Dylan asked her.

"Well, as they say, you get what you settle for, and I guess that's what I did. I mean, for the most part, Tom is a good guy. He helps people a lot, he's a hard worker, and he's friendly enough. It's just the drinking. I know I drink, too; we all do. But Dylan, there's something different about him."

"Yeah, I can see that. Tom is not a nice drunk or a fun drunk. That's a mean bastard there."

"Forget about him!" Carrie snapped, shaking off her thoughts. She started walking toward the pond, her bare feet crunching on the gravel. The moonlight shimmered on the water, casting a soft glow over the night. The stars sparkled overhead, and the warm breeze carried the scent of the river. It was peaceful— almost romantic.

Reaching the pond, they kicked off their flip-flops and dipped their feet into the cool water. It was refreshing against the heat of the evening, a perfect contrast to the balmy air. The two of them began splashing each other, laughing. But when Dylan's splash hit a little too hard, Carrie squealed and darted away, laughing, "Stop it! You're getting me wet!"

Dylan grinned and chased after her. He caught her quickly, pulling her back and tackling her to the ground. They tumbled through the grass, their laughter mixing with the rustling of the grass. Eventually, Dylan pinned her to the ground, her arms above her head. She lay on her back, breathless, while he hovered over her, his face just inches from hers. The electric moment hung between them.

Carrie's heart raced as she looked up at Dylan. His gaze was intense, filled with an unspoken something. His warm and slightly intoxicating breath brushed across her neck, and she could feel the softness of his lips just a hair's breadth away from her skin. She instinctively lifted her chin, drawing closer, but Dylan abruptly pulled back, standing up quickly.

"What the hell are we doing? Let's head back to the trailer. They're going to start wondering where we are."

They walked back to the trailer and saw that everybody was inside.

"Well, I'll see you tomorrow morning," Carrie said as she went into her room, where Tom was lying dead drunk and snoring.

She couldn't fall asleep because her thoughts kept taking her back to dinner on the deck and how humiliated she felt, and how Tom always made her feel that way. Her mind drifted even further back.

It was the end of the 90s, and all the famous sitcom couples were settling down—Daphne and Niles, Chandler and Monica. Carrie wasn't ready for marriage but felt pressured to marry. Tom swept her off her feet when she had been lonely. He was handsome, handy, funny, and pleasant when sober. Carrie felt sorry for Tom because he grew up with an alcoholic father in a bad neighborhood and had low-life friends. She thought she could give him a better life.

Carrie knew Tom was a drug addict and alcoholic, and he was different from other guys because he drank at home, even on weeknights. Some days, she came home from work to find the brandy bottle already out. She knew it wasn't his first drink by how much was left in the bottle. Despite all of this, Carrie still felt the need to be with Tom, but she wasn't sure why.

Trying to make sense of it, she refleced further on thoughts she had written in her journal.

What was I thinking?

He has called me fat for the last time. He thinks I'm fat now? He should have seen me in high school, wearing size 14 jeans, longing for a 10 or at least a 12. Or how about at age ten, right after my parents' divorce, all bloated, non-matching clothes, a welfare kid with sadness beyond comparison? I worked hard to shed those memories, and the pounds melted away with them. Thank you, Jane Fonda, and your magic step aerobics. I think I look good now, and so do others. Like my high school crush when he came into the bar while I was working with his soon-to-be wife. I saw it. What was I thinking? The smell of burnt hamburger in the air, which I later learned was crack, should have been a warning sign. But he took me to a Packers playoff game. Gave up his brother's ticket for me.

Then, the drunken abuse flowed in like a tidal wave—my peaceful home in a quiet town. Rain falling on a beautiful starry night while listening to Echos, and the monster comes home from the garden party so drunk that he pissed in the bed. I thought it was raining. Then the fight, the kick to my kidney after I had kicked his fucking balls. But I love you; I didn't mean to hurt you; it's what we do; it's the garden party—a new house, old house, but new to me, across from my sister, safe zone. Thirty looms in like a dark cloud, and Monica and Chandler, Daphne, and Niles are getting married, so why aren't we married? Let's get married then; here we go, no ring, no romance.

Carrie's thoughts began to annoy her, so she shut them down and tried her best to ignore the annoying sounds coming from the drunk lying next to her. Dreaming of Dylan next to her instead of Tom sent her drifting off to sleep.

CHAPTER 5

The trailer was still and quiet the next morning, except for the low hum of the fans circulating the sticky air. Carrie stirred awake, momentarily disoriented, as if she didn't quite know where she was. The cramped bedroom felt unfamiliar, but glancing at her surroundings brought everything back into focus. Her clothes were tossed haphazardly across the chairs, a mess she didn't remember making. At least she'd had the sense to change into pajamas before crashing.

Her eyes felt dry, a reminder of the contacts she'd neglected to take out the night before due to being too buzzed and lazy to bother. She rubbed them with a sigh, trying to wake up. The bed beside her was empty, which meant Tom had already slipped out and was probably down by the river with his fishing gear.

Carrie's thoughts pivoted away from Tom as she remembered the unexpected moments with Dylan. She couldn't shake the image of his face so close to hers, his presence lingering in her mind. A shiver ran down her spine, a mixture of confusion and something else. Was it desire? She'd always considered her connection with Dylan harmless, just playful flirtation. But now, in the quiet of the morning, she couldn't help but wonder if there was more to it. Maybe the tension between her and Tom fueled her desire, or perhaps it was just the alcohol. But something had shifted, and she wasn't sure what to make of it.

A wave of guilt washed over her as she thought about Tom. What if the roles were reversed? How would she feel if he had moments like that with other women? Maybe he did. He often stayed late at the shop, always claiming he was working. But what if there was more to it? What if there was another woman? The thought lingered, and it stung. She knew all too well that their relationship lacked the passion it once had.

Carrie dragged herself out of bed and shuffled to the small bathroom. Staring at her reflection in the mirror, she thought she didn't look half-bad, all things considered. Her dark, wavy hair still held its shape, a testament to the "Rachel" style she'd been wearing lately. She had carefully styled it with her curling iron, and it seemed to be holding up for at least another day before the inevitable need to tame the unruly mess. She splashed water on her face and tried to fix the smudged eyeliner beneath her eyes. With a quick dab, she decided she looked as good as expected at this hour. Her cotton-striped pajama bottoms and a white tank top with a built-in bra felt casual yet comfortable enough to face Dylan.

Jen was already in the kitchen making coffee. When Carrie appeared in the living room, she put her finger to her mouth, "Shhhh," and pointed at Dylan sleeping on the couch. He had shorts on but no shirt, and a blanket half draped across him.

Jen poured coffee into a mug for Carrie and held up a bottle of vanilla creamer to question if she wanted any in hers.

"Yes," Carrie whispered.

They grabbed their cups and quietly made their way out to the deck.

"Wow, this doesn't look too bad considering the damage we did last night," Carrie said as she sat down with her coffee. They both pulled out a cigarette and lit up. "Who cleaned up?"

"Tori did after you and Dylan went for a walk," Jen replied.

Carrie's cheeks flushed, but Jen didn't seem to notice.

"I tried calling my booty call last night, but he must not have heard his phone if he was at the bar."

"Who is the guy?" Carrie asked.

"Just a guy who lives around here. I thought we'd see him, but maybe tonight." She looked at Carrie and sighed, "That man is so good at..." Jen said as she pointed down to her lap. "Like, he is a pro, if you know what I mean."

"Oh God, I wish. It's been forever since Tom has gone down on me, and honestly, I don't even want him to. He's so bad at it, it's almost embarrassing."

Carrie thought about the beginning of her and Tom's relationship and how they would lie around in bed for hours pleasuring each other. That faded away so quickly; it was a distant memory.

"He's a fence painter, I take it?" Jen asked.

"A what?"

"You know, back and forth, back and forth."

They both busted out laughing.

"Who's a fence painter?"

They both looked at the door and saw Dylan hanging halfway out of it.

"No one," they both said in unison.

Dylan barely paid attention and sat down with a cup of coffee, rubbing his hair and eyes.

"What time is it?" he asked.

Jen looked at her watch. "8:30, which means I have to get started on my salsa. Marcy's party starts around noon."

"We'll get there when we get there," Carrie exclaimed, already annoyed by this woman for some reason. She didn't want someone dictating where they should be. Plus, she wasn't even sure if she had mentioned the party to Tom, and if he'd be back from fishing.

Jen went into the kitchen and bustled around getting the ingredients for her salsa. She pulled out onions and jalapenos and began chopping away. Carrie and Dylan sat in silence on the deck by themselves. Dylan lit up a cigarette and looked around. Hardly anyone was out at this time of the morning around the resort, so it was quiet and already starting to get hot.

"Do you want something to eat? I can make you an English muffin," Carrie said to Dylan.

He looked at her and smirked, "You know how to cook?" He asked in a sarcastic tone.

"Haha, I can use a toaster."

They both got up and went into the trailer. Dylan walked over to Jen and started rubbing her shoulders.

"Oh, that feels so good. My back is killing me from that drive," Jen told him.

"Really? I can fix that." Dylan pulled her to the living room and told her to lie on the floor. She lay face down, and Dylan put his knee on her back and kneaded her shoulder blades. Carrie looked at them and tried to push aside her slightly jealous feelings. She pulled the English muffins from the package and placed them in the toaster.

Just then, Tori walked out of her back bedroom, rubbing her eyes. She looked down at Dylan and Jen and giggled. "You guys!"

Tori dragged herself into the kitchen, poured herself a cup of coffee, and looked around to see what Carrie was doing.

"Making toast?" Tori asked, sniffing the air.

"Yep, I'm pretty good at making toast. Well,

English muffins. You want one?" Carrie asked while buttering a piece.

"No, I need to wake up," Tori answered, reaching for a cup to pour her coffee.

She looked around and saw the tomatoes and peppers Jen had started chopping for the salsa.

"Oh, that's right. We have that party today," Tori said while pouring her coffee.

"Yeah, we're going to take our time getting there," said Carrie as she buttered the English muffins. Dylan stopped massaging Jen, got up, grabbed a buttery muffin from Carrie, and shoved it into his mouth. Jen got up and joined them.

"Maybe we should go to Brett's for a Bloody Mary before we head out there," Jen suggested.

"That sounds good to me. You know I love a Bloody Mary!" Carrie said. She smiled at Dylan and wiped the dripping butter off his chin. Jen was back at the chopping block, so she didn't see the flirting.

"So do I!" said Dylan

"You guys go ahead. I'm going to stay back here to freshen up and have some alone time," said Tori, walking back to her bedroom.

"Suit yourself," replied Carrie, and she went into the bathroom to freshen up a little. It was so hot that she only needed a little dusting of eyeshadow, eyeliner, and mascara. Any more makeup would sweat off. She tied her hair into a clip and put on a cute Fourth of July outfit. She decided on her little gray baby doll T-shirt with a kitten wearing an American flag bandana. It wasn't too cutesy but edgy enough. Plus, the fit was flattering. She pulled on her cut-off denim shorts, threw on some flip-flops, and figured it was good enough. Carrie felt incredibly relaxed and at ease at Riverbanks. She didn't even feel like taking a shower. Why bother, she thought. It's not like she had sex or anything, requiring a shower to feel better.

Jen was ready to head out. She had her hair pulled back in a hair tie and wore a navy blue and white skort—she seemed to be sporting them these days. She also had on a white T-shirt with a stick figure playing softball. Dylan threw on the clothes he had worn the day before.

Carrie couldn't help but think Dylan bore a striking resemblance to Charlie from Party of Five. His light brown hair, longer on top and cropped shorter at the sides, fell into his face in a way that seemed effortlessly sexy. It always seemed to have a glossy sheen, as if he used some product, though she knew it was just his natural, youthful charm. There was an edge to him—a slight imperfection in his crooked teeth that gave his words a faint whistle when he spoke. Most women, including Carrie, found it endearing. His lean frame, all sinewy muscle and wiry strength, had a way of making women feel self-conscious, as if they might break him if they got too close. Yet, somehow, it only added to his allure.

CHAPTER 6

Once the group was ready, they set off toward Brett's, anticipation buzzing. The legendary spot they'd heard so much about was finally within reach.

The door creaked open, and the darkness struck them as they stepped inside. It was almost cave-like, contrasting with the sunny dining area near the front, where guests enjoyed breakfast. The back bar felt like a cooling sanctuary from the scorching day despite the faint, musty smell that seemed to permeate most places in the area.

Behind the bar stood a man who perfectly matched Carrie's mental picture. Stocky and short, with tough, weathered skin and thick, wide glasses, his slicked-back red hair gleamed with what had to be grease or oil. He moved with purpose, wiping counters and rearranging bottles with gruff efficiency.

Looking up briefly from his work, he barked, "What can I get you?" in a tone as brusque as it was indifferent.

They settled at the bar, and each ordered a Bloody Mary served with the customary beer chaser. The back bar felt intimate, with a small bandstand tucked into the corner and about half a dozen gambling machines lining one wall. A few older regulars, clearly seasoned patrons, were already perched at the machines, sipping Bud Lights and looking like they'd been there since sunrise.

Curious to explore, Carrie and Dylan wandered off to take in the place's quirky charm. As they roamed, they noticed a back door leading toward the other trailers. Nearby, a narrow stairway descended steeply, likely to a storage area or some other hidden corner of the establishment. The discovery added an air of mystery to the already peculiar ambiance.

The friends enjoyed their Bloody Marys and chugged their beer chasers. The first drink of the morning always tasted best. After settling the tab, Brett gazed at the group and asked, "Who brought the dog?"

Carrie's cheeks warmed. Brett had that effect on people. "We did," she meekly admitted.

"Well, see that you clean up after it," he barked, his eyes narrowing. "Don't want to see any… surprises. Understand?"

Carrie rolled her eyes, the gesture barely concealed. "Of course we will," she muttered, glancing at Jen. Once Brett walked away, she whispered, "What's his deal?"

Jen shrugged with weary amusement in her eyes. "Brett being Brett, I suppose. He must have a bug up his butt about other dogs. Don't let him get to you.

Did you guys check out the pond last night?"

Dylan and Carrie looked at each other, their eyes slightly wide.

"Yeah, it was pretty dark, though. We put our feet in the water, which felt nice." Carrie answered.

"We need to go swimming today. It's going to be a hot one. How about we get Tom, grab my salsa, go to Marcy's party for a while, and then hit the pond?"

They tossed a few quarters on the bar for Brett—barely enough, but fitting. Stepping outside, the beauty of the rolling river greeted them. The pier buzzed with activity as guests prepared their boats for a fun day on the water.

Scanning the scene, they spotted Tom farther down the pier, casting his line with Brandy loyally by his side. As they approached, Tom turned at the sound of their footsteps. A broad smile spread across his face as he walked over, pulling Carrie into a warm hug and kissing her lips. His upbeat mood was unmistakable, a refreshing change from the night before.

"How's it going out here? Catching anything?" Carrie asked, shielding her eyes from the sun as she looked at him.

"Yeah, a few here and there," Tom replied casually, reeling in his line to check the bait.

Carrie noticed there weren't any open beers in sight, just the ones tucked away in his cooler. Well, that's a good sign, she thought. Maybe today will turn out alright.

"I think I forgot to tell you yesterday, but we're invited to a party over at a friend of Jen's, Marcy. It's a Fourth of July party. We're planning on going maybe a little before noon. Are you coming?"

"Of course. Sounds like fun. I know there will be fireworks later tonight. I heard Bobby talk about it yesterday."

Carrie wiped the sweat from her upper lip. "It sure is hot already," she exclaimed. "Does anybody want to dip in the pond before we go to the party?"

Everyone agreed and they headed back to the trailer to change into their swimsuits, keeping their regular clothes on top so they'd be ready to head to Marcy's afterward. Carrie grabbed the bottle of margarita mix and some cups—why not start the day off right? They also tossed a few beers into a bag before going to the pond.

Stripping down to their swimsuits, the group jumped into the cool, refreshing water. The pond was small but picturesque, surrounded by cornfields and bathed in sunlight. In the middle stood a small pier with a mysterious pole. No one knew what it was for. Dylan, ever the joker, decided it was a stripper pole and spun around on it. Everyone burst out laughing.

The friends enjoyed the moment, splashing around and dunking each other. The water offered a perfect escape from the heat, and the margaritas went down easily as they sat on the pier, soaking up the sun.

Tom broke the calm, his stomach leading the

charge. "I'm getting hungry. Maybe we should head to the party and see what kind of food they've got." He glanced at Dylan and added, "Wanna smoke a bowl with me before we go?"

While Tom and Dylan sat at the picnic table on the grass, passing a bowl back and forth, the girls lingered on the pier, sipping their margaritas.

"Jen, who's going to be at this party?" Carrie asked, her voice tinged with unease. Meeting new people always put her on edge, so she'd already started working on her buzz.

"Probably the usual crowd—people who stay here all summer. I'm sure Marcy's friend Michelle will be there too," Jen replied, then added with a hint of urgency, "We should get moving. I don't want her getting annoyed with me."

Carrie gave her a sly smile. "Is your friend going to be there?"

Jen shrugged, a slight grin forming. "Maybe. Guess we'll find out."

They all slipped their clothes back on over their swimsuits, packed up their things, and made their way to the trailer to drop off their bags and top off their drinks. Dylan and Tom grabbed a beer while Jen picked up her salsa. Once ready, they headed toward the party, looking like a mismatched crew on a mission.

As they approached, Marcy strutted over, her hands planted firmly on her hips. "Well, well! Look who finally decided to show up. If it isn't the Rat Pack."

Carrie couldn't help but roll her eyes internally. Rat Pack? Seriously? That's so outdated. Her mind wandered. Brat Pack? Still too old. No, we're more like the All That Pack, because we're all that. She made a mental note to share the thought with Jen later, suppressing a grin. God, this woman is such a dork.

Marcy's trailer was located in the newer section of the resort, tucked away in the back. Carrie noticed it was well-kept, with a tidy yard that featured a good-sized patio table and plenty of chairs scattered around for guests. The party was already in full swing, with groups of people chatting and balancing plates of food.

Off to one side, a group of women who appeared to be Carrie's age caught her attention. Among them, she spotted Marcy and another woman talking. This woman, taller than Marcy with long, flowing, light-brown hair, immediately struck Carrie as familiar. With a jolt of recognition, Carrie realized it was Michelle, her high school nemesis.

The memory of their past rivalry surfaced. In middle school, Michelle's lustrous hair had been the envy of Carrie, who came from a lower-income family and lacked access to the styling products Michelle seemed to have in abundance. Carrie vividly recalled sitting behind Michelle in class, watching her constantly run her fingers through those long, feathery locks, contrasting with Carrie's more modest hairstyle.

Michelle had a cigarette in her hand and was talking with some women while casting curious glances in their direction. It became apparent that she recognized Carrie, and after a moment of hesitation, she began making her way over to the table they were sitting at, her gait as graceful as she remembered it.

"Carrie, I didn't know you would be here!" she exclaimed as she approached. Now that she was up close, Carrie could tell the years had been good to her. Her hair was still as striking, voluminous, and perfectly styled, almost begging to be touched. Her sun-kissed face gave her the vibe of someone who belonged on a California beach rather than at a campground.

Flawless makeup framed her large, expressive eyes. Carrie couldn't help but wonder why anyone would go to such lengths with makeup for a casual summer day at the resort. Still, there was no denying her beauty.

Carrie nervously sipped her margarita, forcing a smile as she greeted Michelle. "Hi Michelle! It's been ages!" She stood for an awkward hug, the obligatory embrace between 'old friends.'

"I came with Jen, who's friends with Marcy," she explained, gesturing towards Tom. "This is my husband, Tom."

Michelle mumbled a distracted "hi" to Tom, her eyes immediately drawn to Dylan, who was deep in conversation with Tori. He barely acknowledged her presence, a curt hello before returning to his discussion. Irritation flickered across Michelle's face. She tossed her hair back dramatically, announcing, "See y'all around," before bumping into a tall, handsome stranger who seemed to materialize out of thin air. "Oh, excuse me!" she exclaimed, quickly recovering with a dazzling smile. As she rejoined her friends, she couldn't resist stealing another glance at the stranger.

Carrie and Jen exchanged a knowing look. She will be one to contend with.

"Jen, it's good to see you! I'm glad you could make it," the man said warmly. He had a rugged, boyish charm, his dirty brown hair tucked beneath a cowboy hat. His outfit screamed classic country: well-worn Wrangler jeans, a big belt buckle, and a white sleeveless T-shirt with neatly cut-off edges. In one hand, he casually held a can of Coca-Cola, completing the laid-back look.

"Fritz, these are my friends—Carrie, Tori, Dylan, and Tom," Jen said, gesturing to the group.

Fritz smiled, looking a little uncertain as his gaze darted around the table. "Uh, Carrie, um, um… what was it?"

"Tori!" Tori interjected, standing up and extending her hand. "Nice to meet you."

Tom glanced up from his plate, set down his fork, and got to his feet. "Dude, nice to meet you." He reached out to shake Fritz's hand.

Fritz hesitated, looking between Tom and Tori with a confused expression before awkwardly shaking their hands. "Ah, yeah. Sorry about that."

The group exchanged puzzled glances as Fritz turned his attention back to Jen. His expression softened. "Meet me tonight?"

Jen lit a cigarette, inhaled deeply, and blew out a slow stream of smoke. "Maybe. We'll see."

Fritz shuffled his feet, looking a little deflated. "Okay, well, I hope so. See you later." Turning to the group, he added, "Nice, um, meeting you all." Then he walked off, leaving behind an air of unease.

As soon as he was out of earshot, Carrie, Tori, and Dylan turned their questioning eyes on Jen. Feeling their stares, she finally caved and looked up.

"That's my friend Fritz. He lives up here and stays with his buddy Doug—Dodger, they call him. Dodger's parents have a trailer way back by the cornfields. We met a few years ago, and, well, he's my friend." Jen stubbed out her cigarette, immediately lighting another, and took a sip of her drink.

Tori, never one to filter her thoughts, asked bluntly, "Is he slow or something?"

Carrie kicked her under the table, and Dylan gently squeezed her leg, signaling her to tone it down.

Jen sighed heavily, looking down at her cigarette. "He's a recovering alcoholic. He had an accident," she made air quotes with her fingers. "He fell and hit his head pretty badly. Probably has some brain damage. So, yeah, he's a little slow. But he's a nice guy, and I like him."

The group fell silent for a moment. Finally, Tori broke it with a soft smile. "Well, I like him. He seems nice enough. And if Jen likes him, we like him."

They all held up their cups and toasted, "To Fritz."

A sudden splash of water hit Carrie square in the face, making her gasp and step back in shock. Tom instinctively grabbed her arm, pulling her close.

"What the—?" Tom's cheerful demeanor vanished in an instant, replaced by a scowl. His eyes darted around, searching for the culprit.

Two boys darted past, laughing and wielding squirt guns, oblivious to the trouble they'd caused.

"Bobby! Get those damn guns away from the boys!" Marcy yelled, her voice sharp.

Standing by the grill and flipping bratwursts, Bobby turned his head lazily toward them, a mild annoyance crossing his face.

Carrie couldn't help but notice Bobby's appearance. Though shorter in stature, he was undeniably well-built, with muscular biceps and perfectly toned calves. His tanned skin glowed under the sun, and his teeth flashed white as he laughed, the sound carrying over the sizzle of the grill. His short-cropped hair was tucked neatly under a red Nike cap.

"They're just having some fun," Bobby replied with a casual shrug, clearly unbothered.

Tom clenched his jaw. "Yeah, well, they sprayed my wife in the face!"

Bobby sighed, tossing another bratwurst on the grill before holding his hands in mock surrender. "All right, all right. I'll be the bad guy and put an end to their fun."

He walked off with exaggerated reluctance, muttering under his breath, while Tom grumbled, still visibly irritated.

"Come on, Carrie. Let's go get some food." He took her arm gently.

"I'll join you guys. Brats!" Tori yelled over to the boys with the squirt guns. Jen walked over to the table to set out her salsa with the rest of the food.

Dylan looked at them suspiciously. "I'm going to go over to talk to Michelle." Carrie looked back at Dylan, wondering if he was suddenly jealous of how Tom was protective of her. She felt a pang of jealousy as she watched him walk towards her.

Carrie and Tom filled their plates and found an empty picnic table off to the side. Jen returned with a plate full of her salsa and some chips, sat down, and began eating it with gusto. Carrie looked at her, thinking, Wow, that must be some good salsa, or she must be really hungry.

"Who are the kids that squirted Carrie?" Tom asked Jen. His anger was still apparent, but Carrie wanted to forget it.

"That's Marcy's son Brandon and one of his friends."

After a while, Dylan joined her, carrying a plate and sliding into the seat beside her. Carrie leaned towards him, her voice barely above a whisper. "Did you get to know Michelle better?" He smiled, a mischievous glint in his eye. "Not really. She seems a bit boring." Carrie smiled back, the shared amusement creating a fleeting sense of intimacy amid the noisy party.

Marcy approached their table, "Jen, I heard you made some extremely hot salsa. You shouldn't bring such hot stuff to a party without a warning." Jen looked up, embarrassed and humiliated.

"Marcy, shut it. It's not that hot." Jen shoved a large chip of salsa into her mouth without flinching. Marcy ruffled Jen's hair to make it seem like she was kidding. Jen looked up at her and smiled sarcastically, then quickly lit a cigarette and blew the smoke in her face. Finally, Tori interjected, "Well, this is a fun group of people. First, we get hit by a squirt gun and then insulted. I don't know about you, but we should beat it."

CHAPTER 7

Feeling disgusted, humiliated, and way too cool to be at that party, the group went back to the trailer and spent the rest of the afternoon eating leftovers and hanging out on the deck. Tori hooked up her new iPod, the latest technology, and they cranked music. "Bye Bye Bye" came on, and both Jen and Carrie tried their best to recreate the dance that the group performed in the video while the guys shot Frisbee in front of the trailer.

"Hey ladies, come into the kitchen," Jen called with a mischievous grin, motioning for Carrie and Tori to follow her.

"What's with Jen?" Tori whispered to Carrie.

"No clue. Let's find out," Carrie replied, intrigued.

Jen stood by the fridge, her expression downright devilish. She reached into the freezer and triumphantly pulled out a bottle of Mezcal—the same one Carrie had noticed the day before.

"Shots, anyone?" Jen said with a mischievous look in her eyes.

Tori rolled her eyes. "Oh geez," she muttered, clearly not as eager a drinker as the other two. But after a beat, she shrugged. "Ah, what the hell."

Jen grabbed three retro shot glasses, the colors of which had faded from years of use, and filled them to the brim.

"To summer!" they toasted, clinking their glasses together before throwing the shots back.

The tequila burned going down, leaving them coughing and grimacing.

"God, this stuff tastes like a damn band-aid," Carrie choked out, making the others burst into laughter despite their disgust.

Just then, the guys walked in.

"What the hell is going on?" Dylan yelled, yet intrigued.

"Tequila!" replied Jen as she pulled out some red Solo cups to fill for the guys. They all stood together in a circle and downed another shot of the horrible-tasting liquid.

Dylan took Carrie's hand and pulled her onto the makeshift dance floor. They swayed together, their movements syncing with the sultry beat of the song, "Man, it's a hot one" pulded through the speaker. The others joined hands, weaving and spinning in a loose circle around them, laughter and music filling the warm evening air.

Carrie pressed closer to Dylan, her body moving instinctively with the rhythm, but her attention quickly turned to Tom. Out of the corner of her eye, she saw him tip back the bottle of Mezcal, finishing it off in one long pull. The worm slipped out at the end, and without hesitation, he swallowed it.

Tom's gaze locked onto hers, his eyes dark and wild. He pointed at her with a slow, deliberate motion that felt more like a warning than a drunken jest.

A chill ran down Carrie's spine despite the heat. She forced herself to keep dancing, but a gnawing unease settled in her chest. How was this day going to end?

As night fell, the resort came alive with the buzz of Fourth of July celebrations. The crackle of sparklers and distant pops of amateur fireworks echoed through the air. The group grabbed their drinks and settled around a picnic table in the grassy common area, where other residents had gathered in anticipation of the fireworks display.

Seating arrangements were haphazard at best. Carrie avoided sitting near Tom, let alone on his lap. She tried to keep busy, moving from one spot to another, often gravitating toward Dylan.

Tom, visibly drunk and teetering on the edge of obnoxiousness, was starting to wear on everyone's nerves. His slurred words and loud outbursts cut through the festive air, making it clear he was well past his limit. Carrie exchanged a glance with Dylan, rolling her eyes slightly, silently communicating what everyone seemed to be thinking: This is going to be a long night.

"Um, you know my dad spent a lot of money on these fireworks." Marcy's son Brandon said as he walked over to the picnic table. "He wants to collect, uh, like twenty bucks a trailer."

They all looked at each other as if thinking, the nerve of this kid. What is he, fifteen? Carrie immediately thought that this was her first time at this place and that she shouldn't have to pay for some stupid fireworks. Tom dug in his pocket and pulled out a crumpled wad of bills. He flicked out a twenty and handed it to Brandon, who snatched it up immediately.

"Bro, make sure you give that to your dad." Tom laughed. Brandon snatched the bills and headed toward his dad. Bobby was finishing up the fireworks setup on the concrete slab by the shelter where the fishermen cleaned their fish. They were the simple kind you could buy at a roadside stand.

While everyone patiently waited for the show to start, Carrie wandered into the trailer to fix another drink. She didn't see Dylan and had a feeling he might be inside; she couldn't imagine where else he would be. Inside, she found him standing in the living room watching the recap of American Idol.

"Dylan, are you going to skip the fireworks?" Carrie asked as she headed to the kitchen to pour some margarita into her cup.

"No, I'll be out there. I'm just checking out what happened on American Idol." He turned and walked into the kitchen to join Carrie. It felt way too small and hot for Carrie, and she felt the sweat forming on her face. Dylan got close to her and whispered, "It's getting pretty hot. Maybe we should go for a dip?"

Jen and Tori barged in laughing. "Come on, you two, the fireworks are about to start," Jen said as she and Tori came arm in arm. "After that, we're all going skinny dipping!" They didn't seem to notice how close Carrie and Dylan were talking, both of them being pretty drunk.

"Yeah, we're just fixing a drink," Carrie replied as she pushed Dylan away. She grabbed his hand and pulled him towards the door. "Let's go watch these fireworks."

They all stumbled towards the picnic table, where the others were sitting. There was enough room for all of them, except Tom wandered around with Brandy and a flask of Korbel in tow. Brandon was setting up the cakes for Bobby to light. The fireworks blasted sparkling lights into the sky as a crowd of resort goers oohed and aahed at the spectacular sight. Marcy and her friends were on lawn chairs off to the side, and we could hear Marcy's loud mouth yelling, "Careful, Bobby! You're going to hurt someone!" The finale went off without a hitch and turned out to be much better than neighborhood driveway displays.

After the final fireworks lit up the sky, the group dashed back to the trailer to grab their supplies—beers, towels, and a can of mosquito repellent.

"No lights!" Tori hollered. Her voice was playful but firm. "Ain't nobody here catching a glimpse of these beauties!" She cupped her ample chest with a dramatic flourish, giving them a playful jiggle for emphasis.

The room erupted in laughter, her bold humor cutting through the chaos as everyone scrambled to get ready.

They had the pond all to themselves. A luminous moon hung high above, casting a soft, romantic glow over the scene. Everyone quickly shed their clothes, laughing as they sprinted into the water. The air still felt balmy, and the pond retained the warmth of the scorching day, making a perfect, secluded oasis.

"Oh my God, this is awesome!" Carrie exclaimed. The water felt so freeing and wonderful with nothing on. She looked around for Tom but did not see him in the water. He must have stayed back, but it was no surprise she didn't notice or seem to care what he was up to. She looked for Dylan and caught his eye, but they knew not to get close to each other with everyone else around.

"Oh shit," yelled Jen. "The damn biting fish."

"Yeah, I've had enough of this," Tori said, and, in agreement, they all swam back to shore. The girls were pretty sure it was dark enough to hide their naked bodies when, all of a sudden, a bright light shone on them from the wooded area.

"What the fuck?" yelled Tori.

Tom stood on the shore, shining a large flashlight at them. He laughed hysterically, obviously finding it amusing.

"Dude, put that shit away," yelled Jen.

Dylan wrestled Tom for the light to save the ladies from being seen naked.

"Tom, you're a dick; this is not cool!" Dylan pinned Tom down after grabbing the flashlight from him.

"Get the fuck off me!" Tom pushed Dylan off him, stood up, and brushed himself off.

"You assholes are no fun," Tom replied and walked off towards the trailers.

Jen, Tori, and Carrie put their clothes back on. Practically in tears, Tori grabbed as much as she could and started towards the trailer. Jen joined her. Carrie stayed back with Dylan, trying to figure out what had just happened.

Dylan put on his cargo shorts. He approached Carrie at the picnic table, and she lit a cigarette.

"I didn't see anything, I swear," Dylan said with a devilish look. He situated himself between her legs and took the cigarette out of her mouth.

"I know Tom is a jerk, and he pissed everyone off, but I liked seeing you," Dylan said.

He cupped her face, gently tilting it up before pressing his lips to hers. Carrie didn't resist. His tongue slipped into her mouth, and she traced it with her own, feeling the edge of his teeth. Dylan's hands roamed over her, sliding from her thighs to her shoulders and finally to her breasts. The sensation felt electric throughout her barely clothed body.

"We should go back and see how Tori is," Carrie said as she pushed Dylan's hands away.

"Okay, I'll go to bed with this," he motioned to the prominent bulge in his shorts.

CHAPTER 8

Carrie and Jen were lying on beach towels, trying to get some sun. They came to the pond early, while everyone else was sleeping, with bottles of water in tow to help alleviate their hangovers. Sheryl Crow's "Favorite Mistake" played quietly on the boombox Jen brought; a perfect description of what occurred between her and Dylan the night before.

"What's going on with you and Dylan?" Jen asked, lying on her back.

"What do you mean?" Carrie inquired.

"Really? You think I don't see what's in front of my eyes? I can't believe Tom doesn't see it."

"Come on, it's just playing around," said Carrie. "Besides, Tom could give two shits about what I'm doing. It's just drunk flirting."

"Well, that's not good when you're always drinking."

"Hey, we're not the only ones! We all drink up here all the time. It's pretty much the culture here. I mean, we're surrounded by bars. What else is there to do?"

Jen sat up. "Yeah, I know. But Carrie, what's going on with you and Tom? You don't see me going around flirting with every guy I can while I'm drinking."

"That's because you are having sex, I assume. Sometimes I think I hate Tom. I can't even stand the thought of him touching me, so we never have sex."

"If it's about sex, you can fix that."

"He drinks all the time at home and is not a nice drunk," Carrie replied. "I can't tell you how many fights we've gotten into about this."

"Well, all I know is that you can't go around having affairs."

Jen and Carrie decided they had had enough morning sun and deep conversation, so they headed back to the trailer. It was around 10 a.m., and they figured the rest of the group would be up and about. Tom was packing his belongings and equipment in his pickup.

"See, I told you he notices," Jen said to Carrie, nudging towards Tom.

Carrie walked over to Tom cautiously while Jen went up to the deck.

"What's going on?"

In her head, Carrie thought it was because he felt bad about last night's antics, but then she partly thought he probably didn't even remember. She dismissed the idea of him being upset that she was flirting with Dylan because, most of the time, he wasn't even around.

"I'm going home," he said as he continued to load up fishing rods and tackle boxes.

"Why?"

"This just isn't my thing. The fishing sucks, maybe because it's too hot. It would be different if we had a boat. Besides, I have a bunch of cars waiting for me at the shop to fix and make some money." Carrie thought, sure, because you spent a ton gambling!

"Well, okay, I mean, if that's what you want to do." Carrie felt the tension leave her body, knowing she would be able to relax. Maybe she wouldn't drink as much now if she didn't need to numb her emotional pain. On the other hand, she also knew she could get in more trouble with him gone.

"That's everything. In the truck, girl." Tom patted the seat on the driver's side, and Brandy jumped in.

Carrie gave him a quick peck on the lips to say goodbye, but Tom tended to push a little harder. She pulled away. He turned, got in the truck, and drove off, not even saying goodbye to anyone.

Inside the trailer, Tori set out the muffins she had brought along with some plates and plastic silverware. Jen sat on the couch, touching up her nails and blowing them to dry. She looked up at Carrie when she walked in. "Well?"

"Tom's going home. He's got cars he wants to work on." Jen raised an eyebrow. " Is that a good thing?" Tori looked up at her friends under her baseball cap, wondering what was going on.

"Yeah, I think so. Tom said he wasn't having a good time and thought the fishing would be better."

"That's true," Jen replied. "I think I'm going to get a boat for next year. I've been wanting one for a while."

"I think it's good he left," said Tori." He can be an asshole. A real buzz kill."

Carrie looked around the trailer. "Where's Dylan?"

"I don't know. He might be at the bar." Jen answered, still working on her nails.

"At the bar so early?"

"He's probably having a Bloody Mary. We were all busy when he got up, so he just left."

"I'm going to run to the store to get more beer. Does anyone need anything?" Tori asked.

"You might want to grab another bottle of margarita mix—we're out," Jen told Tori.

"Could you pick up another bottle of vodka and some lemonade? I'll give you cash for it. Oh, and grab me a pack of cigarettes, please," said Carrie. She wasn't like Jen, who never left anything to chance regarding her cigarettes; she always brought a carton of them.

Carrie popped open the cooler Tom had left behind and spotted a few Smirnoff Ice bottles still chilling inside. Perfect, she thought, since they are light and a good way to start a long day of drinking.

Carrie glanced around the room, her hands on her hips. "So, what's the plan for today?" she asked.

Jen looked up with a grin. "Beach day!"

Carrie went into her bedroom and changed into her black bikini. She wasn't confident enough to wear it alone, so she pulled on her Victoria's Secret sarong cover-up pants. She looked in the mirror, gathered her hair, and clipped it. Even though she hadn't washed her hair, it still looked good. She applied black eyeliner and mascara, and decided she looked good enough for the pond.

Jen came out of her room looking the same, wearing her suit with a terry-cloth wrap. She added some drinks for herself to Carrie's cooler until Tori came with Jose Cuervo.

Some kids were swimming in the pond when they arrived. "Damn kids," Carrie said quietly. The picnic table was empty, so they set their cooler, tubes of Pringles, and lotion on top to claim their area.

Dylan came walking up to the table from out of nowhere. He had on his swim trunks and a Motley Crue T-shirt and was holding a red Solo cup, a carry-out from one of the bars, no doubt. He unwrapped his beach towel, pulled two beers out, and tossed them into their cooler.

"We were wondering where you were," Jen said and lightly punched him in the arm.

"Hey, keep that up, and no more massages for

you. I spent some time with the locals over at Brett's. Bobby was running his mouth about Marcy." He looked straight at Carrie. "I saw Tom drive off. Is he coming back?"

Carrie reached into the cooler and pulled out a Smirnoff Ice. "Nope." Jen pulled out a cold one for herself, and they all toasted.

The noon sun, with its oppressive heat, blazed overhead. The chirping of heat bugs filled the air. The friends tossed their towels aside and waded into the water. Jen had brought a couple of swimming noodles from her trailer, and they each grabbed one to float on as they relaxed on their backs. The girls bobbed gently while Dylan swam around, playfully dunking each of them. He swam over to Carrie, yanked her off her noodle, and splashed her under the water. Their laughter, carefree shouts, and a few curses filled the air. Soon, a group of parents—likely around their age—arrived, ushering their kids away, probably to grab lunch.

"Hey, look, Tori is back." Jen spotted her friend putting her bags down on the picnic table. She had changed out of her clothes and was wearing her swimsuit and a wrap.

Jen began to swim back to shore, and the rest followed. They were intrigued to know what Tori had bought. She unloaded a bottle of Margarita and an interesting bottle containing a bluish-green liquid.

"Hey guys, I got this new stuff called Hpnotiq. It's a fruity drink made with vodka and cognac. What could be bad about this?" Tori exclaimed, proud of her purchase.

Jen opened a Pringles carton, took a stack of chips, and passed them around. They all sat at the picnic table, and Tori poured a small amount of the magical liquid into five red Solo cups.

"You guys, let's play the name game," Carrie said as she put a stack of three chips in her mouth.

"What's that?" Dylan asked, scooting next to Carrie and putting his hand on her thigh under the table so no one could see.

"We go around the table and name a famous person. The next person has 30 seconds to name another famous person whose first name starts with the letter of the previous person's last name. If you can't come up with a person, you drink."

"That sounds fun," Jen replied.

"I'm not so good with celebrities like you all are," Tori interjected.

"Well, I guess that means you will be drinking more, young lady," said Dylan. Tori gave him a snarly look, placing her beer on the table with a thud. "Game on!"

"I'll start," said Carrie. "Jennifer Aniston." They all rolled their eyes, knowing she was obsessed with the show Friends.

Dylan was next, "Paula Abdul." They all laughed because even though Dylan was a rock and roll guy, he had a thing for her.

"The name has to start with an A, drink!" Carrie yelled, and they all laughed.

Tori was next, and she hesitated a bit. "Drink!" The group yelled.
Tori grumbled, grabbed the cup of the pretty liquid, and slammed it. "Ooh, that's good!" she said, wiping her mouth.

"I want to try it," added Carrie as she grabbed her cup.

They all followed suit and slammed the small amount in the red cups. Tori refilled all of them for another round.

"Adam Sandler," Tori blurted out. Dylan was next to her, and he quickly responded with "Steve Stricker."

"That's not a person!" yelled Tori.

"Wanna bet?" Dylan replied, sat back, and crossed his legs, looking at her sternly.

Carrie whispered in Dylan's ear, "Is he a person?"

"Yes, he is a famous golfer," he whispered back in her ear while caressing her thigh.

The game continued for about an hour as they all got tipsy from the Hpnotiq. The alcohol made it even harder to come up with a name on command as time went on. When the game had run its course, they all headed back into the water to cool off. The waterlogged friends returned to the trailer to fix up for a night out at the bars.

Back at the trailer, they all scattered to their rooms. They were buzzed but not too drunk to function. Carrie headed to her bedroom to change out of her swimsuit. She rummaged through her duffel bag and pulled out her margarita girl shirt. Her hair was still damp, so she worked in some beachy waves with the putty she had just bought. The sun had added some glistening highlights to her brown hair. She washed her face and reapplied her eyeliner and mascara, which had smudged from the heat and mischievous play in the water. Just as she finished, the door opened, and Dylan walked in.

"Dylan, what the heck?" Carrie snarked as she applied mascara using the mirror attached to the dresser.

"I need a place to change. Do you want me to get naked in the living room?"

"Fine," she put her cosmetics away. "You can change here."

Carrie's powder blue margarita girl shirt and favorite baggy cut-off denim shorts looked sexy against her sun-kissed body, which caught Dylan's eye.

"You look cute," Dylan said, tugging at her shirt. "I like the T-shirt."

"Thanks! I need a margarita!" Carrie pulled away from him and lifted his shirt slightly, revealing his flat stomach. "Put on something nice. We're going out," and she walked out of the room.

Jen stood in the kitchen with her hand on her hips when Carrie came out of her bedroom. "Really?" she asked.

"He needs a place to change. Geez, Jen, you expect him to change out here?" Carrie joined her and poured a margarita. Jen was still wearing her black and white bikini top but had added a yellow tank top with bright floral surf shorts. Her blond hair was dry, and she had it pulled up gently in a clip.

"Cheers," they tapped their glasses together.

"Let's go smoke," Carrie suggested. They didn't like to smoke in the trailer since Tori was opposed to it. Plus, they didn't want to fill the small trailer with smoke.

Jen grabbed her iPod, which blared Nickelback, one of her favorite groups, and headed to the deck. Carrie sat back on an old, cracked, and faded resin patio chair and took in the view as she puffed on her cigarette. You could see both bars and the other trailers from the deck. She inhaled the smell of grilled burgers and hot dogs as she watched various groups of families and friends play frisbee, bags, or cornhole, as the professionals call it. The background noise of different melodies filled the air. The meandering river revealed boaters heading into the shore and tying up at the docks for dinner.

"I like this place," said Carrie. "But it would be cool to be out on the river. I'm a bit jealous," she said as she pointed to the river.

"I know," Jen said. "I'm thinking about getting

a boat. Not a pontoon, but a fishing boat that will fit about six. Next year will be different."

Dylan's freshly showered smell interrupted Carrie's boating thoughts when he walked out the door. She felt a tingle down below as she noticed how his soft hair, tousled with the perfect amount of gel, hung over his eyes. His Nike t-shirt and usual cargo shorts completed his simple yet stylish look.

"What's up, angels?" he asked as he sat down and lit a cigarette.

"We should probably get something to eat since all we've eaten so far are Pringles," Jen said.

Tori emerged from the trailer with her hair pulled up into a ponytail beneath her usual baseball cap. She wore a simple gray tank top and khaki shorts.

"Did someone say food? I'm starving!" she exclaimed.

CHAPTER 9

Brett's was packed when they walked in. The dark bar provided the perfect escape for sun-drenched vacationers to escape the sun. The group found a great spot at the bar to accommodate all of them. They knew they needed to soak up all the alcohol from the day of partying, so they ordered chicken tenders and mozzarella sticks to share, and Dylan decided he also needed a sandwich.

Despite the crowd, Brett's wasn't the vibe they were looking for, so they left after eating and headed to The Edge. As they walked over, they passed a row of fancy, cool cars in the parking lot—Mustang convertibles, Corvettes, and more. It seemed that some folks with money had made their way to Riverbanks. Dylan couldn't resist, so he went and posed beside the cars while Carrie snapped photos with her camera. Meanwhile, Tori and Jen linked arms, singing, "All I wanna do is have some fun!"

When they walked into The Edge, Led Zeppelin blared on the jukebox. The windows behind the bar revealed the glistening river.

"Photo Hunt looks free!" Jen yelled over the

music, and they all headed to the game. Jen put her quarter in, and they all gathered around, helping out and pointing at photos. Tori spotted the wheelchair again and entertained herself spinning around, laughing nonstop.

Carrie pulled Dylan away to the bar while Jen and Tori continued to play. "Let's do a shot!" She asked the bartender to make Kamikazes. They both slammed the shot, and Dylan pulled Carrie close to him.

"I want to kiss you so bad," Dylan murmured, his face inches from Carrie's. She felt his boozy breath brush over her cheeks as she gazed at him. His hair fell messily over his eyes, obscuring his expression.

Carrie slowly exhaled. "So do I, but not in front of the girls.. Maybe when they go back." She glanced at the clock—it was almost 11 p.m., so Jen and Tori wouldn't be out much longer.

Before long, Jen and Tori approached the bar to join them. Jen waved the wad of cash in her hand.

"I'm tired," Jen said with a grin. "I'm Photo Hunted out. Let's do a shot, then I'm heading back."

"Same here," Tori added with a tired sigh. "I'm exhausted. Too much sun today."

Everyone in the bar seemed to give off a sun-kissed glow from hours spent at the pond. The sweltering heat and blasting music created an electric buzz, and a mix of drunkenness and unspoken desire filled the air.

The bartender sighed with irritation when Dylan ordered four snakebite shots. That meant he had to make an effort to mix them up instead of just pouring them from a bottle. He set the shots down on the bar, and they all grabbed theirs.

"Cheers to our last night in Riverbanks!" Jen raised her shot glass, and they all clinked their shots and drank—each one wincing after downing the sour and pungent shot made of Yukon Jack and lime juice.

"Ok then, that's enough for me," Jen said and picked up her cigarette case.

"I'm with you, girl." Tori gathered her belongings and looked at Carrie and Dylan. "You guys coming?" she asked.

They looked at each other, and Dylan spoke up first.

"I'm gonna try my hand at one of the machines at Brett's. I still have some cash left to burn." He ran his hand through his sweaty, tousled hair, and it fell over his eyes, disguising the guilty look in his eyes.

Carrie quickly thought of an excuse to stay since they all knew she didn't like to gamble. "I think I'll go too and see what all the fuss is about. Plus, I'm a little hungry. I may get a bite to eat."

Jen and Tori's exhaustion must have clouded their judgment, as the bar didn't serve food that late, and it was unusual for Carrie to eat so late after drinking.

"Okay, then. See ya." Jen tapped them both on the arm, and she and Tori left the bar.

Dylan looked down at Carrie, brushed a wave of hair away from her eye, and caressed her cheek with his thumb.

"Should we go check out those machines?"

A tingle shivered throughout her body as she heard her mischievous inner voice pushing her to go, even though she knew she shouldn't.

"Yeah, let's go," she replied.

They started walking to the next bar, singing Carrie's favorite Motley Crue song, "Don't Go Away Mad (Just Go Away)," that had just been playing on the jukebox.

Dylan sped up ahead of her and turned around to face her.

"Some people tell me I look like Tommy Lee." He air drummed as he walked backward.

"Don't flatter yourself," she replied, running ahead of him while he chased her.

They entered Brett's after the short walk to find it was crowded, though not as packed as The Edge. They scanned the room, searching for anyone they knew, particularly that nosy Marcy. Carrie spotted Bobby in the far corner, sitting opposite the machines with a group of guys. They quickly made their way to the other side of the bar and managed to squeeze into a small corner, where Carrie slid in, and Dylan leaned against the bar behind her. She turned around in the tight space, their bodies brushing together.

Looking up at him, Carrie asked, "What are you having?"

"I think we need whiskey shots," Dylan replied with a devilish look.

"You think?" She stumbled a bit towards him, already feeling the shots from the last bar. He put his arms around her waist to steady her, and they stood still for a second, gazing at each other. Just then, the slow and seductive lyrics of the song, Linger, poured out of the jukebox, and their chemistry grew fiercely intense as if they could spontaneously combust.

Dylan closed his eyes briefly, then leaned down and put his lips on Carrie's as the lyrics started. There was no rejection on her part; she leaned right in, and they kissed for a few seconds like no one else was in the room. Carrie opened her eyes and spotted Bobby walking towards the back of the bar where they were. He was talking with his friend, so it didn't appear he had seen them, but Carrie stopped Dylan and pushed him away lightly. "Bobby," she whispered in his ear.

He took her hand, "Come with me," and guided her to the stairway behind the popcorn machine. The light from upstairs provided just enough illumination for them to make it down the stairs to a storage room with shelves full of large cans, bags, and bins. They found a spot lit by an overhead light above a utility sink. Dylan pressed Carrie up against a shelf and took her face in his hand. He placed his mouth on hers, both of their tongues seeking each other's, his tongue running over her teeth. He pulled away slightly, only to suck on her lower lip while she reached down and put her hand on his zipper. "Mmmm," he moaned and ran his hands through her hair.

A loud commotion stopped them when they heard a person or two coming down the stairs. Dylan and Carrie squeezed behind one of the shelves and saw two figures quickly descending the stairs. Carrie paused briefly, not sure if they had been spotted. The unknown invaders passed by them, heading further into the storage room. Dylan and Carrie immediately slid out and ran up the stairs, practically falling. Carrie saw the hat one of them was wearing, but couldn't remember where she had seen it. They slipped out the back doorway, hoping no one saw them.

"Oh my God," Carrie yelled. She patted her body to make sure she still had her purse. "Fuck, I dropped my purse in there! I wonder who that was? Goddammit!"

Dylan doubled over, laughing hysterically.

"It's not funny, Dylan. I'm married. If anyone finds out…"

"Calm down, Carrie. Come on, let's—"

"No. Let's not. We're not doing this. The light's on in the trailer. Jen must still be up."

Dylan reached for her hand. "Please, that was incredible…"

"No, Dylan, I can't. I just can't." She pulled her hand away and turned toward the trailer.

Dylan stood, frozen, as he watched her walk away, his eyes fixed on her retreating figure.

"I'll go back and try to get your purse."

"Please," she said as she headed towards the trailer.

~ ~ ~

A knock on the trailer door went unnoticed, followed by the loud bang of the door opening and several people entering. Carrie jolted awake, glancing at the clock—it was 2:26 a.m.. She quickly pulled on some pajama bottoms and rushed to open the door, wanting to see the commotion.

As she stepped into the hallway, she bumped into Jen, who had just stumbled out of her bedroom. Jen's hair was disheveled, and she was still wearing the clothes from the night before. Carrie gave her a quick once-over, then turned toward the door, eager to figure out what was happening.

"I'm sorry, ma'am, but we've seen this guy at your place. Is he your friend?"

Two young men dragged Dylan into the room; his head dropped down and was not visible at first. Carrie and Jen ran over and pulled his face up so they could see. His eyes were shut, swollen and bruised, and blood ran down from his mouth, which hung open just like a boxer who had lost the round.

"Dylan, oh my God!" Jen screamed. She and

Carrie took hold of his arms, releasing him from the two strangers, and did their best to drag him to the couch. Jen scurried into the kitchen and dampened a towel while Carrie caressed Dylan's hand and tried to wake him.

"Dylan, Dylan, are you okay?" Tears fell from Carrie's face as she tried to shake him awake. She listened and found his pulse. He was alive. Jen came over with the towel and started wiping the blood off his face. He struggled to open his eyes because they were so swollen. They were glassy and unfocused.

Carrie looked up at the men standing over them. They looked concerned.

"Who did this?" She whispered, careful not to wake Tori.

"We don't know," one of the men replied. "We found him on the ground outside of Brett's."

Jen walked over and got right in their faces.

"Did you ask anyone if they saw anything? How could this happen with no one noticing?" She asked in a sharp voice.

The two men backed off a little. "The bar was closing, and everyone had left. We took the back way out because we're staying right over there," one of them said, pointing toward the door. That's how they knew where Dylan was staying. They had seen him with our group, tossing bags around.

"Come on, man, let's go. She's freaking out," the guy with the trucker hat said, pulling his friend away from Jen's interrogation. The two men walked out, leaving the trailer silent. Jen stepped closer, resuming where she had left off, gently cleaning Dylan's face.

Carrie's mind flashed back to just a few hours ago, to the figures who had passed by her and Dylan, their bodies pressed against the shelf in heated passion. Dylan had gone back to grab her purse, but now, it was nowhere in sight. She would worry about that later. For now, she kept calling his name, trying to wake him. His eyes finally focused, locking onto hers.

"Your purse," he murmured.

Carrie stopped him, pressing her hand on his chest to quiet him before he could say anything else. "Don't worry about it. I can look later. What happened? Who did this?"

"I went back to get your purse, and these two guys jumped me before I could even get in the bar."

"I don't understand. How did no one see or hear anything? People are coming out the back door all the time!" Jen uttered in confusion.

"Let's let Dylan sleep. It's late. We need to see if my purse is at the bar. We can ask questions then." Carrie covered Dylan with a blanket and placed a pillow under his head. He closed his eyes, and she and Jen turned out the lights, went to their rooms, and tried their best to sleep.

The following morning, Jen and Carrie carefully turned Dylan onto his side, positioning him to face the couch so Tori wouldn't be alarmed if she saw him.

Tori was leaving that morning because she was eager to get back to her husband.

After saying their goodbyes, Jen and Carrie made their way to Brett's. As usual, Brett was behind the bar, tending to the morning crowd.

"Great," Jen said. "He's going to be a jerk." Brett looked up as they walked in and continued to wipe down the bar. He reached under the bar and produced Carrie's tiny purse.

"Did you come for this?" Brett asked as he grabbed a purse and put it on the bar. "It was outside the back door. You're lucky no one else found it."

"Did you happen to hear about my friend getting jumped last night?" Jen asked with an attitude while Carrie shuffled through her purse to see if anything was missing.

"No, can't say I did." Brett didn't seem to care one bit.

Jen looked around the bar to see if anyone had heard her. There were only a few people at the bar that she didn't recognize, and one man was on a machine. It was still pretty early, but the restaurant was full of customers having breakfast.

"Come on, Carrie, let's go. Time to leave this place."

Back at the trailer, they packed up their belongings, cleaned, and shut down the trailer quietly, letting Dylan sleep. When the girls were ready to leave, they carefully got Dylan up and gave him some ibuprofen and water. He looked slightly better than he did hours ago, but his eyes and lips were still swollen and bruised.

As Jen's car pulled away, they took one last look at the river. The sun sparkled on the water, and guests prepared their boats for one final Sunday filled with fun.

Jen glanced at Carrie and Dylan, a hint of uncertainty in her voice. "I know this sounds silly, but did you guys have fun? I mean, up until last night?"

Dylan gave a slight smirk and looked over at Carrie. "Yeah, I did," he said, his eyes lingering on her momentarily.

"So did I," Carrie smiled, "but it's time to beat it." She reached into her purse, searching for her missing Van Halen lighter.

PART TWO

2003

CHAPTER 10

Jen arrived first at Riverbanks on Thursday, with the rest of the group working throughout the day and planning to arrive in the evening. Her cousin, Benny, came with her; he was part of their dart league, so everyone knew him and liked him. Jen had taken over her father's jewelry store, which was thriving, so she bought a boat earlier in the year. Jen said Benny was always handy when it came to launching and tying the boat. It wasn't brand new, but it was in great shape and seated six—perfect for their group.

Since Jen loved fishing, the plan was for her, Benny, and Tom to head out early in the morning to fish while the other girls would spend the day cruising on the river. The Riverbanks area had several bar restaurants along the river, each with docks where you could tie up your boat, grab some food, enjoy cocktails, and sometimes even catch a live band, especially on holiday weekends. Everyone was excited to have access to the boat for the summer.

Jen was anxious about Carrie and Tom's arrival. She was well aware of the problems they were having, especially the "butt dial" incident from earlier that year. Carrie played the answering machine message back to her over and over, and it was clear that a woman was giving Tom a blow job. He had accidentally dialed Carrie on his track phone in the heat of the moment. Even after Carrie threw a large stone ashtray at him, Tom denied it, but what she heard was undeniable. Jen also knew about Carrie's after-work escapades at a bar near her work, where she frequently hung out, which did not make Tom very happy, if he even cared. Their relationship was a ticking time bomb, and despite her friendship with Carrie, Jen was worried the drama would ruin the weekend.

Benny took Jen out on the boat and taught her how to drive it. She had bought an MP3 player, so they cruised down the river, enjoying the music and the calm before the afternoon traffic started. After docking, Jen and Benny began decorating the deck with citronella candles and American flags. Tom and Carrie pulled up in their truck as they were finishing up. Carrie immediately jumped out, ran over to Jen, and wrapped her in a warm hug.

"Hey, you look relaxed and happy," Carrie said.

"Benny just took me out on the boat and taught me how to drive it. It was nice, and I learned a lot. He's a good teacher; I think I got this!" She smiled, and her face flushed. She was smoking her cigarette and sipping on a small cocktail. It seemed like cocktail hour was always in full swing at Riverbanks.

"Tom and I will unpack, and then I'll join you. When is Tori getting here?"

Carrie and Tori got to know each other better over the past year after last summer's stay. They had recently gotten together at Jen's to watch the first few seasons of Sex and The City, since neither of them had watched it, and Jen had HBO on Demand. It was a fun girls' night drinking Cosmopolitans, the show's signature drink. The three of them also got together several Saturday nights for karaoke while Tom stayed home after a long day of brewing batches of beer and drinking.

"Tori will be here tomorrow," Jen replied. "Since Drew isn't coming, she wants to spend the night with him."

"He has to work?" Carrie asked.

Carrie couldn't help but wonder why Tori and Drew never seemed to be together outside of darts. They weren't the type to make public displays, but they always seemed content in each other's company. They showed up separately, both after work, never arriving together. After all the shots and dart-throwing, Drew would head out immediately, while Tori stayed behind until the rest of the group started to leave. She was always a flirt at darts, sometimes sitting on the laps of some of the younger guys in the league, enjoying the attention.

"Not sure," Jen replied. "But she will have a bedroom all to herself. Benny has to sleep on the couch."

Carrie started bringing her bags into the trailer while Tom walked Brandy down to the river to check out Jen's new boat. Benny was sitting on the deck, tying some lures on his fishing poles. The smells of the grills wafted in the air, signaling dinnertime.

Benny stepped off the deck, a bottle of beer in hand, likely one of the high-octane varieties he preferred. His larger-than-life attitude made him the type of friend women loved, but a bit of a turnoff when it came to being a serious boyfriend—he could be a little too boorish. Handsome, with thick reddish-brown hair, dark brown eyes, and a well-groomed mustache and goatee, he had the kind of rugged appeal that turned heads. He made a decent living as a sports writer for the local newspaper, so his wardrobe was a mix of casual sportswear and sharp, preppy pieces straight out of GQ. His chosen attire for the day was a Cubs hat, a white tank top, and red basketball shorts, which gave him an effortlessly laid-back look.

"Well, well, now the party can start," Benny exclaimed, walking down the steps from the deck.

"It looks like you've already started the party," Carrie said. Benny hugged her neck and kissed her on the cheek. "I didn't know you liked the Cubbies."

"I like all teams, Care, you know that. Plus, I predict they will take the division this year. Maybe even the league." He tapped her arm. "And you can quote me on that. Where's Tom?

"He's down at the pier looking at Jen's boat."

Benny seemed to get along well with Tom. Although they had similar personalities, Benny was not a mean drunk. He was pompous and crude at times, but also very kind.

"Damn, there have to be some hotties up here! I didn't tan this bod for nothing." Benny exclaimed as he put on his Ray-Bans and headed toward the pier.

Jen rolled her eyes, witnessing the whole interaction.

"He thinks he's God's gift. You should see the duffel bag he brought. It takes up the whole corner of the living room!"

"He's fine. It will be a nice addition. I will start bringing our stuff in so I can relax with you. After the drive with Tom, I'm already tense."

Jen helped Carrie bring in their bags and coolers. After Carrie unpacked her bags and set them up in their bedroom, she made a stiff vodka lemonade and joined Jen on the deck to catch up.

"How's it been with you two? Any more incidents that I should be aware of?"

Jen couldn't shake the memory of the butt dial earlier that spring. The message had been so ridiculous, it was hard to forget. How could any man be that careless? To have his phone clipped to his side while being pleasured by some floozy—was he that stupid? It replayed in her mind repeatedly, making her cringe even more at the thought.

"What can I say? It's a shit show at our house. He stays late working at the shop and drinking with his buddies. It's that, or he is at the neighbor's house creating the next great brew. I must say, he has produced some wines that I like. They can knock you out!"

"Sounds lovely," Jen said as she put out her cigarette. "Come on, let's go to Brett's. We can get a couple of pizzas to bring back for dinner. I don't think anyone is in the mood to cook."

Brett's was not too busy, as it was close to dinnertime, but soon enough, guests would shuffle in for dinner if they weren't doing a cookout. Jen and Carrie walked to the back end of the bar, where they usually gravitated.

Jen placed the food order at the bar while Carrie ordered a couple of beers for them. Two men were sitting at the bar, and one turned to face her.

"Carrie, is it?" Bobby asked, eyeing her tan body from head to toe. Carrie blushed under his gaze, and it only took a second for her to recognize the red hat he was wearing. It was the same one she had seen flash by her and Dylan in the storage room the previous summer. A chill ran through her—he knew. He knew exactly what had happened.

"You here by yourself?" Bobby asked, breaking her thoughts.

"No, with my husband, Tom." Bobby's expression shifted to one of quiet questioning, clearly recalling the scene from last summer when she was with another man.

"We're staying with Jen. You know Jen, right?"

"Yeah, of course. So where's that other guy you were all with last year?"

"Dylan? Oh, he didn't come." Carrie shifted uncomfortably, eager to change the subject. "Where's Marcy?"

Carrie quickly turned the conversation, feeling put on the spot.

"Don't know. I don't keep tabs on Marcy."

Her mind briefly flickered to her earlier conversation with Jen about children. Marcy was probably with her son while her husband sat at the bar with his buddy, zoning out to sports.

Just then, Jen approached them after placing the pizza order, and Carrie quickly handed her a bottle of beer, grateful for the interruption.

"Thanks, Carrie. Hi, Bobby."

"Hey, Jen. It's a shame what happened to your friend last summer. But you have to be careful when you're drinking." Bobby warned.

"I'm not sure what happened, but the investigators around here don't want to spend any time on it," Jen replied, clearly frustrated.

"Oh, come on, Jen. What do you expect from how your group drinks?" Bobby shot back, a smirk playing on his lips.

"You should talk, Bobby! I never see you without a drink in your hand. Hell, you're here at nine in the morning for Christ's sake," Jen retorted.

Jen grabbed Carrie's arm, pulling her toward the other side of the bar. "Come on, let's finish our beer and get out of here."

They made their way to the far corner, Carrie doing her best to avoid Bobby's gaze. She could feel his eyes on her, making her uncomfortable. Jen lit a cigarette, inhaling deeply before blowing out the smoke in a sharp exhale.

"The nerve of him!" Jen muttered, shaking her head as she looked at Carrie. "He's at this bar—or the Edge—just about every weekend morning. The days he's not here, he's probably too hungover to get up, all while his kid runs wild."

Carrie shrugged, trying to stay calm. "Don't let it bother you. It's not like we'll hang out with him or his wife anyway."

"Yeah, but this is a small area, and everyone goes to the same places up and down the river. Bobby will be out boating, so I'm sure we will run into him enough." Jen butted out her cigarette angrily.

Carrie's nerves tingled as she considered potential encounters with him. Her thoughts were interrupted by the bartender delivering their pizzas wrapped in paper.

"Here you go, Jen," the cute bartender said, handing her the stack. The pizzas smelled delicious, like pepperoni.

"Do you need some money?" Carrie asked Jen while smiling at the bartender.

"I got it already. Come on, let's go."

~ ~ ~

After finishing the pizzas, Jen took out a container of jello shots she had made. It was unlike her to "give 'er" on the first night, but she was in a mood from Bobby's earlier comments about Dylan. There was an assortment of small plastic shot glasses in various colors: yellow, blue-green, bright blue, and orange.

"Wow, Jen, with only two more colors, you'd have a rainbow," Carrie pointed out as she poured herself a strong vodka and soda.

The group already felt a buzz from starting cocktail hour early. Tom and Benny had been talking politics at the table for quite a while. Jen and Carrie changed into their adorable margarita girl t-shirts even though they had been refraining from drinking too many margaritas due to the heartburn it gave them. Carrie had suggested to Jen earlier that they should wear them for a photo, so Jen put on her cowboy hat, and Carrie wore her signature cut-off shorts.

"Okay, some of these are vodka, and some are Malibu. I'm not sure which is which, but you'll know when you drink it. I used what I had in the cabinet. I think some might even have lemon vodka. You know I have an assortment." Jen proclaimed proudly as she pulled the large container out of the refrigerator.

She brought the container to the table, and they all sat around, taking the Jello shots one by one. You had to stick your tongue in and guide it out of the small cup. They were sour and powerful, yet delicious. They all laughed because after a few, no one could tell which flavors were which.

"I think this one is a walibu," Benny stated after he tasted a blue-green shot.

"There's no walibu, dumbass!" Jen yelled, and they all laughed. The snacks began flying, bag after bag of chips, all over the table.

"Come on, Jen, let's go out on the deck and snap a photo of us taking a shot," Carrie suggested with a grin.

Jen raised an eyebrow but smiled, tossing her cigarette away. "You're on."

The two of them went out on the deck, the sun casting a warm glow over the water. Jen grabbed the bottle of tequila and two shot glasses from the table, pouring generous amounts into each.

"Here's to us," Jen said, holding up her glass.

Carrie clinked her glass against Jen's with a smile. "To us."

Benny stumbled over and said, "I'll take a photo of you beautiful girls." He clicked it with Carrie's disposable camera. Carrie and Jen stumbled to the kitchen to make another drink. Not seeing anyone in the kitchen, they realized the guys had left and probably gone to the bar. They finished mixing their drinks and returned to the deck for a cigarette.

"Did I tell you I saw Dylan the other night?" Jen

asked Carrie, her voice soft under the moonlit sky. The stars sparkled above them, and in the distance, they could see The Edge bathed in a hazy neon glow.

Carrie's heart skipped a beat at the mention of his name. She took a slow breath, trying to remain calm. "Really? Where?" Carrie asked, keeping her tone casual, though her curiosity was piqued.

Carrie sat back, her gaze fixed on Jen, hanging on to every word. She hadn't seen much of Dylan since that chaotic summer; truth be told, she hadn't tried to. She didn't have his phone number, not that she'd ever use it if she did. They'd barely spoken since then—just a few quick exchanges at the bar when their paths happened to cross when he was with his girlfriend. Casual hellos, a polite "nice to see you," but nothing more. It felt like the chemistry they had shared that weekend had been nothing more than a fleeting combination of hot weather, too much alcohol, and the absence of any other woman around to complicate things.

Carrie exhaled slowly, a sense of resignation washing over her. She had repeatedly told herself that she and Dylan were not meant to be and that night had been an anomaly—just a moment in time, a blip that had no lasting power. But hearing Jen talk about Dylan again stirred up something inside her— something she hadn't expected to feel.

"I went to the Pub on wing night a while back. He was there alone, so I got to talk to him without Sue being there. Ugh, I can't stand her! I asked him if he knew who beat him up that night, but he got all quiet and said no. I think he knows, and he's just not saying. Anyway, I hope he ends it with Sue. Doesn't she have a kid or two? What is he thinking?"

CHAPTER 11

The early morning sun shone into the trailer, lighting up a substantial mess of chip bags, dirty ashtrays, and empty plastic shot glasses. Carrie woke up to an empty bed and an empty living room, meaning the guys had gone fishing. No one bothered to clean up, so Jen threw out shot glasses, cleaned up, and wiped down the sticky table.

The night before, the girls had lingered on the deck, sipping their drinks and swapping stories, as the warm evening air wrapped around them like a comfortable blanket. They laughed as they recalled the concert back in June, a night of pure chaos and fun. They had gone to see Styx, Journey, and REO Speedwagon, and by the end of the night, they were blissfully drunk on light beer. Strolling through the arena arm in arm, they belted out "Roll with the Changes," their voices off-key but full of joy, drawing amused looks from fellow concertgoers.

Carrie chuckled as she remembered how she had the foresight to bring an overnight bag, knowing she'd be in no shape to drive home. Tom, of course, was furious and raged about her not calling, but Carrie had been too drunk and carefree to care. She had stumbled through the next day, barely getting through the work day before cutting out early with Jen. The two of them ended up at the Pub, nursing greasy burgers to cure their hangovers. As the office manager for a construction company, Carrie had the flexibility to leave without anyone questioning it. She told them she was getting office supplies, and no one was the wiser. Jen, owning her own business, had the same freedom. They both had the luxury to escape when needed, even if it was just for a day.

Carrie walked into the kitchen, poured herself a cup of coffee and a large glass of water, and started helping Jen clean up.

"Morning. I see the guys left already?" Carrie asked Jen while dumping out dirty ashtrays.

"Yeah, I didn't even hear them leave or come in. I think I drank too much last night. I planned on fishing with them, but that's not happening."

The girls heard a noise outside and saw Tori's car pull up. She walked into the trailer carrying a red, white, and blue Tommy Hilfiger overnight bag and set it on the table. She looked fresh and wide awake, wearing a ponytail in her Audi hat, a slick Harley Davidson tank top, and tan cargo shorts. She smelled like fresh, clean soap, and her presence livened up the stale, sleepy trailer.

"Morning, ladies. How are we feeling?" Tori assumed they had given it good the night before, based on the trailer's appearance, even though Jen and Carrie had tidied up quite a bit. The bottles and cups of booze were still on the counter, half empty.

She spied the couch, with blankets and pillows strewn about as if someone had been sleeping on it, along with a large open bag on the counter containing clothes in a disorganized mess.

"Who's sleeping on the couch? Dylan?" Tori questioned.

Jen replied, holding her coffee close to her mouth, "Benny, my cousin. You know, from darts."

Tori snarled. "That guy? Oh, come on!"

Her eyes went to the television, where a pair of boxer shorts lay next to it. She pointed at them.

"Eeew, his underwear is over there. Crotch out!"

Jen and Carrie laughed hysterically, and Carrie grabbed a pen from the counter. They poked the boxers and carried them over to drop into his bag.

"It's like he literally stepped out of them and left them just like that," Carrie said, and she shoved them into his bag.

"How disgusting," Tori said under her breath. "Where is that buffoon anyway?"

"With Tom, fishing. Let's start preparing food because we're going on a cruise down the river when they return." Jen set her mug down and went to her room.

Tori went out to her car to gather her bags and cooler. Carrie opened a can of diet Mountain Dew, emptied some of it, and added a little vodka to ease her headache and take the edge off. She opened the refrigerator and pulled out the bags of deli meat and sliced cheeses she had brought. Before the weekend, Jen created an Excel spreadsheet listing items for everyone to contribute over the weekend.

Tori came back in, dragging her bags behind her, and began unpacking, placing items in the refrigerator and taking out the fixings for sandwiches. Carrie scanned the kitchen for Ziploc bags and found them tucked away in a bag Jen had brought. The room was silent as they worked, except for the sound of crinkling plastic and the clinking of jars. Then Tori turned to Carrie, her gaze lingering for a second.

"Nice shirt," she remarked, a playful smile tugging at her lips.

Carrie glanced down at her melon-colored t-shirt, the words "If I don't remember, it didn't happen" emblazoned across the front. She grinned, feeling a bit cheeky.

Jen walked into the kitchen, still looking disheveled from her morning routine. She stopped when she saw Carrie's shirt and, without missing a beat, muttered, "Ain't that the truth."

Carrie laughed for a second, as she realized Jen was right—sometimes it was easier to forget than to remember.

"Is it time for a bloody?" Carrie asked Jen and Tori.

"Not me," said Tori, "but have at it."

Carrie grabbed a red Solo cup and poured a generous amount of vodka, then added the Bloody Mary mix and a splash of Tabasco. She stirred it gently, and the familiar scent of the spicy concoction filled the air.

"Jen?" Carrie called out, glancing over to see if her friend was nearby.

"No, I'm still recovering. I'll stick with water. You need to drink some water, too."

Carrie chuckled, nodding as she took a sip from her cup. "Yeah, I probably should," she said, glancing at her drink with a grin. "But you know how it is, one more won't hurt." She winked, already feeling the warm buzz starting to creep in.

Carrie grabbed a bottle of water and her drink and sat at the table to assemble sandwiches for the boat.

While Carrie and Tori fixed the sandwiches, Jen filled coolers with water, beer, and other snacks that would be easy to eat on the boat. They had brought imitation crab sticks, cut-up sausage, and cheese. Jen also filled a bag with Pringles and crackers. Carrie took a half-full bottle of lemonade and added vodka to make drinks. She made a vodka lemonade, ready to take on the boat with her.

Benny and Tom returned around 11:30, and they all quickly gathered their bags with towels and lotion and headed to the pier. Benny cleaned up the beer cans and had the boat nice and neat for the ladies. He took their hands and helped the girls onto the boat. Carrie laughed as her drink sloshed a little as she stepped on.

"Easy there," Benny said as she made a rough descent on the boat.

"Come on, Carrie. Give me your drink," Tom said, taking the cup out of her hand.

"I think we all had a little too much to drink last night. Think you can drive, Benny?" Jen asked.

"Sure can!" Benny exclaimed and helped her aboard.

Everyone settled on the boat. The guys lounged in the shaded back while the girls sprawled out in the sun-soaked front, soaking up the rays. The boat bounced over the river's waves, splashing water into their faces and filling the boat with laughter. Music played faintly from the MP3 player, struggling to compete with nearby boats' roaring wakes and loud conversations and laughter.

You could feel the river's energy filled with boats—large cruisers, sleek speedboats, and pontoons—piloted by people enjoying drinks and the summer sun.

They cruised to the sandbar at the river's end, a known hotspot. Boats were anchored in clusters, creating an impromptu party on the water. Groups of young twenty- and thirty-somethings stood in the shallow water, tossing balls, drinking, and blasting music. The boat beside theirs brimmed with twenty-year-olds in bikinis, laughing as they passed around beer bongs.

Jen's group maneuvered awkwardly into the water, laughing as they steadied themselves. The riverbed felt soft and squishy beneath their feet, and the water was cool against their skin. Tom and Benny tossed a Nerf football, their aim occasionally splashing the women. Meanwhile, Carrie, Jen, and Tori clustered, chatting about everything from work to family.

After a while, Benny swam back to the boat, pulling himself up with a grunt. "Forgot my smokes," he called out, digging into the small cooler where he'd stashed them.

"Make me a drink, dear?" Carrie yelled toward the boat and handed Benny her cup.

Benny handed Carrie her drink with a cigarette lit in his mouth, then gave her a cigarette. He tended to her with a big smile as he glanced at the bikini ladies in the next boat. Tori yelled from the water, "Benny, can you get me a sandwich?"

He took one out of the cooler, opened it, and took a bite before grinning and handing it to her.

"Jerk!" Tori yelled as she grabbed the sandwich. He took another one for himself and asked if anyone else wanted one.

Tom offered Carrie a sandwich, but she declined, so he bit into it instead.

The group spent the rest of the afternoon at the sandbar, basking in the carefree atmosphere. They waded through the warm, shallow water, drinks in hand, their toes sinking into the mushy sand. Jen's

MP3 player provided a soundtrack of classic rock and pop hits, its faint tunes competing with the laughter and conversations of nearby boaters.

Tom and Benny continued tossing the Nerf football, their playful competitiveness drawing occasional cheers from nearby boats. Carrie, Jen, and Tori stayed close to the boat, lounging in the water and talking as the sun blazed overhead.

Fueled by several vodka lemonades, Carrie found herself loosening up. Her laughter and words flowed easily. She leaned toward Tori and lowered her voice.

"Okay, so there's something I never told you," Carrie said, a conspiratorial smirk on her lips.

Tori raised an eyebrow, intrigued. "Oh, this should be good. Spill."

Carrie glanced at Jen, who shrugged and said, "Might as well. It's too juicy not to share."

She took a deep breath and launched into the story of the infamous butt dial incident. As she recounted the absurd details, Tori's face shifted between shock and amusement, her laughter erupting at the most outrageous moments.

"No way!" Tori exclaimed, clutching her stomach as she doubled over with laughter. "How does someone even manage that? And he didn't realize?!"

Carrie shook her head, giggling uncontrollably. "Nope! He had no clue. Can you imagine the audacity?"

Jen chuckled and added, "I still can't believe it

either. Men are idiots sometimes."

The three women laughed until their sides ached, momentarily forgetting the rest of the world as the sun dipped lower in the sky.

"And look how fat he's getting?" she pointed to Tom. His gut protruded so much that he appeared pregnant.

Tori remained relatively quiet about her personal life, sharing only snippets as the conversation unfolded. She mentioned that she'd recently started an esthetician class and was thrilled about the opportunity. Her company was covering the costs of her attendance at seminars throughout the United States, and she seemed excited about the opportunity to travel.

However, as much as she talked about her career and upcoming trips, she didn't say a word about Drew. Not one mention of her husband, their life together, or his thoughts on her new endeavors. Carrie noticed the omission but decided not to press her. Tori was always good at keeping certain aspects of her life neatly tucked away, and today seemed no different.

Instead, they focused on the moment—laughter, sunshine, and drinks in hand—leaving unspoken topics to linger in the background.

A loud commotion erupted, and Tom abruptly stormed over to Carrie. Without a word, he aggressively grabbed her shoulders and shoved her down into the water.

The group fell silent, watching in shock as Carrie disappeared below the surface. The water was deeper than the sandbar they had been wading in, and she flailed for a moment, trying to orient herself. The vodka lemonades hindered her mediocre swimming skills.

She pushed upward, desperate for air, her hands clawing at the water until she finally broke the surface, gasping and coughing.

"Tom, what the hell are you doing?" Jen snapped, her eyes blazing with anger.

Carrie wiped water from her face, coughing and catching her breath. "What is your problem?" she shouted at him, her voice trembling with fear and fury.

Tom shrugged, a smug grin plastered across his face. "Just having a little fun," he said dismissively, as if his actions were harmless.

"That's not fun; that's dangerous!" Tori chimed in, her tone biting.

Carrie glared at Tom, anger simmering beneath her drenched exterior. She wanted to say more, to call him out in front of everyone, but she bit her tongue. Her body shivered from adrenaline and embarrassment.

Jen stepped between them, her hands on her hips. "Why don't you go cool off somewhere else, Tom?" she said sternly, her tone leaving no room for argument.

Tom snorted, shaking his head as he waded away in the water toward the boat, muttering under his breath. Silence fell over the group, their carefree afternoon dampened by his outburst.

Carrie, still catching her breath, turned to Jen. "I think I've had enough water for today," she said softly, her voice betraying the hurt she tried to conceal.

CHAPTER 12

The sun hung low in the sky, casting a golden glow over the river as it neared dinnertime. The group decided to head back before the rush of other boaters created chaos on the water. Benny hoped to avoid navigating through heavy traffic and its choppy wake since he had drunk several beers that day.

They packed up their belongings and gathered the empty cans, towels, and the remains of their snacks. They refreshed their drinks one last time, and Jen queued up her favorite playlist, turning the boat ride into an impromptu sing-along. Laughter and off-key lyrics echoed over the water as they cruised back down the river, the cool spray hitting their faces with every wave.

As they neared the pier by Brett's, the mood shifted. The wake had calmed, and Benny focused on guiding the boat into the slip without incident. The group fell silent again, watching intently as he maneuvered carefully, Jen standing by to assist if needed.

Benny docked the boat flawlessly with a steady hand, and a collective cheer erupted from the group. They quickly disembarked, tossing their bags and towels onto the dock. Beer cans were discarded into the large receptacle by the pier, and everyone pitched in to tidy up the boat.

The group headed up the pier, the sun dipping lower behind them, painting the horizon in hues of orange and pink. It had been a day full of highs and lows, but for now, they focused on the promise of a good meal and the comfort of the evening ahead.

In the trailer, Jen went to her room while Tom took Brandy for a walk. Carrie lay down on the couch and drifted off to sleep. Jen and Tori took the opportunity to freshen up.

Jen approached Carrie and saw her head uncomfortably placed on the arm of the couch.

"Oh, look at Carrie, she is out! Too much sun and alcohol," Jen said sympathetically.

She took a pillow from the end of the couch and placed it under her head. "I don't want her to get a neckache."

The door slammed open, and Tom stormed in. He stumbled toward Benny, who was calmly mixing a Bacardi and Coke at the counter.

"Dude, you missed it!" Tom blurted, nudging Benny roughly on the arm. "There's a group of hotties down by the pond with no tops on. You gotta see it!"

Benny gave him a skeptical look, glancing at the

flask in his hand. "Man, you've got to be imagining things. No way there's nude sunbathers out here."

"Yeah, well, it'd be cool if there were," Tom muttered, spinning around. His gaze fell on Carrie, who was lying on the couch. "What's my wife up to? Sleeping?"

Without warning, Tom staggered over to her and plopped down on her head.

"Get up! It's dinnertime," he barked.

"Dude, get the fuck off her!" Benny shouted, rushing over to pull Tom off.

Jen and Tori joined the commotion, yelling, "Get off her! Get off her!"

Tom let out a drunken laugh, finally standing up as Carrie groggily pushed herself upright, her face flushed and her expression dazed. Without a word, Tom turned and stumbled out the door.

Tori immediately followed, catching up to him outside. "Tom, what the hell is wrong with you?" she demanded, grabbing his arm.

Tom spun and yanked her arm so hard it wrenched painfully.

"Don't you dare!" Tori yelled, her face twisting with rage.

Without hesitation, she swung her fist and punched him in the face.

Tom staggered back, clutching his nose. Tori stood her ground, her fists clenched, breathing hard.

Inside the trailer, the group remained unaware of the confrontation that had just taken place outside. Tori quietly came back in, subtly rubbing her arm, trying not to draw attention to herself. Her expression was calm, but her clenched jaw hinted at the tension bubbling beneath the surface.

Jen, noticing Carrie's dazed state, took her gently by the arm. "Come on, let's get you to bed," she said softly, a cup of water in her other hand.

Carrie nodded sluggishly, leaning into Jen for support. The two of them made their way to the small bedroom, Jen guiding her like a protective older sister.

"Here, drink this," Jen instructed Carrie, handing her the water. "You need to hydrate."

Carrie sat on the edge of the bed, cradling the cup in her hands. "Thanks, Jen," she mumbled, her voice barely audible.

Jen crouched in front of her, placing a comforting hand on Carrie's knee. "Try to rest, okay? We'll deal with everything else tomorrow."

Carrie nodded again, her tired eyes meeting Jen's momentarily before she took a slow sip of the water. Jen brushed a strand of hair away from Carrie's face before leaving.

In the kitchen, Tori grabbed a drink for herself, keeping her movements casual, though her mind replayed the scene outside. She glanced at Benny, still nursing his Bacardi and Coke, blissfully unaware of the turmoil.

"You good?" Benny asked, raising an eyebrow at Tori as she leaned against the counter.

"Yeah," she replied with a tight smile. "Just a long day."

Jen returned from Carrie's room, her face a mix of concern and exhaustion. "She's down for the night," she said quietly. Then, glancing at Tori, she asked, "You okay?"

"Yeah, I'm fine," Tori replied quickly, brushing off the question. She took a long sip of her drink, staring out the window as the last rays of sunlight dipped below the horizon.

Benny decided to head outside, and Tori looked out to see him arguing with Tom on the grass. He kept his distance because, even though they were friendly, he knew he could be as vicious as a rattlesnake when drunk like he was. They both separated, and Benny returned to the trailer, while Tom wandered off to his truck.

"Are you okay?" Benny asked Tori, lightly touching her arm. "I saw what happened out there." She turned to him and looked away.

"I'm fine, he's just a jerk." She walked away and headed to the kitchen to start preparing dinner.

~ ~ ~

Carrie emerged from the trailer onto the deck around 8:30 p.m.. Jen and Tori were on the deck, relaxing with drinks; there was no sign of dinner in sight, as they had already cleaned up. It was still light out, but they had a citronella candle burning, and the music from Tori's iPod played low. Carrie had changed out of her swimsuit into her Journey T-shirt from the concert she and Jen had attended, along with her cutoff jean shorts. Her tousled hair was up in a clip.

"You look better," Jen said, motioning for Carrie to sit beside her on the deck.

"Sorry for sleeping through dinner. I had such a headache," Carrie replied, settling into the chair.

Jen and Tori exchanged a knowing glance, fully aware of what likely caused her headache.

"Where is everyone?" Carrie asked, looking around.

"Tom's out on the boat fishing," Jen replied. "Benny is at The Edge."

"Why didn't Benny go with him? Oh, wait—he's probably blowing off some steam."

"That, and I told him to go to the bar to get beer for himself," Tori said with a sharp edge. "He's been drinking mine and Jen's Bacardi. What a leech."

Jen sighed, leaning back in her chair, her voice defeated. "Next year, we'll make sure he brings his own stuff to drink."

Carrie smiled faintly. "Well, I appreciate him sticking up for me. I appreciate all of you. I can't believe Tom did what he did."

Jen nodded slowly. "Yeah, well… it's done now. We decided that us girls are going into town tomorrow for the parade. We'll keep it low-key. It's tomorrow since it's Saturday."

"That sounds good," Carrie said, standing up. "I'm going inside for a drink."

"Make it a weak one—it's already after nine," Jen advised.

"I'm getting a beer," Carrie countered.

"Okay, good," Jen said, a small smile crossing her lips as she watched Carrie head inside.

CHAPTER 13

The small town hummed with lively activity. Fathers hoisted children onto their shoulders while mothers searched through strollers for snacks. The streets brimmed with antique shops, ice cream stands, candy stores, and inviting bars. Folding chairs lined the sidewalks in orderly rows, reserving spots for the upcoming parade. Many sat empty as their owners roamed the festival booths, though some early birds sat, savoring the cooling relief of the shade.

The girls turned a few heads as they stepped out of Tori's car and adjusted their adorable red, white, and blue outfits against their tan bodies. Their elegantly styled hair hadn't frizzed from the day's humidity yet. Tori carried a small cooler with bottled water and some malt beverages to help them battle the heat.

As they wove through the crowd, Jen spotted Marcy near a large van parked along the street. She was bent over, rummaging through a bag, wearing tight white shorts that revealed distinct panty lines.

"Well, look who it is," Jen muttered, nudging Carrie.

Marcy stood up, spotting the group. She offered a tight smile, her eyes scanning them briefly before returning to her task.

"Hey, ladies," Marcy said with a forced cheerfulness, brushing a strand of hair from her face. "Enjoying the heat?"

"Trying to survive it," Tori replied, a subtle smirk on her lips.

Carrie shifted the cooler in her hand. "We're heading to the parade. Are you sticking around for it?"

Marcy shrugged. "Brandon's in it with the summer camp float. I thought I'd watch, then maybe hit The Edge later."

"Well, don't let us keep you," Jen said pointedly, already moving to steer the group away.

Marcy gave a quick wave before diving back into her bag, hoping to avoid the awkward conversation.

As they walked off, Tori glanced at Jen and whispered, "Visible panty lines. In white shorts. Bold choice," she remarked in a snarky tone.

Jen snorted, and Carrie couldn't help but laugh as they headed toward the festivities.

"Hey, Marcy." Jen turned around. Marcy turned back to look at them as she tugged at her shorts, which were starting to ride up her thighs. "Who's fancy van is this?" She asked while lighting a cigarette. Carrie and Tori milled around looking in the van.

The monstrous van featured lounger seats and curtains inside. You could tell somebody had recently used the ashtrays in the arms and cup holders. The girls hadn't seen anything like it! It had to be a custom van. They were surprised they did not see a television for passengers to watch while riding.

"It's my parents' van. We rode with them here. Bobby and Brandon are already at the parade. I came back to grab a bag I had forgotten. You should come by later. Bobby is frying some chickens, and I'm making my famous potato salad."

Carrie found it odd that Marcy had invited them over when it seemed she didn't care for them, but she figured that maybe she didn't have many friends and wanted the cool kids at her trailer.

Jen, the unofficial leader of the group, took a slow drag from her cigarette, exhaled, and replied nonchalantly, "Maybe."

The girls found a spot on the curb to watch the parade, settling amidst a lively crowd of families and children. One little girl wandered close to Carrie with a messy wad of cotton candy. "Back off!" Carrie snarked at her, trying to avoid a sticky encounter.

Jen and Tori exchanged wide-eyed glances before bursting into laughter. "Whoa," Jen said, smirking. "Not a fan of kids?" she pointed to Carrie, who looked annoyed as she inspected her clothes to make sure no cotton candy got on her.

Tori chuckled. "Honestly, same," she muttered under her breath. "Let's go." They gathered their belongings and left to go back to the trailer.

They returned to find the guys sprawled out on the deck, looking worn out. Bottles and cans littered the small table between them, evidence of a long morning. Benny leaned back in his chair, sunglasses on despite the fading sunlight, while Tom nursed what looked like his third or fourth beer, his face flushed.

"Rough day, boys?" Jen teased, setting down the cooler they had brought.

Benny shrugged. "Fishing was a bust, and the wake on the river was brutal."

Tom muttered something incoherent, waving a hand as if dismissing the question entirely.

Carrie raised an eyebrow. "Looks like you worked real hard out here," she grumbled, glancing at the clutter on the deck.

Tori grabbed a chair and sat down, shaking her head at the mess.

Benny sat back in his chair and asked, "What's for lunch?" Tori looked at him in annoyance, but Jen quickly responded, "I guess we're going to Marcy's for fried chicken and potato salad." The guys looked at each other and nodded, "Okay."

The gang arrived at Marcy's trailer around 2:00. The aroma of sizzling chicken filled the air as Bobby stood over an outdoor deep fryer, carefully dropping pieces of battered chicken into the bubbling oil. A small table nearby held bowls of flour, batter mix, and raw chicken, indicating his dedication to the task.

Unlike the previous year's lively gathering, the crowd was sparse. Brandon was scrolling through his phone, looking bored. Some local neighbors lingered nearby, beers in hand, but the atmosphere felt subdued. An older couple joined the table with the neighbors, sitting near Brandon. Carrie presumed they must be Marcy's parents.

Marcy's face lit up with a broad smile when the group approached. "I'm so glad you all came!" she exclaimed, wiping her hands on a dish towel as she greeted them.

"It smells amazing out here," Jen said, glancing at the fryer.

"Bobby's been at it for hours," Marcy announced proudly. "He's perfected the recipe. You are all in for a treat!"

Carrie smirked, leaning toward Jen. "Guess we'll see," she whispered, earning a stifled laugh from her friend.

"Grab a drink and make yourselves at home!" Marcy said, gesturing toward the makeshift cooler filled with beer and soda. "Dinner will be ready soon."

They all made their plates and took a seat at the picnic table. After settling in, Marcy came over and observed them enjoying the food. She must have gone inside because she had changed into a polo dress.

"Did you hear about Darren and Diane? They're getting a divorce," she told the group as she crunched on a celery stick.

Jen quickly replied, "What about the real world, Marcy? What's going on here?"

"Well, you know, I'm taking care of Brandon, but Bobby is getting me a motorcycle, and I'm going to take lessons to learn to ride."

Benny looked impressed. "Cool, you'll look good on a bike," he told her with a wink. He pulled off a piece of his fried chicken breast and handed it to Tori. "Here, Tori, eat this." She shook her head no, and he said, "What? You're skinny as a rail." She smiled and kept eating her salad.

Marcy put her hand on Benny's muscled forearm and asked, "Did you try my potato salad?"

"Yes, I did, and it is delicious, just like my mom makes," Benny said in a fake attempt to compliment her. That was his way of teasing her for being a mom.

"Well," Marcy began, her tone slightly sharper, "I put capers in my salad. It gives it a unique flavor and sets it apart from everyone else's. It's my specialty."

Carrie raised an eyebrow, exchanging a glance with Jen. Jen took a long drag from her cigarette, clearly amused but holding back a smirk.

"Capers, huh?" Tori said, a playful edge to her voice. "Fancy."

"Exactly," Marcy shot back, not missing a beat. "It's not just any potato salad!"

"Well," Carrie replied, "I can't wait to try it.

Capers or not, it smells incredible."

Marcy nodded, her shoulders relaxing slightly. "Good. Because it's gonna be the best thing you've had all summer."

Tori chimed in, her tone teasing. "Benny wouldn't know anything about cooking. No skills in the kitchen for this guy!"

Benny leaned back, grinning smugly. "That's because the ladies like to cook for me."

Tori crossed her arms and shot an eye roll. "Oh, right. Because you've got all kinds of girlfriends lining up to take care of you, but the only thing you've got going for you is your ability to annoy everyone equally."

Carrie noticed Brandon off on the side of the trailer with a friend his age, one of the locals, burning ants with a magnifying glass. Bobby came to their table, wiping his hands on his apron. He put his knee on the picnic table and said, "Carrie, I'm putting off some fireworks tonight. Want to help me light them?"

"I don't think you need my help. Looks like your son likes to light things up."

Just then, a tall woman approached their table, captivating their attention. Her curly black hair, curvaceous bosom, and long, slender legs further enhanced her striking appearance. Her presence exuded confidence, and her deep, sultry voice only added to her allure.

"Tom, I thought that was you," she said, her

words dripping with familiarity.

Tom's eyes lit up as if he'd just seen a ghost from a fond memory. "Sherry? What the hell? I haven't seen you since well, back in the day. What are you doing here?"

Sherry placed a hand on her hip, leaning slightly toward him. "I've got a trailer just around the bend. You look great!"

Carrie watched the exchange, trying to keep her expression neutral, though her thoughts were anything but. *What is this woman thinking?* she wondered. Sherry's flirtatious demeanor couldn't have been more apparent, and it was clear that she and Tom were happy to catch up.

Before anyone could say anything, Tom and Sherry drifted away from the group, walking toward the edge of the gathering and speaking in hushed tones.

Carrie stayed rooted in her seat, her vodka lemonade now feeling heavier in her hand. She watched them for a moment, then looked away, feigning disinterest. She couldn't care less about Tom's little reunion—or at least that's what she told herself.

Tori leaned over and whispered, "Who the hell is that?"

Jen shrugged, keeping her voice low. "Apparently, someone from back in Tom's 'glory days.' Let him have his moment."

Carrie forced a laugh, taking a long sip from her drink. "Let him. Doesn't bother me."

But as she stared off toward the horizon, the sun casting long shadows across the campground, she couldn't help but feel the faintest twinge of something she couldn't quite figure out. Was it annoyance? Curiosity? Or just the ache of yet another reminder of how far gone her marriage truly was?

Jen slapped her hand on the table and said, "We gotta go. I'm taking us to Boon Bay."

CHAPTER 14

Boon Bay was a cove along the river that Jen and Benny discovered. Navigating the river at dusk captivated their senses. The picturesque orange and black sky resembled a tiger, and the marshy waters gave off a mysterious feeling of the bayou. Jen captained the boat with Benny alongside her, guiding her the whole way.

"This looks just like Vie-et-nam," Carrie exclaimed. "Just like Forrest Gump."

They tied up the boat and climbed out, heading toward the small bar tucked away behind the pier. The weathered building's wooden façade was a faded reminder of better days, yet it exuded a quiet charm.

Stepping inside took them back in time—straight into the 1970s. The dim lighting, amber-toned decor, and faint smell of cigarette smoke clinging to the walls added to the atmosphere. The bartender, an older man with graying hair and a well-worn flannel shirt, gave them a brief nod before returning to wiping down the counter.

The few patrons scattered at the bar were an eclectic mix of ages, but none seemed to belong in the present. They sat hunched over their drinks, in quiet conversations, like a murmuring current.

The jukebox in the corner crooned an old Rolling Stones song, its crackling speakers adding a vintage warmth to the tune. The outdated establishment emanated a welcoming feel, like an unpolished gem that didn't try to be anything but itself.

Carrie took it all in, the scene oddly settling her feelings of uncertainty. She exchanged a look with Jen and Tori, who were already grinning as if they, too, appreciated the bar's unique charm. The place might have been a relic, but it was the perfect escape they needed.

Benny ambled up to the bar and ordered a round of drinks. The group watched in amusement; Benny wasn't known for his generosity, so this was an unusual gesture. When the drinks came, they each raised an eyebrow and a glass, silently acknowledging the rare occurrence.

Drinks in hand, they returned to the pier, which had mismatched tables and chairs set up to form a makeshift patio. It didn't have the polish of the popular bars farther down the river—those with polished decks and fairy lights—but it held a certain charm. This place belonged to the river's quieter side, serving patrons who lived just off its winding waters or camped nearby.

The chairs creaked slightly as the gentle breeze washed over them. The sinking sun brushed the sky in deeper orange and amber streaks that rippled across the water, fierce and beautiful in its fleeting brilliance.

The serenity produced a long silence as the friends sipped their drinks and stared at the river, each lost in their own thoughts, yet somehow connected in the quiet. It was one of those rare moments when the weight of life seemed to dissolve.

Carrie didn't think about Tom, her failing marriage, or the destructive cycle she felt trapped in. Jen let go of all thoughts about her jewelry store, with its constant demands and financial worries. Tori, for once, let her mind drift away from the passionless routine her marriage had become.

Even Benny, who always seemed to carry the air of a hustler, let his usual bravado slip. He gazed out at the glowing horizon, feeling a rare gratitude. In a world he often found fake and cutthroat—full of people chasing power, money, and status—this group and these moments were genuine.

"We'd better get on the river before it gets dark," Jen said, breaking the tranquil silence. The group slowly stirred, gathering their glasses and bottles to return them to the bar.

Jen handed the keys to Benny. "You can drive. I'm still a virgin captain," she noted with a playful grin. Benny didn't hesitate, taking his spot at the helm like it was his rightful throne.

The boat skimmed swiftly and smoothly over the water as they headed downstream. Jen cued "Eminence Front" on her MP3 player, the steady rhythm and moody vibe perfectly syncing with the glowing horizon. The breathtaking sunset cast long, golden streaks across the water, as if nature were putting on a show just for them.

Using her mixologist skills, Carrie poured another round of robust vodka lemonades, and it didn't take long for the effects to kick in. The group's chatter grew livelier as they sipped, the topics of conversation becoming more elevated, or at least more absurd as the night crept closer.

They reminisced about old stories, swapped outrageous theories about the locals, and even debated the merits of modern music versus the classics they were listening to. For the first time all day, the tension and drama had dissipated. They all reveled as the sun sank into the horizon over the meandering river.

"What's for dinner?" Benny interjected with a smirk, knowing the question would get under Tori's skin.

"You would ask that," Tori shot back, rolling her eyes. "Well, we just had lunch, but I brought a tenderloin that can feed us all, as long as Benny controls himself."

"I can control myself around food," Benny replied. "It's just other things I can't."

Tom, never one to miss an opportunity to stir the pot, chuckled and chimed in, "Such as booze and women!"

Tori shook her head and muttered, "You guys are impossible." But she couldn't help the slight grin tugging at her lips.

"Well," Carrie said, raising her drink, "here's to booze, women, and tenderloin—may we all survive the night!"

They toasted with their glasses, laughter carrying across the river as the boat glided back toward the pier.

The sun had set entirely by the time they returned to the trailer to make dinner. Tom pulled out the portable Smokey Joe and started the coals while everyone refreshed their cocktails and relaxed on the deck. Tori seasoned the tenderloin with salt and pepper and tossed it on the grill after the coals were heated. After fifteen minutes, she asked Tom to take it off the grill.

"It's done," Tori told him. "I like mine medium rare."

Tom cut into the bloody, red meat. "This thing is practically still alive!" Tom exclaimed and placed pieces on a plate. Benny grabbed a couple of large pieces and threw them in the microwave to make them edible. They all stood around the kitchen, nibbling on their pieces of meat, while Tori stole a piece off each plate. "Mmm, this is delicious!"

"Hey, get your own. You said you wanted it rare." Benny bellowed.

Tori walked over to the platter, cut off a hunk of the bloody, rare meat, and shoved it in her mouth.

"Deeelicious," she proclaimed, wiping her mouth.

"Ohh, gross!" the guys all blurted in unison.

After their piecemeal dinner, the group gathered outside on the deck, the faint glow of their phones and the ember tips of cigarettes punctuating the darkness. Mosquitoes buzzed relentlessly as they passed around a joint, their conversations blending with the faint hum of the river and the low beat of music from Jen's iPod.

Tom emerged from the trailer carrying a plate piled with chunks of grilled meat. He set it down in front of Carrie with an uncharacteristically gentle tone. "Here, eat something," he said, gesturing at the plate.

Carrie looked at him, unfazed. She took a slow sip of her vodka lemonade, followed by a long drag of her cigarette, then glanced at the plate dismissively. "That's okay," she replied, reaching for a familiar red can. "I have Pringles."

She popped open the lid, pulled out a thick stack, and dramatically shoved half into her mouth, crunching loudly.

Jen snorted. "Living the gourmet life, I see."

"Pringles are gourmet," Carrie quipped with a smirk. "Stackable, portable, and pair perfectly with vodka. What more could a girl want?"

The group chuckled, their laughter mingling with the nighttime sounds. Tori swatted at her arm and mumbled, "What I want is for these mosquitoes to leave me alone."

Benny exhaled a cloud of smoke and leaned back in his chair. "Welcome to the wild, ladies. Nothing says vacation like being eaten alive."

"Cheers to that," Jen said, raising her beer. "And cheers to Pringles."

Carrie raised her can in response, shaking it triumphantly. "To Pringles!"

Tom gave a half-smirk as he walked over to Tori, who was swaying to the rhythm of the music playing on Jen's iPod. Without hesitation, he slid his arms around her from behind, his hands dangerously close to her chest. A little buzzed from the drinks, Tori didn't immediately pull away as she might have otherwise.

"Carrie, your friend makes steak for everyone, and you can't even eat any." Tom's daggers stared at her..

Carrie, unimpressed, rolled her eyes. "Jen isn't eating any either," she uttered flatly.

Jen shrugged. "Oh, I will in a little bit," she said nonchalantly, not looking up from her iPod scrolling.

"I just don't want to eat big globs of beef before bed," Carrie replied with a sharp edge. She took another sip of her drink, then stubbed out her cigarette. "And on that note, I'm calling it a night."

She stood, grabbed her can of Pringles, and walked inside without another word.

The group fell into a brief silence, the tension lingering. Jen watched Carrie disappear into the trailer, then turned to Tori. "Well, at least someone's got her priorities straight," she joked, attempting to lighten the mood.

Tori laughed nervously, then gently pulled herself away from Tom's grasp. "Yeah, I think I'll grab some steak now before it's gone," she said, stepping toward the table to distance them.

Tom didn't move, watching the group with a glassy expression before sitting back down. "More for me, then," he said, reaching for the plate of steak.

Carrie flopped onto the bed in her room, still fully dressed, and buried her face in the pillow. The alcohol buzz dulled her senses, but the weight of frustration and exhaustion pressed harder. She'd had enough of Tom—his antics, cruelty, and ability to drain the joy from any moment. Outside, the muffled sounds of laughter, music, and conversations mingled with the bass thump of tunes from The Edge. She began drifting off to sleep, but her thoughts wandered to Dylan and how things were so different the year before.

Back then, she had passion—a fire that ignited every night before she lay her head down. She missed him, missed the feeling of being desired and connected. It was a stark contrast to the hollow shell her marriage had become.

In the morning, sunlight streamed through the thin curtains, illuminating the cluttered room. Carrie moved purposefully, packing her clothes while Tom clattered around in the bathroom. She shoved her belongings into her bag without a care for wrinkles or organization.

When she turned her attention to Tom's clothes,

strewn haphazardly across the floor, irritation bubbled up. She picked up his jeans and started emptying the pockets, expecting crumpled bills, loose change, maybe an old joint or two.

Instead, her fingers brushed against something unexpected. She pulled out a neatly folded piece of paper. Her forehead creased as she unfolded it.

In bold handwriting, there was a name and a phone number: Sherry.

Carrie's stomach churned. Seeing it felt like a punch to the gut, erasing any doubt about Tom's behavior the night before. Her grip tightened around the paper as emotions stormed within her—anger, humiliation, and resolve.

PART THREE

2004

CHAPTER 15

The Fourth of July weekend would be different this year. Carrie was going solo—no Tom, no tension. She had left him in the fall of 2003, finally freeing herself from the destructive cycle of their marriage.

It all started with a weekend up north at her sister Carly's boyfriend's cabin. One night, after a few drinks at a local bar, Carrie couldn't help herself and flirted with a rugged hunter. By the night's end, Carly caught her kissing him outside, under the dim glow of the bar's neon lights. She wasted no time confronting Carrie and pushing her to acknowledge her unhappiness. "If you're already looking elsewhere, then it's time to leave him," Carly told her.

That weekend ignited the catalyst for change, and when Carrie returned home, she mustered the courage to tell Tom it was over after years of unhappiness. Within a few months, she moved out and stayed with her father during the divorce proceedings, and Tom negotiated to buy out her share of their home.

Adjusting to living with her father came with its challenges—boredom, awkwardness, and a deep need for independence. Carrie signed up for an aerobics class at a local fitness center to keep herself occupied, where she met Stacy. Her bubbly and outgoing personality drew Carrie to her, and they instantly struck up a friendship. The class was more about camaraderie than exercise.

Stacy was petite, with a dark brown pixie haircut that framed her bright blue eyes. She radiated an electric energy, and her adventurous spirit was precisely what Carrie needed after her divorce. Stacy's single, carefree lifestyle and wild streak matched Carrie's own—something she had stifled for years in her marriage to Tom.

Their friendship quickly deepened. After aerobics class, they'd often head out for drinks, diving headfirst into the singles scene. The local bars became their playground, a place to laugh, let loose, and rediscover themselves. Carrie hadn't felt this free in years, and Stacy's fearless attitude became infectious.

One evening over drinks, Carrie introduced Stacy to Trip, a cocky yet charismatic financial planner she knew from her dart league. Despite the awkwardness of continuing to play darts with Tom still on her team that spring, Carrie stayed in the league for the social connection. Trip had always been a bit of a player, but he and Stacy had undeniable chemistry.

It didn't take long for Stacy and Trip to hook up. Their relationship proved to be fiery and fast-paced, much like Stacy herself. Carrie couldn't help but smile at how quickly her new friend had shaken up the group's dynamic. Stacy's presence was precisely the spark that Carrie needed to feel alive again.

~ ~ ~

As Carrie packed her things for the weekend at the river, she felt the excitement building within her. This year wasn't about enduring Tom's antics or playing the role of the unhappy wife. This year was hers to enjoy.

Carrie and Tori were the first to arrive at the trailer. Jen hid the keys under a rock for whoever got there first. The air felt still and was filled with the scent of pine as they stepped out of the car, stretching after the long drive. This year, they had decided to come up together since Drew couldn't make it again. Tori had casually brushed off his absence, claiming this weekend was hers to unwind and recharge.

Carrie didn't feel close enough to Tori to press for details about her marriage, but she suspected there was more beneath the surface. She made a mental note to keep the wine flowing later—maybe after a few drinks, Tori would open up.

Benny pulled in at the same time they did, but this time, he wasn't just lugging his usual duffel of clothes and toiletries. He had extra bags loaded with food and drinks, a clear sign that he listened for once and brought something to share.

Tori eyed the bags, arching a brow as a smirk played on her lips. "Well, well, Benny—looks like you're finally growing up."

Inside the trailer, the scent of new carpeting lingered faintly, mingling with the aroma of a beachy scented candle. A small breakfast bar now separated the kitchen from the living space, where a sleek flat-screen TV hung on the wall beneath a cheeky "Trailer Life" sign. Tori plopped down on the couch. "Guess I'm sharing this room with Carrie," she called, glancing toward one of the modestly sized bedrooms with freshly washed curtains.

"Stacy and Trip claimed the middle room," Carrie said, arranging a set of mismatched mugs on the counter. "Benny—sorry, couch for you." She shot him a pointed look as he grumbled, flopping onto the cushions.

"Hey, at least it's clean this year," Carrie joked, nudging an old photo frame Jen had straightened on the mantle. "I barely recognize the place."

They wasted no time unpacking their overnight bags, coolers, and assortment of snacks and drinks. The familiar routine felt comforting, grounding them in the easy rhythm of the weekend ahead. Carrie glanced around, taking in the mismatched furniture and faint scent of old cedar, which felt oddly welcoming.

"Alright," Tori said, breaking the silence as she hoisted a bag onto the counter. "First order of business—drinks?"

Carrie smirked. "You read my mind."

With the cooler stocked and their drinks poured, they stepped outside to settle into the weekend's vibe.

Jen arrived shortly after, lugging a large cooler and multiple bags that threatened to topple as she stepped inside.

"Ugh," she groaned, setting everything down with a thud. "The coolers get bigger and bigger every year!"

Carrie and Tori laughed, already relaxed with drinks in hand.

"Well, maybe if you didn't insist on bringing every condiment known to man," Tori teased, eyeing the overflowing bags.

Jen rolled her eyes but grinned. "Excuse me for being prepared. You know how Benny gets if we don't have barbecue sauce for every meal."

Carrie walked over to help, unloading the bags and lining up their contents on the counter. "What's in here? Half the grocery store?"

"Close," Jen replied, pulling out bottles of wine, fresh vegetables, and enough snacks to feed a small army. "I figured I'd come bearing gifts since I got here later. I brought extra ice for the coolers because you two never think of that."

Tori raised her glass. "You're a saint, Jen. A sarcastic, over-prepared saint."

"Damn right," Jen said, cracking open a beer and raising it in return. "Now, where's the music? This place feels way too quiet."

Carrie grabbed her phone and connected it to the portable speaker. As the first notes of a classic rock playlist filled the air, the trio settled into their familiar dynamic, the buzz of another Fourth of July weekend officially underway.

~ ~ ~

Jen stood on the freshly built deck, a proud smile tugging at her lips. "What do you think? Bigger, right?" she said, gesturing to the wide planks that wrapped around the trailer, offering a perfect spot to watch the bustle outside Brett's tavern.

Carrie stepped onto the deck, her sandals clicking softly on the polished wood. "Looks like someone hit the jackpot," she teased, running her hand along the smooth railing.

Carrie ran to hug her. "Jen, did you see the new bar they built on the river?"

Brett's had recently acquired a license to build a tiki bar on the riverbank, steps away from The Edge. The new addition must have ruffled some feathers with The Edge's owner, as it was already drawing a steady crowd.

True to its name, Brett's tiki bar looked like a Hawaiian tropical paradise. Bright string lights crisscrossed overhead, and bamboo accents framed the bar area. Tiki torches flickered along the perimeter, their flames dancing in the evening breeze. The tables had colorful, weather-resistant umbrellas, and the seats ranged from barstools wrapped in faux straw to Adirondack chairs painted in vibrant island colors.

The atmosphere buzzed with energy as patrons mingled with drinks in hand. Exotic cocktails served in carved coconuts and colorful ceramic tiki mugs flew out of the bar as fast as the bartenders could make them. A small stage off to the side hosted a local band playing reggae covers, adding to the laid-back, beachy vibe that made Brett's feel like a world away from the Midwest river resort setting.

"We have to check it out tonight!" Jen said.

"It's a good thing I brought something fancy to wear." Carrie referred to the hot pink slip dress she bought from Target, an Isaak Mizrahi.

Jen grabbed her arm. "Come with me to Brett's. We need to check in."

They walked into Brett's just before prime dinner time. It was still pretty empty, aside from some regulars on the gambling machine and a few at the bar. They headed to the back, and Jen asked for Brett so she could check in. Carrie sat down and ordered a drink, not noticing anyone at the bar.

Carrie sank into a chair, ordered a drink, and absently scanned the television. Suddenly, a familiar voice cut through the background noise.

"Hey, Carrie."

Her head snapped up. Standing at the bar, drink in hand, was Conner. Her heart lurched. Conner. Her high school crush.

"Conner! Oh my god, what are you doing here?"

The sheer delight must have been plastered all over her face, though she frantically tried to mask it.

He leaned in, his gaze lingering on her face. "Carrie, wow. Ten years? You look incredible. I'm staying with Bobby. You know, Marcy's husband? We're good friends."

"Oh, well, we should hang out." Her face got red, and she felt all hot and bothered.

Jen interrupted, "I have us checked in. Let's go back and see if Stacy and Trip are here. Oh, hey, Conner. We're going to the tiki bar tonight. You should meet us."

"Yeah, maybe," he replied, and smiled at Carrie.

Jen casually asked Carrie on their way out, "Did you meet Conner? He's a friend of Bobby's. He's up here a lot."

Carrie hadn't seen him in years, but time had been kind to him. His soft, hazel eyes still held that warm depth she remembered from their fleeting moments in high school, though now there was an added gravity to them. His neatly cropped light brown hair framed his face, which hadn't lost its definition. The sharp angles of his jawline and high cheekbones complemented the boyish charm of his dimples, which appeared when he smiled, along with the faint crinkle at the corners of his eyes. That smile had always disarmed her back then; now it felt just as potent.

"I did," Carrie replied, her voice a little breathless.

"Well, I know him. We went to high school together."

Jen's eyes widened. "Oh, did you date?" She added. "He's really cute!"

Carrie shook her head, no, as memories of her teenage crush came flooding back. She almost dated him. Almost.

The deck buzzed with activity as they stepped out of Brett's and walked toward the trailer deck. The lively hum of conversation mingled with the gentle sounds of the nearby river. Jen immediately noticed Brandon, Marcy's teenage son, lingering a little too close to Trip. She raised an eyebrow, surprised to see him there.

Brandon had started bussing tables at The Pub, where they all played darts, and it was becoming clear that he liked hanging around Trip. Everywhere Trip went, Brandon wasn't far behind, seemingly hanging on his every word. Tonight was no different— Brandon leaned against the railing, nodding eagerly to whatever Trip said, his youthful enthusiasm contrasting sharply with Trip's calm, self-assured demeanor.

Jen nudged Carrie and whispered, "Do you see this? The kid's like his shadow."

Carrie chuckled, taking in the scene. "Trip always did love an audience. Guess he's got a fan club now."

Tori, overhearing, smirked and added, "Let's just hope Trip doesn't start giving him life advice. One narcissist in training is enough."

They all shared a laugh as they headed toward the deck's tables, the air buzzing with energy and the promise of a long summer evening.

"Ladies, you're back. Would you like a shot?" Trip stood there, balancing a stack of plastic shot glasses in his arms, a playful grin on his face.

"Isn't it a little early for Jägermeister?" Jen quipped, though she reached out and took one anyway.

Trip smirked and looked right at Carrie. "Well, I don't have shots of Chardonnay."

Carrie rolled her eyes, a small laugh escaping her lips. That joke had been running between them since the dart season. She'd started showing up to happy hour after work, sipping wine before heading to darts. It wasn't ideal, but driving to her apartment only to turn around and come back felt pointless. It had become her new routine after leaving Tom, though the transition hadn't been without its hiccups.

Tori stepped up, grabbed a shot, and chimed in with a grin. "Yeah, no Chardonnay! I think the dart league had enough of that drama for a while."

Carrie gave her a playful glare. "You act like I burned the place down."

"You almost did—figuratively," Jen added with a smirk. "Remember when you told Drew he couldn't hit a triple if his life depended on it? Then you threw and nailed it?"

"That was skill, not Chardonnay," Carrie said,

tossing back the shot with a confident smirk.

The group burst into laughter, the tension from earlier lifting as they settled into the carefree camaraderie that had always been their glue.

Stacy stepped out of the trailer, the screen door creaking behind her as it swung shut. She sauntered onto the deck, her presence impossible to ignore. She wore snug army green cargo shorts and a coral tube top, accentuating her athletic frame. Her short, dark hairstyle looked flawless, each strand in place as though she'd stepped out of a magazine.

She made her way over to Trip and the girls. Her casual sway in her walk drew Brandon's gaze immediately. He didn't even try to hide it, his eyes traveling up and down as if memorizing every detail.

Noticing Brandon's not-so-subtle attention, Trip smirked and gave him a nudge with his elbow. "Eyes up, kid," he said, chuckling as he reached for his drink.

Brandon flushed, scratching the back of his neck awkwardly. "Just admiring her style," he muttered, trying to play it off.

Stacy caught the exchange and grinned knowingly. "Relax, Brandon. You're not the first," she teased, her tone light and playful as she leaned casually against the deck railing.

Tori and Jen exchanged amused glances, sipping their drinks as the scene unfolded. Carrie, leaning back in her chair, raised an eyebrow at Stacy. "You sure know how to make an entrance."

"Always," Stacy replied with a wink.

Stacy, with her beer in hand, strolled over to where Jen, Carrie, and Tori were seated. She leaned against the railing and said, "I'm so glad you're back. I've been dying to go to the tiki bar. It looks amazing lit up at night."

"Me too! I'm going to change and freshen up," Carrie announced as she grabbed her bag and headed into the trailer.

Once inside, she closed the door and let out a breath she didn't realize she was holding. She was anxious to see Conner again, and the anticipation bubbled up in a way that made her pulse quicken. She rifled through her bag, pulled out her simple yet flattering pink slip dress, and slipped it on.

Standing in front of the tiny mirror, she plugged in her curling iron and tried her best to tame her brown waves, coaxing them into soft curls that framed her face. She dusted on some shimmery eyeshadow, applied a fresh coat of mascara to make her hazel eyes pop, and finished with a swipe of peachy lip gloss.

Satisfied but not overdone, she grabbed her Tommy Girl perfume, spritzing a light mist on her wrists and neck. She gave herself a final glance in the mirror, adjusting the straps of her dress.

"Okay, Carrie," she whispered to herself. "You've got this."

CHAPTER 16

Carrie grabbed her sandals and joined the others who were already conversing and laughing on the deck. The golden light of early evening cast a warm glow over the scene.

"You look nice. I mean, casual nice. You must be planning on meeting someone tonight?" Stacy asked as she turned to face Carrie and accepted the bottle of Guinness beer she brought out for her.

"Here, nah. I'm sure it will be nothing but a bunch of drunks."

"Trying to set a new summer fashion trend?" Tori asked Benny with a smirk, sipping her drink.

Benny grinned, brushing off their remarks. "Gotta stay versatile. Never know who might show up at this classy establishment." He gestured broadly at the deck and the tiki lights strung above, earning a round of chuckles.

"You look like you're heading for a golf course, not a tiki bar," Stacy quipped as she joined the group.

"Style is about being ready for anything," Benny

replied, striking a mock model pose that sent the group into another wave of laughter.

"You look nice, Carrie. A little fancy for The Edge, but nice." Benny complimented.

"It's the tiki bar, and this is just a summer dress. No big deal." Carrie replied.

"She sure does look nice. I better go change," Jen said, heading toward the door.

"Oh, come on, is everyone getting all fancy? I don't give a shit about that." Tori exclaimed. She wore her usual attire: a black t-shirt, khaki shorts that accentuated her long legs, and a baseball cap, with her hair pulled back in a ponytail. Like Trip, she dressed professionally all week at the spa where she worked, so she liked to be casual on weekends.

Benny moved close to her and whispered, "I bet you have a fancy bra under that t-shirt."

Tori punched his arm and pushed him away. "Shut up, you pig!"

They all walked to the tiki bar together with drinks in hand. The tiki lights accented the bar, and the music filled the air. The sparkling river behind the bar provided the perfect backdrop. The simple setup consisted of a large plank of wood laid out next to the river with a bar on one end. Tables were scattered throughout as resort patrons mingled. The music came from a speaker at The Edge, piping music out from inside the bar area. As the friends approached, they all couldn't help but dance as Usher's "Yeah!" blared.

"I fuckin love this song!" Jen shouted, and she and Tori attempted to move like Usher. "You should stick with rock, because this rap stuff is crap." Trip told her. Stacy rolled her eyes. Benny went to the bar to get the ladies some drinks and returned with a few bottles of beer and several plastic cups filled with a pretty bluish-green liquid.

He handed one to Carrie. "This is their specialty—Bug Juice. It has all kinds of hooch in it!" It looked like the Hpnotiq shots they had taken by the pond the previous year. She took a sip of the sweet yet tart drink. It didn't taste strong, which was dangerous because it could sneak up on you. They all scattered about, finding space to sit or stand, moving to the music. Jen spotted Marcy and Bobby at one of the tables and approached them. Bobby stood next to the table. When he turned to go to the bar, Carrie spotted Conner sitting at the table, talking to Marcy. He turned and caught her eye. Marcy got up and followed Bobby to the bar. Conner got up and walked toward Carrie.

"Carrie, we meet again," he announced in a smooth yet casual voice as he stepped up to the table.

Carrie turned at the sound of his voice, her heart skipping just slightly. She smiled, trying to mask the nerves that fluttered in her stomach. "Conner," she said, her voice steady. "Twice in one day. You must be following me." She immediately felt stupid for saying that.

"Come on, Trip, let's go see what Tori and the others are up to," Stacy gestured, pulling his arm. She could sense they probably wanted to be alone. Trip didn't know Conner, so he didn't object.

"Sure, I need another beer anyway," Trip agreed.

"You look good," admitted Conner.

Carrie felt her cheeks warm under the compliment. She took another sip of her drink to hide the slight smile creeping across her lips. "Thanks. You're not looking so bad yourself."

His gaze lingered on her momentarily, his hazel eyes soft but intent. "It's been a while. You've changed. In a good way."

Carrie leaned back in her chair, twirling the glass stem between her fingers. "Life has a way of doing that. You seem, well, different, too. Quieter."

He laughed softly, looking down at his beer. "Maybe. Or maybe I'm better at keeping my trouble under the radar these days."

"Still causing trouble, huh?" she teased, raising an eyebrow.

Conner met her eyes, his dimples deepening with his smile. "Some habits die hard. What about you? Still keeping everyone on their toes?"

Carrie smirked, feeling a little of her old confidence bubble up. "Always."

The conversation around the table faded into the background as they exchanged glances, the unspoken tension between them thick enough to sense. Carrie couldn't help but wonder what kind of trouble Conner could still bring—and why she cared.

Glancing around, Carrie felt the weight of potential gazes on them. She leaned slightly closer to Conner, keeping her tone casual but inquisitive. "So, what's your story? I haven't kept tabs on you. Are you married, with kids?"

Conner hesitated, taking a long sip of his beer before replying. "I am. No kids. We're, well, not in a good place right now." His voice was calm, but there was a flicker of vulnerability in his eyes. "Honestly, haven't been for a while."

Carrie nodded, her fingers absently tracing the rim of her glass. "I get that," she confessed softly. "It's not the same, but Tom and I…" She trailed off and gave a slight shrug. "Divorced. Well, in the process. But it's definitely over."

Conner's gaze didn't waver. "Good for you," he stated. "I heard about him. He wasn't good enough for you."

Carrie couldn't help the small smile that tugged at her lips. Had he kept tabs on her? "That's generous, coming from my old high school crush." She shot him a playful glance, hoping to lighten the mood.

Conner grinned, his dimples deepening. "High school feels like another lifetime, doesn't it?"

"Some things don't feel that far away," Carrie replied, her voice soft but weighted.

Their eyes locked for a moment, the connection between them undeniable. Carrie felt a flutter of something she hadn't felt in a long time—hope, maybe, or just the thrill of being seen.

"Carrie, I didn't know you knew Conner," Marcy slurred as she stumbled toward them, her bright red cup of bug juice sloshing along. Bobby joined her, one arm looped awkwardly around her waist to keep her upright. You could see a mix of mild embarrassment and amusement on his face.

"We went to high school together," Carrie explained smoothly, glancing at Conner with a small smile.

Marcy squinted at them, her lips curling into a knowing smirk. "Well, isn't that something?" she drawled a little too loudly. "Old friends catching up, huh? Small world."

Conner gave a polite nod, his expression guarded but polite.

"Yeah, just saying hi."

Marcy leaned heavily on Bobby, her eyes flickering between them with drunken curiosity. "You're married to Jill, right?" she asked Conner, her tone nosy.

"Yep," Conner answered, taking another sip of his beer.

Carrie could feel the heat rising to her cheeks, but kept her face neutral. "It's always nice to see a familiar face," she interjected, hoping to steer the conversation away from the awkward edge it was teetering on.

"I'm having a cookout tomorrow, and you guys have to come. I want the Rat Pack there!" Marcy mumbled, almost falling over, but Bobby kept pulling her up.

"More like the all that pack, but sure, I think we can make it."

"Carrie, I hear you're divorced now. Conner, watch out for her!" Bobby sneered.

Bobby tugged at Marcy's arm, clearly ready to move on. "C'mon, Marce, let's get you some water," he muttered.

"Oh, fine," Marcy grumbled, letting him pull her away. But not before she threw one last glance over her shoulder, her tipsy smile lingering like an unspoken question.

Conner turned to Carrie and exhaled with a soft chuckle. "Guess I'm officially on the radar now."

"What a jerk. Sorry, I know Bobby is your friend, but I don't know what he meant by that." Carrie looked embarrassed and pulled out a cigarette to calm her nerves.

Conner leaned in, his breath warm against her ear. "Maybe he thinks I'm going to get carried away..." He trailed off, letting the implied suggestion hang heavy in the air.

Carrie tilted her head. "We're just talking," she assured, her tone light but laced with a hint of defiance.

He gave her a knowing smile that made her stomach flutter and her heart race faster. "For now," he added, his words teasing but loaded, carrying an undercurrent that lingered in the space between them.

Before she could respond, he turned and walked toward Brett's, his steps casual but deliberate, leaving Carrie rooted in place, staring after him.

She blinked, her mouth slightly open—the words she wanted to say caught somewhere in her throat. For now—the phrase replayed in her mind, echoing louder with each beat of her heart. Speechless, she glanced down at the drink in her hand and took a long sip, hoping to steady the swirling mix of emotions Conner had left in his wake.

Carrie watched him walk off for a few seconds, and then she walked towards the crowd to find the gang. A waitress from Brett's was walking around with a tray full of coconut shrimp from the restaurant for the guests to try. The Edge only offered pizza, making it a nice treat for everyone at the tiki bar.

"Larry can't be too happy about this," Jen commented between bites. "This bar, too. I mean, geez, this is practically on his property."

Benny returned from the bar with rounds of bug juice. They all felt tipsy after the second drink. Benny and Trip started arguing about politics, with Tori caught in the middle. Carrie grabbed Stacy's arm to go to the bathroom at The Edge, which was dead inside since most guests were outside at the tiki bar or over at Brett's. No one was in the bathroom, so they had the freedom to talk.

"Who was that guy you were talking to?" Stacy asked, her voice cutting through the low hum of the restroom fan. She stood leaning against the sink, her arms crossed, her expression part curiosity, part accusation.

Carrie emerged from the stall, adjusting her dress and meeting Stacy's gaze in the mirror. "What? You mean Conner? I went to high school with him," she answered casually, though her tone betrayed a hint of defensiveness.

Stacy raised an eyebrow. "Well, it looked pretty intense. I got a vibe."

Carrie turned to face her, rolling her eyes. "Oh, stop it. It was nothing. He's married."

Stacy shook her head. "That doesn't mean anything," she advised, pushing off the sink and straightening up. "Come on, let's get back before Trip starts up with Tori."

Carrie raised her brows in confusion. "What? Don't be silly. Tori's a married woman."

"Uh-huh," Stacy noted with a knowing smirk. "Come on, let's go."

Carrie grabbed her bag and followed Stacy out, but her thoughts lingered on Conner's last words.

Carrie and Stacy approached the tiki bar, which had come to life with lights, a buzzing crowd, and the pulsing rhythm of Outkast's "I Like the Way You Move" blasting from Brett's speakers. The energy felt infectious. They spotted Jen, Benny, and Tori on the makeshift dance floor, moving like they were in their twenties.

Being the showman, Benny broke away from the group, still swaying to the beat as he made his way to the pier for a cigarette. Boats were cruising in, docking for the night, their engines a low hum beneath the music and chatter.

A sleek pontoon pulled up to the pier in front of the tiki bar, but the driver miscalculated, bumping the dock with a resounding thud. The impact knocked Benny, mid-dance, right into the river with a dramatic splash.

The crowd collectively gasped, laughter rippling through the air as Jen bolted toward the pier, half-concerned and half-laughing. Benny surfaced, his soaked silhouette illuminated by the tiki lights, holding his beer high above the water like a trophy.

He took a long, exaggerated sip and declared, "Still drinkable."

The crowd erupted into cheers and applause. Jen shook her head, laughing. "Leave it to Benny," she exclaimed, her voice tinged with affection and exasperation.

Carrie and Stacy joined the others at the pier's edge, grinning as Benny climbed back up, dripping but utterly unfazed. "Well, at least he knows how to make an entrance," Stacy quipped.

"Or a splash," Carrie added with a chuckle.

"Time to go," Jen growled.

After Benny and Trip had gone to bed, Jen managed to reach Fritz despite the spotty reception on her old Nokia. She told the others she was heading to Brett's to meet him. Carrie had wanted to tag along, hopeful for another glimpse of Conner, but Tori and Stacy convinced her to join them for a moonlit swim at the pond.

Late-night swims had become their favorite tradition for kicking off the weekend—something carefree and exhilarating, especially now that Tom wasn't around to sour the fun. They each mixed another drink, sprayed themselves liberally with bug spray, and headed to the pond. The night air felt thick with humidity, the sky a blanket of stars, and the water sparkled with moonlight.

After a few sips of liquid courage, they shed their clothes and waded into the cool, dark water, laughing as they swam out toward the center. Their voices carried softly over the stillness, punctuated by giggles and the occasional yelp when one of them swore something brushed against their leg.

Meanwhile, Jen walked into Brett's and immediately spotted Fritz leaning casually against the bar, waiting for her. His broad shoulders and cowboy hat made him stand out in the crowd, and when he saw her, his face lit up.

"There's my girl," Fritz announced, pulling her into a bear hug before lifting her off the ground and spinning her around. Jen couldn't help but laugh, her tough exterior momentarily giving way to the warmth of his affection.

The honky-tonk music was in full swing, and Fritz wasted no time pulling her onto the dance floor. Jen liked being in control at work or among her friends, but with Fritz, she could let go. They danced to every song, his hands firm on her waist as they moved to the twangy rhythm.

When the bar finally wound down, they left together and went back to his place. The night ended in his bedroom, the distant sounds of frogs and crickets outside the window blending with their laughter and whispers. For Jen, it was a reminder that even in the chaos of life, there were still moments of pure joy.

CHAPTER 17

The next morning, Benny and Trip drove to the farm down the street where Jen stored her boat for the winter. They found it buried behind some tractors and other farm equipment. Benny wasn't sure how to get it out, so he and Trip went to the house and knocked on the farmer's door. They waited for a few minutes, then walked around to look in the windows. It didn't appear anyone was home.

"What the hell!" Benny shouted. "How am I supposed to get the boat?"

Beep Beep! Just then, Trip came riding down the driveway in one of the tractors.

"What the heck, Trip? You can drive a tractor?" Benny asked amusingly,

"Of course," he replied, flinging off his hat, "I grew up spending summers on my grandma's farm."

"Well, that's a fun fact I didn't see coming," Benny answered with a smirk.

Trip grinned as he maneuvered the tractor into position. "There's a lot you don't know about me, Benny. Summers on the farm taught me how to drive everything from this beast to an ATV by the time I was ten."

Benny chuckled and leaned against the rusty old fence post. "I'm impressed. Now, how about you impress me further by getting that damn boat out of there?"

Trip adjusted his sunglasses and revved the tractor for dramatic effect. "Watch and learn."

The tractor rumbled forward, kicking up a small cloud of dust as it edged closer to the maze of farm equipment. The boat was wedged awkwardly between an old combine and a flatbed trailer, its tarp partially slipped off from the winter storms. Trip expertly positioned the tractor, hooked the tow line to the boat trailer, and slowly began to pull it free.

"Not bad, huh?" Trip called over his shoulder as the boat emerged, its red paint gleaming under a layer of grime.

"Not bad at all," Benny admitted, genuinely impressed. "I didn't think we were getting that thing out of here without a miracle."

Trip hopped down from the tractor and dusted off his hands. "No miracle needed, just some good ol' farm boy know-how."

They both laughed as they inspected the boat, giving it a quick once-over to ensure it was still in decent shape after being stored for months.

"Alright, let's get this thing hitched and hit the river," exclaimed Benny, imagining their group lounging on the boat with drinks.

"Done and done," Trip agreed. "I'll drive it out, and you can owe me a beer or two for saving the day."

"Deal," Benny smiled. "But you're not touching the grill later—farm boy or not."

Trip laughed as they worked together to hitch the boat to Benny's truck, both already looking forward to the day on the water.

Stacy woke up to Trip being gone. She vaguely remembered him mentioning going somewhere with Benny to get Jen's boat, but things were a bit foggy this morning. Stacy looked around their cluttered bedroom, all the clothes strewn about. She noticed the outfit she had worn the previous night. She recalled the skinny-dipping escapade, rubbed her eyes, and pulled herself out of bed to tidy up. She picked up her tube top and shorts and noticed her panties were not in the pile. She must have left them by the pond. They were Victoria's Secret, so she was not about to leave them there. She looked at herself in the mirror, wiped away some leftover mascara from under her eyes, and then put on a pair of shorts and a tank top to fetch her panties.

Jen and Carrie awoke shortly after, around 8:00. Jen started a pot of coffee and turned on the television. Once brewed, they filled their cups, and Jen poured vanilla creamer in each one. They grabbed their cigarettes and went on the deck. The heat bugs were already buzzing, and the hot, humid air filled the atmosphere. They both sat and lit their cigarettes to enjoy their coffee.

"How was your night with Fritz?" Carrie inquired with raised eyebrows.

"Fun," she answered dismissively.

"Come on, fun? Just fun? You didn't come in until at least 2 a.m."

She blushed and looked down into her coffee, as if hiding something. "We had fun at the bar, danced a little, went back to his place, and had sex. Very good sex."

"Don't you want to be more than just bed buddies? I can tell that you like him a lot. Do you talk to him outside of these weekends?"

"No." Jen looked down, almost as if to avoid the question.

"Is it because of his accident?"

"Come on, Carrie, we're different people. He is a country boy, and I'm all city."

"You like country music," Carrie giggled, realizing how ridiculous that sounded.

Jen laughed, shaking her head. "Liking country music doesn't mean I want to live out in the sticks and go mudding on weekends. We're just different."

Carrie took a sip of her coffee, giving Jen a side-eye. "You can't tell me there's nothing more there. You're always glowing after you see him."

Jen exhaled a stream of smoke and leaned back in her chair. "I'm not saying I don't like him. I do.

He's sweet and he's good to me. But let's be real, Carrie—what kind of future would we have? He's got his ranch and life, and I've got my jewelry store and everything else."

"Everything else? You mean the constant stress and no social life?"

Jen rolled her eyes but smiled. "Okay, fair. But I don't think he's looking for more, either. He's got his baggage, you know."

Carrie nodded, taking another drag of her cigarette. "I get it, but maybe you're overthinking it. Sometimes people surprise you. I mean, look at me—I never thought I'd leave Tom, and now I'm out here drinking bad coffee and chain-smoking with you."

Jen laughed. "The coffee's not that bad!"

Carrie shrugged. "Eh, it's tolerable."

They sat quietly for a moment, sipping their coffee and listening to the buzz of the cicadas.

Jen broke the silence. "So, what about you? You and Conner seemed pretty chummy last night."

Carrie sighed, flicking ash from her cigarette. "It was nothing. We just caught up. He's married, so nothing's going to happen."

Jen gave her a knowing look. "I saw the way he was looking at you."

Carrie shook her head. "Don't start. It's complicated enough without you stirring the pot."

Jen grinned mischievously. "I'm just saying... maybe you should let yourself have a little fun. You deserve it."

Carrie smirked. "Fun always seems to come with consequences around here."

Jen raised her coffee cup. "Here's to a weekend full of questionable decisions."

Carrie clinked her cup against Jen's. "Cheers to that."

Jen took a sip of her coffee, and Carrie dropped the subject. She sat back in her chair and looked out over the pond, squinting her eyes to get a better glimpse of the person sitting on the pier.

"Is that Stacy?" Carrie blurted. The woman on the picnic table had her back to her, but her short, dark hair was undeniable. Carrie thought she was taking some alone time, but suddenly, Brandon stood up from what appeared to be her feet.

Jen turned her body so that she could see what Carrie saw. "What in the world?" she growled and coughed loudly. They moved chairs around to make noise, and finally, Stacy turned around. She quickly gathered herself and walked toward the trailer while Brandon went in the opposite direction.

She walked up the stairs of the deck, looking a little flushed.

"What were you doing down there? And was that Brandon?" Jen asked. "Geez, you're half dressed, and he's a kid!"

Stacy put her arms around her chest, maybe to cover the fact that she wasn't wearing a bra.

"First of all, he's eighteen, and I am wearing clothes. Don't we all wear shorts and tanks around here? Not that it matters. We were only talking."

Carrie tried to diffuse what seemed to be an argument. "We were just wondering what you were doing there so early."

"I left my bra and underwear by the pond last night." She looked embarrassed and pulled them out of her pocket.

"What was Brandon doing there? Did he find your panties first?" Jen sounded irritated.

"He was running. He is training for a marathon or something. No, I got to my underwear first. So, what's the plan today?" Stacy asked, trying to change the subject.

Jen stood up and crushed out her cigarette. "The guys went to get the boat, and we're going down the river early. We should get started making food to bring." She was ready for a day of fun on the river, but couldn't help wondering what Stacy was up to behind Trip's back.

"I guess I'm on sandwich central." Carrie laughed and stood up, hiding her own secrets.

"Did someone say sandwiches?" Tori asked, smiling through the screen door, none the wiser of what just transpired.

CHAPTER 18

The sun beamed on their bodies, and the wind blew their hair as they cruised along the river. Jen opted for Benny to drive since he was better at it, and she had such a late night. The ladies sat in the front of the boat as usual, in the sun, except Stacy. She sat next to Trip, under the boom awning with the rest of the guys, his arm around her, holding her tight. In his other arm, he had his beer and conversed with the guys.

Benny gripped the wheel with one hand, the other casually balancing a red Solo cup against his knee as the boat skimmed over the water. The ice in his Jack and Coke clinked softly with each turn. Shirtless, his skin already glistening with a mix of sunscreen and sweat, he leaned back confidently, the stylish pattern of his swim trunks catching the sunlight.

"Hold on, ladies!" he called over the engine's hum, his puka shell necklace shifting with the boat's motion. His fedora sat tilted at just the right angle, paired with mirrored sunglasses that reflected the endless stretch of blue water.

As the boat eased into a no-wake zone, Benny

reached into the console and pulled out a pack of cigarettes. He lit one with a practiced flick, taking a deep drag before exhaling a cloud of smoke that disappeared into the summer breeze.

"How's the investment business going, Trip?" Benny asked. His job was going well, and he recently moved into a new apartment building downtown. He was thinking of breaking into the stock market with Trip's help.

"It's good, real good. I can't complain; everything's on the upswing right now. Are you thinking of getting a portfolio?" Trip asked. He always exuded confidence and acted almost pompous when talking about his job.

Benny nodded, leaning back in his chair. "Yeah, I've been thinking about it. Got a little extra cash now because of my promotion. I figured I should do something smart instead of blowing it all at Brett's or golf clubs."

Trip chuckled, swirling the ice in his drink. "Smart move, man. The market's been pretty strong lately. A balanced portfolio, along with some growth stocks and a few reliable blue-chip companies, would be a good start. I could get you set up, no problem."

Benny tilted his head and responded. "You're sure about that? What if it all crashes tomorrow?"

Trip waved his hand dismissively. "That's the thing, Benny. You have to think long-term. Diversify, hold steady. Let me put together a plan for you—it's what I do best."

Stacy finally turned her attention back to the conversation, a faint smirk on her face. "Trip, you make it sound like you've never made a bad call."

Trip glanced at her, his expression firm but slightly amused. "I didn't say that. But when you know the game as well as I do, you're bound to win more than you lose."

Benny laughed, shaking his head. "Alright, Mr. Wall Street, maybe I'll take you up on that. Just don't have me living off ramen noodles because you bet it all on some startup."

Trip grinned, raising his glass. "Trust me, Benny, I'd never let you sink that low. I help people avoid making mistakes that can cost them a significant amount of money. He looked down at Stacy and squeezed her a little harder. "This little lady is saving the world with her massages, aren't you, honey?"

Stacy let out a small laugh, but her smile didn't quite reach her eyes. "Yeah, something like that," she replied lightly, taking another sip of her beer.

Carrie noticed the subtle shift in Stacy's tone. "Massages are lifesavers, though," she chimed in. "Do you know how often I've been ready to snap before a good massage put me back together? You're practically a superhero, Stacy."

Stacy smiled more genuinely at Carrie. "Thanks, Carrie. I guess helping people feel better counts for something."

Trip chuckled, clearly not noticing Stacy's

discomfort. "Counts for a lot. You've got magic hands, babe." He gave her a playful nudge, but the comment made Stacy glance away toward the river.

Jen leaned forward. "Speaking of saving people, Trip, what's the craziest financial blunder you've seen someone make?"

Trip's eyes lit up at the chance to share a story. "Oh, where do I start? One guy poured his entire savings into a penny stock because a buddy told him it was the next big thing. He didn't bother to check the company—it was a front for a scam. Lost every dime in two weeks."

"Wow," Benny said, wincing. "Sounds brutal."

Trip nodded, his grip still firm on Stacy's shoulder. "That's why you need someone who knows the ropes, like me, to steer you clear of those disasters."

Stacy shifted slightly, pulling her hair behind her ear. "Maybe not everyone needs saving, though. Some people want to figure things out on their own."

Trip looked down at her, slightly surprised. "Sure, but why make mistakes when you don't have to? That's why I'm here."

Carrie caught Stacy's eye and gave her a small, understanding smile. Stacy smiled back faintly, but the moment passed quickly as Benny slapped Trip on the back. "Alright, Mr. Financial Savior. How about saving me from another drinkless moment and grabbing us another round?"

The group laughed, and Trip reluctantly released Stacy to head to the cooler. Carrie leaned toward Stacy and whispered, "You okay?"

Stacy nodded, her voice barely audible over the river breeze. "Yeah. Thanks."

At the front of the boat, basking in the sun, Jen, Carrie, and Tori sipped on a wine spritzer that Jen had made. They were discussing the series finale of Sex and The City that occurred earlier that year, and noticed that Stacy seemed out of place with the guys, looking disgusted with the conversation.

"Come up here with us, Stacy. It's not so windy now, and you can get some sun." Carrie instructed, patting on a section of the boat seat next to her.

Stacy quickly broke away from Trip's grip without his notice. She plopped down beside Carrie, who put her arm around her shoulder.

"Trip always acts like his career is so much more important than mine. I hate how he belittles my job and me. I have a bachelor's degree and am considering pursuing a master's in physical therapy." She exclaimed.

Carrie gave Stacy a reassuring squeeze. "You absolutely should. You're amazing at what you do. And physical therapy? That's no small feat. Trip has no idea how hard it is to help people heal."

Jen leaned over, holding her spritzer up like a toast. "Hear, hear! Don't let him get to you, Stacy. Guys like Trip are all about puffing themselves up to feel important. You're better than that."

Stacy gave a small smile, but her eyes still held frustration. "Thanks, you guys. It's just that sometimes it feels like he talks down to me in front of everyone, like I'm some cute accessory. I worked hard for my degree and built a loyal client base. I love what I do."

Tori chimed in, flipping her sunglasses up. "And that's what matters. You're helping people and making a real difference. Trip's jealous because he knows you're out of his league."

The group laughed, and Stacy's smile grew wider. "You're probably right," she said, the tension in her shoulders easing a little.

Carrie handed Stacy her cup. "Here, have a sip. Jen makes a mean spritzer."

Stacy took the cup and tried it. "Okay, that's amazing. Maybe I'll start making these instead of margaritas."

"Perfect for a summer day," Jen said with a grin.

As the boat glided over the water, the conversation turned lighter, and Stacy seemed to relax in the company of the other women. Carrie glanced back at the guys, laughing loudly over something Benny said, and felt a wave of gratitude for the easy camaraderie she shared with her friends.

For a brief moment, her mind wandered back to Conner. She wondered where he was at that moment and what he might be doing. But as the sun warmed her skin and Stacy leaned into her, laughing, Carrie reminded herself to quit wandering and stay present.

Benny anchored the boat at the sandbar, a lively scene packed with boats and young partygoers. It looked like an MTV spring break special, and even though most of them were in their early thirties—except for Stacy—they were more than ready to join the fun.

Jen and Carrie wasted no time, slipping off their sarongs and easing into the cool, inviting water. Tori stayed back on the boat, carefully applying sunscreen to her shoulders.

"Drinks, ladies!" Benny called, handing down their cups from the boat.

Trip remained under the shade of the boom awning, meticulously rubbing sunscreen onto his arms. Meanwhile, Benny rummaged through his cooler and pulled out a bag of green grapes with a triumphant grin.

"Look what I brought, Tori. Want some?"

Tori glanced at him with mock surprise. "Wow, Benny actually brought something to share. I'm impressed." She reached toward the bag, but Benny snatched it back with a mischievous smirk.

"Hold on, babe. How about I feed them to you instead?" he teased, holding a grape between his fingers.

"Ugh, you're disgusting!" Tori shot back, rolling her eyes as she got up. She climbed down the ladder into the water, ignoring Benny's laughter.

As she waded into the water, Benny's eyes

lingered a little too long on her figure, clearly admiring the view. Tori, catching his glance, turned back with a sharp look. "Eyes up, Benny. You're not that charming."

"Just appreciating the scenery," he replied with a grin, tossing a grape into his mouth as if to seal the deal.

They splashed and floated in the water, enjoying much-needed relief from the scorching sun. Laughter filled the air as they cooled off, and they reveled in the sandbar's carefree atmosphere.

After meticulously applying sunscreen, Trip finally eased into the water. He immediately scooped Stacy into his arms, holding her close as if shielding her from wandering eyes. She giggled, seemingly enjoying the attention as he floated her around.

Nearby, Jen, Carrie, and Tori tossed a ball back and forth with Benny, the playful splashes adding to the fun. The water shimmered around them, sparkling like a thousand tiny mirrors in the midday sun.

As the group started to feel hunger pangs, Benny swam back to the boat and climbed up the ladder, water dripping from his hair. He rummaged through the cooler and emerged triumphantly, holding up individually wrapped sandwiches.

"Lunchtime!" he called out with a grin, waving the sandwiches like a prize.

"Look at you so graciously handing out sandwiches that we made," Tori snickered and took one.

After lunch, Benny suggested docking the boat at one of the piers along the river so they could explore the local bars. Excited to check out some bars, the girls put on shorts and T-shirts over their swimsuits, while the guys threw on their shirts.

Their first stop was a small, quirky spot called Gamblers. They knew they'd found the perfect place to linger as soon as they stepped inside. The bar was a conversation piece, with countless pennies encased under glass. The soft hum of gambling machines mingling with the tunes from a jukebox in the corner accompanied the lively atmosphere.

"Now this is a vibe," Jen said, sliding onto a barstool and glancing at the glowing jukebox.

"Drinks are on me for the first round!" Benny declared, already making his way to the bar.

The group quickly settled in, captivated by the establishment's charm. The combination of rustic decor, the clinking of coins, and the sound of laughter made it an irresistible spot to start their afternoon adventure.

They bellied up to the bar, laughing as they ordered a round of shots and tried their luck with Shake of the Day. The jukebox hummed with classic tunes—Led Zeppelin and The Cars—setting a laid-back, nostalgic mood. When the music stopped, Jen took charge of the jukebox. She dropped in a few bills, and moments later, her all-time favorite song, Boot Scootin' Boogie, came on.

"Come on, Carrie!" Jen yelled, grabbing her

friend's hand.

The two burst into laughter as they swung each other around, singing at the top of their lungs and stomping their feet in rhythm. Seeing the fun, Benny seized the chance to pull Tori onto the makeshift dance floor. At first, she hesitated, but Benny's exaggerated twirls and goofy grin won her over, and she joined in, laughing as he spun her clumsily around.

Meanwhile, Stacy remained perched on Trip's lap, sipping her drink as they watched the others. She rolled her eyes with a smirk but couldn't help smiling at the chaos unfolding in front of them.

As the song ended, Benny finished his beer, wiped his forehead dramatically, and declared, "Let's beat it before this becomes a full-on rodeo."

With laughter still echoing in their ears, they strolled across the parking lot to the next spot, a buzzing riverside bar called Sandbar. Known for its sprawling deck and energetic vibe, they had a massive outdoor setup featuring a central bar and plenty of tables for sharing appetizers and cocktails. It was a destination for boaters, always packed with sun-kissed, well-dressed patrons enjoying the vibe.

Jen pointed to the deck. "This is the place. I need a mojito."

As they walked in, the girls couldn't help but notice how different they looked from the crowd. Their wet hair clung to their shoulders, and their casual shorts and T-shirts stood out against the other guests' polished outfits and carefully styled appearances.

But none of them cared. They laughed as they made their way to the bar, radiating an easy confidence that turned a few heads anyway. They weren't concerned about fitting in. All that mattered was having fun, and they were determined to do just that.

"What's everyone drinking?" Jen asked, flagging down a bartender.

"Something cold," Carrie answered, wringing out the end of her damp ponytail.

"Whatever she's having," Tori added, gesturing to Jen.

Jen grinned. "Mojitos all around, then!"

The group approached the bar in a loose, jovial cluster, their carefree energy contrasting with the slick, polished crowd that surrounded them. As they edged closer to the counter, Benny noticed someone familiar standing with two other guys near the far end of the bar. It was Bobby.

Bobby and his companions were sipping elaborate cocktails garnished with mint sprigs and citrus twists. They wore fitted tank tops and sported perfectly styled, moussed-back hair, looking far more put-together than Bobby usually did.

"Bobby!" Benny called out. "Didn't see you on the river. Where'd you dock your boat? And where's Marcy?"

Bobby turned away from his friends, a slow grin across his face. "Ben, my man!" he said, reaching for a handshake. His voice was overly enthusiastic, almost performative.

Bobby glanced at the rest of the group, giving them a brief nod. "Hey, the gang's all here. Marcy's back at the trailer. She's getting ready for the barbecue later."

"Guess we'll see you there," Benny responded.

After the brief exchange, Bobby returned to his friends, who glanced at Benny and the group with subtle but unmistakable disdain.

At the bar, Benny muscled up to the counter to order six mojitos. The rest of the group had to stand just outside the tightly packed crowd, squished together like sardines.

"What was up with Bobby?" Benny asked as he returned with the drinks. "He was acting all stuck up, and what's up with that outfit? Seriously, a tank top? He doesn't look like that when he's drunk off his ass at Brett's."

Carrie squinted toward Bobby and his friends, who were laughing at something, their gestures overly animated. "Maybe those are his special, fancy friends," she said, her voice laced with dry humor.

Benny snorted. "Special friends, all right. Guy's got layers, I guess."

Jen sipped her mojito and shrugged. "Or secrets."

The group murmured with speculation, but none of them pressed further. They were here for fun; whatever Bobby was up to could wait until later. It wasn't any of their business.

CHAPTER 19

Back at the trailer, the buzz of the blow dryer cut through the quiet, distracting Jen as she mixed a drink concoction for Marcy's barbecue. Curious and slightly bemused, she went down the narrow hall to find Carrie in front of the mirror, holding the blow dryer and smoothing her hair.

Leaning against the doorframe with her arms crossed and a cigarette in hand, Jen raised an eyebrow. "Blow drying your hair? What's the deal?"

Carrie glanced at her reflection and smirked. "What? My hair's shorter now. It's easier to smooth out. Plus, Stacy turned me on to some product."

Jen rolled her eyes. "Whatever. Who do you have to impress?"

"Shut up," Carrie shot back, laughing softly.

Carrie finished drying her hair, which now gleamed with her new highlights, catching the light. She touched up her minimalist makeup just enough to enhance her sun-kissed glow. Then, she slipped into her favorite tan linen shorts and a black floral tank top. The final touch was a spritz of her favorite perfume. As she turned to leave, she nearly bumped into Stacy, stepping out of her room, refreshed and in a chic new outfit.

Stacy paused, looking Carrie up and down with a grin. "Your hair looks great. That shine serum works, huh?"

"It sure does. I'm tired of looking like a ragamuffin up here."

They headed toward the common area, idly talking, until they spotted Trip lounging on the couch, engrossed in a baseball game on the TV. He glanced up, caught sight of Stacy, and immediately stood.

"Oh hey, babe. Didn't realize you were getting all dolled up." He grabbed her arm playfully. "Guess I'll stay as is," he said, gesturing to his casual attire.

Stacy gave him a look but didn't protest.

Benny putzed in the kitchen, stuffing a small cooler with the high-octane beer he liked. Jen was mixing a to-go cocktail with precision, clearly preparing for Marcy's barbecue.

Jen glanced over at Benny, arching an eyebrow. "What the hell, Benny? I'm sure they'll have drinks there."

"Yeah," Benny scoffed, "the faggot stuff that Bobby drinks."

Jen gave him a sharp look. "What's that supposed to mean?"

"Bacardi," he replied, shrugging.

Jen sighed. "Oh, for crying out loud. People drink

Bacardi, Benny. Well, whatever. Better toss something for the rest of us while you're at it."

Benny paused, "We're gonna need a bigger cooler," he winked at Jen—a playful nod to Jaws.

Jen shook her head, rolling her eyes. "Lord, we have issues," she muttered.

Carrie headed for the door and called back, "Can you throw in a couple of Smirnoff Ice for me?"

"Add some Lites for us," Trip added casually.

Benny paused mid-pack, glanced at the already-full cooler, and sighed exaggeratedly. "Fine, fine," he said, standing and grabbing a larger cooler.

As he transferred everything, Jen smirked at him. "Good. Now it'll look like you came prepared."

Benny grinned, waving her off, while Carrie and Trip exchanged amused glances before heading outside.

Jen and Carrie stayed in the kitchen, finishing the to-go cocktail mix. Jen added a twist of lime to the pitcher while Carrie stirred. The clinking of the ice cubes offered a comforting rhythm in the otherwise quiet trailer.

Outside on the deck, Benny and Tori goofed around. Tori, ever playful, snatched Benny's fedora right off his head and plopped it on her own, striking a cheeky pose before darting off the deck.

"Give that back!" Benny hollered, laughing as he took off after her.

Jen leaned out the screen door, cocktail in hand. "Come on, you two! We're going to Marcy's. Enough horsing around!"

Tori paused at the foot of the stairs and adjusted the hat on her head. "Wait—are we seriously bringing a cooler?"

Jen nodded, glancing back at the kitchen. "Yep. Benny packed a variety this time, so we should be covered."

Carrie grabbed the cocktail pitcher, and Jen tucked a stack of plastic cups under her arm. Benny, now fedora-less and slightly out of breath, appeared at the door, Tori following with a triumphant grin.

"Alright, let's lock up and hit the road," Jen commanded, turning off the kitchen light.

The group piled out of the trailer, cooler in tow, ready to make their way to Marcy's barbecue. The sun was beginning to dip low, casting long shadows across the gravel path as they headed off, the anticipation of the night buzzing between them.

Bobby and Marcy's trailer area felt frozen in time, a relic of previous summers. Aside from fewer people and the absence of the smoky aroma from the grill, little had changed. Instead of sizzling burgers and hot dogs, a long banquet table displayed platters of rolls, cold cuts, salads, and chips, giving off a lackluster feel.

Carrie, Jen, Benny, Tori, Stacy, and Trip grabbed plates and settled at an empty picnic table. The atmosphere felt subdued as they picked at their food, quietly observing the scene.

Marcy soon made her way over, a tray of brownies in her hands.

"Friends," Marcy declared, her voice dripping with saccharine sweetness. "It's an absolute delight to have you all grace us with your presence." She placed a somewhat forceful hand on Jen's shoulder.

"Hi, Marcy," Jen replied, her tone light but guarded.

"Did you bring your famous salsa?" Marcy asked with exaggerated enthusiasm.

Before Jen could answer, Carrie cut in, her irritation barely concealed. "No, Marcy. My lovely friend just brought herself this time."

Marcy ignored the edge in Carrie's voice and swayed slightly as she glanced at Jen's drink. "And a cocktail, I see. Did you notice Bobby's friend is here this weekend?"

"I did," Jen answered, her tone even. "Where's his wife?"

"Oh, she's away with the girls at some lake house."

As Marcy prattled on, Carrie kept her head down, stabbing at her salad with her fork. Behind her carefully composed face, a storm was brewing.

Just then, Conner emerged from the trailer and spotted the group. He smiled and made his way over.

"Conner boy!" Benny greeted him, raising his beer.

"Hey, Benny, looks like you survived the night," Conner chuckled.

Marcy finally set down the platter of brownies in the center of the table. "I made these. Have at it, kids!"

The group eyed the brownies suspiciously, waiting for someone to make the first move.

"I've got to get going," Conner said, glancing at Carrie briefly. "I'm taking Brandon golfing."

"There's a golf course here?" Carrie asked, her curiosity piqued.

"Yeah, just down the road," Conner replied. "We'll probably just do nine holes, but it keeps him busy."

"K, bye," Carrie responded, her voice nonchalant, though her eyes lingered on him as he walked away.

As soon as he was out of sight, Carrie reached for a brownie. That was all the encouragement the others needed—Jen, Stacy, and Trip followed suit, digging into the plate.

"Mmm, holy shit! This brownie is the best I've ever tasted!" Jen exclaimed, savoring the chocolatey bite. The others stayed quiet, each immersed in their own brownie experience.

"I'm watching my figure," Tori reported, her tone indifferent.

"So am I," Benny shot back with a grin. No one seemed to notice when he and Tori walked off together.

Trip wiped the crumbs from his mouth and stood up. "This party's lame. Come on, Stacy, let's go to Brett's and watch the game."

"Wash the game, dude?" Stacy repeated with a laugh.

"Watch! You know what I mean. Let's go." He reached for her arm, but Stacy shrugged him off.

"Nah, I don't feel like washing—or watching anything," she giggled.

Trip frowned. "Suit yourself," he muttered before staggering off toward the bar.

Jen pushed her chair back, wobbling slightly. "Wow, I think I drank too much. I gotta go."

"I'll join you ladies," Stacy added, linking arms with Jen and Carrie.

The three of them began walking away, arm in arm, their steps unsteady. Jen tripped on her platform flip-flops, and like a domino effect, they all tumbled to the ground, laughing uncontrollably.

"What a bunch of drunks," Marcy snickered as she turned back toward her guests.

The women got up, giggling and brushing themselves off. Something felt off. They hadn't had too much to drink, but their legs felt rubbery, and their thoughts scattered.

When they reached the trailer, Jen went straight inside.

"Stacy, let's walk around a bit. I need to shake this buzz off," Carrie said, her arm looped through Stacy's for balance.

"My gawd, I feel fucked up," Stacy slurred as they aimlessly wandered through the surrounding area.

They stumbled upon a trailer adorned with a yard full of gnomes.

"Who lives here?" Carrie asked, blinking at the colorful statues.

"No idea," Stacy replied before both collapsed into the gnome-filled yard, laughing uncontrollably.

They rolled around on the ground, clutching their stomachs, until Brandon appeared, towering over them with a look of amused bewilderment.

"What the hell?" he muttered before scooping Stacy up and tossing her over his broad shoulders.

Still laughing, Carrie stumbled back to the trailer. She collapsed onto the couch next to Jen, holding the remote and staring at the TV with glassy eyes.

Carrie got up and went to the kitchen, her movements clumsy. She grabbed a carton of Pringles, stacked three together, and shoved them into her mouth. "Oh my god, Jen! Try these—it's like pizza on a chip!"

Jen reached out sluggishly, taking a few. "I want a

baked badada," she mumbled.

Carrie burst into laughter. "Did you just say baked badada? Dude, what is wrong with you?"

"I don't know!" Jen replied, her words slurring. "I can't even focus on the TV. It's like little lights going back and forth. What the hell? Hey, where's Stacy?"

Carrie looked around, her vision slightly blurred. "I dunno... Oh, wait. Trip came and got her. I think they went back to the bar."

~ ~ ~

As the evening wind picked up, the group continued to talk and drink, some moving inside to cool off, while others hung by the campfire. Benny and Tori stood at the edge of the deck, away from the others. Benny leaned against the wooden railing, sipping his beer, while Tori seemed lost in thought, staring out into the dark.

"You're pretty quiet tonight," Benny remarked, nudging her with his shoulder.

"I'm just... thinking," she said, her voice soft but heavy with something unsaid. She glanced up at him, a fleeting, almost vulnerable look in her eyes. "About everything, I guess. Sometimes I wonder if I'm even on the right path."

Benny paused, his gaze softening. "You always look like you've got it all figured out, though."

"Yeah, well, maybe I'm not so sure anymore," she

replied, turning toward him. She took a step closer, her hand brushing against his. "And maybe I'm tired of pretending."

There was a quiet understanding between them for a moment, as if the intensity they had both been ignoring finally bubbled to the surface. Benny took a slow breath, his eyes locking with hers. "You don't have to pretend with me, Tori," he said, his voice low and a little gravelly.

Tori's lips parted slightly, and the world seemed to shrink. The rest of the group's noise faded, and the only sound that mattered was her heart beating. She stepped closer, tilting her head up to meet his gaze.

"You know, I never thought we'd be here," she murmured, her breath catching.

Benny's hand moved up to her arm, gently guiding her closer. "Sometimes the best things happen when you least expect them."

With that, Tori closed the space between them, and Benny met her halfway, kissing her softly at first, then deeper as the tension between them finally released. They pulled apart for a moment, eyes wide and faces flushed.

"Maybe we should have done this sooner," she whispered, her voice barely a breath.

"I was thinking the same thing," Benny admitted, his lips curving into a sly grin as they shared another kiss under the stars.

~ ~ ~

Carrie woke up groggily, her mouth parched. The trailer felt eerily quiet, aside from faint music drifting in from the bars and the muffled sounds of neighbors enjoying the night. Jen was slumped over on the couch beside her, and Trip snored softly from one of the recliners, completely passed out.

Carrie rubbed her still foggy eyes and shuffled to the kitchen. She grabbed a bottle of water and devoured it, the cool liquid soothing her dry throat. The trailer felt stuffy, so she went to the deck for fresh air.

The stunning night boasted clear skies with countless stars sparkling above, and the bright moon casting a silvery glow over everything. The air felt cooler, and Carrie inhaled deeply, taking in the earthy scent of the nearby pond. She leaned on the deck railing, thinking what a shame the others were missing this perfect moment.

As her eyes wandered, she noticed movement by the pond. Two figures stood close together, their silhouettes cast in shadow by the moonlight. They were locked in an embrace, their bodies leaning into each other as if they were kissing.

Carrie squinted, trying to see better. She mentally ticked off the group: Jen and Trip were inside, leaving Tori, Benny, and Stacy unaccounted for. A strange feeling twisted in her stomach as she continued watching, unsure whether to call out or stay silent.

Her heart raced slightly, and she stepped back from the railing, retreating into the shadows of the deck. She couldn't shake the unease of what she might have just witnessed.

CHAPTER 20

The next morning, Carrie followed Jen onto the deck, shielding her eyes from the morning sun with her hand as she sipped her coffee. The fresh air felt good, but the fog lingered in her head. She leaned on the railing, staring out at the still water.

"Brownies don't do that," Carrie said after a moment, her voice thoughtful. "Unless... they weren't normal brownies."

Jen groaned, rubbing her temples. "You think Marcy spiked them?"

Carrie shrugged. "I wouldn't put it past her."

Jen took a long sip of her coffee and stared into the distance. "Well, that explains the giggles and the munchies, but not why I can't remember half the night. I feel like I was on autopilot after we left." She turned to Carrie, narrowing her eyes. "What about you? Any weird flashbacks?"

Carrie hesitated, her mind flashing back to the shadowy figures at the pond. She could see how they moved—intimate, connected—but still couldn't make out who they were. It had to be Benny and Tori. But why would they sneak off like that? And what would it mean if they had?

"I... remember walking outside for air," Carrie responded slowly, avoiding Jen's gaze. "But that's it."

Jen raised an eyebrow. "You're holding something back."

Carrie shook her head, forcing a smile. "Nothing juicy, I promise. Just trying to piece things together like you."

"Well, good luck with that." Jen leaned back in her chair, letting out a tired laugh. "This place is cursed, I swear. Weird shit always happens here. That's why I don't come every weekend. I don't think I would survive."

Carrie nodded absently, her eyes drifting toward the pond again. She couldn't shake the image from her head, or the uneasy feeling it left behind.

Inside, the sound of shuffling feet signaled someone else waking up. Benny stumbled onto the deck, his hair a mess, still wearing his clothes from the day before.

"Morning, ladies," he mumbled, grabbing Carrie's coffee cup and taking a sip before she could protest. "What's with the long faces? We all made it back alive, didn't we?"

"Barely," Jen said, eyeing him. "Do you remember anything from last night?"

Benny grinned, though there was a flicker of something in his expression—nervousness, maybe. "Enough to know it was a good time."

Carrie studied him carefully, but his face gave nothing away. He wasn't admitting if he was at the pond with Tori. Not yet, anyway.

"Well, good for you," Jen said, rolling her eyes. "Now grab some coffee and help us figure out what the hell happened."

Benny chuckled, heading inside, but not before glancing at Carrie. It was brief, almost imperceptible, but it left her wondering. Did he know what she saw?

Carrie turned back to the pond, her coffee cooling in her hands. Last night's mystery wasn't just a fuzzy memory but something bigger. Something that might unravel them all.

Just then, Tori came out on the deck. She looked perfectly normal, as if nothing strange had happened the night before. Of course, she didn't eat a brownie, nor did Benny.

"What's up, ladies?" she asked. "You were all acting pretty goofy last night. I mean, not your normal goofy."

"We're pretty sure Marcy laced the brownies she served us. Probably weed. She's way too nerdy to get her hands on anything else." Carrie answered. "Where did you and Benny go?"

Tori looked up from the steaming coffee she was cupping in her hand, her eyes shielded slightly from her baseball cap brim. "We were at the bar," she answered calmly. I was playing Phot Hunt while Benny went back and forth to watch the game with Trip."

That seems believable, Carrie thought. As messed up as Trip was, he probably wouldn't remember whether they were there. But what about Stacy? Better to leave it alone and not open up a can of worms.

The rest came out to the deck one by one: First Trip and Stacy, then Benny with an English muffin he was shoving in his mouth. The girls were still in pajamas, and the guys were still wearing the clothes they had on the day before. They all slept later than usual, and everyone except Tori and Benny looked pretty disheveled and out of it.

"Well, good morning!" Marcy yelled from the golf cart as they pulled close to the deck. Bobby was driving. "How are you all feeling this morning? You seemed pretty lit when you left."

"That's because you drugged us!" yelled Trip as he stood up and towered over them from the deck.

"What are you talking about?" Bobby asked, sipping his Bloody Mary from a red Solo cup.

"Your wife laced those brownies she served us. Just us. She only served us!" Trip yelled back, clearly enraged.

"Where would I get drugs from?" Marcy roared.

"I don't know, maybe your son?" yelled Trip, enraged and standing up as if to confront them.

"Don't be silly, he doesn't do drugs," Marcy exclaimed. "Plus, he's training for a marathon."

"Maybe you all should control your booze

intake." Bobby sneered and drove off, Marcy waving goodbye.

"Assholes!" Trip yelled and plopped himself down hard on a chair. Stacy rubbed his shoulder to try to calm him. His face was beet red.

Carrie leaned against the railing, watching the golf cart disappear down the dusty road. She sipped her coffee, letting the bitter taste ground her as the group simmered with frustration.

"Honestly, Trip, yelling at them won't fix anything," Carrie calmly admitted, but she secretly kept her irritation with Marcy just below the surface.

Trip huffed, brushing Stacy's hand off his shoulder. "So, we're just supposed to let it slide? That psycho thinks drugging people is funny."

Benny chuckled, stretching his arms behind his head. "Come on, Trip. What's done is done. Plus, you don't seem worse for wear this morning. Maybe it even did you some good."

Trip shot him a glare. "You think it's funny? What if something happened to Stacy? Or Jen? We could've gotten hurt."

"Relax, dude," Benny commanded. "If you don't want to get messed with, don't hang out with people like Marcy. It's not like she's winning Citizen of the Year."

Jen sighed heavily, clearly tired of the argument. "Benny's right about one thing—let's not waste energy on her. We've got one day left, and I'm not spending it mad at a woman with no social boundaries."

Carrie nodded, though her mind was elsewhere. Visions of the foggy silhouettes she had seen by the pond kept creeping back. If Marcy had laced the brownies, it would explain a lot. But what about Benny and Tori? The idea of them sneaking off together didn't sit right, even if no one else noticed.

"Whatever," Trip grumbled. He stood up, pacing the deck like a caged animal. "But if I see her again, I'm saying something. That woman needs a reality check."

"Cool, good luck with that," Benny quipped, earning another glare. He stood, stretching lazily.

Benny leaned forward, tapping the table to grab everyone's attention. "Hey, did you guys hear? There's gonna be a big fireworks show tonight. Brett's running it—way better than those sad little sparklers Bobby had last year. It's happening right here by the bar."

"Where'd you hear that?" Trip wondered.

"At the bar last night," Benny replied, glancing around the group smugly.

Trip rolled his eyes. "Guess I missed that nugget of wisdom." He leaned back, crossing his arms. "You know what? Why don't the guys golf eighteen holes today? Conner mentioned there's a course nearby. I bet we can rent some clubs. Better than sitting around here."

Benny slammed a hand on the table, making the plates rattle. "Hell yeah! I need to work on my swing anyway. I've got an interview with Steve Stricker coming up." He grinned broadly, clearly pleased with himself.

Jen chuckled, shaking her head. "Perfect. That'll give us some girl time. Just make sure you're back in time for the fireworks."

CHAPTER 21

After the heated discussion, the group decided to split up. The guys headed to the golf course, and the girls went to the tiki bar for lunch. They were determined to embrace the holiday spirit and make the most of their last day in Riverbanks.

The bar was quiet, since most resort guests were busy with cookouts or holiday parties. They snagged a cozy table for four and perused the menu before ordering a round of drinks.

"Let's get a few apps to share," Jen suggested, her eyes scanning for her favorites. They settled on guacamole, nachos—Jen's absolute favorite—and the bar's famous coconut shrimp.

When their drinks arrived, they raised their glasses and clinked them together. "Cheers!"

"To some girl time!" Jen declared, grinning as she leaned back in her chair, soaking up the moment.

"Yeah, especially after the year I've had," Carrie added with a sigh, glancing down at her drink. When she looked up, all three of them were staring at her. "What?" she asked, feigning innocence.

"Well, expand on that," Tori pressed, her tone laced with curiosity. "We know about the crap with Tom. And then there was that Jake guy you brought to Jen's party. What was that about?"

Stacy shifted uncomfortably, glancing away. She was the only one who knew the whole story.

Carrie took a deep breath, brushing a strand of hair from her face. "Okay, fine. I went to The Pub one night, and Jake was working the bar. He flirted with me a lot. He's ten years younger, I think, and very cute. He has a Brad Pitt vibe, don't you think?" She paused, searching their faces for agreement.

"Anyway," she continued, "he asked me out and I felt flattered. Honestly, I was starving for male attention. After Tom, I needed something, someone. We went out a few times and had a little fun. Things were exciting at first. But then it went south."

"What happened?" Jen asked softly.

Carrie hesitated. "Let's just say he tried to take advantage of me. I wasn't in a good place—mentally, emotionally, you name it. I was a mess after leaving Tom."

Tori shook her head, her tone sharp. "I'll say. Those drunk nights at darts? You were pretty much a disaster."

"Tori!" Jen interjected.

Carrie just shrugged, forcing a small smile. "She's not wrong."

"Okay, okay, let's change the subject," Carrie said,

waving her hand dismissively. Her gaze shifted to Tori, her lips curling into a mischievous smile. "What about you and Drew? I never see you two together except for darts, and then he always bails right after. Let's face it—you're no angel. Sitting on Nate's lap, for example."

Tori laughed, throwing her hands up in mock surrender. "Hey! Nate's a cutie, and come on, we all like to flirt. Please don't act like you're above it. Besides, Drew wouldn't care. He's got his own "work wives." The others exchanged curious looks, but no one asked for clarification.

"I'm sure we do," Jen commented, glancing over at Stacy. "But I can't flirt with guys in our dart league. It just feels off."

"That's because you have a BOYFRIEND!" Carrie blurted out, grinning like the cat who caught the canary.

Jen's eyes narrowed into a sharp glare. "Carrie…" she uttered through clenched teeth, her tone a warning.

"Oh, come on, Jen. We're all friends here. You can tell them." Carrie leaned back in her chair, clearly enjoying herself.

The group fell silent, their interest piqued. Still learning the dynamics of this tight-knit circle, Stacy leaned in slightly, eager for the gossip.

Jen sighed, pulling out a cigarette. She lit it slowly, took a long drag, and exhaled the smoke in a slow plume. Then she picked up her drink, took a measured sip, and spoke. In a low voice, she replied. "Fine. But this doesn't leave this table."

"The guy I introduced you to at Marcy's the other day, Fritz. I hook up with him when I'm up here."

"Just on the weekends?" Tori asked, knowing Jen spent more weekends up here since she bought the boat, often bringing Benny along.

"For now!" Carrie shouted, and they all laughed and high-fived. They all agreed Jen needed a boyfriend. She was independent, always working hard to make her jewelry store successful and planning to expand with a new location. They figured a guy might help soften her tough exterior.

Jen mumbled before scooping a giant bite of guacamole into her mouth, "I don't know about that." The girls burst into laughter.

They continued munching on nachos and coconut shrimp, their conversation shifting between the drama of the past few days and the latest episodes of Sex and The City. Jen gestured dramatically as she recounted her favorite scene, causing Carrie to laugh and nearly spill her drink. The distant sound of preparations from the bandstand caught their attention as a DJ began to set up. The beat of the music started thumping through the air, mingling with the chatter, as the outdoor bar began to fill with more guests. When the opening notes of the Spice Girls blared through the speakers, the girls exchanged grins, and without hesitation, they grabbed their drinks and headed toward the dance floor. Their hips swayed to the rhythm, their laughter blending with the energetic music, as they joined others in an impromptu dance party.

They danced arm in arm, their voices belting out the lyrics, completely caught up in the fun. More women joined in, adding to the energy and turning the moment into a full-on girl anthem. The music thudded in their chests as they twirled and laughed, carefree under the bright sun. Carrie glanced over at their table, where their purses and half-drunk cocktails sat untouched. She saw Benny, Trip, and Conner making their way over, their eyes trained on the group of dancing women.

As the song ended, they sashayed back toward the table, their cheeks flushed and hair sticking to their foreheads from the heat. They grabbed their drinks, laughing and trying to catch their breath, their skin still glistening with sweat. The guys greeted them with smirks and a few low whistles, but the girls were too high on adrenaline to care.

"What have we got here?" Trip asked. "You're all too old to be dancing to this song."

The group exchanged looks, shrugging off his comment. They were all in their early to mid-thirties, except for Stacy, who was only twenty-nine. Age didn't matter at that moment.

"This is our jam! We're nineties gals!" Carrie shot back, giving Trip a playful punch in the arm. "Lighten up, old man." She flashed him a grin, her laughter still lingering in the air as the beat from the song continued to pulse around them.

The afternoon's energy shifted as the group scattered. Jen, Stacy, and Tori headed back to the bar to grab fresh drinks, laughing as they pushed through the crowd. Benny and Trip went off to mingle with some other people at the edge of the dance floor. The music played on, the rhythm infectious, but Carrie glanced around, suddenly realizing she was alone.

Conner, who had been chatting with the others earlier, now stood beside her. He gave her a small, knowing smile, his eyes catching hers in that subtle way that felt like an invitation to an unspoken conversation. The air between them thickened as they both found themselves standing in the open space, the sound of the music surrounding them like a bubble that separated them from the world.

Carrie didn't speak immediately. She took a breath, her eyes drifting back to the dance floor where everyone else seemed caught up in the moment, and then back to Conner. They were alone now.

"You look like you're having fun. Have you outgrown Van Halen?" he asked.

"Never," she replied with a wink, acknowledging their mutual love for the band.

"Can I talk to you in private?" Conner asked, his voice lower than usual. He gestured toward the back of The Edge, to an empty area, away from the noise of the bar and the throngs of people dancing. Her friends were distracted, and the thick crowd gave them some privacy.

"Yeah," Carrie replied, her heart skipping as she followed him, a flutter of excitement and anticipation building inside her. She had a feeling this would be a continuation of their flirtation from two nights ago, and she wasn't sure if she was ready for it, but she couldn't resist.

As they reached the far end of The Edge, Conner stopped, turning to face her. He backed her against the cool wall, his presence closing the space between them. His hand landed on her shoulders, a firm but gentle touch that made her breath hitch. He gazed into her eyes intensely.

"Are you with Dylan now?" he asked, his voice steady but hinting at something more.

Carrie's stomach dropped, confusion flooding her mind. She hadn't expected this. What was he talking about?

"What? No!" she answered quickly, trying to mask her surprise. "Why would you think that?"

Conner's gaze softened, but his voice remained steady, almost too calm. "I overheard Bobby at the bar today. He was talking to some people about how he saw you and Dylan in a compromising position in Brett's storeroom. I am just asking to make sure."

"You were trying to make sure what, Conner?" she interrupted, her voice trembling with emotion. "That I'm still available? That I'm not somehow tied up with Dylan? You overheard some gossip and thought you'd confront me in a corner of this place?"

Suddenly, the words hit Carrie like a punch. Her stomach twisted, her mind racing. She pushed his hands off her shoulders, taking a step back. The anger bubbled up before she could control it, her thoughts flashing to Dylan and the pain he'd endured, clouding any romantic feelings she had.

"Bobby?" She couldn't keep the disbelief from her voice. "He's the one who beat up Dylan?"

Her blood began to boil, but the shock felt stronger. She didn't even wait for an explanation. Without hesitation, she turned and started to walk away, her mind consumed by the mess Bobby had created, by the mess everyone had made.

"Carrie, wait—" Conner's voice trailed off as she walked back toward the bar area, but she didn't stop. Her legs carried her forward until she found the others. Confusion still clouded her thoughts.

CHAPTER 22

When Carrie walked up to the outdoor bar, she found her friends clustered together, drinking and mingling. Bobby, Marcy, Brandon, and Marcy's parents were sitting at a table nearby. Her eyes narrowed as she saw Bobby's back to her, and without hesitation, she marched over and tapped her finger sharply on his shoulder.

He turned around, surprised, and she wasted no time.

"It was you who jumped Dylan that night! You and your lowlife friends. And you left him there, bleeding! He could've been seriously hurt! How could you do that?" Her voice shook with a mix of fury and disbelief as she took a step closer, rearing her fist to punch him. Bobby quickly pulled up his shoulder, stepping back defensively.

"Whoa, Carrie, you need to back off," he defended, his voice more irritated than apologetic. "Yeah, I saw you. You were making out with him, and who knows what would've happened if I hadn't walked in."

"Who cares? That's none of your business!" Carrie spat, as her anger flared. "I was in a bad marriage, so what? What right do you have to interfere in my life? And why the hell were you in the storeroom anyway?"

Bobby stiffened, his eyes darting around briefly. "Brian asked me to get something from there. Needed some olives. We're tight. I do stuff for him."

Before Carrie could respond, Marcy's voice cut through the tension. "Carrie, just because you're a slut doesn't mean you can accuse MY husband of anything!"

The group fell silent as everyone —Jen, Tori, Stacy, Trip, and Benny —watched the escalating confrontation. Carrie stood frozen momentarily, absorbing the sting of Marcy's words. She turned away, her blood boiling.

"Oh, for real? None of us here are innocent," she muttered, pushing past the group and storming off toward the trailer, her mind racing.

~ ~ ~

Carrie sat slouched on the couch in the trailer, mindlessly flipping through channels on the television. The noise of the party outside seemed muffled, and the distant rumble of fireworks started to fill the air.

The door swung open, and Jen, Tori, and Stacy stepped inside, a rush of excitement following them. Jen walked straight to Carrie, sitting beside her, and wrapped an arm around her shoulders.

"Carrie, come on, watch the fireworks with us," Jen urged, her voice warm and inviting. Tori and Stacy stood by, watching, waiting for her response. "They're about to start."

Carrie looked up at them, still reeling from the tension of the evening. Her sharp gaze cut like a knife. "Aren't you mad that Bobby beat up Dylan?" Her voice held a mix of disbelief and frustration.

Tori shrugged, trying to deflect. "We don't know that for sure," she replied. "And anyway, we don't want to ruin our last night here?"

Stacy grinned, clearly eager to change the subject. "I hear Jen has tequila for shots!" she exclaimed, suddenly perking up. Before Carrie could respond, Stacy grabbed Jen's arm and tugged her toward the kitchen.

Jen opened the freezer and pulled out an unfamiliar bottle of tequila. She poured shots into mismatched glasses, the amber liquid catching the light. "To friends," she declared, raising her glass with a teasing smile.

Carrie hesitated for a moment, then, despite everything, gave in. She picked up her shot glass and joined in.

"To friends," Jen said with a playful grin, raising her glass high.

The sharp burn of the tequila followed the clink of glasses as they all downed the shots in unison. Each of them winced, some more dramatically than others, but the sting quickly faded as they wiped their mouths, laughing.

As the laughter died, Jen leaned closer to Carrie, her voice dropping to a conspiratorial whisper, "Conner will probably be there for the fireworks. Come on."

Carrie turned to face her, her eyes flashing with curiosity and hesitation. The heat from the tequila still lingered in her chest, making her feel a bit more reckless than usual. She glanced toward the door, the sounds of the fireworks growing louder in the distance.

"Conner?" Carrie asked, her tone skeptical but intrigued.

Jen nodded, her expression playful yet somehow knowing. "Yeah, I think he's looking for you."

Carrie paused, then sighed, feeling the tug of the night and the unspoken possibilities that lay ahead. "Alright, let's go."

With that, she stood up, the evening's energy shifting with the promise of whatever might come next.

The group walked toward the river, the vibrant energy of the tiki bar and The Edge spilling into the evening air. The sound of laughter and camaraderie mixed with the gentle hum of music. They found a table just outside The Edge, where the lights dazzled on the river, and they felt the cool breeze brushing against their skin. Benny headed inside to grab the drinks, leaving the others to settle in.

The stars above contrasted sharply against the dark sky, and the moon hung low, casting a soft glow over the water. It was a serene moment, but the buzz of excitement from the impending fireworks was undeniable.

Fritz stood casually against the wall of The Edge, his arms crossed as he scanned the crowd. When Jen walked toward him, her eyes locked on his, and they quickly fell into a quiet conversation, their voices barely rising above the loud conversations at the bar.

Carrie noticed them and then scanned the crowd. Before she could focus on her thoughts, Brandon suddenly appeared. His sharp, youthful energy almost felt disruptive against the group's more relaxed atmosphere. His presence made the conversation feel more frantic, like a jolt of electricity.

"Wassup, guys?" he inquired casually, pulling out a chair and sitting down. His eyes flicked to Stacy, an easy smile forming on his lips.

Trip shot Brandon a glare. "Buzz off, dude. This bar is for adults," he snapped. Without waiting for a response, Trip grabbed Stacy by the arm and tugged her toward the river, away from the table—an apparent attempt to distance himself from Brandon's intrusion.

Carrie watched them leave, a faint smirk tugging at her lips. It wasn't like she had any real stake in the drama, but Trip's overprotectiveness was always a bit much. She turned her attention back to the table, where Tori and Benny were playfully poking fun at each other, their easy laughter filling the air. For a brief moment, Carrie felt like an outsider looking in on a scene she didn't quite belong to.

Suddenly, Conner appeared next to her, his expression unreadable. He mouthed a single word and tilted his head: "Over there."

Carrie's eyes flicked over to where he indicated—towards the back of the bar, behind the crowds of people, where shadows seemed to linger in the dim lighting. A knot tightened in her stomach as her pulse quickened, a mix of anticipation and wariness filling her. She glanced at Tori and Benny, then in the direction Conner had pointed, trying to weigh her options.

Carrie followed Conner around the back of The Edge. The thumping bass from the bar was now muffled, leaving only the quiet night air between them. She crossed her arms, waiting for him to speak. The tension between them was as thick as mud.

Conner shifted, his hands in his pockets, his gaze flicking nervously toward the ground before meeting her eyes. "I didn't mean to upset you before, I just thought…"

She raised an eyebrow, her voice steady, though her heart raced. "You thought what? That I'm with Dylan?"

Before she could react, Conner stepped forward, closing the space between them, his lips crashing into hers. The sudden pressure left her breathless, her pulse thudding in her ears. His hands found their way to her waist, pulling her closer as she instinctively pressed into him, melting into the kiss. Her thoughts scattered, and time stood still as their mouths moved together, their bodies instinctively responding, as if there were no consequences, no boundaries.

But then she pulled back, her chest rising and falling with the rapid beat of her heart. Her hand instinctively went to her lips, still tingling from his touch. "But you're married," she whispered, her voice soft, yet firm.

Conner's eyes flashed with regret and desire, his breath shallow. "I know, but…" he trailed off, his lips meeting hers again, more urgently this time.

In the distance, the first burst of fireworks lit up the sky, casting a kaleidoscope of color across the dark river. Red, white, and blue blazed above them, illuminating their silhouettes, the crackling echoes of the fireworks filling the air. The contrast between the vibrant lights and the heat between them felt surreal, as if everything else had faded into the background.

After a long, heated kiss that left them both breathless and conflicted, Conner reluctantly pulled away, his forehead resting against hers. The fireworks were still bursting in the sky, but the vibrant colors seemed to dim compared to the weight of the moment between them.

Carrie's heart pounded with her emotions tangled in the aftermath. She stepped back, keeping her eyes on Conner, but her gaze flickered to the fireworks lighting up the river, offering a temporary escape. "I can't do this," she whispered, the words tasting like guilt on her tongue.

Conner gazed at her, his breath shaky. "You're right. This shouldn't have happened."

Carrie nodded. "I need to go back. My friends will be looking for me," she replied from her tightened throat.

He hesitated for a moment, then nodded, stepping back. "Yeah. I get it." He gave her a small, almost apologetic smile, as if trying to convey something unspoken, before turning and walking toward the crowd.

Carrie stood there for a beat longer, watching his retreating figure. She felt the night's chaotic energy shift into something quieter, something that felt more like regret than passion. The fireworks began to fizzle out, and the cool air felt heavier.

Carrie's heart sank as she stepped out from behind The Edge, scanning the area where her friends had been. The table was empty, and the crowd had thinned slightly, though bursts of laughter and conversation floated in the air. She glanced at her watch, her mind racing. How long was I gone?

CHAPTER 23

The fireworks finale erupted above her, the sky ablaze with glittering explosions, but it only amplified the strange unease in her chest. She started toward the parking lot, hoping to catch up with her group. As she rounded the corner, her eyes caught an unmistakable sight—Stacy, giggling and leaning into Brandon, their silhouettes illuminated by the flickering colors in the sky.

Carrie's stomach tightened, the scene hitting her like a gut punch. She quickened her pace, her steps deliberate, and reached them just as Brandon rested a hand on Stacy's waist, drawing her closer.

Carrie grabbed Stacy's arm without thinking and pulled her back sharply, her voice cutting through the night like a whip. "What the hell are you doing, Stacy?"

Stacy stumbled slightly, caught off guard. "Carrie, what—?"

Carrie's eyes darted to Brandon, who looked more amused than alarmed. "Go find someone your own age," she snapped, her tone cold as steel. Brandon shrugged, his cocky grin unwavering as he stepped back, hands raised in mock surrender.

"It's not a big deal," Stacy muttered, trying to free her arm, but Carrie held firm.

"Not a big deal? He's a kid, Stacy," Carrie hissed, lowering her voice but keeping the intensity. "What are you thinking?"

Stacy flushed, her earlier giddiness fading as her gaze dropped to the ground. "I wasn't—"

"Exactly," Carrie interrupted, releasing her arm. "You weren't thinking. Let's go."

"Brandon and I were watching the fireworks since everyone else took off, including YOU. She pointed her finger at Carrie and teetered over a little with a can of beer in her hand. "Where were you anyway?"

"Never mind. Let's go back to the trailer and find everyone else" Carrie grabbed Stacy's arm and pulled her towards the trailer.

Brandon stood there watching them, smiling. "Bye, ladies."

"What's going on?" Carrie asked, narrowing her eyes as she glanced from Stacy to the space where Trip should have been. "Where's Trip?"

Stacy crossed her arms, a flush creeping up her neck. "We got into a fight. He stormed off. I don't know where he went—probably Brett's."

Carrie tilted her head, her curiosity piqued. "What was the fight about?" A flicker of suspicion crossed her mind, wondering if it had anything to do with

Stacy's earlier antics with Brandon.

Stacy exhaled sharply, her tone rising with indignation. "He was drunk—like, really drunk. He stood up, wobbling like an idiot, and it looked like he was going to fall into the river. I yelled at him to sit down, and do you know what he did? He called me a bitch. A bitch, Carrie! Can you believe that? I will not stand for that!"

Carrie's expression softened, her stomach twisting. The word stung, even though this time it wasn't directed at her. She nodded slowly, understanding Stacy's outrage in a way deeper than she cared to admit. Tom had called her that—more than once. The word lingered like an ugly bruise, never quite fading.

"Yeah," Carrie replied quietly, meeting Stacy's eyes. "I get it. You don't deserve that."

Walking through the dimly lit parking lot, their path took them past the campsites behind Brett's, near the fish-cleaning shelter. The faint smell of smoke and something savory drifted through the air. In the glow of a campfire, two men stood talking in low voices, their pipes casting thin trails of smoke into the night sky. A large pot hung over the flames, suspended from a tripod, and the men's clothing had an old-world feel, as though they'd stepped out of another time—or another place entirely.

Carrie instinctively grabbed Stacy's arm, steering her to veer away, but one of the men called out in a booming, cheerful voice. "Ladies, come on over and try our Solyanka! It's delicious!"

"Just keep walking," Carrie whispered, quickening her pace, but the second man stepped forward, blocking their path with a wide grin. "Oh, don't be shy! We're from Russia—come, try our soup! A taste of home!"

Stacy paused, her curiosity piqued. She tugged on Carrie's arm, her voice laced with excitement. "Come on, Carrie. Let's try it—it's probably harmless."

Carrie's stomach knotted as she hesitated, her instincts screaming otherwise. But Stacy, ever the adventurer, accepted the invitation. The first man handed her a tin cup filled with steaming broth. Stacy took a tentative sip, then grimaced.

"You don't like?" the man asked, his tone disappointed. He quickly turned to a small folding table and produced a frosted bottle of vodka. "Then try this—Russian vodka! You'll like this much better."

He extended the bottle toward Stacy, who was reaching for it when suddenly, out of the shadows, Trip stormed forward, his face a mask of fury. Without warning, he hauled back his fist, aiming straight for the man's face.

"Trip, no!" Carrie shouted, but her words came too late.

Before the punch could land, Benny appeared

seemingly out of nowhere, grabbing Trip's arm mid-swing. "Whoa, man! Chill out!" Benny growled, yanking him back as the Russian men stepped away, their hands raised defensively.

"What the hell is wrong with you?" Trip barked, his eyes blazing.

The first man gestured toward the soup pot, his voice indignant. "We are only offering hospitality! Is this how Americans act?"

Carrie tugged on Stacy's arm. "Let's go. Now," her voice quiet yet urgent.

Stacy hesitated, but the tension in the air made her relent. "Okay, okay," she agreed, casting an apologetic glance over her shoulder as Carrie dragged her back toward the path. Trip and Benny lingered for a moment, exchanging heated words before reluctantly following.

"What the hell, Trip? What are you doing?" Tori abruptly asked as she appeared out of nowhere. "What's going on?"

"This asshole is trying to give my girlfriend some vodka, and who knows what? Stacy, do you know these guys?" Trip yelled.

Carrie and Stacy huddled together, freaking out. Tori quickly joined their side. "No, we were just walking past on the way to the trailer, and they stopped us, asking us to try some soup. It was gross, so then he offered me vodka. I wasn't going to drink it! We were about to leave," rebutted Stacy.

"We were trying to be nice. Just came here from Russia to fish—no big deal. We mean no harm," assured the man who offered the vodka in broken English.

"Come on," Benny insisted. "Let's go." He looked them up and down, and as creepy as they appeared, maybe they were trying to be nice, he thought. Not a cool thing to do at 11:00 at night.

They all made their way back to Jen's trailer, the weight of the evening hanging over them like the humid night air. Jen was already on the deck, legs crossed, smoke curling lazily from the cigarette in her hand as she watched them approach. Her eyes flicked over the group, taking in their tense expressions, but she didn't say anything.

Trip marched ahead, leading Stacy inside without a word, and the sound of the bedroom door closing hard signaled they were heading straight into another round of their unresolved fight. Benny trailed behind, muttering something about needing a beer, and disappeared into the trailer.

Carrie dropped heavily into one of the deck chairs, her elbows resting on her knees and her head bowed. Everything from the night was swirling in her mind: the fireworks, Conner's kiss that lingered on her lips, and the pang of guilt that came with it. As exhilarating as it had been, she knew she couldn't let it happen again. She wasn't the kind of person who could destroy a marriage—even if their connection had felt electric.

Then there was the unsettling encounter with the Russian men, their strange, almost otherworldly presence, and the chaos Trip nearly unleashed. It was all too much to process. With a heavy sigh, she leaned back in the chair and ran her hands through her hair, wishing for a moment of clarity.

Tori sank into the seat beside her, kicking her sandals off and propping her feet on the deck railing. "What a night," she exhaled, blowing out an exhausted breath.

Jen flicked her cigarette into the ashtray and lit another one, watching them both with quiet curiosity. "Want to fill me in, or are we just gonna sit here and stew in our drama?"

Before either of them could answer, Benny came out holding three beers. He handed one to Jen and offered the others to Carrie and Tori. "You ladies look like you could use this," he said, his tone unusually light for the tension in the air.

Carrie took the bottle gratefully, twisting off the cap and taking a long sip. "Thanks," she murmured.

Jen leaned back in her chair, blowing smoke into the night. "Well, sounds like I missed a hell of a night. So, who's going to start?"

Carrie exchanged a glance with Tori, unsure of where to even begin.

"Just some russian roulette," Carrie replied, rolling her eyes, irritated by the whole scene.

"What do you mean?" Jen asked, eyes wide, curiously.

"That will teach you to wander off, Carrie. You know there's always drama here." Tori chimed in.

"Whatever," Jen scowled. "I'm sure there will be more."

Carrie woke a few hours later, her throat parched and her head still foggy from the night's incidents. She reached for the glass of water she'd left on the nightstand, but it was empty. Sighing, she slipped out of bed, careful not to disturb the stillness, and headed toward the kitchen.

The darkness was nearly complete, except for the faint, flickering glow of the television casting long shadows across the room. The volume was muted, but the rhythmic shift of light and shadow caught Carrie's attention. As she rounded the corner, she froze.

Two figures sat entwined on the couch. Carrie's heart skipped a beat as she rubbed her eyes to make sure she wasn't imagining things. But there it was, plain as day: Benny, with Tori perched on his lap, locked in a heated, passionate kiss. Their silhouettes shifted against the dim light of the screen, their movements unhurried and oblivious to anything else.

Carrie stepped back, the floor creaking slightly under her weight. They didn't notice. She turned quickly, retracing her steps back to the bedroom. Once under the covers, she stared at the ceiling, her thoughts racing.

The image of Benny and Tori together clashed with everything she thought she understood about her friends. And it wasn't just them. Stacy and Brandon's flirtations, her own impulsive, charged kiss with Conner—it all swirled in her mind, forming a mosaic of tangled emotions and secrets.

She squeezed her eyes shut and rolled onto her side. Some secrets, she decided, were better left unspoken.

PART FOUR

2005

CHAPTER 24

"Do you think she suspects anything?" Carrie asked as she navigated a curve in the road, glancing at the phone nestled in her cup holder. She had her phone on speaker so that she could talk safely while driving.

"I doubt it. Stacy's so wrapped up in her job and Trip these days, I don't think she's even thought about her birthday plans beyond him showing up late," Jen replied. "And besides, I told her I'd bring margaritas, so she's counting on that distraction."

Carrie laughed. "You're good at playing it cool. I hope Brett remembers the decorations and the cake."

"Don't worry about Brett. He's been bragging about the 'big birthday bash' to half the regulars," Jen added with a chuckle. "If anything, he'll overdo it. Wait until you see the balloons I ordered—they're so obnoxious! Stacy's going to hate them."

"I can't wait," Carrie answered in a light tone. "It's nice to have something fun to look forward to. Things have been, well, a lot lately."

Jen hesitated. "You're still thinking about last summer?"

"Not just that," Carrie admitted. "Work's been relentless. It feels like I'm just going through the motions. I miss the days when we could come up here and just be."

"Well, this weekend, we will do just that; no work stress, no drama. At least until the guys get here," Jen teased.

Carrie rolled her eyes but smiled. "Famous last words."

When Carrie pulled up to the trailer around 6:00 p.m., she noticed Jen's car parked out front. She must have gotten out of the store early, Carrie thought, stepping out of her vehicle and stretching after the long drive. Riverbanks was about an hour and a half from the city, but the promise of a relaxing weekend made the trip worthwhile.

She grabbed a few bags from the trunk and headed toward the door. As soon as she stepped inside, her eyes widened. The trailer appeared brighter and more modern, with new lighting that gave the space a fresh, updated feel. The breakfast bar looked great with new sleek mosaic tiles, and there were new barstools tucked neatly under it.

"Wow, Jen! You've been busy," Carrie said, taking it all in.

Standing at the counter blending margaritas, Jen looked up with a bright smile. "Hey, Carrie! Just in time. I've got the first batch of margaritas ready to go. Since it's just us tonight, I figured we'd kick things off with a little party here." She wiped her sticky hands on a kitchen towel and gestured toward the cutting board, where she had prepared freshly chopped ingredients for salsa.

Carrie couldn't help but notice the new sign hanging in the kitchen that read, "I'm a better person when I'm tan and holding a margarita." She smirked. "I love the new sign! So true, Jen. And seriously, the trailer and the updates look great!

"Thanks! I figured it was time for a refresh," Jen exclaimed, walking over to hug Carrie.

Carrie set her bags down and began unpacking. "I grabbed some guacamole on the way here," she said, pulling out a container along with a few bottles of alcohol.

"You're the best," Jen smiled, reaching for the guacamole to add to the snack spread. "Oh, and chips are in the cupboard—grab those for me, will you?"

Carrie obliged and then went down the hallway to the bedroom to put her things away. She and Tori had agreed to share the room again this year, especially since it was clear that Drew wouldn't be coming. Not this year or any year after. Declaring the holiday weekend as Tori's escape had become an unspoken rule among them.

Carrie unpacked her duffel bag, laying out pajamas and the clothes she didn't want to wrinkle. She placed her toiletry bag in the shared bathroom, setting out her contact solution and aspirin for easy access, she thought with a grin. A girl's night guaranteed a headache, but was worth it.

"Yoo-hoo!" Tori's cheerful voice rang out from the front door. She walked in with her duffel bag in hand, her energy as vibrant as ever. "Am I late, or just fashionably on time?"

"Well, well, the gang's almost all here," Jen called from the kitchen, tossing a few ingredients into a mixing bowl.

Carrie poked her head out of the bedroom and pointed toward their shared room. "Put your stuff in here," she instructed with a smile, and walked to the kitchen to help Jen.

Tori dropped her bag in the bedroom and returned to join Jen and Carrie in the kitchen. Jen handed out margaritas in colorful glasses rimmed with salt, the tangy scent of lime filling the air.

"To girl time," Jen declared, raising her glass.

"To no work emails," Tori added with a laugh.

"And to aspirin in the morning," Carrie joked, clinking her glass with theirs.

"Knock-knock," a familiar voice called out just before the door swung open.

They all screamed in delight as Stacy stepped inside, a wide-spread grin across her face.

"Cool! We thought you wouldn't get here until later. This is great!" Jen yelled from the kitchen, her excitement bubbling over as she wiped her hands and waved.

Stacy dropped her bags by the door, striking an effortlessly glamorous figure in a silky camisole top paired with flared, well-worn jeans that hugged her perfectly. Her dark hair, now grown out to a longer length, cascaded in soft beachy waves, enhanced by sun-kissed highlights. She looked like she'd walked off the set of The O.C., her radiant energy commanding the room.

"The office closed early for the holiday, so here I am!" Stacy declared, spreading her arms theatrically. She came ready to kick off her 30th birthday celebrations ahead of schedule.

"Well, someone's ready to party," Carrie teased, her smile widening as she poured Stacy a margarita and handed it over. "You look fabulous, by the way."

"Thanks! I figured this was the weekend to turn it up a notch," Stacy said, taking a sip and making a face as the tequila hit. "Oh wow, that's got a kick. Perfect."

"Come on, join the fun," Tori motioned Stacy toward the kitchen. "Jen's got us fully stocked with snacks and margaritas."

Stacy sauntered over, peeking at the fresh salsa and guacamole on the counter. "You ladies don't mess around, huh? This weekend is shaping up to be epic already."

"To Stacy and her pre-birthday kickoff," Jen declared, raising her glass high.

"To Stacy and the fact that she somehow looks like a Malibu ad while the rest of us are still in traffic mode," Carrie added with a laugh, clinking her glass to Stacy's.

The room filled with laughter as the girls released the tension from the workweek, their shared energy setting the tone for a memorable weekend of friendship and celebration.

After everyone had settled into their rooms and put the food and beverages away, the friends gathered at the newly tiled breakfast bar. Jen stood behind the sink on the opposite side, a self-proclaimed bartender for the evening, expertly pouring margaritas into mismatched glasses. The air felt light and festive as they nibbled on chips, fresh salsa, and guacamole, the sharp tang of lime and cilantro mingling with the smooth saltiness of their drinks.

"So, Tori," Jen said, leaning her elbows on the counter, "how was California? Did you at least enjoy some sunshine while learning how to—what was it again?"

"Body wraps," Tori replied with a laugh, swirling her drink. "It sounds more glamorous than it is, believe me. They flew us out for training on a new technique, and I spent most of the time in a cold hotel conference room. But, on the last night, I snuck out to Santa Monica and got margaritas by the pier." She sipped and added, "Not as good as these, though."

"Well, I'd say that's a win—training and tequila," Stacy added, crunching on a chip. "I could use a work trip somewhere warm.

"As the newly named human resources manager,

I have to do orientation for new employees and buy them lunch," Carrie stated. "Well, I was out sick the day this new guy, James, started. When I offered to buy him lunch the next day, he declined and wanted me to take him out for a drink instead. Can you believe that?" Carrie took a sip of her drink and laughed.

"Is he good-looking?" Tori asked.

"He's nice enough looking. But I have enough on my mind. I don't need any more complications."

"What's that supposed to mean?" Tori inquired in a confused tone.

Jen refreshed their glasses with more Margaritas and said, "Why don't you tell them your secret, Carrie? I mean, we're all friends."

Carrie looked up at Jen and then turned to Tori and Stacy. "I was sort of seeing Dylan for a while until recently," she shared.

Tori and Stacy looked at each other in amazement. "What? Why didn't you tell us?"

Carrie didn't want to lie to her friends. She just kept secrets. It all started a month after the last Fourth of July when she went to the Pub to meet a co-worker. She didn't know why she had chosen that bar, since it wasn't near her condo. Dylan was there. Alone. She and her friend, Tracy, had wings and beers and discussed Tracy's break-up. When her friend left, she stayed for another drink. Dylan walked up to her and asked to talk. They hadn't spoken since that first summer when he came to Riverbanks. He had dropped out of their dart league, started seeing Erica, and had not been seen much since then. They talked for quite a long time and exchanged numbers; Carrie had recently gotten a cell phone, so Dylan didn't have that number.

He called her on a random weeknight, singing the blues about Erica. She listened intently as he talked about her disrespect towards him, expressing his belief that she wasn't genuinely interested in him. All Carrie could think of was how much she wanted him. She went to her office Christmas party without a date, got drunk, and called him on a whim. She went to Dylan's apartment, and the steamy attraction they had suppressed for the last few years bubbled to the surface as they embraced and passionately tore off each other's clothes in the hallway. In a sultry entangle, they had sex against the wall, like she always wanted, like she had seen in the movies. They continued their seductive romance throughout the spring and early summer, but then it abruptly came to an end. Dylan didn't take or return her calls, and things returned to how they had been. She ran into him at the Pub, and he ignored her.

Carrie's voice wavered as she finished, "And that's it. He ghosted me. Like it never even happened." She looked down at her margarita, swirling the drink aimlessly. "I wasn't going to say anything because, well...it's over. And it wasn't exactly something I'm proud of."

Tori leaned back in her chair, her arms crossed, eyebrows raised in disbelief. "You and Dylan?

Seriously? I thought he was off the radar after Sue."

Stacy, wide-eyed, leaned closer. "Wait, hold on. You mean to tell us that you two were together? Like a real thing?"

Carrie shook her head quickly. "No, not a thing. It was, well, I don't know what it was. Comfort? Lust? Maybe both? I wasn't thinking straight. I just knew I wanted him, and for a little while, he wanted me too."

"And then he just ghosted you?" Jen asked, her tone sharp, like a protective older sister.

"Yeah," Carrie admitted, her voice barely above a whisper. "After all that, he just stopped answering my calls. Ignored me at the Pub like I was invisible. It's like it never even happened."

Stacy let out a low whistle. "Damn. That's cold, even for Dylan."

Tori shook her head, a mix of empathy and frustration flashing across her face. "Why didn't you tell us sooner? We could've warned you. He's always been complicated."

Carrie shrugged, her shoulders slumping. "I didn't think it mattered. And it wasn't exactly my proudest moment, hooking up with someone like Dylan, knowing how it would probably end. I guess I just thought..."

"That it could be different?" Jen finished for her.

Carrie nodded silently, her throat tightening.

"Well, forget him," Tori insisted, reaching across the breakfast bar and grabbing Carrie's hand. "He's not worth the energy. You're better off without that kind of baggage."

"Agreed," Jen added, raising her glass. "To leaving the past where it belongs—and to a better weekend ahead!"

Carrie managed a small smile and raised her glass with theirs. But as they sipped their margaritas, she couldn't help but feel the familiar ache of what might have been and the sting of Dylan's rejection. Some secrets, she thought, really do lose their weight once they're shared.

"Well, we are going to have a great weekend. I heard there is a pirate party and brat fry on Saturday down the river at Landing Strip."

"What's that?" they all asked in unison, curiously.

Jen shrugged. "Dunno, something like a bunch of people dress up like pirates and ride around in their boats decked up like pirate ships. Hey, there will be a bunch of hot men walking around."

Just then, Brandon appeared at the door. At nineteen, he was tall and muscular, sporting a five o'clock shadow that made him appear older. Behind him stood Conner.

Carrie froze for a split second when she saw Conner behind Brandon, her grip tightening slightly on her margarita glass. She forced a smile, hoping none of her friends noticed her immediate tension.

"Ladies! Care for some company?" Brandon yelled through the screen door.

The girls all looked at each other and shrugged.

"Sure," Jen said, walking to the door. She opened it and motioned with her arm to enter. "We don't need our girls' night after all." She shook her head and returned to the kitchen while Brandon and Conner came in.

"Oh, come on, this isn't Sex and The City," Brandon said casually. He walked up to the bar, took a chip, dipped it in salsa, and took a bite out of it. "Mmmm, spicy!" He looked around the trailer, which was empty except for the girls at the counter. "Where are the guys?" He put his hand on Carrie's shoulder. "No boyfriend yet, Carrie?"

Carrie looked at Brandon and turned to Conner, pacing around the living room area. "I have many, so I couldn't choose who to bring." All the girls laughed, and Conner came over to the kitchen and accepted Jen's offering of a margarita. "What brings you here, Conner?" she asked.

"Sorry to barge in," he replied, his voice smooth and casual as he leaned against the counter. His eyes lingered on Carrie a fraction too long before moving to Jen. "Brandon said you guys were here. Thought I'd stop by and say hi."

"Hi," Carrie muttered, taking a quick sip of her drink and avoiding his gaze.

"I thought the gang was here, but didn't see any of the guys. Anyway, it was getting boring with just Marcy. Bobby is out somewhere."

Carrie froze as it dawned on her—Conner must know Michelle from high school. "Is Michelle staying with her?" she asked, unable to hide the jealousy in her voice.

"Yeah, she is," Conner replied, "but I got a room at The Edge. Too crowded with two women, and Michelle needs a lot of space, if you know what I mean." He smirked. "You know I'm not into those cheerleader types."

Carrie thought back to how things had been in middle school. She and Michelle had been friendly enough, going to the same birthday parties and sleepovers. But once high school started, Michelle drifted into a different crowd, trading their casual friendship for the world of cheerleaders and jocks.

On the other hand, Carrie found Becky, a kindred spirit who shared her love for rock music. Through Becky, she fell in with a different scene, one filled with BMX riders, heavy guitar riffs, and anthems from the Beastie Boys. Their paths still crossed at parties, the kind with keg stands and the haze of pot smoke, but by then, they were just familiar faces in separate worlds.

Carrie could still picture the night everything changed. Becky had scored an invite to a party celebrating the basketball team making it to state— not that their crowd cared much about sports, but a party was a party. Carrie had been saving up from her job at the local fast-food joint and finally splurged on a pair of Levi's she'd been eyeing for months, along with white fringe boots that made her feel unstoppable. Becky teased her hair just right, making sure she looked perfect. They both knew Conner would be there. Carrie and Conner had spent the semester exchanging glances and inside jokes in literature class, bonding over their shared love of Van Halen. She was going to tell him how she felt at the party.

Tons of people were at the party, the air thick with cigarette smoke, and the bass from the stereo rattling the walls. After a few beers, Carrie slipped away to the bathroom. When she came out, she paused by the window, spotting Conner outside on the patio, laughing with his friends. Their eyes met, a spark of recognition cutting through the crowd. Her pulse kicked up. But Becky materialized at his side before she could move, flipping her hair and leaning in close.

Before Carrie had time to process it, a hand grabbed her wrist. She spun around to find Scott, drunk, grinning, pulling her toward a dark corner. He pressed in too close, the smell of beer heavy on his breath, and went in for a kiss. Carrie jerked away, her heart hammering. He just laughed, shrugged, and sauntered off like it was nothing.

Shaken, she turned back to the patio. Conner and Becky were gone, and by the end of the night, they were a couple. Just like that, her friendship with Becky was over.

Even though Michelle was not at that party, another high school rival was too much to take.

"That and we would rather be around you lovely ladies." Brandon interrupted her thoughts and squeezed between Stacy and Tori, taking Stacy's glass and taking a sip. Stacy slapped his hand. "Brandon!"

"Oh, come on! I'm nineteen." Brandon replied with a boyish grin, but a man's gleam in his eye for Stacy.

"Last I heard, the drinking age is twenty-one, bro," Jen responded as she popped open a can of beer and handed it to him. "You can have a beer. That's it."

The group settled into an easy rhythm. The atmosphere felt light and carefree as they laughed and tossed dice, the clink of glasses and upbeat music filling the air. The margaritas flowed, loosening everyone up as they let their guards down—a rare dynamic, free from the usual tensions.

Stacy, for once, seemed entirely at ease. She laughed louder, leaned into jokes more freely, and didn't care when Brandon's eager attention turned her way. His youthful enthusiasm was borderline comical, as he tried to impress her with exaggerated stories about his summer job and his bench press record.

Tori rolled her eyes but humored him, while Stacy giggled at his antics, occasionally tossing out teasing remarks. "Brandon, does your mom know you're out this late?"

Brandon grinned, unbothered. "I'm nineteen, Stacy. Pretty sure I don't have a curfew anymore." He winked, and Tori stifled a laugh.

Carrie, meanwhile, focused on keeping herself busy. She took her turn at rolling the dice and made a point to refill drinks or grab more chips to avoid sitting idle too long. Now and then, her eyes would drift to Conner, who kept his distance but seemed to feel her presence just as keenly. He was the picture of restraint. He joked with the group and played along, careful not to linger too long near Carrie. Still, there were fleeting moments when their eyes met—quick, charged glances neither dared to hold for fear of giving themselves away.

Brandon's open and relentless attempts to charm Stacy and Tori starkly contrasted with the unspoken tension between Carrie and Conner. He flitted between the two women like an overeager puppy, oblivious to any subtle hints they tried to give him.

Stacy leaned back in her chair, swirling her margarita and giving Brandon a playful smirk. "You know, you'd probably have better luck if you focused on just one of us at a time."

Brandon grinned, unfazed. "Why choose when I can aim for both?"

The room erupted in laughter, Tori throwing a chip at him. "Kid, you've got guts, I'll give you that."

As the hour passed, the conversation grew livelier, and the walls between them seemed to fall away. But beneath the laughter and teasing, there was a sense of freedom, an unspoken acknowledgment that, for this brief time, no one was watching.

Carrie couldn't help but notice the ease in everyone's demeanor—the way Stacy relished the attention, the way Tori let herself relax, and even Conner seemed lighter without a wife hovering nearby. It was liberating, this sense of unaccountability. Still, there was an edge, a sense that this freedom could easily tip into recklessness. Secrets had a way of brewing in moments like these, and Carrie wondered what the rest of the weekend might hold. For now, though, she pushed those thoughts aside and tried to enjoy the night—because if there was one thing she'd learned over the past year, it was that moments like this didn't last.

Jen wiped down the bar, her hands moving quickly as she stacked the empty glasses and pushed leftover chips into a bowl. "Alright, y'all, who's up for Brett's? I'm meeting Fritz."

The response came in a chorus, "Yeah!" The energy in the room built as they prepared to head out.

CHAPTER 25

The warm summer air greeted the friends as they stepped outside, still holding onto the daylight. The trailer park buzzed with activity—people were already gathered for the weekend, grills sizzling with burgers and brats, and music pumping from every corner. A relaxed chaos could be felt, along with laughter, voices, and the occasional pop of a cooler opening.

Carrie couldn't help but take in the scene as they walked towards Brett's. The river sprawled before them, the sun beginning its descent, casting a soft glow over everything. People had their boats tied to the docks, their hulls bobbing gently in the water, while the sky shifted from gold to soft pinks. The river gleamed beneath it all, a slow-moving ribbon of light.

Conner and Brandon kicked a hacky sack back and forth a few paces ahead, their conversation lost in the light-hearted banter. Full of energy, Brandon leapt to catch the sack mid-air, but his enthusiasm waned after a few minutes. He threw the ball aside and sprinted to catch up with the group.

Carrie lingered, her steps slowing, a quiet moment pulling her back. She watched Conner make a few more kicks, casually waiting for Brandon to catch up. There was an unspoken space between them, the tension from earlier still hanging beneath the surface. She let herself breathe in the beauty of the backdrop; the river's glimmering surface reflecting the final moments of daylight.

Connor slowed down and let Brandon catch up with the rest of the group, momentarily leaving him and Carrie alone.

"All your boyfriends, Carrie, what's that all about?" he teased, his hand slipping toward the hem of her jean skirt.

Carrie froze for a moment, unsure whether to laugh it off or brush him off, but she kept walking, her pace slow and deliberate, trying not to give in to the flutter in her stomach. We decided this was not right, she told herself as she moved. His fingers traced the bare skin of her legs in a casual touch that felt anything but casual. His hand lingered just above her knee, as if their unmistakable tension had stopped him. She didn't respond and just kept walking with a mixture of guilt, shame, and something else she couldn't quite put a name to. Her eyes scanned ahead, focusing on the open door of Brett's, the music and laughter spilling out into the warm evening air.

The trailers along the pathway to Brett's were lit up with people cooking out, listening to music, and enjoying drinks. "Brett won't let me in the bar, so I'll see you all later." Brandon walked off to one of the trailers, where he high-fived some young men and joined them on the deck.

The group effortlessly blended in once they entered—Brett's place was alive with the usual crowd, the familiar buzz of laughter, and carefree energy. But even with the noise, Carrie couldn't shake the way his fingers had felt against her skin, and the silent weight in their shared space. She pushed the thought away as they merged with the rest of the gang, her thoughts as tangled as the conversation swirling around her.

Conner waved as he walked over to Bobby, surrounded by his usual crew. "I'd better go join them for a bit, though I'd rather be hanging with you ladies," he stated with a grin. Carrie could tell he wasn't thrilled about splitting up, but it was hard not to appreciate his loyalty.

Jen spotted Fritz at the bar, conversing with a few guys, so they all made their way over, and Jen introduced them. "Fritz, you remember my friends— Carrie, Tori, and Stacy?" Fritz paused for a second, squinting like he was trying to recall. Then his face lit up as if a light bulb went off in his head.

"Oh yeah, the city girls!" He slapped his forehead dramatically. "You all keeping my girl company?"

Jen rolled her eyes, clearly trying to brush off the comment. Still, she leaned in to kiss him on the cheek, her arm slipping around his slim waist. Carrie couldn't help but notice how much the moment had an edge of familiarity and a little possessiveness on

Jen's part.

Carrie looked over at Tori and Stacy, raising her eyebrows in surprise. The whole situation felt a little too comfortable, but Jen seemed used to it.

Carrie's gaze shifted back to Fritz. She could now see what Jen saw in him. He had that rugged, effortless charm—like a country version of Brad Pitt in Thelma and Louise. The white t-shirt, the jeans, the tousled hair—like he stepped off a movie set, and Carrie could see why Jen liked him. His easygoing, cowboy look made everything seem a bit edgier.

Fritz's friend, Dodger, leaned against the bar, his eyes scanning the group of girls with a subtle interest. He wasn't Brad Pitt good-looking, but there was something about him. Tall, like Fritz, but broader, with a muscular build that suggested he might have been an ex-football player—strong and solid, not the lean cowboy type. His long, curly hair looked windblown, making him look like someone who'd just rolled out of a frat house and didn't give a damn about it. Carrie could sense a laid-back, confident energy about him, like he knew exactly what he wanted and wasn't in a rush to get it.

"I hear you all are some dart players there in the city. How about we play a game?" Fritz grabbed Jen's arm quickly, claiming her as his partner.

"Come on, let's show these guys how it's done!" Carrie said.

Stacy shook her head. "I don't know. You're the hat-trick queen."

"You can be my partner!" Carrie replied as she approached the bartender to get some bar darts.

"What about me?" Tori whined. Dodger quickly intercepted and said, "You can be my partner, darlin"

"Watch it there, big guy," Tori replied, but she took him up on his offer, and they started shooting 301—the group of six shot darts for the next hour, cheering and high-fiving. After a concerted effort by Carrie and Stacy, and a close score, Fritz and Jen emerged victorious, winning the game. They all went to the bar to have the losers, Dodger and Tori, buy a round of shots.

After the shots, Tori suddenly stood up, rubbing her temples. "I have a headache," she proclaimed, her voice soft and strained. "I'm going to head back to the trailer."

The group murmured their understanding as she left. A few minutes later, Stacy stood up, glancing at the others. "I'm going to check on Tori," she announced, but Carrie noticed the subtle shift in her expression. She knew where Stacy was headed.

Jen, not missing a beat, turned to Fritz. "Let's go play darts," she said. The two walked off toward the dartboard, laughing and talking. After a few more games and drinks, they eventually headed toward Dodger's trailer, leaving the rest behind.

Carrie stayed put for a while, nursing her drink. She glanced around, realizing a lot of people had left. Bobby was gone, and the atmosphere had thinned. She considered following Tori to the trailer but hesitated. Instead, she found herself walking back to where Conner was, leaning against the bar, talking with a few others. Without a word, she sat beside him, the noise fading into the background.

Carrie and Conner silently sat together at the bar, the air between them charged. Every minute that passed only seemed to make the sexual tension more undeniable. Carrie knew better than to let herself think about Conner like this—he was married. But somehow, being back in Riverbanks, with everything that had happened the previous summer, had shifted something between them.

She moved uncomfortably in her seat, trying to ignore the pull she felt toward him, before finally breaking the silence. "Conner, why isn't your wife here?"

He glanced at Carrie, his expression casual. "Jill's working. She does the Friday fish fry."

Carrie raised an eyebrow. "She doesn't mind you being here by yourself?"

He shrugged, not missing a beat. "No, I don't think so. She's got a pretty good crowd at the bar, and I think she enjoys herself."

Carrie's mind briefly wandered to his wife. What was she like? Was she pretty? Was she nice? Why do they seem so distant? Is Conner a bad husband? She didn't know him that well, but he appeared well-to-do. Maybe it was his expensive clothes, perpetual tan, or how he seemed to love golfing. It was hard to reconcile that image with the idea of his wife working at a bar.

"What are you doing these days? Investment banking like Trip?" she asked, trying to steer the conversation to safer waters.

He laughed, shaking his head. "No." He turned slightly to face her, a glint of amusement in his eyes. "This is the first time you've ever asked me what I do."

Carrie smirked but stayed quiet as he continued.

"I've got my own business," he answered, his voice lowering. "Carpentry."

Carrie's eyes widened, genuinely impressed. "Ooh, that's impressive. You like working with your hands, huh?"

Conner's hand slid under the bar without warning, brushing against hers on her knee. He stroked it lightly, his touch slow and deliberate. The simple gesture sent a wave of heat up her spine, making her heart race. Carrie swallowed, trying to maintain control, but the moment felt too heavy to ignore

"Well, well, well," Bobby's voice cut through the air as he appeared behind them.

Carrie and Conner quickly pulled their hands apart, turning to face him. Bobby reached the bar and grabbed his keys, which he had left behind.

"I see the fun continues here," he said with a smirk, clearly enjoying the moment. "Came back for my keys, but I'd better get back to Marcy." His smile lingered, and Carrie and Conner knew precisely what he was implying.

Connor stood, his hand resting on Bobby's shoulder. "Come on, man, we're just talking. No need to say anything to Jill." Conner pleaded with his eyes, implying that a guy should understand.

Bobby eased up and smiled cunningly. He looked around to see if anyone he knew was nearby and calmly said, "I hear you. Your secret's safe with me. We are all entitled to have fun. Carry on."

Bobby walked out the back door, and Conner quickly grabbed Carrie's hand. "Come on, let's get out of here," he insisted. They worked their way through the crowd and headed out the front door.

"Let's go to the pier to talk," Conner suggested. Carrie didn't say a word but followed him. Her steps hurried to keep up with him. The pier near The Edge was empty now; all the boats had already docked. Being nearly midnight, the place felt eerily quiet.

Once they reached the edge of the pier, Carrie finally spoke, her voice tinged with anxiety. "Conner, what was all that about?"

He laughed softly, grabbing her waist and pulling her closer. "Don't worry about him," he said, with his lips just inches from hers. He leaned down as if to kiss her, but Carrie pushed him away slightly, taking a step back.

"What are you doing?" she demanded. "We almost got caught in there. I mean, we did get caught! Aren't you afraid Bobby will tell your wife, Jill, that's her name? Doesn't that concern you?"

Conner sighed and took a step back, giving her space. "He won't tell her. Trust me." His gaze darkened as he spoke again, more seriously. "I know what happened in the basement that night Dylan was jumped."

Carrie turned away, facing the dark water, trying to process his words. "You mean that it was Bobby and his thug friends? Yeah, we called him out last year, remember? And he denied it."

Conner gently turned her around to face him, his eyes fixed on hers. "He was down there with a man. And not for the reasons people might think. Not drugs, not anything like that." He paused, his voice dropping to a whisper. "Something he doesn't want anyone to know."

Carrie's eyes widened as realization hit her. "You mean…"

"Yeah," Conner confirmed, his gaze steady. "He's gay."

They stayed by the pier for a while, laughing at the absurdity of it all—how Bobby, married with a son, still tried to act so macho all the time. The moonlight cast a romantic glow on the river, softening the air between them. The night felt timeless, as if the rest of the world had disappeared, leaving only the two of them. Eventually, they wandered to the pond, finding themselves alone once again.

The silence hung between them comfortably as they stared at the moon's reflection on the still water.

"It's so beautiful out here," Carrie said, her voice soft, almost lost in the night. She turned to Conner. "Do you remember high school?"

Conner looked at her, his gaze thoughtful. "Yeah, I remember. We hung out in the same group, didn't we?"

Carrie nodded, her fingers tracing the hem of her sleeve. "I always liked you. We shared that one class together."

"Chemistry?" Conner asked, a playful grin on his face.

Carrie shook her head with a laugh. "No, Literature. We both liked Lord of the Flies. You sat in front of me. I had such a crush on you." She paused for a moment, her smile fading a little. "Then there was that basketball party… I can't remember whose house it was. I came with my friend, and planned to tell you how I felt, but I was too shy. I never said anything. You ended up with Becky."

Conner's eyes softened, a knowing look crossing his face. "I remember. I liked you too. I saw you come to the party, and I know you saw me looking at you. But then Becky, well, she wasn't exactly shy, was she? She just came at me."

Carrie slapped his hand playfully. "You pig!"

Conner laughed, raising his hands in mock surrender. "Hey, come on. I was just a teenage boy. Hormones were in charge back then." He paused and gently took her hand. "I'm a different person now," he continued in a serious tone.

Carrie felt her pulse quicken, the old chemistry between them undeniable. He reached for her face, cupping her cheeks gently as he leaned in. Their lips met, slow at first, then deepening, soft and urgent. Carrie closed her eyes, letting herself feel it all—the connection, the electricity, the longing. But as much as she wanted this, something within told her she couldn't give in.

Her mind screamed in protest, but her heart ached for him. She pulled back slightly, still holding on to him but with a distance that wasn't there before. "This can't happen. As much as I've always wanted to and still want to, it can't." Her voice cracked, torn between the years of wanting and the reality of the consequences.

Conner's expression faltered. "Oh, come on, Carrie. It doesn't have to be this way. We should have been together back then. You were just too shy." He came close to her, his breath hot in her ear. "You're not shy anymore."

Carrie shook her head. "No, but you're married. I was married, and I left him. Not to be with you, but because I needed to be independent. I needed to be free. You can do that too, Conner. You can leave her if you're unhappy."

The words hung between them, heavy with truth. Conner took a step back, his expression unreadable for a moment. Then Carrie dropped his hand, the connection breaking as she turned and began walking away, the regret flooding in. She felt the weight of her decision and the pain of walking away from something that could have been. But she couldn't destroy a marriage, not even for this.

She had always longed to be with Conner and felt a deep pull toward him, but she couldn't see herself breaking up a marriage. She also couldn't help but think that she had done the same thing to Tom without a thought. Would it be so bad if she gave in to her desire?

CHAPTER 26

Carrie woke up with a heavy heart, feeling sad, disappointed, and confused. The events from the night before swirled in her mind, especially her encounter with Conner. She regretted how things had ended between them, but even more so, the uncertainty haunted her. When she walked into the trailer just after midnight, she expected some resolution, but Tori was the only one there and sound asleep. She knew where Jen was—at Fritz's, no surprise there—but she couldn't shake the feeling that she knew where Stacy had gone, and it wasn't exactly comforting.

Carefully, she slipped out of bed, glancing at Tori's peaceful form, and quietly made her way to the kitchen to brew some coffee, trying to ground herself in something familiar.

Carrie's thoughts turned to Brandon as the rich smell of coffee filled the air. She couldn't understand what kept drawing Stacy into these reckless encounters with him. Stacy had always been the wild one, but Brandon had this unpredictable energy that seemed to ignite something in her. Trip, on the other hand, wasn't like that. He was older, more settled, and more predictable than Brandon, who was tall, muscular, and attractive to many, but Trip lacked the youthful excitement that Brandon exuded.

Stacy, seven years younger than Trip, was still trying to figure out who she was. She wasn't ready to settle down. Stacy had so much more life to live, especially while still in school. She came from a poor background, much like Carrie, while Trip was obsessed with his pursuit of wealth. There was a disconnect, but what had Carrie's mind racing was how Riverbanks had this way of bringing out a particular kind of rebellion in people; "while the cat's away, the mouse will play" attitude. Carrie knew that attitude all too well. It had been a part of her life for years.

Stacy emerged from her bedroom looking a bit disheveled but with a smile that didn't quite reach her eyes. She scanned the living room, gauging who was awake, and accepted a cup of coffee from Carrie without a word. Both women stepped onto the deck, where the early morning sun began kissing the wood. The others were still asleep, leaving them in the quiet of the morning.

Carrie sipped her coffee, watching the sunlight dance on the water, before turning to Stacy. "Where were you last night?" she asked, her voice casual but pointed. "When I came back from Brett's, Tori was already in bed. I checked in on you, and your room was empty."

Stacy hesitated for just a beat too long before responding. "I went to The Edge. Since Tori was crashing early, I figured I'd keep the party going. Bobby and Conner were there, so I hung out for a little bit."

Carrie raised an eyebrow, sensing something was off. "Stacy, you were not there. I went looking for you. The bar was practically empty, and Bobby and Conner were not there either. You were with Brandon, weren't you?"

Stacy's face faltered, but she quickly recovered. She leaned back in her chair and sighed dramatically, her eyes flickering toward the trailer to be sure Tori wasn't listening. She got up, peeked through the screen door to confirm no one was awake, and then sat back down. "Okay, you got me," she admitted, her tone a little defensive. "But it's not what you think. We were hanging out by the pier. He wasn't allowed in the bars, and he was bored. We talked. That's it."

Carrie folded her arms, her eyes narrowing. "I'm not buying it. Brandon's got the hots for you. Tell me you didn't kiss him."

Stacy's cheeks flushed with embarrassment. "Well, we did kiss," she confessed, looking away. "I don't know why I did it! It just happened. The moon cast a glow over the water, and he's just so tall, young, and good-looking. I couldn't help myself."

Carrie felt a knot tighten in her stomach, but held her ground. "So what? That makes it okay?"

Stacy leaned forward slightly, a sly grin playing at the corners of her mouth. "What about you? Don't tell me you were at Brett's all night. I saw you and

Conner walking toward the pond. A little moonlight passion?"

Carrie froze momentarily, her eyes darting toward the trailer as she heard a rustling inside. She lowered her voice, almost a whisper. "Shhh. Tori's getting up. And as for me and Conner, that's nothing. You need to stop whatever it is you started with Brandon. He's Bobby and Marcy's son—think about the trouble that comes with that." She leaned in, her voice low and serious. "And what about Trip? Do you want to ruin that?"

Stacy's face dropped, and Carrie saw a flicker of uncertainty in her friend's eyes for a second. But then the smile returned, albeit a little more guarded. She took another sip of her coffee. "I'll figure it out, Carrie. I always do."

Just then, Tori poked her head out of the door. "What's all the whispering about?"

Carrie and Stacy quickly composed themselves and stood up to distract Tori from their conversation.

"Trying not to wake you." Carrie turned to see Trip and Benny's cars approach the trailer. "Wow, looks like they left at the same time," Carrie remarked, a little surprised by the synchronicity.

Trip got out of his car, didn't bother to grab his bags, and made a beeline for Stacy. With a grin, he hugged her, lingering for a moment too long before kissing her deeply.

Stacy pulled away with a laugh, brushing her hair

back. "I haven't even brushed my teeth yet!"

Trip chuckled, eyes twinkling with mischief. "I can tell. You taste like alcohol." He gave her a playful swat on the butt. "Glad you had fun last night. I'm going to unpack, and then we're going for a morning boat ride."

Stacy looked confused. "We usually go later, after breakfast."

Trip squeezed her tight, lifting her off the ground slightly, his voice teasingly low. "I want some alone time with my girl since we didn't have any last night." He grinned, clearly expecting her to go along with it.

Jen, overhearing, interjected from the doorway. "Besides, Stacy, we're taking the boat out Saturday for the pirate party."

Stacy's smile faltered for a moment, revealing she wasn't thrilled by the idea of an early boat ride, but she nodded, trying to hide her irritation. "Oh, yeah. I forgot." She smiled forcedly, then headed inside to freshen up, her steps deliberate as she went inside to change.

It was a necessary distraction, especially after the tension that had built up between Brett and Larry, the owner of The Edge, over the tiki bar situation the previous summer. The town had ordered the bar removed due to safety concerns. Too many drunk patrons had ended up falling into the river, which had caused more than a few headaches. So, early this season, Brett built a new bar with a cement slab for tables and space for live music just outside the parking lot, across the street from the river. Larry didn't make a fuss about it. He was relieved. The tiki bar had been more trouble than it was worth. He kept the small bar running, hosting live bands in the evenings, but the big outdoor parties were now in Brett's domain.

Benny walked up the stairs, his cell phone pressed to his ear. He ended the call with a quick flip of his phone and grinned at the group. "Hey, party people. Let's get this weekend started," he said, dropping his bags by the door.

He leaned in to kiss Carrie and Tori on the cheek.

Carrie exchanged a glance with Tori, silently trying to gauge her reaction. Are they having an affair, or was the kiss on the couch last time just a one-time thing? Tori's face tightened, her usual mix of disdain and discomfort. She gave Benny a light shove, her voice edged with forced cheer. "Not in the mood for your shit today, Benny," she said, pushing him away.

Carrie's stomach churned. She wondered if she was more in the dark about what was happening between them than she realized.

Jen emerged, looking a little worse for wear. No one knew exactly when she got back the night before since everyone had already gone to bed, but it was late.

"Well, well, look what the cat dragged in," Carrie teased.

"Jen pulling an all-nighter?" Benny chimed in

with a smirk. "Good for you, girl." He leaned in and kissed her cheek in greeting.

Jen waved off their comments with a tired grin. "Fritz and I crashed at Dodger's place. I walked back around 5:00. I'm fine, though." She clapped her hands together with mock enthusiasm.

"Stacy and Trip are gone for a bit, so let's get moving—time to decorate!"

They headed to Brett's and hung up black and gold streamers, adding clusters of balloons emblazoned with "Dirty Thirty" to create a festive but classy vibe. The decorations turned the corner of the new outdoor bar into a cozy celebration spot. They planned an intimate gathering with their group, along with Fritz and Dodger. But Jen, over everyone else's objections, insisted on including Marcy and Bobby, claiming it was only fair since they always invited her to their cookouts. Naturally, this meant Brandon and Conner would likely tag along too.

Carrie was sure that Marcy's friend, Michelle, would be tagging along for the weekend. Marcy always brought Michelle—her "cool" friend— probably to compete with Carrie, Jen, and Tori, whom she clearly envied. But Michelle's presence felt like an obstacle to Carrie's newfound freedom. After all, Michelle still remembered Carrie as the shy girl from high school, the one who had "never been kissed." And now? Carrie knew Michelle would be quick to label her a "slut," eager to expose her flaws and remind her of the girl she used to be. Michelle had a way of pulling out the worst in her.

After the setup, the girls headed back to the trailer to get ready. They agreed on matching outfits: camisoles and jean skirts, their hair styled into gleaming beachy waves. Benny, ever the stylish one, opted for a crisp cotton button-up shirt and cargo shorts. He tied his long, wavy hair into a half-back ponytail, adding to his effortlessly cool look.

Jen whipped up her famous salsa in the kitchen while the rest lounged in the living room, sipping Benny's expertly made pre-party Bloody Marys.

"Are you dating anyone these days, Benny?" Carrie asked, her tone teasing.

"Yes, many women," Benny replied with a mischievous grin.

Tori rolled her eyes and leaned back in her chair. "A different one every week, from what I hear. Especially with that stud pad of yours."

"A real Jerry Seinfeld, huh?" Carrie added, smirking.

"Yeah, but better looking," Benny shot back, flipping his hair dramatically.

~ ~ ~

As Carrie stepped into the cool, dimly lit storeroom, the familiar hum of the refrigerators and the faint tang of cleaning supplies transported her back to that fateful night with Dylan. She caught her breath as the memories surfaced, unbidden. The stolen moments, the whispered laughter, and the overwhelming sense of danger—it all felt so close, like it had just happened yesterday. She closed her eyes, her thoughts drifting to him. Where was Dylan now? Was he thinking of her?

Shaking herself free from the weight of her reverie, she spotted the cake and carefully lifted it off the shelf. The walk up the narrow stairs felt longer than it should have, her thoughts swirling in uneasy circles.

As she reached the top, voices reached her ears, muffled but distinct. She froze mid-step, her body tensing as she realized she'd stumbled upon a private conversation.

"I can't believe Conner took a room at the hotel. You went to high school with him, weren't you friends?"

Carrie's heart sank. Marcy's voice was sharp, nosy, and all too eager for gossip.

"Not really. Conner ran with a different crowd. Our paths didn't cross much." She hesitated, then added, "But damn, he's cute. Guess I should've paid more attention back then." A voice she recognized: Michelle

"I know he's married, but I hear it's on the rocks. I say go for it!"

"Oh, I would," Michelle said, her tone low and edged with bitterness. "But he just can't seem to stay away from Carrie. I'm sure he knew exactly where she'd be this weekend."

Carrie's chest tightened as the air seemed to thicken around her.

"They're having a party for Stacy today. Are you going?" Marcy pressed.

"You bet," Michelle snapped. "He's married, but his wife isn't here. Besides, now that I'm here and staying with you, we'll have plenty of opportunities to find out how loyal he is."

A knot of unease tightened in Carrie's stomach. Michelle was staying with them? The thought sent a jolt of icy dread through her. She remembered his disappointment and how his eyes clouded when she turned him down. With Michelle staying at Marcy and Bobby's, the possibility of them connecting loomed large. Carrie couldn't bring herself to let that happen. Yet, a sense of urgency pushed her forward. There was no time for idle speculation; she had to get to the party.

Clutching the cake tightly, Carrie turned and bolted toward the outdoor bar, her thoughts spinning. She had to find a way to keep Conner away from Michelle. Her showing up could ruin everything— Stacy's party and her fragile dynamic with Conner.

When she reached the bar, the area was already buzzing with activity. Stacy, glowing in a floral sundress, held a cocktail in her hand as she swayed to the music from the nearby speakers. The sight briefly grounded Carrie. She plastered on a smile and placed the cake on the table.

"Oh, Carrie! This party is SO nice!" Stacy gushed, breaking away from Trip, wrapping her in a warm hug.

"Happy Dirty Thirty!" Carrie replied, forcing a lightness into her voice. But her eyes quickly sought out Jen, who was busy talking with the group near the drinks.

"Jen, can I borrow a smoke?" Carrie asked, tugging her friend aside.

Once they were out of earshot, Carrie wasted no time. "Michelle's here."

Jen's brow lifted. "So? I thought you were friends?"

"Not really. Michelle was my nemesis. I hated her. But I overheard her at Brett's when I went to grab the cake. She's going to try to seduce Conner."

Jen leaned in. "I know you have—or had—a thing for him, but he's married. You can't be the one to cross that line. If Michelle wants to wreck a marriage, at least it's not on you."

Carrie's expression fell. "I know, but I can't stand the thought of him being with her. You get it, don't you? She was my nemesis—I couldn't handle it."

Jen's expression darkened briefly before shifting to a calm, almost sly demeanor. "I get it. I know exactly how to deal with her. Leave it to me."

Carrie wanted to believe her, but her nerves were fraying. She glanced around the gathering crowd, scanning for any sign of Michelle. She only saw the regulars—locals mingling with drinks in hand, passing through to catch the free outdoor band or to head to the river.

But the air felt charged, like a storm brewing just beyond the horizon: the small covered area filled quickly, the festive atmosphere at odds with Carrie's growing unease. The band was about to start, and the locals, eager for music and drinks, swarmed in. The sunshine reflected off the water in brilliant flashes, contrasting with the shadows growing in Carrie's mind.

She grounded herself. Whatever happened next, she'd have to keep it together—for Stacy's sake, if nothing else.

Carrie, Jen, Stacy, Tori, Trip, and Benny sat at the table, nibbling on food and waiting for the band to start. Finally, the lead singer tested the microphone a few times, then belted, "Hello Riverbanks, we are The Rovers." They began playing an old country song, and the crowd erupted in cheers. Benny looked around and asked, "Are we the youngest here?"

"It looks like a geriatric happy hour," Carrie replied.

Benny stood up. "Okay, then it's time for some real drinks!"

The opening notes of Ring of Fire crackled

through the speakers, and Benny let out a "whoop" pulling Tori onto the small dance floor. Stacy laughed as Trip grabbed her hand and spun her around clumsily, almost knocking over a chair. The lively beat of one of their favorite songs that followed had the group fully immersed in the music.

Benny swayed dramatically, gesturing to Tori like a Vegas lounge act, while she rolled her eyes and mimicked his exaggerated moves. Across from them, Stacy leaned into Trip's arms, her head thrown back in laughter as he attempted an awkward two-step.

"What's taking Fritz so long?" Jen muttered, craning her neck to scan the crowd. She tapped her foot impatiently, the condensation from her drink dripping onto her hand as she gripped the glass.

Carrie followed her gaze, but three figures were walking toward them—Bobby, Brandon, and Conner.

"Look who's here," Jen exclaimed, nudging Carrie's arm. "You boys solo again?"

Conner's smile was warm and easy, his hands tucked into his pockets, while Bobby's piercing blue eyes locked onto Carrie with a glint of something unreadable—disdain, maybe, or just a bad mood. Brandon, however, barely noticed them, his eyes darting over the crowd as if scanning for someone. Probably Stacy, Carrie thought.

"You wish," Bobby replied, his tone dry. "Marcy and Michelle are on their way. They just got sidetracked. I think they ran into your boyfriend, Jen."

Jen took a long, deliberate drag of her cigarette, the ember glowing brightly. Carrie recognized the move. Jen was irritated. That sharp inhale, the tap of ash, and the slight narrowing of her eyes were all signs.

Carrie barely had time to follow Jen's gaze before Bobby and Conner turned their heads, their smiles shifting to smirks. From across the bar, Michelle and Marcy were approaching. Michelle looked like she had come off a California beach in her cut-offs. She was the picture of confidence, bold and unapologetic.

Beside her, Marcy looked understated in her crisp white Capri shorts and pastel polo, as if she had accidentally wandered off a golf course.

"We heard you were having a party for Stacy. Mind if we join? We are old friends," Michelle asked, her tone light but her eyes turning towards Conner.

"Of course," Carrie replied with a tight smile, her voice dripping with forced enthusiasm. "The more, the merrier."

Michelle and her group found seats, while Bobby, Conner, and Brandon lingered near the bar.

"Bobby, get me a glass of wine, will you?" Marcy requested, crossing her legs and flashing a practiced smile.

"Sure. What do you want, Michelle?" Bobby asked, already heading toward the bar.

"Oh, how thoughtful of you. Just a light beer, thanks," Michelle answered.

Bobby and Conner walked to the bar, but Michelle's gaze stayed firmly on Conner, her lips curving slightly.

Trip stood and stretched. "Need anything, Stacy?"

Stacy glanced up at him and smiled. "Sure, I'd love some wine."

As Trip headed toward the bar, Brandon slid smoothly into the seat next to Stacy, earning a raised eyebrow from her. She turned toward Michelle, breaking into a polite smile.

"So," Stacy said, "Carrie tells us you two went to high school together."

Michelle gave a laugh, more rehearsed than genuine. "Yes, and Conner too. Carrie and I met in middle school. In high school, though, we drifted— different crowds. Carrie was the shy one back then, while I was more outgoing." She paused, her smile sharpening. "But it sounds like she's not shy anymore, so I've heard."

"That's enough," Benny snapped from across the room, his voice cutting through the growing tension. "Who is this chick, anyway?"

"Oh, I know—that wasn't a very nice thing to say," Michelle said, her tone feigning innocence but laced with condescension. "I just heard Carrie's been, let's say, a little wild since her divorce. But who am I to judge? I've never even been married."

She abruptly pushed back her chair, standing with

mock nonchalance. "Come on, Marcy, let's join the guys at the bar."

As she walked away, she glanced over her shoulder. "Happy birthday, Stacy," she added, her tone edged with irritation.

The afternoon buzzed with music and chatter as the group gathered. Laughter mingled with the band's rhythm, and the dance floor stayed alive. Fritz arrived, beaming, and wasted no time pulling Jen onto the floor, spinning her around with each new song.

At the bar, Trip, Bobby, and Conner nursed their drinks, their conversations punctuated by glances toward Michelle, who seemed to bask in their attention, tossing her hair and flashing coy smiles.

Meanwhile, Brandon seized his chance. With the bar crowd distracted, he leaned close to Stacy, his voice low as they shared jokes and swayed to the music together.

Carrie stayed rooted in her chair, her eyes constantly drifting to Michelle. Her stomach twisted as Conner leaned in closer, their heads bent together in what appeared to be an intimate exchange. Were they connecting, or was he doing this to get under Carrie's skin? The thought gnawed at her, but Benny appeared at her side before she could spiral further, grinning as he grabbed her hand.

"Come on, let's dance!" he said, pulling her toward the floor just as "Slide" started to play.

At first, her smile was hesitant, but Benny's

exaggerated spins and goofy moves soon coaxed a laugh out of her. She let herself get swept up in the moment on the dance floor—if only for a little while.

There was no bathroom in the outdoor bar, so Carrie made her way to Brett's. She slipped into the dimly lit restroom, the smell of stale beer and floral air freshener hanging heavy in the air. Choosing a stall, she locked the door behind her.

A sharp, wet sniff cut through the silence. It came again, louder this time, from the stall beside hers. Carrie froze, her breath catching. The unmistakable sound of someone snorting cocaine made her stomach tighten.

She flushed quickly, her movements rushed, and headed to the sink to wash her hands. As she turned to leave, the stall door next to hers creaked open.

"Carrie," Michelle drawled, stepping out with a sly smile, her eyes glassy. "Want a bump?"

"No," she barked back at Michelle.

Michelle's smile widened, sharp and mocking. "What, you're a good girl now? That's cute. But I don't think that's what Conner likes. Pretty sure he's into my type."

The words hit like a slap. Before Carrie could think, her hands shot out, shoving Michelle hard into the sink. The clang echoed in the tiny bathroom.

Michelle laughed, a cold, cutting sound. "Oh, Carrie," she sneered, straightening herself. "Still jealous. Always jealous."

Her irritating laughter followed Carrie as she bolted from the bathroom, her heart pounding and her vision blurred with rage.

CHAPTER 27

The so-called party for Stacy fizzled out
after Carrie returned from the bathroom incident.
Truthfully, it had never felt like a celebration—just an
excuse to gather at the bar while a local band played
for an older afternoon crowd. With plans for a long
day on the boat the next day, no one argued when the
group decided to leave and head back to the trailer.

The deck offered a quieter reprieve compared to
the crowded outdoor bar area. Carrie and Jen settled
into the worn lawn chairs near the railing, their drinks
sweating in the humid evening air. From the other
side of the deck, laughter and music spilled over as
the rest of the group danced and mingled, cocktails
sloshing in their hands.

Carrie lit a cigarette; her hands were still
trembling slightly from the earlier confrontation. She
exhaled a thin stream of smoke, her eyes fixed on the
orange glow of the horizon.

"I still can't believe she does coke," Jen muttered,
breaking the silence. She swirled her drink, ice
clinking against the glass.

Carrie gave a humorless laugh, flicking ash into a

makeshift ashtray. "But still, I knocked her on her ass. Or at least I wanted to."

Jen smirked but shook her head. "Unreal. Who saw that coming?"

"Not me," Carrie replied quietly, taking another drag.

Jen leaned forward, her elbows resting on her knees, cigarette balanced between her fingers. She exhaled slowly, the smoke curling in the humid air. Her voice was low but firm, cutting through the faint hum of music in the background.

"I can see why Michelle's so jealous of you, Carrie," she said, her gaze steady. "You and Conner are always sneaking off, whispering like nobody notices. But people see. Even if you don't think so, there are eyes everywhere around here."

Carrie winced, looking down at the condensation pooling on her drink. She traced a circle around the rim of the glass but said nothing.

Jen pressed on, her tone softening slightly. "I know you're trying to find someone, especially after things ended badly with Tom... and then Dylan. But Conner? He's not the one. He's married, Carrie. You know that."

"I know," Carrie replied in almost a whisper. She looked out at the darkening river, the glow of distant boat lights reflecting in her eyes. "It's just... it feels so easy that it's tempting. He's always around, and when we talk..." She paused, searching for the right words.

"It's like he sparks something in me. Something I haven't felt in so long."

Jen shook her head, a rueful smile tugging at her lips. "Oh, I get it. Believe me, I do. But easy and tempting doesn't make it right. And it sure as hell doesn't make it worth it." She reached over and tapped Carrie's arm lightly, drawing her attention. "There are other men out there. Good men. You have to open your eyes and stop chasing what you can't have."

Carrie bit her lip and nodded, though her expression betrayed the turmoil swirling inside her. She took a long sip of her drink, hoping it would dull the ache she couldn't quite name.

"Maybe you're right," she answered at last, though her voice carried no conviction.

Jen sighed and leaned back in her chair, taking another drag of her cigarette. "I know I'm right," she muttered, her tone half-joking. "Now, let's just hope you figure it out before things blow up."

They sat in silence for a moment, the weight of unspoken fears settling between them, as the faint laughter and music from the other end of the deck carried on obliviously.

Later in the evening, as the sun dipped below the tree line, the deck party came alive with music and laughter. Fritz and Dodger had joined in, and even Brandon slipped away from his mom and dad, collapsing onto an empty chair, his face a mix of frustration and relief.

"You have no idea what's going on over there," he announced, shaking his head.

"What now?" Jen asked, setting her drink down.

Brandon took a long swig of beer before answering. "Michelle is buzzing around like a crazy woman, sitting on Conner's lap. It's ridiculous."

Carrie froze, her stomach tightening.

Brandon continued, "Michelle is totally into Conner. She started accusing him of being into you, Carrie, and said you two have been sneaking around, and everyone can see it. Conner tried to deny it, but she wasn't having it. She said he's married but all over Carrie, and if he wants to cheat, he should cheat with her."

The group exchanged uneasy glances.

"Then what?" Jen asked.

"Then Conner snapped," Brandon replied, shaking his head. "He told her she was acting crazy and embarrassing herself. That's when she flipped. She started yelling about how Carrie is just trying to get back at her for how she treated her in high school. He must have had enough and just walked out. Michelle threw a vase at the door after him."

"Marcy's in there trying to calm her down, but it's not working. Michelle keeps going on about how Conner is probably with you, Carrie. She even said she saw you two talking at Stacy's party before the whole push happened."

Carrie's face turned red. "We weren't doing

anything wrong. We were just talking."

"Tell that to Michelle," Brandon said, finishing his beer. "Anyway, I had to get out of there. It's too much drama for me. It's time to celebrate Stacy more!" He grabbed a beer and joined in on the dancing with the rest.

Carrie stayed quiet, her mind spinning with everything Brandon had just said. She slipped to the far corner of the deck, needing a moment alone. She immersed herself in the moon's soft glow as it reflected off the pond, casting a picturesque haze over the night, and wrapped her arms around herself, staring at the rippling water. Her chest felt heavy; guilt mingled with confusion. She hadn't meant for anything to happen with Conner, and now everything was a mess.

Her thoughts drifted to Michelle, crazed and furious. The memory of her looking all coked-out replayed in Carrie's mind, and a pang of regret settled in her stomach. But a familiar voice broke her trance before she could sort through the tangle of emotions.

"Carrie. I need to talk to you."

Her heart sank. She turned slightly to see Conner standing in the grass just beyond the deck, out of sight from the rest of the group. His figure shadowed, but she recognized him instantly. Without a word, she stepped off the deck and grabbed his arm, pulling him behind the trailer so no one could see. The cool night air felt heavier back there, pressing against her as she faced him.

When they were far enough from the others, Carrie spun around to face him, her voice a harsh whisper. "How could you? Michelle? Of all people? You had to flaunt your attraction to her right in front of me?"

Conner stepped closer, his hands resting firmly but gently on her shoulders. "Carrie, calm down," he said, his voice low and urgent. "I'm not attracted to her. She's not my type."

Carrie's eyes narrowed. "She does drugs, Conner. Cocaine."

"I know," he admitted, a flicker of frustration crossing his face. "Michelle is leaving tomorrow. Marcy doesn't want that at her trailer, especially with Brandon around. Even Bobby agrees."

Carrie let out a breath, her shoulders sagging slightly. "Good," she murmured, a hint of relief in her tone.

"Do you think she's pretty?" Carrie asked cautiously, her voice barely above a whisper.

Conner smiled softly, taking her hands in his. "She's pretty, sure. But not even close to you." He held her gaze, his tone steady. "Carrie, she's fake, shallow, and stuck in the past. She peaked in high school and never moved on. She'll never come close to the woman you are."

Carrie's heart raced as the pull between them grew stronger. Every nerve in her body begged her to give in, but Conner was married. A loveless marriage, which she knew all too well what that's like. She'd already crossed lines before with Tom; how was this any different? Didn't they both deserve a chance at happiness?

Her resolve crumbled as she stepped into his arms, tilting her head up just as he leaned down. Their lips met in a deep, hungry kiss that sent a shiver down her spine.

"Let's go somewhere private," he whispered, his breath warm against her ear.

She pulled back slightly, searching his face. "Are you leaving your wife, Jill?"

His eyes darkened with a mixture of sadness and guilt. He hesitated, the weight of his words pressing between them.

"It's... complicated," he answered finally. "Jill's pregnant."

Carrie stepped back, shaking her head.

"Carrie, wait—" Conner reached for her again.

"Good luck with that," she snapped, turning on her heel and walking away before he could say another word.

She didn't stop until she was back on the deck, her breath coming in shallow bursts. The noise of the party felt distant now, and their heated exchange clouded her focus. For the rest of the evening, she avoided looking toward the shadows behind the trailer, where Conner remained.

CHAPTER 28

The next morning, Jen emerged from her bedroom, her phone still in hand, a playful grin lighting up her face. "You'll never guess what Fritz and Dodger are up to!" she announced, her voice full of amusement.

"They're driving a pontoon boat for the boat association and turning it into a full-blown pirate ship. Costumes, props, the whole nine yards! They're even dressing up as pirates themselves," she laughed.

"They're on their way over now to get their makeup done. Anyone want to help me get them decked out?"

"Sure, I'll help you," Carrie answered quickly, eager for any distraction from her conversation with Conner the night before. She stood at the stove, a spatula in hand, as she scrambled a large pan of sizzling eggs for the group, filling the trailer with the aroma throughout.

"Does this mean we can ride on the boat too?" Carrie added with a hopeful smile, glancing over her shoulder.

Tori and Stacy were sprawled across various spots in the living room, still lounging as they waited for breakfast before starting their day. From the deck outside, Benny and Trip heard the chatter about the pirate boat plans and came inside, curiosity pulling them into the conversation.

"A pirate boat? Count me in!" Benny declared, rubbing his hands together.

"A couple of us can ride in the boat, Jen said, "but they also have some other friends joining. Benny can take my boat with a few of us, too."

"You got it!" Benny exclaimed with enthusiasm, already envisioning himself at the helm. He loved any chance to drive the boat and show off his skills.

"Breakfast is ready," Carrie announced, setting the pan of scrambled eggs on the counter alongside a stack of plates. "Let's eat so we're ready when Fritz and Dodger get here."

Before she could finish her sentence, Benny and Trip were already grabbing plates and piling on the eggs, eager to fuel up for the day ahead.

"What about ladies first?" Tori commented, walking in. She pushed them both out of the way, grabbed a plate, and added some eggs. "There, now Stacy, come and get some." The guys stood to the side, looking irritated, but let the girls get theirs.

After eating, Tori grabbed Benny by the arm and said, "Come on, let's clean up so Carrie and Jen can work their magic on the pirate boys."

"Fine," Benny sighed dramatically, "but I need to get myself ready. Gotta look my best for all the bikini-clad babes hanging out at The Landing." He glanced around. "I need a bathroom since this one's full. Can I use yours, ladies?"

"Sure," Carrie smirked, "but don't make a mess in there."

Carrie rummaged through her closet, a whirlwind of skirts and blouses swirling around her. Jen entered the room, closing the door behind her with a soft click. She sat on the edge of the bed, her gaze fixed on Carrie's frantic movements.

"So," Jen began, her voice a low murmur, "how did it go with Conner last night? I never got a chance to talk to you with all the birthday chaos."

Carrie paused, a silk scarf slipping from her grasp. "It was… complicated," she admitted, the word hanging heavy in the air. "I told him I was upset that he was flirting with Michelle."

Jen's forehead wrinkled. "Oh my god, seriously? That woman is still a nightmare."

"I know, right?" Carrie shuddered, the memory of Michelle's icy glare from their school days still vivid. "It hit a nerve."

"Did he… deny it?" Jen asked, her voice laced with concern.

Carrie hesitated, "He said she's not his type at all."

A flicker of relief crossed Jen's face. "Good."

"Things got much better after that," Carrie continued, a small smile gracing her lips. "We had a nice moment."

"That's good," Jen said, leaning forward.

Carrie's smile faded. "But then I asked him about leaving Jill, and he told me she's pregnant."

Jen's jaw dropped. "Oh wow, I did not see that coming."

"Me neither," Carrie confessed, a wave of dizziness washing over her.

"So, what are you going to do now?" Jen asked gently.

Carrie sank into a chair, her clothes' vibrant colors suddenly muted. "Nothing," she whispered, her voice barely audible. "I know this can't go anywhere. He's not an option for me."

Jen reached out, her hand resting lightly on Carrie's arm. "I know," she agreed softly. "Try to put that aside. We're going to have fun today."

Fritz and Dodger eased the pontoon into the dock by The Edge, the engine humming softly as they tied it securely to the post. It was just after 9 a.m., and the morning sun reflected off the water, promising another hot day. Both men stepped off the boat dressed casually in their bathing trunks and t-shirts, each carrying a bag stuffed with pirate costumes and props.

"Hey, babe," Fritz gushed as he walked into the trailer, his eyes lighting up at the sight of Jen. She greeted him with a beaming smile and a long kiss, standing on her tiptoes to reach him.

"I'm so excited you guys get to take one of the boats out today!" she said, her enthusiasm contagious.

Fritz chuckled, running a hand through his silky brown hair. "Yeah, well, my dad pulled some strings. He's tight with one of the guys from the boat association."

Dodger stepped in behind him, his tall, broad frame filling the small living room. He set his bag down with a thud and clapped his hands. "You've got the best man for the job. I'll be driving."

"He's a better driver than I am," Fritz admitted, pointing a thumb at Dodger with a grin.

Jen grabbed Fritz's arm and pulled him toward the kitchen. "Come on, Captain, sit on the bar stool, and I'll work on your pirate makeup here," she said, rifling through her makeup bag.

Dodger leaned casually against the counter, watching Jen get set to work. "Just don't make him too pretty. He's supposed to be a fearsome pirate, not a beauty queen," he smirked.

Jen shot Dodger a playful glare. "You're next, sailor. Don't think you're getting out of this."

Carrie grabbed Dodger's arm and steered him outside to the deck, makeup bag in hand.

"Come on, let's get this started so we can hit the water," she declared with a grin. She and Jen were still in their usual morning attire of pajama shorts and tank tops. It was Riverbanks, after all, where casual mornings were the norm. The built-in bras in their tank tops were just enough to keep them from feeling completely underdressed.

Dodger plopped down on one of the deck chairs and stretched his long legs. "Alright, let's do this. Turn me into a fearsome pirate," he joked, leaning back and smirking.

Carrie pulled out a black eyeliner pencil from her bag. "We'll start with some eye makeup to make you look mysterious and scary. Lean back and try not to blink."

Dodger did as instructed, but flinched the second the pencil touched his eyelid. "Ah, this feels weird," he said, shifting slightly and instinctively placing his hands on her waist to steady himself.

Carrie froze for a second, then stepped back with a small laugh. "It's okay. I get it. Not everyone's used to this kind of stuff."

"Yeah, no kidding. Just don't poke my eye out."

She leaned back in, carefully smudging the eyeliner to give it a rugged, smoky effect. "I think we'll skip the mascara," she teased, pulling back to examine her work.

Dodger raised an eyebrow. "Oh, hell no to that anyway."

"Alright, how about some dirt or soot? Pirates are supposed to look a little rough, right?" She used her fingers to smudge black streaks on his cheeks and forehead. "There. Rugged and dangerous."

He grinned. "Not bad. You might have a future in pirate cosmetics."

"Thanks. Now, what did you bring to wear? Let's see if we can complete the look," Carrie said, crossing her arms with mock seriousness, ready to judge.

Dodger handed her the bag with a sly grin. "Here's the stuff. But heads up—I'm not wearing pants. It's way too hot for that."

Carrie glanced down at his muscular thighs and calves, firm and toned from years of outdoor work and sports. Definitely keep the trunks on, she thought to herself, suppressing a smirk.

Without hesitation, Dodger tugged his t-shirt over his head, revealing six-pack abs and a chest straight out of an action movie. "Man, it's getting hot already," he muttered, running his hands through his hair, his biceps flexing as he did. Carrie couldn't help but notice a long scar running along the side of his stomach.

She quickly averted her gaze and pulled a gauzy white shirt from the bag. "This isn't going to be very cool, but it's a must for the pirate look," she said, handing it to him.

Dodger slipped the shirt on, the loose puffy sleeves contrasting with his muscular frame. Carrie reached into the bag again and pulled out colorful bead necklaces. She draped them around his neck and then handed him a fake sword.

Dodger shifted his weight, looking down as she adjusted the beads. His gaze lingered on her brightly painted pink toes before trailing up to her legs. "You've got runner's legs," he remarked casually. "Do you run?"

Carrie blinked, caught off guard. "Uh, yeah, I do. I've been running for a while now. Do you?"

"Yeah, I do," Dodger replied, his grin widening. "We should run together sometime."

"Maybe. Sit tight while I get some hair products."

Dodger raised an eyebrow but obeyed, sitting on the deck chair. Carrie quickly stepped inside and returned with a can of mousse in hand. She shook it up, squeezed a generous amount into her palm, and ran her fingers through his hair.

As she worked it into his loose waves, she couldn't help but notice how thick and soft his hair was, falling in natural waves that would make any hairstylist jealous. She tousled it to give him a carefree, windswept look, making him seem even more effortlessly handsome.

"I would leave the hat off with hair like this," Carrie smiled. "Girls are going to want to take photos with you."

Dodger paused, looking up at her with an amused grin. He shook his hair out, causing it to settle even more perfectly. "Me?" he asked, clearly surprised.

"Yes, they will," she admitted, blushing slightly as she finished. "Well, I'd better get ready. We'll meet you on the boat."

Dodger chuckled, running his fingers through his

hair one last time. "You sure about that?" he teased.

Carrie turned quickly, trying to mask her flustered expression. "Definitely," she promised, clearing her throat. "You're good to go, pirate."

As she walked back toward the trailer, she couldn't help but feel the weight of his gaze on her. Was she reading too much into this, or was there more to his teasing than just a friendly exchange?

CHAPTER 29

As usual, getting everyone ready at the same time was a challenge. Benny, Trip, and Stacy had already gotten a head start, each finishing up their prep with an air of casual confidence. Tori, however, was still lounging around in her pajamas, engrossed in the TV. She finally rolled off the couch and joined the chaos, though she wasn't in a hurry.

The already cramped bathroom became a battleground for face washing and teeth brushing as the group squeezed in together. Carrie, Tori, and the others tried to make do, bumping into each other while attempting to freshen up. Meanwhile, Carrie and Tori had claimed their respective bedrooms as personal beauty stations, making room for hair styling and makeup applications.

The small trailer felt even more cramped as the temperature soared. With the windows closed to keep the heat at bay, the only relief came from the fans, which blared in every corner. Still, it wasn't enough to offset the heat of so many people and the mounting anticipation of the day ahead. Carrie tried not to let the sweaty discomfort get to her, focusing instead on getting ready, though part of her mind was still preoccupied with the lingering tension from the night before.

"All who are ready, go outside on the deck. It's bloody hot in here with all of our bodies!" Jen yelled from the bathroom.

"Okay, okay, boss. Come on, Trip, let's go hit some wiffle balls." Benny suggested.

"In a minute," Trip replied distractedly, his fingers dialing his phone as he stepped into the kitchen. "I have to check the stock market. I'll be out in a second." His voice became muffled as he started making calls, focusing entirely on the financial updates.

Standing near the fridge, Stacy grabbed a beer with a sigh, her patience thinning as she watched Trip get absorbed in his work again. "I'll hit some with you. What the heck," she said, trying to mask her irritation with a casual shrug. "It can't be hard. You play, right?" She threw Benny a half-hearted smile, already regretting that she'd agreed to play but deciding it might be better than standing around feeling ignored.

As the rest of the girls finished getting dressed and putting the finishing touches on their hair and makeup, they gathered their beach bags, coolers, and sunscreen for the boat trip.

"We don't have to bother with sandwiches," Jen announced, tossing various snacks and drinks into the cooler. "There's a brat fry at The Landing, and it's cheap too."

"Darn, I do love our sandwiches," Tori added with a laugh, clearly disappointed but not hiding her amusement.

"We should make some roadies," Carrie suggested, pulling out cups and mixing up a few travel cocktails. They each filled a cup with their favorite drinks, preparing for the day ahead.

Through the door, they could see Stacy laughing as she played wiffle ball with Benny, who ogled her every time she bent over to hit the ball. Tori, who had been watching, looked away quickly, her face tense, hiding the frustration she was trying to suppress. Jen and Carrie exchanged looks, silently agreeing that he was acting like a pig.

"Total neanderthal," Carrie muttered, her eyes narrowing as she heard Benny make another leering comment. Jen nodded in agreement. "I don't know how Stacy puts up with it," Carrie whispered, not wanting Tori to hear.

Fritz and his friends did a bang-up job decorating the pontoon like a pirate ship, which couldn't be missed, even from a distance. Two large black flags hung and were draped across the front and back, adorned with a skull and crossbones. There was a skeleton hung on one side, and even a rope plank they could pull out and stake into the water.

Jen looked at Carrie and Tori. "Wow, this will be fun."

Trip looked around. "Where's Stacy and Benny?" He looked annoyed that Stacy wasn't waiting for him in the trailer.

"They must be down by the pond. They were going to hit wiffle balls with Benny's club." Carrie answered as she walked toward the pond. "You guys, we are getting on the boat!" she hollered out. Trip stayed where he was, still on his phone but now looking at a text message.

Benny and Stacy came running back to the trailer, golf club in hand. "You guys have a cooler? Let me grab some things." Benny said.

Trip looked at Stacy. "Put some shorts on, Stacy. I don't need you walking around with your cheeks and crotch showing to everyone."

"God, lay off, I will! I have to get my beach bag anyway."

"Who walks around like that?" Trip asked, as if he were disgusted.

"Someone who has a body like that does," Tori replied.

Benny and Stacy emerged from the trailer, closing the door behind them. "Okay, let's go."

After loading up Jen's boat, Benny helped Tori and Stacy aboard, while Trip jumped in to help guide it off the pier. Jen and Carrie made their way over to Fritz's boat, where he and Dodger stood tall, ready to help them.

Dodger extended a hand to each of them. "Welcome aboard, ladies," he grinned.

Fritz was already lounging on the deck, casually

holding a beer, surrounded by a few of their friends—guys their age, with a couple of girlfriends scattered around. Fritz waved them over. "You didn't need to bring any drinks," he declared, nodding toward several coolers stacked on the boat, filled with beers and a variety of spirits.

Carrie and Jen set their bags down and took a seat. The boat was still for the moment, calm enough that they could talk. They introduced themselves to the two other girlfriends, who seemed nice enough, but were a little plain-looking. Nothing that would threaten Jen and Carrie's confidence. Jen exchanged a glance with Carrie, a silent acknowledgment passing between them: no competition here.

As they rounded the final bend, Landing Strip came into view, a riot of sound and color. Boats decorated as pirate ships bobbed on the water, their makeshift sails and pirate flags flapping in the breeze. The thumping sounds of a band rolled out from the bar, mingling with the hum of the crowd spread across the sprawling lawn. People milled between tents lining the waterfront—some serving food, others hawking raffle tickets for the fifty-fifty draw. The scene buzzed with energy, promising a day packed with revelry.

Dodger maneuvered the boat to a pier slowly while the rest of the group stood to watch. Carrie and Jen grabbed their tops since they had taken their tube tops off to get sun. Some other boats pulled up at the same time, including Bobby's. Conner was driving, while Bobby leaned back holding a large water gun and shot it directly at Carrie, hitting her drink and knocking it to the floor, liquid spraying all over the place. Marcy sat on the boat laughing hysterically and pointing at Carrie. Conner looked up and yelled, "Bobby, what the fuck?"

Bobby laughed, "It's okay, Conner. Your girlfriend found another man. Get over her."

Carrie and Jen hopped off the boat, their sandals crunching against the gravelly shoreline. They waved to Fritz and Dodger, who adjusted their pirate hats and made their way toward the bar deck. Their swagger drew giggles from a cluster of women nearby. Posing for photos and charming the guests in their costumes was part of the deal.

Carrie scanned the lively scene as she and Jen wandered through the crowd. Laughter and the clinking of beer bottles filled the air, mingling with the faint smell of grilled brats. They wove between groups of people lounging in lawn chairs and kids darting around with plastic swords.

"Over here!" Jen nudged Carrie, pointing to one of the tents. Inside, they spotted Stacy and Tori, deep in conversation with a vendor. Tori held a handful of fifty-fifty tickets, while Stacy leaned over a clipboard, inspecting a list of items for the silent auction.

Stacy grabbed Carrie by the elbow and steered her a few steps away from the others, a playful yet curious look on her face as Jen and Tori continued browsing the auction items.

"How was the boat ride?" she asked casually, though her tone hinted at something more.

Carrie shrugged. "It was fun, until Bobby nailed me with his water gun."

Stacy smirked, her voice dripping with mock innocence. "Oh, I bet that big, strapping man rushed to your rescue."

Carrie blinked, taken aback by the comment. Was Stacy being nosy? Jealous, maybe? She tilted her head slightly. "Dodger? He was driving."

"Uh-huh," Stacy replied with a knowing smile, her eyes lingering on Carrie for a moment longer before she turned on her heel and sauntered back toward the others.

The bar's deck pulsed with life, a maze of sun-kissed faces and bodies packed shoulder to shoulder. Fritz and Dodger stood out in their pirate costumes, grinning as bikini-clad women draped themselves over their arms for photos. Nearby, Benny and Trip huddled with a group of women, shot glasses clinking in succession, their boisterous cheers blending with the music thumping from the speakers.

Carrie weaved through the bustling crowd, dodging elbows and weaving around groups deep in animated conversation. She glanced around, scanning for Jen or the others. No luck. Feeling lost, she headed for the outdoor bar, her sandals tapping softly against the worn wooden planks. A bartender juggling orders caught her eye, and she leaned against the counter, waiting for a moment to catch his attention.

She ordered a cup of bug juice. Dodger approached the bar as Carrie stood waiting for her drink.

"Aren't you supposed to be out mingling, Mr. pirate celebrity?" Carrie asked nonchalantly.

"I have been, and doing it well, I might add, but even pirates need a drink." He took a few steps to be closer to her.

"What, you don't have a flask of rum in your pocket?" She shuffled her feet nervously as Dodger turned his attention back to her.

"No, but that would have been a great idea!" The bartender appeared and asked what he was having. Dodger replied, "Bug juice, Matey," leaning into the pirate theme as he tipped an imaginary hat.

"What do you do, Carrie?" Dodger asked.

"For fun?" she replied, playing with the cigarette she had just pulled from her pack. "You're looking at it." She cracked a slight smile and lit it, letting the smoke curl between them.

Dodger laughed softly. "No, I mean for a living."

Carrie paused. It struck her how rare it was for someone, especially a guy, to ask her that. She studied him for a moment before answering. "I'm a human resources manager."

Intrigued, Dodger asked. "Where do you manage this office?"

"It's a construction company," she replied, shifting slightly. "I started there at a young age and just kind of worked my way up."

"Nice," he replied with genuine interest. "Are you from around here?"

"No, I'm from the city," she answered, her tone casual as her eyes briefly darted away.

"Ah, right, the big city girl," Dodger teased lightly, raising his glass for another sip, his dark eyes twinkling at her.

Carrie laughed softly, correcting him. "Not really—it's just a suburb." She tilted her head. "What about you? What do you do?"

"I'm a map maker," Dodger said, leaning against the bar. "Well, a surveyor, technically."

"Really? What does that mean?"

"I gather and analyze data for surveys—things like deeds, maps, easements, and highway plans. I set boundaries and measure the land between them. I work in construction, too, so we've got a lot in common." His smile widened, and he added, "I like your hair, by the way. It's dark like mine. Same with your eyes. We could almost be brother and sister." He winked.

Carrie blinked, caught off guard by the compliment. She studied his face, noticing how his kind eyes softened under the smudges of faded black makeup. The sweat had worn away most of the pirate disguise, revealing someone surprisingly down-to-earth. It struck her how little she really knew about him—or even Fritz, for that matter. For the first time, she felt the urge to change that.

CHAPTER 30

After leaving Dodger, Carrie wove through the crowd, crunching sand beneath her flip-flops. Her gaze landed on Tori and Jen, who were with a group of rowdy men dressed as pirates. One wore a plastic cutlass tucked into his belt and leaned too close to Jen as she threw her head back in laughter. Tori twirled the end of a plastic lei around her finger, smirking as another pirate leaned in to whisper something in her ear. Fritz was nowhere in sight.

Carrie's stomach churned as she turned toward the grassy area bordering the beach. There, she spotted Stacy with Brandon. Stacy swayed slightly as she laughed, her bikini top catching eyes with every exaggerated motion. Brandon stood close, a beer bottle dangling from one hand and a crooked smile playing on his lips as Stacy clung to his arm like it was the only thing holding her upright.

Carrie decided to approach Stacy first. She walked up to them, her footsteps sinking slightly into the sand. Brandon spotted her and immediately straightened up.

"Oh hey, Carrie," he said with an awkward grin. "I was just leaving." Without waiting for a response, he turned and hurried off, leaving Stacy standing there with her arms crossed, her face flushed.

"Stacy, what are you doing?" Carrie asked sharply, trying to keep her voice low but firm.

"What do you mean?" Stacy shot back, swaying slightly as she teetered on her flip-flops. "You act like you're so damn innocent all the time. I saw you with Dodger. What now, you're moving from Conner to this guy?"

Carrie blinked, caught off guard. "You're the ones who told me to back off from Conner. And for the record, I don't have a boyfriend. You do. Besides, Dodger and I are just friends."

Stacy squinted at Carrie with a skeptical expression. Her voice dropped into a slurred whisper. "Trip, my boyfriend, is not who you think he is. He has lots of women. Why do you think he's always on his phone?" She wobbled as she pointed a shaky finger toward the deck. "See? Look at him with Benny and those girls. Those two are one and the same."

Carrie followed her gaze. Sure enough, Trip and Benny were laughing and leaning close to two women, their heads bent in conspiratorial whispers. She sighed, suddenly feeling the weight of the night pressing down.

"Come on, Stacy. You don't know what you're saying. Let's get back to Jen and Tori."

Reluctantly, Stacy let Carrie guide her away. They approached a small circle of people near the bonfire, where a group of guys surrounded Jen and Tori; some had on pirate hats and faux eyepatches. Jen had stolen one of the pirates' hats and took a swig from a flask he handed her, a red cup of bug juice dangling precariously from her other hand.

Carrie stopped in her tracks. "What's going on, ladies? Where's Fritz?" she asked, her voice cutting through the crowd with a pointed edge.

Jen turned, her eyes slightly glassy but still sharp enough to catch Carrie's tone. "Oh, Carrie, hey! Where've you been?" she asked with exaggerated cheerfulness. She took another swig from the flask and waved the cup around. "Fritz is having a party—can't you see?"

Carrie followed Jen's gaze toward the pontoon. Fritz was surrounded by a bunch of girls in bikinis, laughing and pouring drinks. Her jaw tightened as she scanned the scene. She spotted Dodger nearby, leaning against a cooler and talking to a group of people.

Without a word, Carrie strode over to him. He noticed her approach and immediately straightened, parting from the crowd.

"Can we go back to the boat?" Carrie asked, her voice low but urgent. "Jen is getting sloppy, and I don't want to run into Bobby or Conner again."

Dodger studied her for a moment, then nodded. "Sure. Let's go."

Carrie turned back toward the group, motioning to Jen and Tori. "Come on, guys. Let's head back to the boat," she called, her voice firm but steady.

Jen blinked at her, confused for a moment before reluctantly handing the flask back to its owner. "I'm not going. I'm staying here with my friends. He can have his fun with those whores." Jen snarled.

"I'll go with you, Carrie," Tori replied. "I don't want to go back with Benny and Trip."

"Jen, come on, are you sure? You know Fritz is just being nice."

"Yeah, Jen, Fritz doesn't play around like that," Dodger added.

She shook her head. "It looks like he does. Go on, I'm staying," she said, walking off toward Benny and Trip. Stacy joined her.

Dodger led Carrie and Tori to the pontoon, his hand lightly brushing Carrie's back as they stepped aboard. The boat swayed gently under their feet and was lit up by strings of fairy lights that wrapped around the railings. The unmistakable buzz of laughter and music filled the air, mingling with the occasional splash from the water below.

"Drinks first," Dodger announced, reaching for a cooler near the helm. He cracked open the lid, revealing a colorful assortment of cans and bottles chilling in ice. He poured amber liquid into red Solo cups, handing one to Carrie and another to Tori.

Carrie took a sip, the sweet and tangy taste immediately hitting her tongue. She glanced around, noticing at least ten people on the boat, scattered across benches and the deck, their voices competing with the music blasting from the speakers.

Tori's eyes lit up when she spotted a guy leaning casually against the railing. His sandy hair glinted under the string lights as he laughed at something someone said. Without a word, she slid past Carrie, weaving toward him.

Carrie turned her attention to the dance floor—or what passed for one. Fritz was in the center, moving awkwardly to the beat while two girls in crop tops danced around him, their hands raised high as they swayed. If Fritz noticed their giggles, he didn't seem to care.

Dodger nudged Carrie's arm, a sly grin spreading across his face. "You're up, Maria," he said, queuing My Maria on his MP3 player.

Before she could protest, he pulled her onto the makeshift dance floor. The familiar twang of the guitar filled the air as Dodger spun her in a quick circle. Carrie laughed, the motion dizzying and exhilarating.

"Hold on tight!" he teased, lifting her off the ground. She shrieked as he twirled her around, her arm instinctively wrapping around his neck to steady herself.

The boat rocked slightly with their movements, but the crowd cheered them on. Carrie's laughter mixed with the music as Dodger set her back down, holding her hand as he led her into another spin.

One of the guys was sprawled across the bench seat, grinning as a group of girls gathered around him. With a cheer, they began pouring shots into his belly button, taking turns to sip them out amid laughter and squeals. The line of eager participants grew, each more animated than the last.

After several rounds, the guy sat up with a playful smirk and shouted, "Who's next?"

"I will!" Tori called out, stepping forward with a mischievous spark in her eye. With a dramatic flourish, she lay down on the bench and slid off her shorts, exposing her bikini bottom. The handsome guy from earlier stepped up with a bottle in hand, pouring a shot into her navel as the rest of the guys whooped and lined up to take their turn.

Meanwhile, Dodger stayed close to Carrie, spinning her around as they danced to the pulsing beat. She glanced over at Tori's impromptu belly-shot session and shook her head in disbelief, laughing. The day was quickly spiraling into chaos, and Carrie wasn't sure whether to feel scandalized or entertained.

~ ~ ~

Benny got behind the wheel to drive Jen's boat back. Like the rest, he had already had too much to drink. He attempted to follow the shoreline but ended up steering towards the weeds. Jen, Stacy, and Trip were throwing potato chips at seagulls diving down at them and laughing the whole time. They ended up in the weeds, and the boat bottomed out in the mud. Benny had to get out in the waist-high water to push them out.

Trip helped him back in the boat. "Dude, you need to sober up."

Benny drove back slowly in the wake zone, watching out for DNR the whole time.

Carrie waited for her friends on the pier while Tori went to the trailer to sleep. Carrie worried they would be stopped and ticketed or even worse. *I shouldn't have let them drive.*

Fritz and Dodger came over after tying up the pontoon. "Where's Jen?" asked Fritz.

Carrie could see he wasn't drunk. "She's pissed off at you! Why were you partying with all those girls? She saw you."

"I was just having fun," he replied defensively. "It was only for a little while. I didn't even see Jen."

Carrie realized that, due to his accident, he may not have been aware of how much time had passed, which wasn't his fault. She suddenly felt sorry for him.

Dodger approached Carrie and took her hand, sensing her concern for her friends. "It's alright, Carrie. I'm sure they'll be safe. Jen can drive the boat just fine, and Benny can too."

"She is drunk, and so is he. Hell, they all are." She was thankful that she only had one drink while on the boat, so she had her wits about her, which was unusual.

Their boat glided slowly toward the pier, Benny gripping the wheel with focused determination while the girls belted out the lyrics to the song blaring from the speakers. Dodger and Fritz sprang into action, calling out directions and guiding the boat with steady hands until it nestled snugly against the dock. They secured the ropes with practiced ease, the pier creaking slightly under their movements. The group gathered their bags as they energetically chattered. Fritz extended a hand to help the girls onto the dock, but they waved him off with confident smirks, hopping out with effortless grace.

"Leave us alone!" Jen shouted at him in frustration. Carrie extended a hand to help Stacy, but Stacy swatted it away. "Yeah, Carrie, just go," she snapped.

The two women climbed out of the boat and stormed down the pier, their footsteps echoing against the wooden planks as they made their way toward the trailer. Benny and Trip exchanged a glance before stepping off the boat themselves. Trip turned to Fritz with a shrug. "She's mad. You'd better give her some space," he advised. Without another word, they trailed after the girls, leaving Fritz standing by the boat, his expression unreadable.

Dodger glanced at Fritz. "We should go, man. Let her cool down. You can talk to her tomorrow," he assured, tapping Fritz on the shoulder.

Fritz hesitated, his eyes following Jen and Stacy as they disappeared down the pier, their angry voices fading into the night. With a sigh, he turned and walked toward the pontoon, his movements slow and heavy as if weighed down by unspoken words. Dodger stayed behind for a moment, watching Fritz retreat, then turned his gaze out over the water, his face lit by the moon's faint glow.

"Carrie, how about a run tomorrow?" Dodger asked with a casual smile.

"Sure," she said, her lips curving into a small smile. "Come and get me?" Carrie met his gaze, realizing he also wasn't drunk.

Dodger's grin widened, lighting up his face. "Perfect. I'd better get Fritz back—no way he's driving that boat in his state. I'll see you tomorrow. And Carrie," he added softly, his voice carrying a reassuring weight, "it'll be okay."

CHAPTER 31

The morning light filtered through the thin curtains of the trailer, casting a muted glow on the cramped space. The fans buzzed, circulating the hot air but doing little to alleviate the lingering tension. Carrie's eyes flicked open, the dull ache in her head matching the uneasy weight in her chest. She turned her head and saw Jen sprawled beside her, still wearing her clothes from the night before, passed out cold. The stale scent of booze clung to the air, a sharp reminder of the night's chaos. It was the first time they'd all gone to bed angry with each other—except for Tori, who had retreated early.

Carrie suddenly recalled her dream with vivid clarity: Dodger had pulled her into his arms, and the world around them had shifted into a dreamlike haze. It wasn't Riverbanks, but a place that felt foreign and intimate, as though they were alone in a world built just for them. She turned, straddling him, her hands fumbling with the buttons of his shirt, pulling it off to expose his scar. Her fingers traced the jagged line of it, the rough texture beneath her touch, before she leaned down, her breath hot against his skin, and pressed a soft kiss to the mark. The warmth of his body beneath her sent a shiver down her spine, as though their connection had reached a new, unspoken level.

Carrie shook off the lingering effects of the steamy dream, shaking her head as she pushed it aside. She splashed cold water on her face, trying to clear her thoughts, then went to the kitchen to start breakfast for the group. But before she could gather the ingredients, there was a knock at the door. Her heart skipped a beat as she opened it to see Dodger.

"Ready for our run?" he asked, looking as fresh and energized as if he'd just finished an intense workout. His athletic build, honed from his football days, was evident even in the early morning light.

Carrie blinked, still half-dazed. "Oh, you were serious?"

"As serious as a heart attack." His smile was wide, warm, and impossibly bright, as though it could rival the sun rising over the river.

"Give me a minute," she muttered, her nerves flaring. She quickly closed the door, her heart fluttering, and hurried back to the room she shared with Jen. She rifled through her things, desperately trying to find something to run in, her thoughts racing as fast as her pulse.

Carrie rummaged through her bag, pulling out an oversized NYC T-shirt and snug biking shorts. It wasn't exactly a runner's ensemble, but it would have to do. At least she'd packed her running shoes, though she'd hardly expected to use them. She glanced at

Jen, still sprawled across the bed, blissfully unaware. Can't you go instead? Carrie thought bitterly, but she knew the answer.

With a sigh, Carrie stepped onto the deck, where the morning sun was already beating down, promising a sweltering day. She squinted at Dodger, who stood relaxed and ready, his easy smile somehow energizing and unnerving.

"I'll do my best," she announced with a half-laugh, sitting down to lace up her shoes. She felt Dodger's eyes on her, warm and appreciative, and she tried to ignore the way her pulse quickened under his gaze.

They set off along the field bordering Larry's, the tall grasses shimmering in the heat of the morning sun. The air felt thick and buzzed with insects that clung to the humidity. Carrie pushed herself to match Dodger's effortless stride, her sneakers crunching against the gravel road. Her breath came harder with each step, her chest rising and falling as she fought to keep pace.

From time to time, their eyes met—a fleeting exchange of determination and encouragement—but neither broke the silence, focused on the rhythm of their feet hitting the ground. The sun bore down relentlessly, and the heat bugs seemed to intensify with every passing minute, a chorus of summer's unforgiving weight.

About a mile in, Carrie felt her legs grow heavy, the world blurring slightly at the edges. She slowed, her pace faltering until finally, she stumbled to the side of the road and collapsed onto the grass, gasping for air.

"Ohhh, I have to stop," Carrie groaned, as she fell onto the grass lining the county road, her chest heaving as she struggled to catch her breath.

Dodger, already far ahead, turned and jogged back to check on her. He crouched beside her, straddling her as he reached out a hand. "Come on, Carrie. You've got this."

She gulped for air, barely able to shake her head. "No... I can't."

Dodger grinned, undeterred. He stood and pulled her to her feet with ease. "Alright, let's walk back," he told her gently.

Carrie wiped the sweat from her face with the hem of her oversized T-shirt, squinting at the shimmering road ahead. "We really should've brought water," she muttered, breathless.

Dodger chuckled. "Next time, we'll plan better."

"Next time?" Carrie shot him a look, half-smiling despite herself. "Maybe I'm getting too old for this. How old are you, anyway?"

"Thirty-one," he replied, his tone light. "And for the record, you're not too old."

"You're not much younger than me," Carrie admitted, her breath starting to even out. "So... I suppose you're right."

Dodger shot her a sideways glance, his voice

softening. "Does that mean we can be friends?"

Carrie smirked, wiping her damp palms on her shorts. "Yes, I think so."

"Good," he smiled. "Because I like you."

"I like you too," she admitted, a faint blush creeping into her cheeks. She glanced at him curiously. "But I have to know—Dodger. Is that your real name?"

He laughed, "No. It's Doug."

~ ~ ~

Carrie stepped into the quiet trailer and tiptoed around, careful not to wake her sleeping friend. She grabbed her toiletry bag and a fresh change of clothes.

After a cool, refreshing shower, Carrie went to the kitchen to find Tori stirring a cup of coffee. She glanced at the tidied couch where Benny had been sleeping and noticed the blanket neatly folded, the pillows fluffed, and his bag zipped shut—nothing like the usual explosion of clothes and belongings he left behind.

"Wow," Carrie said, running a towel through her damp hair. "Benny's starting to clean up after himself. You can barely tell he slept here. Where'd he go?"

Tori looked up from her coffee, her eyes lingering on Carrie for a moment as she wiped a smudge from the rim of her mug. "He and Trip left in the car a little while ago. Not sure where they went," she replied with a shrug. "Honestly, I feel bad for him having to crash out here like that. Must be uncomfortable."

Carrie nodded thoughtfully, glancing back at the couch. "Still, it's an upgrade from the first year. You remember—stuff everywhere, like a tornado hit."

Tori chuckled. "True. Benny might be evolving."

"Look at you, changing your opinion of Benny," Carrie teased with a sly smile as she poured herself a cup of coffee. "Years ago, you couldn't stand him. Maybe you should offer to let him sleep in the room with you next time."

Tori raised an eyebrow, smirking into her mug. "Oh, I'm sure Drew would love that idea."

Carrie chuckled as they made their way to the deck, the early sun warming the wooden boards beneath their feet. They settled into chairs, the soft breeze carrying the sound of chirping birds and distant boat motors.

Tori stretched out her legs and took a sip of coffee. Carrie hesitated, turning her cup in her hands before speaking.

"Can I ask you something?" Carrie asked in a cautious tone.

"Sure, but I think I already know what you're going to ask," Tori replied, taking another sip of her coffee.

"Oh yeah? Why doesn't Drew ever come to Riverbanks with you?"

Tori leaned back in her chair, her expression calm but reflective. "Yeah, that's the one. I've wondered if anyone would ever ask me outright." She paused, glancing at the horizon. "Drew and I have an open relationship. We always have. Between our work trips, we're apart more than we're together. I'm pretty sure he's got a 'special interest' in Marilyn—the flight attendant he's always traveling with."

Carrie blinked, caught off guard. "Really? That's not what I expected. Are you seeing other people, too?"

Tori nodded, the corners of her mouth quirking into a faint smile. "I am."

"Benny?" Carrie's tone held a mix of curiosity and disbelief.

"Yes," Tori answered.

Her quick and simple reply almost didn't seem scandalous.

"Does Drew know?"

Before Tori could answer, the rumble of Trip's car broke the moment. Both women looked over as Trip and Benny stepped out, carrying a box of donuts. The two men strolled up the deck steps, Benny grinning like he had something to brag about.

"Morning, ladies," Benny announced, holding up the box like a peace offering. "We brought breakfast!"

"Looks like someone's trying to make up for bad behavior yesterday," Carrie responded.

"Oh, come on, everyone was misbehaving, not just Trip and me. I recall this one here having a good time," Benny said, patting Tori on the shoulder. Tori looked at Carrie with a face as if not to let her secret out at this time.

Jen and Stacy emerged from their rooms together, the aroma of fresh coffee greeting them.

"Ooh, donuts!" Jen exclaimed, grabbing one immediately. Stacy followed suit, both women settling down with steaming mugs of coffee.

Trip wandered over to Stacy, holding out the box. "I picked out your favorite—the French ones," he said with a slight grin.

Stacy took a bite and sighed contentedly. "Mmm, this is amazing. Good call on the donuts."

Carrie stood up, brushing off her hands. "I'll whip up some eggs for everyone. We need a little protein before hitting the road."

Jen and Stacy exchanged glances before setting down their coffee. "We'll help," Stacy offered, standing up.

Inside the kitchen, Jen grabbed a glass and filled it with water, then turned to Carrie, her expression soft. "Hey, Carrie...I'm sorry for being such a bitch yesterday. The heat and Fritz just got to me."

"Yeah, me too," Stacy added. "We had no right to treat you like that."

Carrie shook her head, a warm smile spreading across her face. "It's okay. You guys put up with me and all my antics. We're all allowed to have our moments." She pulled them both in for a hug.

"Aww, love fest in the kitchen!" Tori teased as she walked in, coffee mug in hand. She joined the hug with a grin. "The guys just said they're planning one last trip down the river to see if they can catch some smallmouths. That is, if it's okay with you, Jen."

"Yeah, go for it," Jen replied with a wave of her hand. "We'll get some girl time again."

Tori turned to Carrie. "Think you can help me make a few sandwiches for them to take?"

Even though it seemed like an odd request— so much so that Stacy and Jen exchanged puzzled looks, as if Carrie had just volunteered to wash their laundry or do something equally unpleasant—a knock at the door interrupted them. Jen walked over and cracked it open, revealing Fritz standing on the other side. He was staring down at his boots, his cowboy hat clutched to his chest, the picture of a humble gentleman.

"J...J...Jen, I'm so sorry," Fritz stammered, lifting his eyes to hers, wide and apologetic like a chastened puppy. "I don't know why I let those girls on the boat. You know you're my girl."

Jen sighed with a soft expression, and without a word, she stepped out onto the deck and grabbed his arm. She pulled him toward a corner out of sight from the others. Although they couldn't hear Jen's words, it was clear from her gestures and his nods that they were working things out.

The door flung open again, and Benny and Trip

walked in. "Looks like those kids are making up. I don't suppose she'd mind if we took the boat out to do some fishing?" Benny asked.

Stacy replied with a big smile, "Tori already asked Jen and she said yes."

The excitement Stacy exuded meant she was happy to have the morning with the girls.

"We are making you both a sandwich to take along," Tori told them, looking up from spreading mayonnaise on bread. "You could invite your girlfriends from yesterday. Did you get their numbers?" Tori was clearly stewing over Benny's antics and partying with girls at the pirate party the day before, and also his hanging out with Stacy and practically pinching her butt while playing wiffle ball.

Benny walked over to Tori and hugged her. "Aww, are you jealous? Just making new friends.

"Is that what you were doing, Trip? Stacy asked.

"No, I was drumming up some clients."

"Oh, I am sure those slutty looking women are interested in investing."

"Took some convincing, but I think yes. Besides, you didn't look too lonely yourself." Trip's irritation with her flirting showed heavily, and he walked over to the counter to fix a Bloody Mary. "Want one, Benny, before we head out?" The girls all looked at him with a scrutinizing gaze.

"No man, I'd better stick with water. It was rough getting the boat back yesterday."

"Good," Tori said, smiling and handing him the two sandwiches.

After the guys left for their fishing adventure, the girls got ready and then headed to their favorite spot at the outside bar, overlooking the glistening river. The heat of the day still lingered in the wooden slats beneath their feet. They claimed their seats with practiced ease, three of them tucking into the partial shade offered by the overhanging umbrella, while Carrie deliberately slid into the sunlit chair. The warmth kissed her skin, and she tipped her head back, soaking it in like it was her lifeline. They sipped their drinks, the condensation beading and dripping onto the table. For a while, they watched the slow churn of the water, a breeze occasionally teasing their hair.

Jen leaned back in her chair, taking a long drag from her cigarette and exhaling slowly as she turned her gaze toward Tori. "So, Tori, where's Drew flying this weekend?"

Tori didn't flinch, her expression casual as she replied, "East Coast, New York, and Philly, I believe."

Jen gazed back at her, clearly not satisfied with the simplicity of the answer. "Must be hard for you with him being gone all the time."

Tori shrugged nonchalantly. "Not all the time, just long stretches here and there. And besides, I've got my own thing. I've been doing some consulting at the house."

Jen's eyes narrowed as she took another drag from her cigarette and opened her mouth. But before she could press further, Tori quickly shifted the conversation. "Stacy, how's school going?"

Stacy grinned, leaning in a little. "Good! I've got enough credits to graduate in the spring. My instructor owns a rehabilitation facility, and she has asked me to work for her, providing rehab and massages. I'll have my own massage room and everything!"

Carrie leaned forward, clearly impressed. "Wow, that's exciting. She must be impressed with your work." Carrie then shifted the focus and asked, "Jen, how's the business going?"

"Oh, great," Jen replied, her voice tinged with exhaustion. "But it's draining. I'm trying to open a second shop, but it's proving to be more challenging than I expected. I found a location, but there's remodeling, finding staff, the list goes on. I don't have time for anything else these days."

"Maybe you should get a partner," suggested Carrie. "What about Fritz?" she half-teased.

Jen laughed, a short, dismissive sound. "Carrie, he lives here. You think he's just gonna pack up and move down by me to help run a business? Not a chance. Besides, he couldn't handle it."

Carrie grinned sheepishly. "Guess I have a rich fantasy life, as I heard once in a movie. But wow, you guys have such impressive careers. Meanwhile, I feel like I'm stuck in the complaint department at my job. The only benefit my work offers is summer hours, but that means I have to work nine hours on Mondays through Thursdays. That is such a long day, especially in the summer."

Stacy nodded sympathetically. "That sounds rough. Have you thought about starting your own business?" She asked. "I'm sure you could get a small business loan, especially being a female entrepreneur."

Carrie tilted her head thoughtfully. "Yeah, I've got ideas, but nothing solid yet."

Tori chimed in with a teasing smile. "Well, you've got time. You're what, thirty-five? I'd say you've got until forty to make it big."

Carrie laughed, a little self-deprecating. "I better get on that five-year plan, huh?"

"Let's change the subject to something a little more fun," Stacy proclaimed, leaning in with a mischievous glint in her eye. "What's up with you and that boy toy, Carrie?"

Carrie rolled her eyes but smiled. "He's not a boy toy. He's thirty-one."

Stacy raised an eyebrow, clearly amused. "Oh, he just looks like a frat boy."

Before Carrie could respond, Stacy's attention drifted to something behind her. "Speak of the devil," she muttered.

Carrie turned to see Fritz and Dodger strolling up to the back of the deck. Dodger flashed a grin and asked, "Hello, ladies. Can we join you?"

Jen glanced at the group, silently checking if everyone was okay with their conversation being interrupted. After a moment of agreement, she nodded, "Sure."

Fritz and Dodger walked around to the entrance of the deck. The sound of laughter and light conversation filled the air as they pulled up a couple of chairs, squeezing themselves into the circle with the women.

"Man, that pirate party was something else," Dodger exclaimed, leaning back in his chair and taking a sip from his drink. "These boating association events always seem to turn into anarchy. Everyone lets loose; no filters, no rules. It's like a free-for-all."

Fritz shook his head, a slight smirk playing at the corner of his lips as he ran his hand through his thick, windblown hair. The sun had caught his waves, giving them a glossy sheen. "Yeah, sure does," he agreed, his tone more resigned than amused. "You never know what's going to happen, but that's half the fun of it. Always chaotic, but never boring."

Dodger chuckled and nodded, his eyes scanning the group. "I guess that's the charm of these events. People come for the spectacle, but leave with stories." He leaned forward, resting his elbows on his knees. "But I gotta admit, I wasn't expecting that level of madness last night."

Carrie's vodka lemonade was nearly empty when Dodger gently placed his hand on her arm. "Carrie, can I get you another drink?"

She looked at him, then glanced at her glass. "Sure," she replied, offering him a small smile.

"Come with me?"

They made their way down the stairs to the outdoor bar. Dodger ordered a drink for both of them, his easy charm still in full swing. "Looks like you all are good now," he said, recalling the tension from yesterday. "See? I told you it would smooth over."

Carrie nodded, stirring her drink. "Yeah, we're fine. Things got out of hand yesterday, but I had a good time. It's always like that when we get together. We all know how to push each other's buttons."

Dodger's smile softened as he watched her, his gaze lingering a little longer than usual. He stepped a bit closer, lowering his voice. "I had a great time, too. Look, I was thinking. Can I call you sometime? I know you live a bit further away," he added, with a slight laugh, "but I do have a car, and I do drive. Unless, uh, wow, I never thought of this—unless you have a boyfriend?"

Carrie felt a flutter in her chest as their eyes locked, but something made her glance away. Her gaze fell on Conner and Bobby walking toward Brett's, probably heading for brunch. Conner's eyes flicked over to her, but she quickly turned her attention back to Dodger.

"No," Carrie shook her head. "I don't have a boyfriend. You can call me."

Dodger's smile deepened, a mix of relief and something else passing through his eyes. "Good. I'll take you up on that."

PART FIVE

2006

CHAPTER 32

Carrie stood at the bar. The conversations of patrons filled the air at The Edge as she waited for the bartender to hand her the key to the room she'd rented. Dodger and her planned a quick getaway, but they'd decided to share the space with Stacy and Trip, who were also looking for privacy from the chaos of the weekend. This new arrangement worked out well. Benny would be crashing in Jen's trailer, giving him a place to sleep without cluttering up the space. Fritz would stay in Jen's bedroom, while Tori had a bedroom to herself. It was the perfect solution—a bit of space for everyone, no one on top of each other, and plenty of time to relax and have fun.

Carrie smiled as the bartender slid the key across the counter, tucking it into her bag with a sense of relief. The weekend was shaping up to be just what they needed—a chance to escape the usual hustle and unwind. The thought of a quiet evening with Dodger, perhaps followed by a late-night drink with friends, brought a sense of anticipation. She could already feel the weight of the weekend's potential—a mix of freedom, fun, and the slight undercurrent of something more.

As Carrie gazed out at the river, she couldn't

help but feel how surreal it was to be spending the weekend with Dodger. After their departure last summer, they had started talking on the phone regularly; however, the long-distance relationship meant they had limited time together. They did enjoy a couple of dates—memorable weekends that lingered in her mind like vivid snapshots.

The first one they spent together was in the fall. Their calls had become a nightly ritual, each conversation more intense than the last. Carrie found herself counting down the minutes until she could leave work and dive into their late-night talks. His voice had an effect on her she couldn't explain—familiar and comforting, yet undeniably charged. She craved those moments, escaping into their conversations, which took her far away from the monotony of her job and the dull rhythms of her everyday life.

Sometimes Carrie couldn't believe that someone as captivating as Dodger wasn't involved with anyone else, but he had assured her he wasn't. She didn't pursue any other connections during their long-distance romance. She even stopped going to the Pub, not wanting to risk running into Dylan, in case some old spark ignited.

Their conversations never crossed into anything overtly sexual, though there was a constant undertone of flirtation that made her stomach flutter each time they spoke. They kept it light, playful—almost teasing in a way that kept her anticipating the next call. Dodger was brilliant, and Carrie couldn't help but be drawn to the depth of his thoughts. He shared stories about his job, his ideas, and the projects he worked on, each one more fascinating than the last. It wasn't just his expertise that intrigued her, but the way he spoke about it, with such passion and insight.

What captivated Carrie even more was their talks that veered into uncharted territory. Dodger shared his struggle with religion, how he found the teachings he grew up with to be confining and contradictory. She listened, fascinated, as he described his exploration into different philosophies, especially Buddhism. He attempted to understand the world in ways she never thought about—questioning everything, seeking answers in places she had never even considered. Carrie had never known anyone like him. His perspectives were so different from anything she'd seen, and they made her feel that her own life and friends, with their simple routines and predictable beliefs, were almost everyday in comparison. She admired his search for deeper meaning, and it stirred something inside her, challenging her narrow views. Inspiring growth within her.

One evening, after an intense conversation about relationships, sex, and religion, Dodger's voice softened as it did when he discussed anything significant. He hesitated for a moment before asking, "When can I come see you?" It wasn't just the typical, casual question—they'd both been feeling the heightened intensity between them, a pull that had been building with each phone call, each shared thought.

Carrie's heart skipped a beat at the thought of him being there, physically close to her, in her space. She'd imagined it countless times, how it would feel to finally be together in person, to see what their chemistry would be like beyond the phone calls and texts. She quickly suggested, "How about you come down here for the weekend? Stay at my place. The couch is all yours, promise." Her words were playful, but underneath was a layer of excitement she couldn't hide.

They made plans, setting the date with a mixture of anticipation and nervous energy. Thoughts of Dodger being in her world, in her apartment, thrilled her and left her feeling unsettled at the same time. But they were both ready for the next step, for the chance to explore whatever this connection between them might be, away from the distance of the phone and the weight of their own separate lives.

Their first date proved to be everything they had imagined and more. On Friday evening, they enjoyed an intimate dinner at a trendy restaurant downtown, perched on the edge of the river. The warm breeze drifted in from the water as they sat outside, sipping chilled white wine and savoring oysters that were far fresher than anything Carrie had ever had. As they exchanged playful glances and shared soft smiles, the connection that had sparked last summer reignited between them, stronger than before.

The conversation flowed easily, but their attention to each other grew more intense. Carrie felt the pull of Dodger's gaze, the way his eyes locked onto hers as if they shared some secret, some unspoken understanding. Without even realizing it, their hands found each other under the table, fingers interlaced. The food, once the focus of the evening, slowly faded into the background as the chemistry between them grew palpable.

After dinner, they stood hand-in-hand overlooking the river. The soft lights from the boats below reflected on the water, casting a romantic glow around them. Dodger stroked Carrie's hair, sending a shiver down her spine, before his hands slid to the back of her flowered slip dress. He gently tugged her closer, his touch sending waves of warmth through her.

She turned to face him, and the space between them vanished as he leaned down to kiss her. They engaged in a slow and tentative embrace, a gentle exploration of their longing. But soon, the kiss deepened, tongues mingling, their breaths coming faster and more urgent. Neither of them wanted to make a scene, to be the center of attention on the crowded patio, so without another word, they left the restaurant, driven by the magnetic pull between them.

Carrie and Dodger were silent for most of the drive back to her apartment. Their hearts pounded with anticipation as the wind blew through their hair, cooling them before the impending heat.

The apartment door clicked shut behind them, and for a moment, they just stood there. Dodger watched her with a calm, steady gaze—no rush, just quiet confidence. His large, muscular body towered over Carrie, and she quivered at the mere touch of his strong hands.

They shredded their clothing, both eager to give in to the passion building between them. Carrie took in his body, chest broad and solid with just a dusting of hair across his pecs. She ran her fingers across it, tracing the hard lines, feeling the warmth of his body beneath her touch.

Dodger knew just where to touch her and how to please her. Carrie responded without hesitation, running her hands through his long curly hair while she pulled his mouth to where she wanted him. She enjoyed every moment of their embrace. His strength made her feel desired and left her breathless.

Her mind briefly drifted back to Dylan. With him, things had been chaotic, electric, overwhelming, messy, and real. But with Dodger, things felt smoother, cleaner, almost too perfect.

Still, when he pulled her close afterward, his heart pounding against her cheek, she knew things were real, and it wasn't with Dylan. She didn't regret a thing.

~ ~ ~

"Hi Carrie." She got out of her thoughts and turned to see Conner standing next to her.

Conner's presence felt like a sudden shift in the air, pulling her attention away from everything else. He looked different—more rugged, somehow. His hair, once neatly styled, was now grown out, giving him a more relaxed look. The stubble on his face added an edge she hadn't noticed before. It wasn't just his appearance that had changed, though; there was something in the way he carried himself, a quiet confidence that caught Carrie off guard.

"Conner. I wasn't expecting to see you here this weekend. Don't you have a child now?" She asked in a slightly harsh tone.

He winced and took a swig of his beer. "I do, but I come here every year at this time. Jill is at home with Trevor. I'm leaving tomorrow. Marcy and her friends are having a bachelorette party."

Conner's reply comforted her. She did not need any complications with him as she tried to get to know Dodger.

"I do have some news for you, though. I'm not sure if you've heard, but your ex-husband is coming this weekend. Marcy has a friend up here, Sherry, who knows him from a long time ago. She said he's coming with some friends, staying at Anglers down the river."

Carrie remembered Sherry all too well, especially her phone number, which she found in Tom's pants pocket. She summoned the bartender over and ordered a vodka lemonade. Just thinking about Tom gave her the urge to drink. She took a long sip and looked over at Conner. "I didn't hear."

Just then, the hostess came over to confirm Carrie's room and let her know if she needed more towels or paper products, to stop back. Carrie thanked her and turned back to Conner.

"You're not staying at Jen's?" Conner asked, looking confused.

"No, it was getting too crowded. I rented a room here. Stacy and Trip, and me, and...," she stopped herself, because it was none of his business. She took a big drink, finishing the small drink. "I have to go," Carrie stated as she walked out the back door that led to the rooms.

Conner quickly replied, "I didn't mean to hurt you, Carrie."

Carrie's lips curved into a faint smile as she strolled down the hallway, her heels clicking softly on the tiled floor. She felt lighter, freer. For once, she didn't feel the restless flicker of "what if" shadowing her thoughts, no stolen glances searching for Conner in a crowd. That was over now—he had his life, his family.

Reaching her door, she slipped the key into the lock, turned it, and pushed it open. The faint scent of lemon cleaner greeted her. She stepped inside, her eyes scanning the two full-sized beds with their plain comforters, the small TV perched in the corner like an afterthought. The narrow bathroom door stood ajar, revealing just enough to suggest it would be a squeeze for two women sharing the space. She chuckled softly, imagining the morning chaos.

Dropping her bag on one of the beds, she pressed her palms against the worn bedspread. The room wasn't much—shabby walls and simple furnishings—

but it would work for them. It felt like a clean slate, one she could make hers for the weekend. She exhaled, feeling a rare sense of ease settle over her.

A loud car horn announced the arrival of her roommates. Carrie glanced over to see Stacy and Trip unloading bags, arms full as they made their way toward the room. With a sigh, Carrie realized she still needed to grab her bags. She turned toward her modest Saturn, parked right beside Trip's sleek, shiny BMW—a stark contrast that made her smile. Trip's career was clearly thriving. She remembered Stacy gushing about the winter cruise he had surprised her with—a sign that things were going well for him.

"This place is a pit!" yelled Trip, his face scrunched in disapproval as he set down his bags. He peered into the bathroom. "Do they even clean in here? Stacy, I hope you brought some disinfectant spray."

"Oh, geez, it's not that bad," Stacy replied, unloading her bag of goods to make a cocktail. Come on, this is our favorite; the Fourth of July weekend! It may not be the cruise ship or a fancy hotel, but this is Riverbanks."

Riverbanks planned to kick off the Independence Day celebrations early since the holiday fell on a Tuesday, and the buzz of excitement hinted that someone—probably Larry—would be setting off fireworks before long. The group was thrilled about having more space to spread out this year, but the plan was still to gather on Jen's deck, as always.

"Let's fix a drink and head over to Jen's trailer," Stacy suggested.

"Let me change first. I've still got my driving clothes on," Carrie replied, heading to the bathroom.

A few minutes later, Carrie emerged wearing a short denim skirt that showed off her golden tan. Stacy, lounging on the bed with Trip and half-watching something on TV, turned to look at her. Her eyes widened in surprise.

"Wow," Stacy exclaimed, unable to hold back her reaction. "It's surprising you can still rock that look at your age."

Trip glanced up from the TV, his expression shifting to irritation. "Yeah, Carrie, aren't you a little old for that look?"

Carrie paused, one hand resting on the doorframe, and shot him a sharp look. "Well, at least I don't dress like I'm forty-five," she quipped, letting her gaze flick pointedly over Trip's rust-colored button-up Henley and cargo shorts.

Trip frowned, looking down at his outfit. "I do not," he muttered defensively. "You don't have any style, Carrie. Anyway, you girls finish up. I'm heading over to Jen's." He grabbed his drink and walked out, his irritation trailing behind him.

Stacy rolled her eyes as she refreshed her glass. "Don't listen to him, Carrie. You look at least five years younger than you are. He's just in a mood."

"That's probably because I don't have any

children," Carrie answered and went back in the kitchen to check her hair and makeup.

"That's why I'm not having any children," Stacy yelled back to her.

Carrie poked her head out of the bathroom door. "Doesn't Trip want kids?"

Stacy set her drink down with a clink and placed her hands on her slim hips, giving Carrie a disbelieving look. "You honestly think I'm marrying Trip? Get real." Her tone was incredulous, but Carrie saw the teasing glint in her eye. Then, as if to change the subject, Stacy spun on her heel and posed playfully. "How do I look?"

She wore what had become her signature Riverbanks outfit: a silky camisole top paired with loose, cargo-style pants rolled up to her knees, accentuating her curves in just the right way.

"You look great," Carrie told her as her thoughts wandered. This weekend was already off to a curious start—what else could it have in store?

"I'm heading to Jen's," Stacy said, grabbing her drink. "You coming?"

"No, I'm going to wait for Dodger," Carrie replied, leaning back against the doorframe.

Stacy's grin widened. "Oh yeah, your boy toy. I bet he makes you feel young." She shot Carrie a knowing look before sauntering out, her hips swaying as she went.

He certainly made Carrie feel young. When

Dodger arrived, he filled the doorway like a scene out of a dream, a bag dangling from each hand as his muscled arms flexed beneath a tank top. The sunlight framed him, highlighting the tousled curls that fell across his face, partially obscuring his playful grin. His smile broke through the shadows, warm and unguarded, as he exclaimed, "Hello, gorgeous," in that low, teasing tone that sent a shiver down her spine.

Before Carrie could respond, he strode across the room, dropped the bags, and swept her up. She landed on the bed with a breathless laugh, but the playfulness shifted quickly. His hand slid beneath her skirt, his fingers brushing against her skin with a touch that was both tender and deliberate. His lips found hers, slow and savoring, before trailing down to her neck, his breath hot and urgent. Every caress, every kiss dissolved her thoughts until there was no Conner, no Tom—only the sensation of Dodger and the way he made her feel alive again.

~ ~ ~

When Carrie and Dodger strolled up to Jen's trailer, the savory aroma of grilled meat filled the air, mingling with the thrum of music that set the tone for the evening. Stacy was in Lala Land, dancing solo, her hips swaying and her arms in the air as she moved to the irresistible beat of Gnarls Barkley's Crazy. The bassline seemed to vibrate through the entire scene, adding energy to the warm summer night.

At the patio table, Jen and Fritz sat looking completely at ease, their conversation punctuated by laughter. They each nursed margaritas in colorful glasses, the rims dusted with salt, as they dipped chips into a bowl of chunky salsa. Jen leaned back in her chair, her sunglasses perched atop her head, while Fritz, as usual, looked unhurried and amused.

The screen door creaked open, and out came Benny, sporting a crisp apron over his button-down and chinos. In one hand, he carried a platter piled high with sizzling meat, but the music got the better of him. He paused mid-step to bump hips with Stacy.

"Carrie!" Benny called out, his voice cutting through the music. "You made it! We were waiting for you, hon." Balancing a platter of burgers, he walked down the steps and kissed her cheek. "Hey, uh, Dodger, right?"

"Yeah, man." Dodger extended a hand, giving Benny a firm shake. "Good to see you again."

"Same here." Benny nodded with a grin. "I've got brats cooking, and the burgers are about to go on. Tori's inside working on the sides."

Carrie glanced toward the trailer and then back at Benny. "Wow, what a sound system! What are you guys listening to?"

"Spotify," Benny replied. "Laptop's inside. Go on up and join the party!" He turned back toward the grill, carefully placing burgers over the sizzling flames.

Carrie and Dodger climbed the steps to the deck, passing Stacy, who twirled, still lost in the music. They made their way to the patio table, where Dodger ruffled Fritz's hair and offered a fist bump greeting.

Carrie settled into a chair and glanced around. The atmosphere on Jen's deck felt different this year—more polished, as if everyone had stepped up their game. Perhaps it was the extra space, or maybe something else. She couldn't help but notice Trip was nowhere in sight, and Stacy was dancing alone.

"Stacy, where's Trip?" Carrie asked, leaning back in her chair.

"I don't know." Stacy shrugged, barely missing a beat. "He probably went to the bar."

Just as Carrie thought, great way to start the weekend, Brandon appeared, as if he could sense Stacy was feeling flirty and without Trip. He bounded up the stairs two at a time, a confident grin on his face, and immediately joined Stacy on the makeshift dance floor.

Brandon, now a year older and undeniably handsome, moved with an ease that caught everyone's attention. Stacy's demeanor shifted; her playful dancing became more suggestive as she mirrored his moves. Their chemistry was undeniable as they danced closely. But as the song faded, they casually separated. Brandon collapsed into a chair next to Jen, breathing hard, while Stacy slid into a seat beside Carrie, across from him.

Jen smirked, turning toward Brandon. "You

again? We can't seem to get rid of you, can we?" she teased, but her gaze flicked to Stacy with an edge of knowing. Stacy averted her eyes, taking a long sip from her drink.

Benny appeared on the deck, carrying a platter of grilled meat. Spotting Brandon, he grinned. "My man! Look at you—older, taller. So, does that mean you're finally coming to the bar with us?"

Brandon chuckled, running a hand through his hair. "Not yet, but you better believe I'm sneaking in tonight. I need someone to cover for me." He shot a sly look at Stacy.

Jen sighed dramatically, crushing out her cigarette. "Alright, alright. Let's get dinner on the table. And Brandon, you need to beat it."

Tori poked her head out of the trailer just in time to chime in. "Yeah, scram, squirt!"

Brandon laughed, raising his hands in mock surrender, but didn't budge from his chair.

CHAPTER 33

Later in the evening, after dinner and cleanup, the group headed to The Edge—everyone except Trip, who opted to stay at Brett's to watch the baseball game. The rest were excited about the '90s cover band playing that night. By the time they arrived, the place was already buzzing with energy, but they managed to find a spot at the bar. Jen and Carrie perched on stools, while Fritz and Dodger drifted toward a group of their friends, leaving Benny, Tori, and Stacy swaying along to the band as it warmed up with some familiar tunes.

In one corner of the bar, a rowdy group of women drew everyone's attention, their laughter and cheers cutting through the crowd. One woman, clearly the star of the night, wore a sparkling crown and commanded the room. Shots lined the table in front of them, and they were already halfway into the festivities, dancing and singing along to the warm-up music.

Marcy was among them, as was Sherry, both fully immersed in the chaos. A few men hung around the group, vying for attention. One by one, the men took off their shirts while the queen of the group rotated between their laps, doing shots and laughing uproariously. The whole scene was a spectacle—a wild mix of bawdy humor and unfiltered revelry that seemed to set the tone for the night.

Jen leaned over to Carrie, smirking. "Well, there's Riverbanks for you."

"That's right, Marcy's friends are having a bachelorette party," Carrie replied to Jen, nodding toward the group of women.

"How do you know?" Jen asked, glancing over her shoulder, surprised to see Benny not ogling the ladies.

"Conner told me. I ran into him earlier when I was checking in." Carrie hesitated for a moment, then added, "He also mentioned Tom's coming up for the weekend. He's staying at Anglers with some friends." Her face tightened with concern as she looked at Jen.

Jen's eyes widened. "Wait, backup. You saw Conner? Is he here with Jill and the baby?"

"No, he left today." Carrie's gaze flicked back to the bachelorette party. "Because of that." She didn't elaborate on the baby.

Jen leaned in closer, lowering her voice. "Did you talk to him for a while?"

"Hell no." Carrie shook her head sharply and turned away, her eyes landing on Dodger across the room. He was talking animatedly with his friends, his easy charm on full display. Catching her gaze, he smiled, and Carrie couldn't help but smile back.

As the evening went on, the bar grew more crowded, bodies pressing together in the dim, pulsing light. The crowd's density made it easy for Brandon to slip in unnoticed. Benny spotted him, waved him over, and ordered him a beer. Then Brandon whisked Stacy off to the dance floor as "Slide" blasted from the speakers. The pair moved in sync, their chemistry drawing attention from those nearby.

Not one to miss the action, Benny grabbed Tori's hand and pulled her onto the floor. Soon, Jen, Fritz, Carrie, and Dodger joined in, losing themselves to the music's rhythm. When the band transitioned into Santeria, the energy turned electric. The sultry beat had everyone moving closer, bodies entwined as laughter and the occasional cheer punctuated the steamy atmosphere.

As the song faded into If You Could Only See, the mood shifted. Dodger pulled Carrie into a gentle sway, his hand firm at her waist, while Jen and Fritz moved together nearby. The dance floor felt smaller, more intimate, as couples leaned into each other, absorbed by the slow melody.

When the song ended, Carrie and the others returned to the bar, flushed and grinning. But as they approached, they noticed their seats were empty.

"Where'd they go?" Carrie asked, scanning the room.

Jen frowned, looking around. "Do you see Benny or Tori?"

Dodger shook his head. "Too packed in here."

They all looked around, trying to spot their friends, but the sea of moving bodies and the dim lights made it impossible to tell where anyone had gone. A sense of curiosity and unease settled over them as they exchanged glances.

"Thank God we still have our seats!" Carrie exclaimed as she quickly sat down.

"Maybe they went to the bathroom," Fritz said. "Dodger, come with me to look around?"

"Yeah sure, you girls sit tight," he replied as he kissed Carrie sensually.

Carrie and Jen looked at each other, puzzled. "Where the hell is everyone?" Jen inquired.

"I don't know," Carrie looked around, "but I just don't want to run into Tom."

As the opening chords of "Give It Away" blasted through the bar, a man from the bachelorette party suddenly appeared in front of Jen, a mischievous grin on his face. Without a word, he took her hand and gently tugged her off her chair, pulling her toward the makeshift dance floor.

Carrie watched, wide-eyed, as Jen laughed but didn't resist, her usual composure slipping away. The man swayed close, moving his hips with exaggerated flair, and Jen surprised everyone by matching his energy. She swung her hips to the beat, her hair spilling over her shoulders as she leaned into the rhythm.

Carrie's jaw dropped when Jen upped the ante,

grinding against the dancer with unexpected boldness. The crowd whooped as the man reached for the hem of his shirt, teasingly pulling it up to reveal his toned abs. Jen threw her head back, laughing, her movements seamlessly in sync with his.

Fritz stormed through the crowd in a fury. Before anyone could react, he grabbed Jen's arm and yanked her away from the dancer with such force that she stumbled backward into Carrie, who caught her just in time.

The room seemed to hold its breath as Fritz turned his attention to the dancer, gripping him by the shoulders and lifting him slightly off the ground. "That's my girlfriend!" he roared, his voice cutting through the music. "I ought to bash your head in!"

Fritz's eyes burned with a wild intensity, and the dancer froze, his earlier bravado replaced by sheer panic.

Dodger grabbed Fritz in an instant, wrapping an arm around him and pulling him away. "Fritz, chill out!" he commanded. "They were just having fun— nothing to freak out about."

The dancer backed away quickly, smoothing down his shirt and holding his hands up in a gesture of surrender. "Hey, man, no harm meant," he grumbled, his voice shaky but calm. "I thought she was part of the group. It was just for laughs. I didn't mean anything by it."

Fritz's fists clenched, his chest heaving, but Dodger's firm grip kept him grounded. The tension slowly began to dissolve as the crowd returned its attention to the music, leaving Jen, Carrie, and the others to deal with the aftermath of Fritz's outburst.

Fritz stared him down and then turned to Jen, taking her arm. "Come on, Jen, let's get out of here."

Jen brushed away his hand. "No! I'm staying. He did nothing wrong. You can leave if you want."

Dodger turned to Carrie, who stood next to her barstool. "Are you alright if I take him somewhere else? I don't want him to be by himself."

"Of course. I'll stay with Jen and calm her down, and then we'll find you. At Brett's or the outdoor bar?"

"Yes, thanks." He smiled and kissed her lightly, then grabbed Fritz by the arm and led him out through the crowd.

Bobby slithered up to them with a sly grin, his drink in hand, exuding an air of nonchalance. "Looks like you've got yourself a hothead there, Jen. Better keep an eye on him," he advised, his voice dripping with mock concern.

Jen stepped toward him, her face a mix of irritation and defiance. "Shut up, Bobby! What are you even doing here? Crashing a bachelorette party? Or are the dancers more your thing?" Her eyes darted pointedly to his outfit—tight black shirt clinging to his frame, hair slicked back and tied in a small ponytail.

Bobby chuckled, unfazed. "Nah, I'm just here for

the '90s jams. Always been a fan." He took a leisurely sip of his drink, then winked. "Take care, ladies."

He sauntered off, his tight shorts drawing simultaneous head shakes from Jen and Carrie.

Carrie reached for Jen's hand. "Come on, let's go find the others," she said, pulling her away from the lingering tension.

The parking lot outside Brett's was alive with commotion as Carrie and Jen approached. Raised voices cut through the night, unmistakably Trip's, and as they got closer, they saw him gripping Brandon by the neck. Stacy clung to Trip's arm, desperately trying to pull him off.

"I ought to break your fucking neck, you little punk!" Trip roared, his face red with anger.

"Trip, let go of him!" Stacy pleaded, panic in her voice.

"What the hell is going on? Trip, Jesus Christ, let him go!" Jen shouted as they neared.

"That's right, let him go," came a calm yet menacing voice. Bobby strode forward, flanked by two imposing men.

Trip hesitated, his grip loosening just enough for Brandon to squirm free and dart behind his father. Bobby instinctively threw an arm out to shield his son, glaring at Trip. Despite Trip's size advantage, Bobby's companions looked formidable, and they weren't smiling.

"What's this all about?" Bobby asked, his voice

deceptively calm.

Trip pointed a finger at Brandon, his rage undiminished. "Your no-good son has been sniffing around my girlfriend, and I've had enough. I came out here for a smoke, and there they were, sneaking around together."

Bobby's eyes narrowed, but his tone remained steady. "Maybe you should keep your girlfriend in check."

Trip's face twisted with fury. "Get lost, you faggot."

Bobby blinked, then smiled coldly, holding up his left hand to display his wedding ring. "Faggot? Faggot? Dude, I'm married."

Trip sneered. "I'd go after dudes, too, if I had a wife like yours. You're gayer than a bag of dicks."

That was it. Bobby lunged, fist raised, but Benny appeared out of nowhere and shoved him back before the punch could land. At the same time, Dodger and Fritz rushed in, planting themselves between the two men.

"Bobby, man, we don't need any trouble," Dodger said, hands outstretched in a gesture of peace. "Trip's upset, but no one's hurt. Let him sort it out with Stacy and call it a night."

Bobby glanced at Brandon, who was tugging on his sleeve. "Yeah, come on, Dad. Let's go."

Bobby's nostrils flared, but he relented, taking a step back. "Fine. But if you touch my son again—"

Trip cut him off with a sneer. "And what?"

Bobby didn't answer, his glare doing all the talking. Finally, he turned, ushering Brandon and his men away.

"Just stay away from him," Bobby threw over his shoulder before disappearing into the night.

The men turned and walked off toward their trailer, Brandon glancing back over his shoulder. His eyes lingered on Stacy, who stared back at him.

Carrie and Jen moved to Stacy's side as Tori appeared from the shadows, her timing as impeccable as Benny's. Dodger and Fritz rejoined the group, while Benny guided Trip a few steps away to cool him off.

"You girls okay?" Dodger asked, wrapping Carrie protectively in his arms. Fritz followed suit, pulling Jen into a reassuring hug.

Benny returned with Trip, who still wore the remnants of his anger but seemed composed enough to avoid further conflict.

"Let's all head back and call it a night," Benny suggested, his tone light but firm. "The last thing we need is to get kicked out of the bar for causing a scene."

Jen turned to Benny, irritation sharpening her voice. "Where did you and Tori disappear to earlier? We couldn't find either of you."

Benny glanced around nervously, scratching the back of his neck. "Uh, we went for a walk. It was getting hot in The Edge with all that dancing."

Tori nodded quickly, her head down. "Yeah, you know me—I hate crowds. Besides, you guys were slow dancing. It was cute."

The group walked back to their trailers, the tension of the night trailing behind them like a cloud of smoke. As they reached Jen's, she turned with a wry smile and declared, "I always say, you don't have to give 'er the first night."

CHAPTER 34

Carrie woke early to the quiet stillness of the morning, her head throbbing faintly. Stacy had begged her to stay up for a few drinks after they got back from the fiasco at Brett's the night before, and she'd reluctantly agreed. Dodger didn't mind—he was worn out from the long day at work and the drama of the night. Besides, intimacy wasn't an option with Trip and Stacy sharing their room. Dodger had promised her a surprise in the morning before drifting off to sleep, while Trip, thoroughly drunk, had passed out almost instantly.

Carrie and Stacy had grabbed the half-empty box of wine from Stacy's cooler and decided to head outside. Though the bars were still open, the idea of running into anyone was less appealing than the peaceful solitude of the pier.

It was a warm, still night, the kind that made the river feel alive but calm. They'd brought a light blanket from the room to keep the mosquitoes at bay. Sitting on the pier, they filled their red Solo cups from the box's spigot, the soft gurgle of the wine the only sound breaking the silence. They sipped slowly, gazing out at the dark river as it shimmered under the faint moonlight, their conversation muted.

"Do you want to tell me what's going on with you and Brandon?" Carrie asked, her voice low but pointed. "Did Trip catch you in the act?"

Stacy sipped her wine and gave Carrie a sidelong glance.

"No, he didn't see anything. We were just smoking, but that alone was enough to set him off."

Carrie leaned in. "But what didn't he see? You were gone for quite a while."

Stacy sighed, her gaze shifting to the rippling water before turning back to Carrie.

"All that dancing earlier—it got me worked up, you know? Then you and Jen were off slow dancing with your guys, and I, well, I wanted that too. But not there, not with everyone around." She paused, biting her lip. "So, we went outside. Close enough to the bar where we could still hear the music. We danced close, and then we kissed. A lot."

The irony wasn't lost on either of them when "Promiscuous Girl" started thumping in the distance from The Edge.

"Carrie," Stacy continued, her tone softer now, "I see him from time to time. Trip has no clue. You know the rehab center where I work, right? The one where I do massages? I get an hour-long lunch break—an hour. What do you think I do with that time, sometimes?" She laughed darkly.

Carrie's eyes widened, but she kept quiet as Stacy went on.

"And it's not just at lunch. We plan things, especially when Trip says he's going out of town. I know he's seeing that co-worker of his. He thinks I don't know, but I do."

Stacy's words hung heavy in the air, the faint music from the bar now a surreal soundtrack to her confession.

Carrie and Stacy had grown close over the past year, often spending long afternoons together venting about life, relationships, and the challenges of juggling it all. Stacy had confided in Carrie more than once about her suspicions that Trip was seeing someone else. There were the late nights when he didn't come home, the unexplained "work trips," and the texts he guarded like state secrets. Carrie had always assumed Stacy's bitterness and sly comments about Trip's fidelity were her simmering frustrations—natural when a relationship was as tense as theirs.

But this? An illicit fling with Brandon? It blindsided her. Brandon, of all people—the much younger, cocky son of Bobby and Marcy—was the last person Carrie would have guessed Stacy would turn to. Now, sitting on the pier with Stacy's shocking confession hanging between them, Carrie felt torn. On one hand, she wanted to berate Stacy for risking so much with someone so immature and reckless. On the other hand, she couldn't deny understanding the temptation to seek comfort outside of a relationship that felt suffocating and loveless.

"God, what in the world? Why are you even together?" Carrie blurted out.

"I don't know, but it's not going to last. I don't want to be with Brandon either. He is too young, and his family scares me. Bobby, there's something about him. But for now, Brandon's fun to have sex with."

They laughed and talked for about another hour, sharing bedroom stories about Dodger and Brandon. Carrie didn't mind. She didn't care for Trip too much. He was chauvinistic and hot-headed, and her allegiance was to Stacy. They finished the box of wine and pulled out the guts to squeeze out the very last of it. As they stumbled into the room around 1:30 a.m., they were careful not to wake the men.

Carrie rubbed her temples, feeling the dull throb of a lingering headache. Turning to the other side of the bed, she noticed it was empty except for a folded note on the pillow that read, Went for coffee. She groaned softly and glanced at the clock—8:45. Stacy and Trip were still out cold in the other bed.

Digging into her bag, she pulled out a small bottle of aspirin, popped a couple of tablets, and washed them down with a sip of water from the bottle on the nightstand. Just as she was settling back into bed, there was a knock at the door. Still dressed in her pajama shorts and tank top, she hesitated for a moment but figured it had to be someone from their group.

She swung open the door to find Jen standing there, holding two steaming mugs of coffee and flashing a knowing smile.

"Morning," Jen said, handing Carrie one of the steaming mugs. "Brought you some coffee." She peeked inside, catching a glimpse of Stacy and Trip still fast asleep. "Where's Dodger?"

"He went to get coffee, but I'll take this," Carrie replied, gratefully accepting the mug. She stepped outside, the cool morning air brushing against her bare arms. "What's up? It's kind of early."

Jen took a sip of her coffee, her eyes darting toward the pier. "Come with me," she said. "We need to talk."

"Tom came to my trailer this morning," Jen said, her voice low.

"What?" Carrie replied, her eyes widening in shock.

"I was on the deck having coffee, and he came walking up. Everyone else was sleeping. He came to see you, but I told him you weren't staying with me. He asked where, but I was pretty vague. I'm sure he figured it out. He wanted to know if he could see you today, but I told him we have plans during the day. Tom would like to see you early this evening and asked if you could meet him at the outdoor bar."

"I thought he stopped drinking." Carrie wondered.

"He did, or at least I think he did. He looked good and was very nice. I thought you would prefer a public place. We can all go too and hang out while you talk somewhere. It's up to you. I can understand why you wouldn't want to, but all he wants to do is talk. Maybe make amends. Anyway, did Dodger tell you about the plan for today?"

"No, he told me last night that he had a surprise, but he was gone when I woke up."

"Fritz and I, and you and Dodger, are going to Rocky Point beach. It's about half an hour away, it's amazing. There are rocks all around and even some little caves."

"How come we've never gone there?" Carrie asked curiously.

"I never heard of it. The locals know about it, it's a hidden gem."

"So just the four of us? What about Benny and Tori? And Stacy and Trip?"

"Benny can take them out on my boat. We won't be gone all day. I want to get away from the drama for today."

Carrie thought about it; Stacy would likely be upset being left alone with Trip, but she wanted some alone time with Dodger and didn't feel it was her responsibility to make sure she had fun. She seemed to do fine in that department.

"Okay, but let's not be gone all day. We came here this weekend to be together, and I don't want the rest to feel left out."

Jen put out her cigarette and stepped on it. "You

got it. We'll have some lunch, maybe swim and throw a frisbee around, and then we'll be back. Just in time for you to talk to Tom."

~ ~ ~

The sun glistened bright in the sky as they drove to the beach in Fritz's truck, cruising through miles of open farmland. Carrie wore a sundress over her swimsuit, her knees pulled up and feet resting on the front seat, her flip-flops kicked off. Dodger's hand slid gently up her calf, teasingly brushing her skin before creeping higher. She lightly swatted his hand away with a playful grin, lowering her legs.

Up front, Jen and Fritz were belting out the lyrics to a country song playing on the radio, their voices blending with the music. Fritz glanced in the rearview mirror and smirked at what he saw.

Carrie couldn't remember the last time she felt so alive, so desired. Dodger's presence lit something inside her, and she couldn't help but steal glances at him. His strong thighs rested under his swim trunks, and a noticeable bulge was beginning to press against the fabric. She leaned closer, unable to resist. Her lips met his for a tender kiss, their connection deepening for just a moment before she pulled back, a little breathless. His head dipped, his hair falling across his face, and the musky hint of his cologne lingered between them.

They arrived at the beach to a packed parking lot,

but Fritz managed to find a spot. They unloaded their cooler, beach bags, and a couple of large blankets, ready to rest their sweaty skin under the midday sun.

Carrie slipped off her sundress, revealing a modest yet flattering red tankini. She couldn't help but feel self-conscious compared to the younger, toned women on the beach. Jen, on the other hand, confidently rocked a bikini top paired with a short swim skirt. Her blonde hair, pulled into a ponytail, was soon let loose to cascade down her shoulders.

The group wasted no time heading into the water to cool off.

Carrie hesitated at first, reluctant to get her hair wet. Dodger grinned, splashing her lightly. "Come on, your hair already looks great—kind of beachy."

With a reluctant laugh, she finally dunked under, only to surface and tug him down with her. They both came up sputtering and laughing, and Dodger caught her in his arms. They floated together, their lips meeting in soft, unhurried kisses.

Nearby, Jen swam toward Fritz, who stood waiting with open arms and pure adoration as she leapt into his embrace, both of them laughing like teenagers.

After an hour of swimming, they worked up an appetite and returned to their blankets for lunch. Carrie and Jen had packed a spread of hummus with fresh vegetables, crusty bread, cheese, olives, and slices of salami. They even brought a chilled bottle of white wine, which Jen poured into small plastic cups for herself, Carrie, and Dodger. Fritz stuck with a can of Coke, eyeing the wine with mock disdain.

"What, no salsa, babe?" Fritz teased, dipping a carrot into the hummus. Jen scooped up a handful of sand and tossed it lightly in his direction, laughing.

Once they'd eaten and packed up, Carrie grabbed Dodger's hand. "Let's go for a walk," she suggested, the warmth of the wine adding a rosy glow to her cheeks.

Jen pulled Fritz up as well, the two couples heading in opposite directions along the shore. The golden evening light stretched across the sand as the beach began to quiet. Dinner hour was approaching, and the crowd started to thin, leaving the shore bathed in peaceful stillness.

"Do you think there will be fireworks tonight?" Carrie asked as they walked hand in hand, barefoot in the sand.

"I can arrange some fireworks," he snickered, looking at her devilishly.

"We share a room with Stacy and Trip. How is that going to happen?"

"Come this way." He led her off the beach to a wooded area, far away from the parking lot and hidden from the beach. He sat down and leaned against a tree, spreading his legs slightly.

"No blanket?"

"We don't need one. Come here," Dodger pointed to his lap.

Carrie obliged and straddled his lap, facing him. She lifted his t-shirt off and tossed it to the ground. He picked her up slightly to move her swim bottom over and pulled himself out of his swim trunks to enter her. She cupped his face as their lips touched, and Dodger murmured, "You're already wet." She moved around enough for them both to climax; it didn't take long. After they finished, he leaned back against the tree. "Holy shit, that was so hot."

She stood up and brushed dirt off her legs, looking around for something to wipe herself with. "Damn, I wish I had my towel."

Dodger grabbed a big leaf off the ground and handed it to her. "Use this," he said, smiling. He stood up and took her in his arms, kissing her. "Here, use my shirt. I don't care."

"Thanks," Carrie replied and grabbed the shirt to wipe down between her legs. "Let's get back before they wonder where we are." She balled up his shirt and offered to carry it back.

They headed for the parking lot and could see Jen and Fritz off in the distance. They were standing on the blanket where they ate, dancing to music from a small radio they must have gotten from Fritz's truck. They held hands, pulling each other back, swinging to the music in a circle. Jen was singing, and Fritz looked up to the sky, smiling, almost childlike.

Carrie turned to Dodger and asked, "What does Fritz do?"

He looked down at her curiously. "What do you mean?"

"I mean for a living, a job," she replied.

Dodger kicked some rocks in front of him and answered, "Nothing really. He does odd jobs, deliveries, and other tasks. But he can't do much; he's on disability. That's why he lives with his mom. But it's okay, he's got Jen."

Carrie wondered, Does he actually have Jen? She only sees him on weekends in the summer, maybe a few times in the winter, but she's so busy with her store. He must be happy with what he gets, she thought.

CHAPTER 35

When they arrived back at the trailer, the deck was empty. They noticed their friends gathered on the grassy area across from Jen's trailer. Stacy stood poised on the makeshift pitcher's mound, a ball in hand, while Benny held a bat, crouched and ready to swing. Tori and Brandon stood in the outfield, baseball caps tilted low, looking like a casual team cobbled together for fun.

Stacy wound up and pitched the ball. Benny swung hard, sending it soaring into the sky. Brandon dove, his arms outstretched to catch it, but the ball slipped past him and landed in the grass.

"Whooooow!" Benny whooped, tossing the bat dramatically. He took off in an exaggerated run around imaginary bases, grinning like a kid. Tossing his cap to the ground, he grabbed Brandon in a playful headlock. "You thought you had that one, didn't you? Haha!"

The game ended, and they wandered back toward Carrie, Jen, Dodger, and Fritz, shaking their heads at Benny's antics. Carrie scanned the scene, her eyes darting around. Something—or someone was missing.

"Where's Trip?" Jen asked, her gaze settling on Stacy.

Stacy shrugged, tossing the ball back and forth in her hands casually. "He left. We were out boating earlier and tied up at the lake. Brandon came over to join us, and we started playing a game of water baseball. Trip played along for a bit, but then he got annoyed about something. When we got back, he called me a liar and a tramp, packed up, and stormed off. Guess I'll need a ride home with you." Her tone was so detached that it was hard to tell if she even cared.

Jen folded her arms, her brows furrowing. "Why is Brandon hanging out with you guys? After what happened last night, I don't think that's very smart." Her stern gaze landed squarely on Stacy.

"Nothing happened last night." Stacy's tone was firm as she locked eyes with Jen. "And Brandon likes hanging out with Benny. That's all."

Jen crossed her arms, her voice tight. "Well, he shouldn't be here. Bobby's bound to come sniffing around for him."

Brandon leaned against the trailer and sighed. "Fine, Jen. I'll leave."

Benny, clearly annoyed, threw his hands up. "Aww, come on. He's a fun dude! And now that Trip's gone—"

Before he could finish, Stacy turned and marched into the trailer, slamming the door behind her. The rest of the group stood in the awkward silence that followed, shifting uncomfortably.

Jen stepped closer to Benny, grabbing his arm to make her point. "Don't you think it's shitty how Stacy's acting? Flirting and flaunting it in front of Trip like that? No wonder he left."

Benny pulled his arm free and frowned. "No, I don't. Because Trip can be an asshole—you know that, Jen." Without waiting for a response, he walked off toward Fritz and Dodger. "So, how was the beach?" he asked, slipping easily into a conversation as the guys huddled up, falling into easy conversation.

Meanwhile, Carrie, Jen, and Tori headed toward the deck. Jen shook her head, clearly still fuming. "I don't know," she said, "but Stacy? I don't trust that girl. Trip might be an asshole, but she came with him. She could show at least a little respect."

"Speaking of assholes, Tom came looking for you earlier." Tori cut in, stopping what could have been an argument.

Carrie froze mid-step. "What?"

"Yeah," Tori continued, "Apparently, you were supposed to meet up with him?

"That's right—I was expecting to see you at the outdoor bar."

The voice came from behind them, and everyone turned in surprise. Tom stood by the stairs, his presence like a ghost from the past but distinctly changed. He didn't step up onto the deck, just hovered at the bottom, looking up.

Tom was slimmer now, fit and tan, wearing dark blue swim trunks and an old Led Zeppelin t-shirt that clung to his chiseled frame. His face had thinned, giving his features a sharper, more defined look. His hair was still cropped close and dark, but his eyes stood out—once hardened and haunted, they now held a softened, sober clarity.

Carrie glanced toward the guys. Dodger had noticed Tom but didn't intervene, keeping his distance and chatting with Fritz and Benny. She turned back to Tom, unsure of what to say, and finally walked to the edge of the deck. Jen and Tori stayed where they were, their expressions guarded.

"Tom, I heard you were here," Carrie said, her voice quiet and uncertain.

"You look great," Tom replied, his gaze steady. "Did Jen give you my message?"

"She did," Carrie nodded. "But we had plans today, and we just got back."

As if on cue, the guys started wandering over toward the deck. Benny was the first to greet him, slapping Tom lightly on the back.

"Hey, man! I heard you were around. You look good."

"Thanks, Benny," Tom said with a faint smile. "I gave up the hooch—you've probably heard. Does wonders for the body and soul."

"Well, that's great, Tom." Benny looked down at

the beer in his hand and chuckled awkwardly. "Hope you don't mind if I keep enjoying mine. Can't let a brewski go warm."

Dodger stepped beside Carrie, casually slipping an arm around her waist. Carrie felt the gesture anchor her. "Dodger, this is my ex-husband, Tom. Tom, this is Dodger, my, uh…" She hesitated.

"Boyfriend," Dodger finished smoothly, holding out his hand.

Tom took it with a firm shake. "Nice to meet you." He let his hand drop and looked at Carrie. "Hey, would you mind if we talked in private for a bit? We need to catch up."

Dodger glanced at Carrie, his expression calm. "Sure. Fritz and I were going to catch some of the game at Brett's anyway."

Benny leaned toward Carrie and asked quietly, "Do you want me to stick around?"

Carrie shook her head. "No, it's okay. You keep them company." She cast a reassuring glance at Jen and Tori. "I won't be long."

Jen paused and sighed. "All right, come on, girls. Let's go for a night swim."

Tori grabbed a towel with a huff and muttered under her breath, "This should be interesting."

As the group scattered, Carrie turned back to Tom, bracing herself for whatever conversation awaited.

~ ~ ~

Carrie and Tom walked along the road separating Brett's and The Edge from the river, heading toward the cabins where Tom was staying. Angler's was about half a mile down, and the evening was quiet, with no cars to worry about. Carrie sipped a cocktail from a cooler cup, needing something to calm her nerves. Tom, of course, didn't drink, but that didn't stop her. Their small talk filled the silence.

"So, what have you been up to, Carrie? Besides finding yourself a new boyfriend. Isn't he a little young for you?"

Carrie smirked. "He's only a few years younger. And he's kind. A hard worker."

"So am I," Tom replied quickly, then hesitated. "Well, maybe I wasn't always kind. But a hard worker. Are you still at the same job?"

"I am. But it's not what I want to do forever. I'm thinking about starting my own cleaning business. A friend of mine has one and wants to retire—she's offered me some of her clients."

Tom raised an eyebrow. "Oh really? That's what Sherry does. She's got her own cleaning business."

Carrie froze at the mention of Sherry. The name hit her like a slap. She stopped walking and turned to him. "Did you hook up with Sherry? Because I found her number in your shorts pocket once."

Tom glanced away, guilt flashing across his face.

He stopped walking as they reached Angler's cabins.

"Let's go sit on my deck," he suggested quietly.

He opened the door to his cabin, and Carrie stepped inside. The space was small but cozy enough for two. A man was sitting on the couch, scrolling on his phone.

"This is my friend Randy," Tom gestured.

Randy looked up and smiled. "Oh hey, you must be Carrie. I've heard about you."

Carrie's stomach tightened. She wondered just what Randy had heard.

"Tom, I'm heading to the campfire," Randy said and stood up. "Catch you later."

Tom led Carrie through the kitchenette to a sliding door that opened onto a deck. Just beyond was a small pier with a fishing boat tied to it. The river shimmered as the last of the sunlight reflected off its surface.

"Shall we?" Tom gestured toward the pier.

Carrie hesitated. "I know this sounds bad, but… do you have anything to drink?"

Tom grinned. "I've got tea. Oh, and this." He pulled a joint from his pocket. "I haven't given up everything."

Carrie laughed nervously. She thought sobriety meant giving up everything, but right now, she was thankful for the exception. Tom lit the joint, took a long puff, and handed it to her.

"Let me get you that tea," he said, disappearing

inside. He returned with a bottle of Snapple just as she exhaled her first puff, feeling its calming effects.

They walked down to the pier together, and Tom motioned to the boat. "Let's go out for a bit. It's such a nice night."

Carrie climbed into the boat, settling into the seat as she gulped the tea, her throat suddenly dry.

"So, Sherry…" she began, breaking the quiet. "You slept with her, didn't you?"

Tom sighed, leaning back. "Yeah. I know—I was a jerk. But I knew something was going on with you and Dylan. I could feel it. It was in the air. Everyone knew. And don't forget about Don."

Carrie's head spun. He knew about Don? And Dylan? She had always thought he was too drunk to notice what she was doing since he spent his days yelling at her or trailing after his dog.

"I guess we were both assholes," she finally admitted. Then another thought struck her. "Wait—where's Brandy?"

"She's at the campfire. Let's go for a little ride down the river," Tom suggested as he started the motor.

The boat glided over the water, slipping by other boats adorned with their nightly lights. The river felt mysterious in the dark, with only the glow of their boat's light cutting through the shadows.

"You should start that business," Tom broke the silence. "I think you'd be good at it."

Carrie turned to him. His eyes were different now, as they flickered with kindness. At that moment, she realized she didn't love him anymore, but she didn't hate him either.

By the time they returned to the pier, it was nearly 1 a.m. Carrie squinted at the clock on the microwave as they stepped into the cabin.

"Oh my God, it's late! Dodger's probably wondering where I am." She felt a jolt of guilt as her buzz wore off. Lightning flickered in the sky.

"I'll walk you back," Tom offered. "Looks like a storm's rolling in."

They walked in silence until they reached the parking lot between The Edge and Brett's. Carrie stopped and turned to him.

"You know, you're not a bad guy," she said softly. "The alcohol just got in the way."

Tom smiled faintly. "I know. Don't let anything get in the way of you and Dodger, if he's the one."

Carrie slipped her key into the motel room door and turned it slowly, her heart thudding in her chest. She pushed the door open just enough to peek inside, her breath catching in her throat. The room was dimly lit, the glow of the television flickering across the walls.

Her gaze darted to the bed. There was Dodger—his bare shoulder visible above the sheets. Relief washed over her for a moment, thinking he was alone. But then she saw it—a tangle of dark hair spilling over the pillow next to him.

Carrie froze, her stomach tightening as if she'd been punched. She took a shaky step closer, her heels sinking into the carpet. The figure stirred slightly, turning just enough for Carrie to see Stacy's unmistakable face, her lips parted in sleep.

"Stacy! What the hell?" Carrie yelled loudly.

Both of them jolted awake. Stacy shot out of bed, her face flushed, while Dodger rubbed his eyes and looked around, dazed.

"Carrie! This is not what it looks like," Dodger stammered.

"What am I looking at, then? Why are you in bed with her? Did you sleep together?" Carrie barked.

Dodger blinked, his confusion evident, as if piecing the situation together himself. "No! I went to bed, and—"

"And what?" Carrie's voice rose, cutting him off. She turned sharply to Stacy. "Why are you in bed with my boyfriend?"

Stacy hesitated, her face crumpling in discomfort. "I... I must have been confused."

"Confused? You didn't see an empty bed?" Carrie's fury bubbled over, her words sharp. "Trip is right—you're a liar. I don't even know why I bring you here every summer. You do nothing but sneak around and screw anyone but your boyfriend."

Stacy's expression hardened, her tone laced with venom. "You know why you always bring me, Carrie. Because what I do makes you look better. Let's start with Jake, then Don, then Dylan—while your husband was still around, by the way. And let's not forget Conner, the married man you're still sneaking around with. Or your little reunion stroll with Tom tonight."

Carrie froze, stunned into silence.

Stacy pressed on, her voice rising. "Face it, Carrie—everyone here is a mess. Jen fools around with poor Fritz, who has no idea why she ghosts him the rest of the year. Tori cheats on her husband. Christ, Benny's the only one with any character around here."

Carrie's hands shook as she pointed at the door. "Get out. Go to Jen's, if she'll even take you. Anywhere but here."

"Fine." Stacy grabbed her bag and angrily shoved her belongings inside, leaving some scattered behind. Without another word, she stormed out, slamming the door behind her.

The silence hung thick in the room, broken only by the sound of distant thunder. Lightning lit up the room, casting jagged shadows across the walls as the storm rolled in.

Dodger spoke quietly, his voice tinged with a hint of guilt. "Where were you, Carrie?"

CHAPTER 36

The storm raged through the night, rain hammering against the windows and lightning slicing across the sky as Carrie and Dodger sat up talking. She recounted her walk with Tom, describing how they aired their grievances, acknowledged their bad behavior, and agreed to put the past behind them. The moment had ended with the sharing of a joint—a rarity for her, something she only did to steady her nerves.

Dodger, who didn't use drugs himself, listened quietly. He nodded in understanding, recognizing the emotional weight of the encounter, even if it wasn't his style.

When the conversation turned to Stacy, Carrie's tone sharpened. She grilled him on what had happened while she was gone, demanding to know why he ended up in bed with her. Dodger swore nothing had happened—that he'd gone to bed alone and woke up to find Stacy there. His insistence sounded genuine, but Carrie couldn't shake the sick feeling that they were hiding something.

Still, she let it go for the night, knowing she didn't have much moral ground to stand on. Exhausted and emotionally spent, they finally crawled into bed, the clock creeping toward 3 a.m.

Before getting into bed, Carrie opened the door to check the storm. The wind whipped the rain sideways, tree branches bent and groaned, and the sky flashed in quick, dazzling bursts. "It's like The Wizard of Oz out there," she murmured, shutting the door against the chaos.

Finally, they fell into a restless sleep, the sound of thunder rumbling like a distant drumbeat as the storm carried on.

The morning revealed a landscape of chaos, the aftermath of one of the worst storms to hit Riverbanks. Large puddles reflected the bright sunlight that had replaced the rain, while broken branches and debris littered the ground. Both Brett's and The Edge were still without power, leaving Carrie and Dodger disoriented about the time when they finally woke.

After getting dressed, they stepped outside and headed toward Jen's trailer to check on the rest of the group. The air felt crisp and smelled of damp earth, the kind of freshness that comes only after a powerful storm has passed.

As they walked, Dodger's phone buzzed. He stopped and answered, his tone shifting to one of concern as he listened. When he hung up, he turned to Carrie.

"That was Fritz. His mom's place got hit pretty hard—there was flooding and some damage to the house. She needs us to help with repairs."

Carrie nodded, and just as they neared Jen's trailer, Fritz appeared, striding toward them with purpose.

"Let's get moving," Fritz instructed, gesturing toward Dodger. "It's already 10:00!" He checked his watch and barely slowed his pace.

Dodger turned to Carrie, his expression apologetic. "I'll see you later. Hopefully, it won't take too long." He kissed her lightly before hurrying off with Fritz, leaving Carrie to continue alone toward Jen's trailer.

Carrie walked up to the deck, a flicker of disappointment crossing her face as she thought about Dodger leaving to help Fritz's mom. She understood the urgency, but with all the damage at the resort, wouldn't his help be needed here too?

She sighed, opened the door, and stepped into the trailer without knocking. Jen stood at the kitchen counter, chopping what looked like ingredients for salsa. The television played quietly in the background, a reassuring sign that the trailer still had power.

"At least you've got electricity," Carrie noted, dropping into one of the chairs. "The bars are still out."

Jen glanced over her shoulder with a small smile. "Yeah, we lucked out."

Carrie tilted her head toward the television. "What are you watching?"

"Some dumb show," Jen replied with a dismissive wave. She wiped her hands on a dish towel, then came around the counter to tug on Carrie's arm. "Come on, let's sit on the deck before Stacy gets out of the shower."

She didn't wait for Carrie to settle before launching into the conversation. "I heard about the mistaken bed situation. I wanted to tell you—Stacy was all over him last night."

Carrie's face scrunched in disbelief. "What do you mean?"

"Like, she was always hovering around him, pulling him to dance. I swear, at one point, she fell right into his lap."

"Was he drunk? I have no doubt she was." Carrie responded.

"Yeah, he had a few drinks, but I think he was just mad that you were gone so long."

"Did you or Fritz say anything? Tori, Benny?"

"No, the four of us were playing cards. I don't even think they noticed, but I did. I wouldn't say anything to her, though—at least not yet. Keep your enemies close, right?"

Carrie frowned. "I think that's a little harsh. I wouldn't say she's my enemy now."

"Well, see what she says. I'm just saying, I don't trust her."

They went back inside, and Stacy emerged from

the bathroom with a towel wrapped around her head, wearing short shorts and a skimpy tank top.

"Hey, Carrie, about last night," Stacy began, holding up her hands in defense. "Nothing happened. You have to believe me. We were drunk and just passed out."

Carrie waved it off dismissively. "Ah, never mind. I'm sure it was just a mistake." She turned to Jen, shifting the subject. "Are you mad they had to run off and help Fritz's mom?"

Jen's smile seemed a little forced. "No, not at all. We can have fun on our own today. Let them go to work." But there was something in her eyes— something was bothering her.

Stacy, sensing the change in mood, glanced around the room. "Where did Tori and Benny go?"

"To the Farmer's Market in Bentonville," Jen replied.

"What?" Stacy asked, confused.

"You know they're a couple, right?" Jen added casually.

"No, I had no idea. What about Drew?" Stacy inquired, still processing.

"They have an open marriage."

"Wow. I guess you never really know people," Stacy said, shaking her head in disbelief.

"Yeah, I hear that," Carrie murmured, exchanging a look with Jen.

Jen put the salsa away and wiped her hands. "I'm going to find something to do while the bars are closed. The rain stopped, but it's still pretty crummy out, and it looks like it might rain again."

Just as she finished speaking, Benny and Tori walked in, carrying small baskets filled with blueberries and a large bottle of tequila.

"Hello, hello!" Benny beamed at his friends. "We're making blueberry margaritas! The bars are closed, so we figured we'd bring the party here. Look!" He held up the bottle of tequila—a better quality than the cheap stuff they usually had.

"I hope you made your salsa, Jen," Tori called into the kitchen as she made her way inside.

Jen emerged from her bedroom, holding a box. "I sure did, and I found this." She held up a cardboard box containing the game Twister.

Benny clapped his hands. "Oh boy, this is gonna be a fun day!"

The girls worked on the margaritas while Benny set up the Twister board. They weren't exactly sure how to make blueberry margaritas, so they improvised—boiling the blueberries with sugar to sweeten them up, then blending them with a generous amount of tequila. Just as they finished, there was a knock at the door. They all looked up to see Brandon standing outside, holding a case of ice-cold beer and some snacks.

"It looks like more fun here than at my place. Can

I join?" Brandon grinned.

Jen glanced at Stacy, then shrugged. "Oh, what the hell. I can't stop you."

Jen finished the first batch of margaritas and poured them into glasses. Stacy and Carrie took the first tastes.

"Mmm, very good... and strong!" Carrie exclaimed, grinning.

"Oh no," Jen giggled, "you've got seeds all in your teeth."

Carrie and Stacy rushed to the bathroom to check out their smiles in the mirror. Their laughter echoed from the hallway.

"No sense in wasting that batch," Jen said, turning to Tori. "How about if they finish it, and we make another one—but strain out the seeds?"

"Good idea," Tori agreed. They rummaged through the cabinets until they found a strainer.

Carrie and Stacy stayed at the counter, finishing off the pitcher. Stacy, already feeling the buzz, poured herself another glass.

"These are so good, I can't stop drinking them," Stacy said, grinning as she downed the last of her glass and refilled it.

"I know. Let's finish this pitcher so we can get the seeds out of our teeth," Carrie laughed, taking another sip.

The new batch was soon ready, and they all

indulged, washing it down with the ice beer Brandon had brought. The alcohol hit quickly, especially for Stacy and Carrie, who'd been sipping the extra-strong batch.

They laid out the Twister mat, and Benny and Brandon took turns spinning the arrow, positioning Carrie and Jen in ways that made them twist and contort in exaggerated poses. Their laughter filled the room, and the playful tension built as Benny spun again, placing Stacy and Brandon in a way that gave Brandon the perfect excuse to grope her breasts and crotch. He did the same to Benny, positioning Tori in a similar, awkward, and suggestive pose.

As the game wound down, Carrie started to feel dizzy and overwhelmed from all the drinks. She plopped into one of the living room chairs, closing her eyes for a moment.

Benny and Tori were sprawled on the couch, entangled in a haze of tequila and laughter, while Jen and Stacy, still in the kitchen, started another round of margaritas. Brandon, munching on chips and salsa, kept his eyes on them, enjoying the chaos around him.

"So, Stacy, why were you in bed with Dodger last night?" Jen asked, her tone sharp as she pressed the lid onto the blender and turned it on. The machine whirred loudly, blending another batch of margaritas.

Stacy leaned against the counter, a sly smile playing on her lips. "Oh, I don't know," she said with mock innocence, grabbing a chip and slipping it into Brandon's mouth. Their eyes locked, a current of lust passing between them. "I guess I wanted to see how he measured up."

"Measured up?" Jen snapped, turning off the blender to stare at her.

"Yeah," Stacy replied with a shrug, tilting her head toward Brandon. "To this young stud."

Carrie, slumped in her chair, felt the room spin slightly as the alcohol took hold. The voices around her seemed distant, yet sharp enough to cut through the fog in her head. Her vision blurred, but she could make out Stacy's flirtatious body language. She watched, almost mesmerized, as her mind drifted into a hazy dream state.

Images flashed in her mind of Stacy climbing onto her boyfriend—or was he even her boyfriend? The two of them together in bed, tangled up and sweaty.

Carrie shook her head, trying to snap out of it, but her anger flared. "You're unbelievable, Stacy," Jen exclaimed, her voice trembling with a mix of fury and intoxication. "I saw you all over Dodger last night. And now Brandon? What's your deal?"

Stacy smirked and turned toward her. "What's my deal? Maybe you're just jealous. You're all hung up on a guy who's either screwing around behind your back or too boring to care. That's not my problem." She reached for Brandon's hand, pulling him close. "Come on, Brando. Let's go somewhere more fun."

They started kissing as they staggered toward the door, their laughter grating against Carrie's nerves.

But just as they reached the exit, the door flew open with a loud bang.

Bobby stormed in, his expression dark and his voice cutting through the chaos. "What the hell is going on here? Jen, I'm telling you right now—keep this slut away from my son!" Bobby's angered voice boomed through the room.

Jen threw up her hands. "What are you talking about? I can't control her!"

Bobby jabbed a finger in her direction. "If she goes near Brandon again, I'll make sure your retarded boyfriend pays for it."

The air turned electric with tension just as Dodger and Fritz burst through the door. Dodger's face darkened as he zeroed in on Bobby. "Don't you ever talk about my friend that way!"

Without hesitation, Dodger grabbed Bobby by the collar and dragged him out the door. The deck shuddered under their weight as he shoved Bobby off the edge. Bobby hit the ground hard with a grunt, but before he could react, Dodger was on top of him.

It wasn't much of a fight. Dodger, twice Bobby's size, pinned him easily, straddling his chest. He pulled back his fist and landed a solid punch squarely on Bobby's nose. A sickening crack followed, and blood spurted out, staining Bobby's shirt and pooling on the ground.

"Dodger, stop!" Voices screamed from the deck as the others scrambled outside. Benny threw himself into the fray, pulling Dodger off Bobby with considerable effort.

Marcy came speeding up in her golf cart, leaping off before it even stopped. "What the hell is going on?" she shrieked, her voice cutting through the chaos. She ran to Bobby, who was cradling his nose, his face pale and streaked with blood.

She rounded on the group, her eyes blazing. "You people are deranged!" She grabbed Bobby by the arm, forcing him to stand. "If his nose is broken, you're going to hear from us." She turned to Brandon, who was standing off to the side, clearly torn. "Come on, Brandon. You're not staying with these hooligans."

"Hooligans, Mom? Really?" Brandon rolled his eyes, his tone dripping with sarcasm. He spun toward Stacy, pulled her close, and kissed her deeply, eliciting a gasp from Marcy.

"For God's sake!" Marcy yanked at Brandon's arm, practically dragging him away. She threw a final glare over her shoulder. "That woman is too old for you and a major slut!"

Brandon, laughing, glanced back at Stacy, who smirked and waved coyly, crossing her legs as if lounging in victory.

On the deck, Carrie stood frozen, watching the chaos unfold below. Dodger brushed dirt off his clothes, avoiding her gaze, while Stacy hovered near him, fussing over his shirt.

Fritz approached Jen cautiously. "What the hell happened here?"

Jen jabbed a finger at Stacy. "Her. It's always her. She can't figure out which poor idiot she wants to prey on, and I'm over it." She pointed toward the driveway. "Get out. Don't come back. I don't care how you're getting home—figure it out."

Stacy opened her mouth to argue, but Dodger put a hand on her arm, silencing her. His eyes darted up to Carrie, still on the deck, looking down at him with a mix of anger and resignation.

"I'll take her home," Dodger said quietly, his tone almost apologetic.

Carrie said nothing, but her expression told him everything he needed to know. Whatever apology he thought he could offer, it wouldn't be enough.

PART 6

2007

CHAPTER 37

"How's the kitchen coming along? Do you think we'll be able to stay this summer?" Carrie asked Jen as she gathered her supplies, ready to head out to her first client.

"Pretty much. I don't know if the smell of the smoke will be gone. Probably never will. Uh, I can't believe this happened!"

It wasn't too shocking, especially after the events of the previous summer's last night. But no one would have ever expected it would be as drastic as a fire.

The phone call came the morning after they'd left Riverbanks. It was Jen, her voice a raw, strangled sob.

"It's all burned," she choked out. "The kitchen. It's gone."

Carrie's heart plummeted. "Oh my God, Jen, what happened?"

"Fire. Someone started it on fire." Jen's sobs intensified. "I can't believe this."

Carrie's mind raced. "Your trailer? Did you leave something on, or a candle burning? I didn't see anything before I left. Did you?"

"I did see something," Jen confessed, her voice a hushed whisper. "A handwritten note."

Carrie's blood ran cold. "What did it say?"

Jen hesitated, the silence stretching between them. "Don't fuck with me, Bitch."

Carrie gasped. "Are you serious? Bobby, it had to be Bobby. He was fired up that night! Or Brandon. There's something about him. I think he's a firebug."

"Wait, Carrie," Jen interrupted, her voice trembling. "There's something else I didn't tell you."

"What?"

Jen took a shaky breath. "I broke up with Fritz that night."

Carrie's mouth dropped. "You did? Why?" She asked.

Jen murmured. "It's complicated. He's been acting, well, strange lately. Jealous, always hovering over me. You know I don't like that. And lately, when we are having sex, he's been having seizures."

Carrie's jaw dropped again. "What? Oh my gosh!"

Jen's voice was thick with shame. "Yeah. He has had epilepsy ever since his accident. It's been getting worse and worse. I'm sorry, call me a bad person, but I can't deal with it."

Carrie sat speechless, the weight of Jen's confession settling over her like a shroud.

After the incident at the trailer on the last Fourth of July weekend, Dodger repeatedly tried to contact

Carrie, but she refused to take his calls or return his texts.

Carrie had wondered if she was in love with Dodger. She knew she needed to do some soul-searching, so as the summer gave way to fall and a crispness chilled the air, she spent her mornings with a cup of coffee, pondering the loves of her life. Tom, who had been her husband. She loved him as a friend, but not as a lover or a life companion. She had finally realized she had to leave him because she would have ended up hurting him. Carrie knew if he found out about the others, he would have forgiven her, but she could not forgive herself.

There were many others. It started with Jake. Their encounters were adventurous, daring, and purposely wrong, but he awakened her senses. He would ultimately destroy her.

Then there was her brief but illicit affair with Don—a sexy, older married man she met one sun-drenched evening when she and Jen went to a festival by the lake. He was charming and intoxicating, with a confident smile that hinted at secrets. Carrie knew from the start it was wrong. He wore a gold wedding band that he never bothered to hide, and his eyes sometimes flickered with guilt when he looked at her too long.

Being married and unavailable was part of the draw for Carrie. Don made her feel desired again, not broken. She felt like she still had power over something, someone. Her heart still ached from

Jake—the way he'd made her feel dirty in the end. Don wasn't a solution, but rather a distraction. During their many phone conversations and promises that neither of them meant, Carrie slowly began to pull herself back together.

These were secrets she kept from everyone, except Stacy.

~ ~ ~

Carrie's thoughts were interrupted by her cell phone vibrating. It was Jen calling. "We should be able to stay in the trailer. I had the contractors clean up the smoke smell and the damage, so it's liveable. Are you still coming? What about Dodger? You haven't talked much about him lately."

"No, he is not," Carrie replied. We are done. Maybe it should just be the three of us, Tori, you, and I."

Carrie hadn't been communicating with Dodger, despite his attempts to contact her repeatedly. He finally gave up.

"I'll have to check with Tori to see if she is bringing Benny, although it wouldn't be the weekend without him. But just the girls would be nice."

"We should mentally prepare ourselves for the weekend," Carrie added.

"We always do, but what in particular do you think we need to prepare for?" Jen inquired.

"We still don't know who started the fire."

"You think it was Bobby?" Jen asked. "Or Marcy? Or wait, Brandon?"

"I think it could have been any one of them. I mean, that family is crazy. Remember that summer when Bobby beat the crap out of Dylan? He doesn't admit it, but I know he did it."

"That is true," admitted Jen. "Oh, speaking of Dylan, I ran into him the other day."

"You did? How is he?" Carrie asked.

Do you have to let it linger? Thoughts of Dylan flooded Carrie's mind. His beautiful brown hair, crooked smile, and carefree take on life. Not to mention his strong masculine sexuality.

"He's good, but get this, he started a business— something like wood carving or carpentry. I don't know, but he looked good too. Carrie, maybe you should…"

"Jen, he ghosted me years ago. I think I am done with men. Maybe I should be a lesbo."

"I don't think so, Carrie. I know how you like men," Jen snickered.

CHAPTER 38

Walking into the trailer seemed different, quiet, somber, with a slight smell of smoke, and a feeling of loneliness. Thankfully, only the kitchen had been affected by the fire, but its damage had affected the rest of the house.

As Carrie entered the trailer, memories of the final night from the previous summer came flooding back to her. The image of Stacy in the same bed with Dodger, and then her later blatant flaunting of it. The way the weekend ended, with Dodger taking her home instead of staying with her in her time of need. He chose Stacy over her. Carrie had not spoken to Stacy since that day, and they hadn't worked anything out. Perhaps it was best, in her mind, because she could not move on with skeletons glaring at her.

Jen had enough money from her insurance to repair the kitchen. She had the cabinets and countertops replaced, along with a new bar with stools and room for six. She also had a sound system installed. Carrie turned it on, and "Apologize" came on. The lyrics made her feel blue. She missed Dodger, and it hurt her that Stacy never apologized.

"Hey, you're here already." Jen put down her bags and gave Carrie a big hug. I'm so happy to see you. It's been quite a year."

After Jen's breakup with Fritz, she focused on her professional life and opened another jewelry shop. She now owned three, all located in trendy areas of town to attract young hipsters. Carrie would often visit her shop on the east side where she worked, and they would sit at one of the local restaurants, eating alfresco while Carrie worked on her writing. After breaking ties with Fritz, Carrie urged Jen to pursue other relationships, but Jen wasn't sure. She did not easily open up to anyone and give in to her feelings. Carrie felt jealous in a way because she often gave in to her feelings, even when she knew it wasn't the best thing to do..

"Now that this kitchen is fixed, I need to relax," Jen told Carrie. "Why don't we go to The Edge and have someone serve us?"

The Edge felt cool, a welcome contrast to the heavy summer heat outside. Inside, the bar echoed slightly with the hum of a distant playlist and the occasional clink of glass behind the counter. The place was nearly empty—just a couple of regulars bantering in light conversation.

A young bartender in a snug black T-shirt appeared from behind the shelves, a playful energy in his stride. He had tousled hair and a smile that reminded Carrie of Dylan.

"Well, hello ladies," he said, leaning casually on

the bar. "How're we doing today?"

Jen slid onto a stool and gave him a knowing look. "Enjoying the calm before the storm of another weekend in Riverbanks."

He chuckled, grabbing a couple of glasses. "I hear ya. Never a dull moment in this place." He smiled and winked. "What'll it be?"

Jen turned to Carrie with a grin that tugged at old memories. "Do you make margaritas?" she asked, the corners of her eyes crinkling in amusement.

The bartender straightened up, already reaching for a shaker. "I sure do."

Carrie looked at Jen and commented, "Nice outfit. Did your new boyfriend buy you that?" Jen looked beachy chic, not too fancy for Freeland. A simple, creamy silk tank top paired with beautiful, patterned linen pants and solid gold earrings complemented her classy look.

In the middle of her busy life, Jen met Matt at a trade show. He was a handsome, rich jewelry dealer eager to shower Jen with attention. He took her on a trip to Venezuela that spring.

"He's not my boyfriend, we're just having fun," Jen rebutted.

"Come on, Jen, we're thirty-seven, don't you think it's time to settle down?"

Jen looked at Carrie. "Do I look like the married-with-children type? I'm happy with a steak dinner and great sex."

"Oh yeah, that's right. You're a Samantha." They both laughed, thinking of Samantha's escapades and attitude in their favorite show, Sex and The City.

They sat, looking out at the large window that overlooked the river. Carrie couldn't help but remember the excitement she felt that first weekend when she came to Riverbanks with Jen and Dylan. How many memories they made, and the new ones since then. Some good, some bad, but it was always memorable.

Carrie and Jen sat in silence for a while, perhaps both wondering what memories they would make this weekend.

As they headed back to Jen's trailer, they saw a figure on the deck. He was walking around the deck, running his hands on the railing. As they got closer, they saw it was Dylan. It was almost as if their reminiscing of that first summer together manifested him to appear. He looked different from what Carrie remembered. His long brown hair was now cropped neatly. He was clean-shaven and smiled that wonderful smile when he saw them walking up.

"Angels!" He yelled.

Jen ran up the stairs, and he enveloped her in a big hug. "What a surprise," she gushed as she pulled away from the hug. "What are you doing here?"

Dylan looked at Carrie, who stood in the background, silent and shocked, but happy to see him. "I came up here for business, just a few miles north of here. Thought I'd stop in to see if you were around.

Carrie, aren't you going to come and say hi?"

She walked up the stairs of the deck and hugged him while Jen stepped away. "Hey Dylan, good to see you. You look great. I didn't know you had your own business."

He gazed down at her with a gleam in his eye. "I'll tell you about it later. What's going on with you ladies? You both looked lost in thought. Did I catch you walking down memory lane?" His knowing smile hit Carrie's heart once again.

"We went out to The Edge to unwind and watch the river," Carrie replied softly, her gaze dropping to avoid his eyes. "We were talking about the first time I came here—with you."

Dylan gave a low, amused sound. "Mmm," he said, a mischievous glint in his voice. "Yeah, that was a good time... right up until the end."

"Come inside, Dylan. I made some changes to the trailer since you were here," Jen announced.

They gathered around Jen's breakfast bar, which they used more as a regular bar. Dylan and Carrie on one side, Jen on the other, mixing drinks. She plugged in her new iPhone, which produced music through her new Bluetooth speaker. The pulsing beat of Nelly Furtado's "Say it Right" came sneaking out. "You don't mean nothing at all to me..."

Carrie looked through her peripheral vision at Dylan's legs, then up to his shorts. She tried hard to focus on the song, thinking *you mean nothing to me.* But her thoughts drifted back to that first summer when their secret glances and forbidden touches under the tables led to a passionate encounter that had a lasting impact on the events that followed. As Dylan chatted, all Carrie heard was his beautiful voice. Then she looked at the side of his face and noticed the small scar that lingered under his eye—a souvenir of his first summer in Riverbanks.

"I think it's time you told us what happened that night, Dylan, and who beat you up," Jen said.

Dylan explained in as much detail as he remembered about that night. He had walked down to Brett's storage room to look for Carrie's purse and found Bobby on his knees in front of one of the guys he hung out with a lot. He left out some of the explicit details, but Jen and Carrie understood the undertone. Dylan told them he quickly scampered back up the stairs, but Bobby and his friend had already seen him. He went to the bar to order a beer in an attempt to deter them, but they came up behind him, saying it was already last call. Then they pulled him outside behind the bar. He had a difficult time remembering because they knocked him senseless, but he recalled coming to, enough to see the two of them walking away.

"Wow!" Jen exclaimed. "I never would have taken Bobby to be gay. He always acts so macho and metrosexual."

"He's probably overcompensating," Carrie responded, recalling the time they ran into him and his group of friends at the Bridge bar a couple of summers ago and how they all seemed very strange to her.

"Why didn't you say anything?" Jen asked.

"Because truthfully, I felt bad for him. I know he was a complete asshole to jump me like that, but I'm tough. I healed. He has a huge secret to hide; from his wife, his kid, hell, his whole family!"

"He does seem angry a lot. That last night when he came here last year, and was trying to get Brandon away from Stacy. She's a friend of Carrie's who came here a few summers ago. She's a tramp and tried to scam on Brandon AND Carrie's boyfriend Dodger."

Dylan turned and looked at Carrie, and she looked at him. Jen could sense the heat between them.

"Dylan, why were you looking for Carrie's purse in the storage room?"

"Carrie and I, we..."

"I get it. You had a stolen moment. That was the summer that Carrie had all the problems with Tom," Jen stated.

"Last year, Bobby and Dodger got in a fight on our last night, and Dodger punched Bobby in the nose. There was blood everywhere, quite a scene."

"Sounds like it." Dylan turned to Carrie. "This guy, Dodger, are you still with him?"

"No, he left with Stacy and took her home. I haven't talked to him since. And anyway, what is it to you?"

"Easy, Carrie," replied Dylan. "I was just wondering if maybe he has some information about Bobby that could give us some clues."

"What are we, detectives now?" Carrie asked in a sarcastic tone. "Jen, didn't the police do an investigation?"

"Yeah, they did. The only thing they found was this." Jen walked over to one of the cabinets, reached in, and pulled out a Van Halen lighter, holding it up.

Carrie grabbed it from her hand. "That's my lighter! It went missing that first summer."

"Really?" Jen asked. "Do you have any idea who took it from you? That is a huge clue!"

"God, that was, what, five years ago? I remember being mad that I couldn't find it when we left that morning after Dylan got beat up." Carrie scrunched her eyes. "I do remember seeing Brandon burning ants on the sidewalk, and I thought that was strange. His parents don't smoke, so where did he get the lighter? Oh, I know, from ME!"

"Or, maybe Bobby took it from your purse in the storage room. That would make more sense. He has more reason to burn the place." Dylan rebutted.

"Why me and my place?" inquired Jen. "I'm not the one who found him in the storage room with another man; you did."

"But you are friends with me," said Dylan, "and he probably assumed I told you, and that you would tell others, especially his wife and son."

"True, but you haven't been around here in years. It just doesn't make sense."

"No, it doesn't." Dylan shook his head. "Let's go to Brett's and see if we can get any more information from Brian."

"Shouldn't we wait for Tori?" Carrie asked.

"Oh, I forgot to tell you she called to say she would not make it until tomorrow. She has a work thing to attend. Benny too. I'm hoping they make it tomorrow because that's when the Fourth of July festivities are happening since the Fourth falls on Wednesday this year."

They gathered their phones and purses and headed outside. On the deck, Jen reached into her purse for the key to lock the trailer. "Shit, I must have left the key back at home." She looked around the deck, and on one of the railings was a decorative rock that she turned over, revealing a key. She locked the door as Dylan and Carrie looked at each other.

Carrie asked, "Does anyone else know about that key?"

"Possibly," Jen answered, with a look of amazement on her face, realizing they might have discovered another clue.

CHAPTER 39

Brett's was alive with people eating and drinking, and Brian stood behind the bar serving drinks. They found an area at the bar, located near the back, close to the stairs leading to the storage room. An area they usually gravitated to since it was more hidden.

Jen called Brian over and ordered their usual pepperoni and onion pizza. "I'm glad he's here. We can try to get some information since he no longer works on Saturdays. I heard there is a new bartender, a girl that I haven't met yet."

Carrie and Jen sat on barstools, with Dylan in the middle. "You haven't been up here in a while?" Carrie asked.

"No. Brian called me and told me about the fire, and I got caught up in my business and getting contractors out here to fix it."

Brian set their beers down. "Hi Jen, hey there Carrie. You're Dylan, right?"

"Yeah, man, it's been a while," Dylan replied. "How are things here? Just as wild as usual?"

"You bet. Always something. Jen, how's the kitchen coming along?"

"It's fine, but I still can't get over that it happened. I can't believe the police haven't found anything to prove who started it," answered Jen.

"I'm not surprised. Right after it happened, there was the Tony incident."

"Tony incident?" Jen and Carrie asked at the same time.

"Tony DeMarco. He's one of the ballers who have been coming here the past few years. They usually stay at The Riverbanks Inn, and they have big fancy boats to stroll the river. He and his friends were here one night partying hard. I wasn't working that night, but the rumor is that Tony was flirting with some girls who all had boyfriends here. Long story short, Tony went missing for a while and was found lying in the ditch by the road across from the river. They beat him unconscious. Last I heard, he was in a coma. You didn't hear about this?"

"Wow, no, I didn't," Jen answered. "I guess Riverbanks gossip doesn't travel."

"Anyway, I assume the cops were too busy trying to solve that mess. Your trailer just got brushed off."

"Tragic about that Tony guy. Was Bobby there by chance?" Dylan asked.

"No, I was not there." A voice from behind them bellowed. "But your friend Trip was here," Bobby told them. "He pushed Brandon's friend Nick down the stairs there, pointing to the infamous stairs, and gave him a concussion."

"Trip left. He was pissed at Stacy and left." Carrie said, remembering how she turned to Dodger in his absence.

"That's not what I heard," Bobby replied. "Nice friend of yours. Oh, by the way, Carrie, Conner will be here tomorrow. He and Jill got divorced. I think you ought to reconnect." He beamed a smile and walked away.

It was all too much for them to take in. The tragic story about Tony, and then Trip supposedly pushing Nick down the stairs, and the mystery of why Trip was still there that weekend. They sat on Jen's deck talking about it for a while over drinks, throwing ideas around. Carrie's theory was that Trip left, came back, and went to the bar to find Brandon. Then he pushed Nick down the stairs, thinking he was Brandon. That was after Jen kicked Stacy out, and she went home with Dodger.

Amidst all the turmoil they had just learned about, Carrie had a heavy thought on her mind: Conner.

Jen sighed, crushing out her cigarette. "I'm done. This is too much for one night. Dylan, where are you staying tonight?

"I was going to drive back to the hotel I'm staying in."

"Probably not a good idea. You've been drinking. Tori is not here, so there's an extra bedroom. Or you can crash on the couch. I'm going to turn in. You guys have some catching up to do." Jen looked them both over and sleepily walked inside.

Carrie and Dylan sat there, in the moonlight, alone. Memories of that weekend, when they flirted and teased each other, came flooding back, but now Dylan was different and more serious. That was during her married years, when it was forbidden and fun, but things weren't the same. With that thought, she stood up to go inside.

"Carrie, wait. Let's talk for a while," Dylan requested.

She obliged, so they decided to go to the pond, their favorite spot. The moon glistened on the water, and the sounds of the nearby bars filled the air from a distance, yet their quiet area still seemed hidden. Carrie wasn't looking for a passionate encounter; she wanted closure. She had it with Tom and with Conner, but now she needed it with Dylan.

Dylan sat on a picnic table, and Carrie stood in front of him. She longed to be in his arms and receive a long-awaited kiss, but stood back. She wanted answers. She needed them.

"You look great, Carrie. I like what you did with your hair," Dylan told her. She cringed because she had recently gotten it cut much shorter than she usually wore it, but still kept the highlights.

"You look good, too. Like a different person, but again, I haven't seen you in five years."

He took his head in his hands and ran his hands over his hair to pull back as if it were still long, like he always did. Carrie waited for a response.

"Carrie, I know you can't begin to understand what I was going through, or why I stayed away. But things got really bad. I can't lie. I got into drugs again. I thought about you all the time, but I could not get you involved in that world. I cared, I mean, care too much about you."

"I would be the one person who would understand. I was drinking very heavily back then, for God's sake. I came to your apartment drunk off my ass, and we had sloppy sex, but it still meant something to me. We all went through tough stuff; me, Jen, hell, even Tori, but the one thing we did was stick together. We didn't stay away, like you did," Carrie argued.

"I know, Carrie, I know. I couldn't see a way out."

"So what changed. You have a business that I didn't even know about. Something had to change all of that. A girl? It's always a girl." Carrie's voice went flat.

"Yes. My Grandma. My Grandfather passed away." Dylan looked away, holding back tears. "God, I loved that man. He would sit with me when I was a kid and show me how to mold wood into objects. He was a patient, loving man, and it broke my heart when he died. It broke me. But Grams offered me an opportunity to take over his business with one hitch: I had to get off drugs. It took a while, but I did it. I now run Gramp's furniture business, and I am good at it. Who'd have thought?" He boasted.

"I'm proud of you and happy for you." Carrie

gently touched Dylan's arm. He was her friend, someone she adored and wanted the best for.

"How about you? What's your life like? Are you still a big office manager?" Dylan asked.

Carrie shuffled her bare feet in the grass, feeling as if what he just recalled of her life seemed mundane. "I started a cleaning business."

He raised his arms in the air. "Really? That's great!"

"It is. I like being my own boss. I have some good clients and make a pretty good living. But..." she stopped.

"But what?"

"It's not that satisfying," Carrie looked down. "Nobody aspires to be a cleaning woman."

"You're not just a cleaning woman, you're a businesswoman. There's a big difference. You should be proud." Dylan lifted her chin so she could see his smile.

I suppose so, but I've been writing, and I've submitted a short story to Reader's Digest. It's going to be published in a couple of months," Carrie shared.

"I'm intrigued. What's it about?" Dylan asked.

"It's called "The Closet" and is about a girl who dreams of entering her closet and stepping into her favorite childhood books."

"That's a great idea. I know how much you enjoy reading. Are you considering a career as a writer?

"Maybe. I have a few other stories I started. I'm also going to take a creative writing class in the fall."

Dylan took her hands gently into his. "Sounds like we're both doing what we always wanted to do. This calls for a celebration. Let's go for a dip."

"What? I'm not skinny dipping with you." Carrie pulled her hands away.

"No, I mean go get your suit, and let's go for a swim. Look how beautiful the pond is and the moon beaming down on us; it's like God's love shining down on us."

"What, are you all religious now?" Carrie chuckled.

He laughed. "No, I just think it's pretty."

They both went back to the trailer and quietly changed into their swimsuits. "Yahoo!" Carrie yelled as she hit the refreshing water.

After their exhilarating plunge into the refreshing pond, they surrendered to the tranquility, floating on their back and allowing their eyes to wander across the vast canvas of twinkling stars above. Perhaps they were grateful for their current situations in life, considering what they had endured. As their bodies graced the water, Dylan attempted to hold Carrie's hand, but she resisted, not ready to endure that pain again.

When they returned to the trailer, Carrie softly told Dylan to take the spare room. "Tori's not here anyway, so no need for you to sleep on the couch."

He hesitated, bag slung over one shoulder, then nodded. "Thanks," he replied, his voice low, almost tentative.

They lingered a moment in the narrow hallway, the sweetness of the night swim pressing around them. Their eyes met—just for a second too long—before they both turned away. Dylan disappeared into the spare room, shutting the door with a quiet click. Carrie stood in the darkened hall for a moment, her hand brushing the cool wall, wondering how close she'd come to asking him to join her.

The next morning, Carrie woke to the faint dampness clinging to her skin, a reminder of the previous night's swim. The birdsong outside and the faint creak of the deck settling seemed almost too calm after the restless thoughts she carried to bed.

She paused outside Dylan's door, her hand hovering near the frame. Should I wake him? She bit her lip, then shook her head and moved on, her bare feet padding softly toward the kitchen.

CHAPTER 40

The early morning light filtered through the thin curtains in the living room, casting pale streaks across the countertops. Carrie rummaged quietly through the cabinets, opening one, then another, muttering under her breath when a stack of mismatched mugs nearly tumbled out. Coffee, where does Jen keep the coffee?

Despite her efforts to stay quiet, the faint clatter must have been enough. A door creaked open behind her, and she turned to see Dylan stepping into the kitchen, his hair tousled, sleep still heavy on his face. Jen followed moments later, tying her robe loosely at her waist, both of them wearing the groggy expressions of people drawn out of bed by the promise of caffeine.

"Morning," Carrie murmured, setting three mugs on the breakfast bar. She filled them carefully, the rich scent of coffee filling the small space.

Jen took her cup and leaned against the counter, her eyes narrowing playfully. "So," she said, a teasing edge in her voice, "what did you two do last night?"

Carrie froze for a heartbeat, glancing at Dylan. He raised an eyebrow at her, a slight, almost imperceptible smirk tugging at his lips.

"Just went for a walk," they said in unison, the words too practiced, too quick.

Jen sipped her coffee, watching them over the rim of her mug. Her knowing look lingered for a moment too long before she turned away with a chuckle. "Right. A walk."

Carrie busied herself wiping the counter, her cheeks warming under Jen's gaze, but she didn't dare look at Dylan again.

"Jen," Dylan said casually over his coffee, a teasing lilt in his voice. "What do you think about Carrie's story getting published in Reader's Digest?"

Jen froze mid-sip, her eyes widening as she whipped her head toward Carrie. "What? Carrie, you never told me!"

Carrie's hand tightened around her mug, her cheeks flushing. She shot Dylan a sharp look, her lips pressing into a thin line as if to silently plead, Don't say anything else.

"I... I didn't want to make a big deal about it," Carrie softly admitted. She fiddled with the edge of her sleeve, avoiding Jen's gaze. "Plus, you've had so much going on this year. I was planning to tell you and Tori this weekend."

"Tell me what?" Tori's voice rang out from the doorway as she stepped in, her bags in hand and a grin spreading across her face. "I'm all ears!"

Carrie groaned softly, dropping her head into her

hands as Tori sauntered over, clearly delighted to have stumbled into something juicy. Dylan chuckled under his breath, leaning back in his chair as Jen reached over and gave Carrie's shoulder a playful shake.

"Well?" Jen said, her grin matching Tori's now. "Are you going to tell us, or do we have to read about it in the magazine?"

Carrie waved a hand, her tone dismissive. "Oh, come on. It's that story, 'The Closet,' I told you about. The magazine liked it, and it is scheduled for publication in a couple of months. Big deal." She quickly turned her attention to Tori, her eyes lighting up. "But enough about that. Tori! I'm so glad you're here. We've got so much to tell you. You know about the fire in Jen's kitchen? We've got clues—"

"Hold that thought." Tori dropped her bags by the door and raised a hand, cutting Carrie off with a grin. "I'm dying to hear about it, but let me at least get my stuff unpacked first." She turned to Dylan, her smile widening. "And look who's here. Fancy running into you, huh?" She didn't wait for a response, brushing past him with a playful smirk.

Dylan barely had time to open his mouth before she added over her shoulder, "By the way, you're not taking my room. Find somewhere else, buddy."

Carrie stifled a laugh as Dylan held up his hands in mock surrender. "Wasn't planning to, Tori," he said, shaking his head, a grin tugging at the corners of his mouth.

Tori winked at him before disappearing down the

hallway, leaving Carrie and Dylan in her wake, the faint sound of her humming as she unpacked drifting back toward them.

Tori leaned back in her chair, a curious glint in her eyes as she twirled the stem of her empty glass. "Alright, I'm unpacked. Spill. What's all this about the fire?"

Carrie exchanged a glance with Jen and took a deep breath. "Okay, so, first clue—the Van Halen lighter. We found it in the trailer."

Tori frowned. "Van Halen lighter?"

"It's mine," Carrie explained, leaning forward. "Went missing five years ago. I'm almost positive Brandon took it—he's got a history, you know. A real firebug."

"Wait," Tori interrupted, holding up a finger. "This is the same summer Dylan got beat up, right?"

"Exactly," Carrie replied, her voice dropping. "The lighter was in my purse, and Bobby would have found it, meaning Brandon had access to it. You remember how Dylan caught Bobby with that guy? Motive, right there."

Jen chimed in, tapping her nails on the table. "And don't forget about my hidden key. The one behind the decorative rock. Everyone knows about that hiding spot."

"Oh, and Trip," Dylan added, his voice tight. "Someone saw him the night of the fire, shoving someone down the stairs. You all thought he left after that big fight with Stacy, but maybe not."

Tori blinked, holding up her hands. "Wait, wait. This is a lot. I need a mimosa."

Carrie laughed and stood up, grabbing the champagne bottle. "Coming right up. But don't get too comfortable, Tori. You're not off the hook—we've got more to talk about. Where's Benny? We need him to drive the boat."

"He can't make it until maybe tonight or tomorrow. He's trying to secure a major interview for the paper, but it's all up in the air. But he wants to be here. Plus, Jen knows how to drive the boat."

By late Saturday morning, the buzz of boat engines and bursts of laughter echoed off the banks of the river. Jen's boat bobbed at the dock, its faded cushions ready for another day of tradition—drinks, food, and gossip, all with the backdrop of the bustling river scene.

Carrie tossed a cooler onboard, the ice inside clinking as she grinned. "Ready for the usual? Bars, boaters, and bad decisions?"

Jen laughed, adjusting her sunglasses as she climbed aboard. "It's tradition!"

Dylan leaned casually against the railing, a beer in hand, watching them with an easy smile. Jen looked over at him, tilting her head. "So, are you staying or what?"

He shrugged, taking a sip before answering. "I'll stick around if you want me to. No business this weekend—I just wanted to spend time with you girls."

Tori rolled her eyes dramatically, climbing into the boat. "Oh, you're staying," she teased, nudging his shoulder. "We need someone to help us figure out the mystery."

"Mystery?" Dylan raised an eyebrow, playing along. "I'm in!"

"Besides," Tori added as she plopped into her seat. "Boaters, bar fights, bad flirting—this river has it all."

"Oh, I know," Dylan agreed. "I know."

The boat rocked gently as they cruised along, the smell of sunscreen and river water mingling with the tang of spiked lemonade. Boats sat tied up in clusters along the shore, music blaring from portable speakers. People laughed, danced, and shouted across the water, the party spilling out under the summer sun.

Carrie leaned back against a seat cushion, her toes skimming the edge of the boat. She sipped her drink, half-listening to Jen and Tori swap stories about their workweek. Dylan sat across from her, legs stretched out, his sunglasses hiding the glances he occasionally sent her way. She caught one and quickly looked away, pretending to adjust her sunhat, a faint smile tugging at her lips.

"Not solving the mystery today, I guess," Jen joked, holding up a skewer of grilled shrimp from the cooler.

"Tomorrow," Carrie replied, raising her drink in mock solemnity. "We deserve at least one day off from playing detectives."

By the time the boat glided back to the pier, the golden light of late afternoon painted the river in hues of amber and pink. Their stomachs rumbled in unison, and Jen clapped her hands together. "Alright," she said, hopping off to tie the boat. "Late lunch or early dinner—let's call it both."

~ ~ ~

"Dylan, my man!" Benny's voice boomed as he strode up, patting Dylan on the back hard enough to make him take a step forward. "God, it's good to see you! What's it been, since... 2002?" Benny had arrived just in time for dinner, as usual.

Dylan chuckled, adjusting his hat after the slap. "Something like that."

Benny threw an arm around Dylan's shoulders, grinning ear to ear. "You've changed, man, turned serious. We need to fix that tonight—let's hit the bar while the ladies whip up some dinner."

He shot a dramatic wink at Tori, who was leaning against the railing with her arms crossed. "Just kidding, babe," he added, flashing her a crooked grin.

Tori rolled her eyes but smirked, shaking her head. "You're lucky I know you're full of it, Benny."

"Full of charm," Benny corrected, giving Dylan a nudge. "C'mon, let's get a head start. First round is on me."

The sound of pots clattered as did Jen and Tori's laughter from the kitchen as Carrie slipped out onto the deck, a cigarette in hand. The warm breeze carried the faint scent of charcoal and the earthly aroma of the river. She leaned against the railing, flicking her lighter and inhaling a slow drag, her eyes wandering over the golden light spilling across the yard, soon to be illuminated by fireworks in a few hours.

The creak of footsteps on the stairs pulled her from her thoughts. She turned just as Conner appeared, his familiar face stirring a tangle of memories.

"Carrie, I was hoping to find you," he announced with a small smile tugging at the corner of his mouth.

Caught off guard, Carried asked. "Conner? What are you doing here?"

He stepped closer, his hands tucked into the pockets of his faded jeans. "I heard you'd be up here. And I wanted to tell you I'm divorced now."

Carrie straightened, exhaling a slow plume of smoke. "Yeah," she replied carefully, searching his face for an answer to the questions swirling in her mind. "I heard."

Conner glanced over his shoulder toward the water, then back at her. "Can we... go somewhere to talk? Just the two of us?"

For a moment, she hesitated, her grip tightening around the railing. The way he looked at her made her heart thud faster than she wanted to admit.

"Alright," she answered finally, crushing out her cigarette on the deck's edge. "Let's talk."

At the pond, an awkward silence hung in the air. Finally, Conner broke it. "Carrie, give me another chance. I see you here with Dylan."

"We're just ..."

"And I know things got weird when you found out about Jill," Conner admitted.

"Being pregnant? Why didn't you tell me before I even started to get close to you again?" Carrie asked, clearly agitated.

"I just found out, right before I ran into you, and it was just so good to see you. I didn't want to complicate matters before we could get to know each other again," Conner replied. "We missed out on so much time."

"I guess it doesn't matter now, does it?" Carrie stated with a note of longing in her voice.

"Why?" Conner asked, looking at Carrie as if every note she would say would seal or end their fate.

"Having a child changes everything, even for relationships that start naturally. But why did she divorce you? You seem like a good father."

"I tried to be one, but Trevor isn't even mine," Conner told her.

Carrie's eyes widened. "What? Who's the father?"

"Some guy from the restaurant where she works. It's been going on for a while, I guess. Not that it matters—we hadn't been getting along for a long time."

Carrie frowned. Her confusion was evident. "But why? I don't get it."

Conner let out a bitter laugh. "I put in long hours—bidding jobs, making sure projects stayed on track. She didn't like that, so she started taking on night shifts on weekends, staying late and socializing with her coworkers. That's just how it is in the restaurant industry."

"I see," Carried responded.

"Every Sunday, I'd try to make plans—brunch, golf, anything—but she was too exhausted, always saying she didn't feel quite right. After a while, I stopped trying altogether. I think she did, too. She knew something was off between us. She felt that there was someone else."

"What?" Carrie stared at him. "Why would she think that?"

He hesitated, then looked at her with a kind of resigned honesty. "I don't know. She just sensed it, I suppose. I'm guessing Bobby told her we were sneaking around those summers here."

Carrie felt a jolt of discomfort. "But that's not true," she said softly.

"There's something about you, Carrie." He held her gaze. "You've got… I don't know, you've got that thing. A lot of men notice you. And let's be honest— you do flirt. A lot."

Her mouth dropped open. "I do not!"

He laughed, the tension breaking for a moment.

"Yes, you do. But it's not a bad thing—it's just you. It's part of what draws people in." Before she could respond, he stepped closer, his expression softening. He took her hands in his, his voice quiet but deliberate. "We're both not seeing anyone. Maybe we should see if there's something here."

They made plans to meet at midnight. Carrie's heart pounded as she nodded, torn between the thrill of the moment and the nagging voice in her head warning her of the consequences. Midnight loomed like a crossroads, promising either clarity or chaos.

CHAPTER 41

The smoky scent of sizzling burgers wafted through the air as Jen hovered over the grill, flipping patties with practiced ease. "No need for Benny to take over," she muttered to herself, a small smile tugging at her lips. She felt a swell of pride—not just in her grilling skills but in the way she'd taken charge lately. Even the boat was now her domain, and she liked it that way.

On the other side of the deck, Tori and Carrie worked in sync, slicing colorful peppers and cucumbers onto a platter. "Crudités," Tori declared with a playful flourish, as if the word itself added a touch of elegance. She whisked together a creamy dip, tasting it with a satisfied hum before setting it alongside the veggies and a bowl of pasta salad.

Benny and Dylan reappeared to find the food ready, and the deck table set with paper plates and mismatched napkins. Benny's loud laugh carried across the yard as he and Dylan climbed the steps. They were still in good spirits, their flushed faces betraying just a few beers—nothing out of hand yet.

As the group settled into their chairs, the evening

felt unusually calm. Conversation flowed easily, and laughter rippled through the air, unencumbered by the usual tension that came with too much drinking. The night promised to stay peaceful, at least for now.

After dinner, the group decided to head to Brett's for drinks and luck on the gambling machines, while others just wanted to unwind. They retreated to their rooms to freshen up and change before heading out.

Carrie brushed her hair in the mirror as there was a knock at her door.

"Come in," she called.

Dylan stepped inside, lingering by the doorway. His expression serious, his hands shoved into his pockets. "I just got a call from my distributor. There's an issue with some wood I purchased—I need to go back to my hotel, sift through some paperwork, and make a few calls." He hesitated, his voice softening. "I should be back in time for the fireworks, though." He looked at her intently, his gaze searching hers. "You do want me to come back, don't you?"

Carrie's heart skipped. His voice, his expression—both carried a quiet plea. She hesitated, the weight of the moment pressing down on her.

Dylan had his chance, hadn't he? After she left Tom, she'd been ready—hoping—but he'd pulled away. Now, there was Conner. Conner, with the undeniable pull they had to each other. She wanted to see where that could go. But still, the way Dylan stood there, his vulnerability just beneath the surface, tugged at something deep inside her.

"Yes," she finally answered, her voice hesitant. "I mean, if you can make it. We wouldn't want you to miss the fireworks."

Dylan's shoulders fell ever so slightly. His wistful smile barely reached his eyes. "Right. I'll try."

He turned and walked out, his steps slow and heavy. Carrie watched him go, her chest tightening. She knew he wanted more—needed more from her than she'd given—but she couldn't seem to say the words he was hoping for.

They arrived at Brett's at a good time. Some people were still eating dinner, while a few others were at the bar with no intention of eating. They looked around to survey the crowd, always trying to avoid Bobby and Marcy. Most likely hopeless since Bobby always seemed to be around. They spotted him standing in front of a table in the corner, making it hard to see who else was at the table. They quickly darted to the opposite end, near the machines. There were enough barstools for the girls; Benny grabbed a beer and found a machine to play his hand at.

They spotted the bartender, the new girl, serving at the other end.

"That must be the new bartender," Jen said. "Of course, he hires someone who can sport daisy dukes."

Carrie looked at Jen. "They're jean shorts. I wouldn't exactly call them daisy dukes. You're showing your age. Come on, give her a chance, we don't even know..."

The bartender turned slightly, and they could see

she was talking to Brandon. She then came towards them. It was Stacy.

"Hi Carrie, Jen. I wasn't sure if you would be here this weekend." Stacy commented while wiping down the bar in front of them. "What are you having, the usual?"

They both looked at each other, dumbfounded. Jen spoke first. "What in the world are you doing working here? And how is it possible you are still with Brandon? After that last summer, that family couldn't stand you!"

Stacy looked right at her, piercing blue eyes steady and smug. "Things change. I come up here on weekends in the summer, so I thought I would make a buck or two. I only work a few hours on Saturdays. Marcy is the one who changed her tune once Michelle was out of the picture. She needs a girlfriend to hang around with, and I guess I make her feel cool."

Carrie nudged Jen under the bar. "Good to hear. I'm glad things worked out for you guys. I take it you're not with Dodger?" Carrie replied, deciding it was best to be nice to Stacy so they could get as much information from her as possible.

Stacy put drinks in front of them and stood back with her arms crossed. "Carrie, you overreacted about that. I think you were wasted and assumed the worst. He's here, over by Brandon and Bobby. Maybe you should talk to him."

"Hmm, perhaps," Carrie said. "There were a lot of strange things that happened that night after we left."

"Yeah, I heard about the fire in Jen's trailer. Wow. Any idea who did it?" Stacy asked, looking like the cat that ate the canary as she said it.

"No, but we heard something weird about Trip," stated Carrie. Jen remained quiet and just listened. It was clear she was not fond of Stacy.

"What's that?" Stacy inquired, looking around to see if anyone needed a drink.

"That he came back and came here looking for you and pushed some Nick guy down the stairs? I guess he wound up with a concussion or something?"

Stacy let out a small laugh. "Oh sure, I heard that." She stopped and looked at them straight in the eye. "But it's not true.

"Not true?" Carrie questioned.

"Carrie, people up here lie. That's what they do. They try to make stories sound better." She walked away to help other customers.

Jen and Tori rolled their eyes. "Why you were ever friends with that woman, I will never know," Jen grumbled to Carrie.

The crowd thinned, and suddenly Carrie saw Dodger leaning against the bar with the same careless grace, the same mischievous glint in his eyes. Carrie's heart lurched as she noticed a woman, tall and elegant, with dark chocolate-colored hair, step up beside him. He smiled, that lazy, infuriating smile, and handed her a bottle of beer. Her stomach twisted. They looked so comfortable, like they belonged together.

Carrie muttered a quick excuse to Jen and Tori as she stepped outside. They didn't argue, sensing she needed a moment alone.

The balmy evening air wrapped around her as she stepped onto the porch. The river glistened under the setting sun, dotted with patrons on their boats, laughter and music carrying across the water. Crowds were gathering along the shore, ready for the fireworks. It should have felt festive, but instead, it made Carrie restless. She lit a cigarette, the glow of the flame briefly illuminating her face as she leaned against the wall.

The sound of the door creaking open behind her made her glance over her shoulder. Dodger stepped out. His expression was unreadable.

"Carrie," he said cautiously. "I saw you walk out. Can we talk?"

She turned to face him, exhaling a stream of smoke. "Sure. What's on your mind?"

Her nonchalance seemed to rattle him. He ran a hand through his hair, frustration etched into his features. "Why didn't you return my calls? Or my texts? You honestly thought I had something going on with Stacy? That I took her home that day?" His voice rose slightly, then dropped again. "For the record, I dropped her off at a store. Her friend picked her up. That's it. God, Carrie, I don't know why you were so quick to assume the worst."

She narrowed her eyes, taking a slow drag of her cigarette. "Assume the worst? You two ended up in bed together. I heard how she was all over you while I was gone, trying to get some closure with Tom."

Dodger opened his mouth to respond, but she cut him off. "It all looked pretty suspicious to me."

He sighed, shaking his head. "Same here, Carrie. We were both suspicious, both unsure of what we wanted. Maybe we just weren't ready for anything real."

Carrie flicked ash onto the porch railing, her voice cool. "Maybe not. Anyway, you seem happy now. That's what matters."

"I am," he admitted after a pause. "But Carrie, it was real, what we had."

She smiled, "I know. It was. Just bad timing."

Dodger lingered for a moment as if he wanted to say more, but instead, he nodded and walked back inside, leaving Carrie alone with the river and the night.

~ ~ ~

The friends chose to watch the fireworks from Jen's deck, a quiet refuge from the bustling crowd by the river. None of them wanted to wade into the chaos, especially knowing Bobby, Marcy, Brandon, and Stacy would be out there, camped in their lawn chairs. Fritz had shown up not long after Carrie's tense exchange with Dodger, and they were sure he'd joined the throng as well.

On the deck, the air felt calmer. The sounds of distant laughter and music floated up, softened by the steady rustle of the river. From their vantage point, they would still have a clear view of the fireworks, but without the noise and commotion pressing in around them. It was peaceful—exactly what they needed.

Benny couldn't help but notice Dylan's absence. As the only man left on the deck, he felt a moment of awareness but quickly shrugged it off. He'd always been at ease around women, even relishing the chance to dote on them.

"His loss," Benny declared with a grin. "Jen, let's head inside and whip up a batch of my new summer punch."

"I take it we're steering clear of margaritas this time?" Tori quipped, smirking at the memory of their last tequila-fueled misadventure.

"No shit," Jen agreed with a laugh. "Come on, Benny. Let's do it."

With a playful nudge, Jen led the way inside, leaving Tori and Carrie to exchange knowing smiles as they watched the two disappear into the kitchen.

Carrie's thoughts raced, pulling her in two directions at once. Where was Dylan? Why hadn't he returned like he said he would? And then there was Conner—the thought of meeting him at midnight made her stomach twist. Had she made a mistake agreeing to it?

Her spiraling thoughts were interrupted by Tori's voice cutting through the stillness.

"What's on your mind, Carrie?" Tori asked, her tone teasing. "Oh, wait—don't tell me. I can practically feel it. Here you are, in one of your favorite places, surrounded by old flames. That must be tearing you apart. And, of course, it wouldn't be me if I didn't offer my opinion."

Carrie let out a soft laugh, trying to ground herself. "Please, Tori. Please enlighten me. I'm dying to hear your take."

Tori leaned in, her gaze sharp but not unkind. "You're not drawn to love or contentment, Carrie. You are drawn to lust and intrigue."

Carrie tilted her head, intrigued. "What are you saying?"

"I'm saying you're attracted to men who are familiar yet forbidden. Look at Dylan—he showed up when you were in that disaster of a marriage with Tom. He was comforting, but there was an edge of excitement to him. Then there's Conner, your high school flame. Same story—familiar, exciting, and completely off-limits. And Dodger? He came along when you were free for once, and he gave you something you hadn't felt in years: a spark. He made you feel young, alive. But that fizzled out thanks to a so-called friend who was enabling your recklessness after Tom."

Carrie stared at Tori and paused. "So, what do I do? Who do I choose?"

Tori smiled knowingly. "Carrie, maybe you don't need to choose anyone right now."

Carrie sighed, leaning back against the deck railing. "Good advice. What about you? What drew you to Benny?"

Tori smirked, leaning in conspiratorially. "Oh, you know I couldn't stand him at first. He was messy, loud, and just so Benny. Complete opposite of me. But I realized that's exactly why I needed him. I'm too uptight, too rigid. He balances me out. We have fun together. Plus, he has his own life and career, which gives me space and time for myself."

Carrie raised an eyebrow. "But isn't that how it was with Drew? You two were apart a lot."

Tori's smile softened. "Yes, but there's a difference, Carrie. Benny always comes back."

Carrie pondered her words as Dylan walked up the stairs to the deck.

"Hey angels." Carrie's heart pounded as he set his backpack down on the deck.

"Great, you're back in time for the fireworks," Jen responded.

They watched the fireworks in comfortable silence. The girls sat together on the deck chairs, while Benny and Dylan stood nearby, beers in hand, casually talking about sports. The display wasn't much—just a modest show of roadside firecrackers that Larry had provided for the guests. A few other resort guests added their backyard-style fireworks, scattering bursts of light across the sky. By 10 p.m., the pops and crackles had faded, leaving the night quiet once again.

Benny stretched, tipping his beer toward Dylan. "What do you say we hit The Edge? See if they've got a band tonight."

Dylan nodded, a grin tugging at the corner of his mouth. "Always good to spread the love between both bars, right?"

The girls stayed behind, opting to tidy up the trailer before deciding whether to join the guys. Carrie, however, felt the clock ticking. She had only a couple of hours before her secret meeting with Conner, and the thought made her stomach churn. She felt nervous about what Jen and Tori might say—or how they might look at her if they found out she was meeting him.

As Dylan lingered by the door, he glanced back at Carrie. His expression shifted, a flicker of disappointment crossing his face as if he could sense her distraction. Still, he remained hopeful, giving the group a quick, "See you there," before heading out with Benny.

Carrie's thoughts were muddled as she watched him walk out the door. The night wasn't over yet, and she wasn't sure how it would end. She entered the kitchen, the scent of lingering summer punch still thick in the air. Jen was already at the sink, wiping down the counters.

"Let me help," Carrie offered, grabbing a stack of rinsed glasses.

"Thanks," Jen replied, her voice a little tight. "We should hurry if we want to meet Benny and Dylan at The Edge."

Carrie paused, the glasses slipping slightly from her grasp. "Are you sure you want to go there? Fritz might be there."

Jen released a heavy sigh—a weariness Carrie recognized. "I can't avoid the only bars within walking distance. Besides, tomorrow's our last night. We should spend it together, don't you think?" She looked up at Carrie, her eyes searching. "You're coming, right?"

Carrie hesitated. "Actually, I'm meeting Conner. He's coming by at midnight, and we're going for a drive."

Jen's face fell. "What? Carrie, why?"

Carrie met her gaze, a flicker of uncertainty in her own eyes. "You're the one who told me last year I owed it to myself to see if there was something between us. Now he's divorced."

Jen managed a wry smile. "Yes, but he has a child. That makes a big difference, especially since you don't exactly adore kids."

Carrie felt a familiar pang of defensiveness. "Trevor isn't his son. Michelle got pregnant by some other guy."

Jen's eyes widened. "Well," she replied with a slow smile spreading across her face. "That changes things."

CHAPTER 42

Carrie sat on the porch steps of the trailer, the cool metal pressing against the back of her legs. The others were at The Edge, probably playing Photo Hunt, but she couldn't focus. The air felt charged and heavy with anticipation, as if the night itself was holding its breath.

She glanced at her phone: 11:59.

Then she saw it.

The unmistakable sweep of headlights cutting through the darkness, casting long shadows across the lawn. A pickup truck rolled up the gravel drive, its engine purring low and steady. Carrie's pulse quickened as the car came to a stop, and the driver's side door swung open.

Conner stepped out, the dome light briefly illuminating his face before he shut the door. He leaned casually against the car with his hands in his pockets, as if he wasn't sure whether to approach or wait for her. The faint glow of the headlights bathed him in a soft, golden light, making the moment feel surreal.

Carrie stood, smoothing the fabric of her dress

as she descended the steps. She walked toward him slowly, each step crunching against the gravel.

"You always did like making an entrance," she said, stopping a few feet away.

Conner smirked, the kind of smile that held a thousand unsaid words. "And you always liked sneaking away at midnight."

Carrie tilted her head, trying to hide the way her heart was racing. "Did anyone see you?"

"No," he said, his voice low. "But even if they did, I don't care."

The tension between them felt electric as they stood there, caught in the moment. Conner stepped closer, his eyes never leaving hers.

"I wasn't sure if you'd come out," he admitted.

Carrie shrugged, though her voice betrayed her calm exterior. "I almost didn't."

"But you did." His voice softened, as if the weight of those three words held everything unsaid between them.

The sound of voices approaching made Carrie glance over her shoulder. Her friend's chatters sounded heated, as if something had happened at the bar. She stood for a moment contemplating whether to wait for them or leave with Conner. She decided to avoid drama.

Carrie quickly turned back to Conner, her voice barely above a whisper. "We should go."

Conner nodded, opening the passenger door for her. She hesitated for only a second before sliding inside, her heart pounding. As Conner rounded the car to get to the driver's seat, the sound of hurried footsteps broke the quiet.

"Carrie, wait!" Jen's voice called out, sharp and urgent.

Carrie froze, one foot still inside the car. She turned to see Jen running toward her, Tori and Benny trailing behind, their faces tense.

"What is it?" Carrie asked, stepping out of the car. Her pulse quickened—not from anticipation now, but from dread.

Jen stopped a few feet away, catching her breath. "You need to hear this."

"Hear what? What happened?"

"It's about the fire," Jen told her, her voice barely above a whisper, as if saying it too loudly might make it worse.

Carrie felt her chest tighten. "What about it?" she asked, her voice wavering.

Jen glanced at the others before locking eyes with Carrie. Her voice dropped, serious and measured. "We know who started it."

A hush fell over the group as they instinctively moved to the deck. Conner lingered near the far railing, his hands in his pockets, while Dylan leaned against the opposite side, arms crossed, his gaze flickering between Conner and Carrie.

Jen exhaled deeply. "Here's the story. We were all playing Photo Hunt, and the bar was shoulder-to-shoulder. Dylan went to get refills, and while he was waiting at the bar, he overheard something. Go ahead, Dylan."

Dylan's expression darkened as he pushed off the railing. "Behind one of those wooden pillars, Stacy and Marcy were sitting together, talking. They didn't see me standing there because it was so crowded. But I heard them, clear as day."

He paused, his voice lowering. I heard Marcy say, "You're taking a big risk working here this summer. I'm glad to have you here, and so is Brandon, but what if someone finds out that you and he went to Jen's trailer that night—and left a candle burning?"

Carrie's breath hitched. "She said that?"

Dylan nodded grimly. "Yep, and then Stacy responded, saying she wasn't worried, because no one saw and they didn't know for sure what started the fire."

"And Marcy?" Carrie inquired, her voice tense.

"Marcy told Stacy that her secret was safe with her." Dylan hesitated, his gaze shifting to Conner. "Then they started talking about you."

Carrie's stomach churned. "Me?"

"Marcy brought up Conner," Dylan replied, his jaw tightening. "She said she wants to see what he's up to. She agreed to let him come here because she likes him and because his ex-wife had hurt him pretty badly. Then she said that Carrie needs to be put in her place.'"

Carrie's fists clenched at her sides. "And Stacy?"

"Stacy tried to calm her down," Dylan continued, "telling her that Conner is single and so are you."

Jen folded her arms. "Dylan heard it all. They might have been careless, but there's no question Stacy and Marcy know something about the fire—and they were deliberately targeting you, Carrie."

Carrie's head swam, her emotions a chaotic swirl of anger, hurt, and confusion. She looked at Conner, whose face was unreadable in the dim light.

"What now?" she asked, her voice barely above a whisper.

Conner finally spoke. His tone was steady but calm. "We confront them. Together."

The group returned to The Edge, the bar's dim lighting casting long, unsettling shadows as they approached. Stacy and Marcy, oblivious to the brewing storm, chatted and laughed in a corner booth.

Jen, Carrie, Dylan, and Conner went ahead, with Tori and Benny hovering nearby. Jen slid into the booth, displacing Marcy.

"Mind if we join you?" Jen asked, her tone deceptively calm.

"What's this about?" Marcy demanded, annoyance edging into her voice.

"We need to talk about the fire," Carrie sharply

declared. "And about what you two have been saying behind our backs."

Stacy protested, "We don't know anything about the fire."

"I overheard you, Marcy," Dylan interjected. "You told Stacy her 'secret was safe' – about the candle at Jen's trailer."

Marcy bristled. "You're twisting my words! I didn't mean it like that."

"Then explain it," Carrie insisted, her anger rising. "Because it sounds like you and Brandon might have had something to do with it."

"It was an accident!" Stacy exclaimed, attempting to defuse the situation. "Brandon and I were there, but we didn't mean for anything to happen. We thought the candle was out."

"You thought?" Jen snapped back. "You destroyed my trailer! You could have hurt someone!"

"It wasn't just the candle!" Marcy barked, frustration evident. "The wiring in that place is ancient. It could have been anything!"

Conner stepped forward. "Stop deflecting. You've been targeting Carrie all weekend. What's your problem with her?" he asked coldly.

Marcy spat out, "She thinks she's so perfect, always turning heads, stealing attention. First Dylan, now you. It's pathetic."

"You're the one obsessed with tearing people

down," Carrie countered, her voice trembling with fury. "If you want to blame me for your insecurities, go ahead. But this is on you, Marcy."

"Stop!" Stacy pleaded. "We didn't mean for any of this to happen. We were trying to find a place to be alone. We didn't mean to be careless." She turned to Carrie. "I told her to leave you and Conner alone. I didn't want any of this!"

"Don't turn on me now," Marcy spat back, anger simmering in her eyes. "You're just as guilty as I am."

~ ~ ~

It was late by the time they returned to the trailer after the tense confrontation. The group trudged inside, the weight of the evening's drama pulling them into a heavy silence. Carrie lingered by the truck, her eyes on Conner as he leaned against the driver's side door. Inside, Dylan moved to the window, his silhouette framed by the dim light as he tried to catch a glimpse of their exchange.

"I'm sorry we didn't get to go for our ride," Conner said, his voice low but sincere.

Carrie crossed her arms, hugging herself against the cool night air. She had hoped for something—a moment to hold onto, a midnight kiss to punctuate the chaos of the day—but now wasn't the time. Too much had unraveled, and too much still hung in the balance.

"Neither of us needs more drama tonight," she

replied, her tone tinged with regret.

Conner studied her, his expression softening. "We don't have to do this tonight, Carrie. But I'd still like to see you tomorrow. Maybe we can start fresh?"

Her lips curved into a faint smile. "Tomorrow sounds good, but I have a feeling it's going to be anything but fresh."

Conner frowned, waiting for her to elaborate.

She sighed, glancing toward the trailer. "Bobby's going to lose it once he finds out what happened tonight. There's no way this blows over quietly. If I know him, it'll be a full-on explosion."

Conner nodded, his gaze steady. "Then we deal with it when it comes. Together, if you need me."

Carrie's throat tightened, and she struggled to find the words. She wasn't used to someone offering to stand by her without expecting something in return.

"Thanks," she whispered.

Conner stepped closer, his hand brushing her arm lightly. For a moment, she thought he might kiss her, but he pulled back, respecting the space between them.

"Goodnight, Carrie." He softly touched her arm.

"Goodnight." She watched him climb into the truck. The headlights flared to life, casting long shadows across the yard as he drove away.

Inside the trailer, Dylan stepped back from the window, his jaw tight. He hadn't been able to hear what was said, but he didn't need to. The tension in Conner and Carrie's body language spoke volumes.

Carrie lingered outside for another moment, letting the cool air calm her nerves. When she finally stepped inside, all eyes were on her. The room was thick with unspoken questions and quiet judgment, but she ignored it, heading straight for the kitchen to pour herself a drink.

Tomorrow was coming fast, and she had no idea what it would bring.

CHAPTER 43

A sharp knock abruptly awakened Carrie. She groaned, rubbing her eyes as she glanced at the clock, just after 7 a.m. The door creaked open, and Jen stepped inside, her face etched with worry.

"Carrie, I need to talk to you," Jen said, her tone quiet but urgent.

Carrie stretched, blinking herself awake. "Okay, give me a minute. I need coffee."

She shuffled into the living room, pausing when she spotted Dylan sprawled on the couch, sleeping soundly. She tiptoed past him, mindful not to wake him, and joined Jen in the kitchen, where the aroma of freshly brewed coffee filled the air.

Jen handed her a steaming cup, already mixed with cream. "Thanks," she muttered, taking a sip as Jen led the way out to the deck.

The early sunlight bathed the deck in a golden glow, a stark contrast to the heavy mood Carrie sensed was building. She dropped into one of the weathered chairs, cradling her mug.

"God, Jen, what's so important that we're up this early?" Carrie asked, her voice groggy. "I feel like we just went to bed."

Jen hesitated, biting her lip. "It's about Fritz."

Before Carrie could respond, the screen door creaked open, and Tori's head appeared. Her hair was disheveled, and she squinted against the morning light.

"What's going on?" Tori mumbled, stepping out with a cup of coffee in hand. "Why are we up so early?"

Jen exhaled, motioning for Tori to join them. "I need to talk to you both."

Tori sank into a chair, her curiosity outweighing her exhaustion. She cradled her mug and eyed Jen expectantly. "This better be good," she moaned, half-joking.

Jen's usual easy-going demeanor was absent. Instead, she seemed tense, her hands gripping her mug tightly. The early morning sun might have been warm and inviting, but the atmosphere on the deck was anything but.

Carrie exchanged a glance with Tori, their silent communication saying everything: Whatever Jen had to share, it wasn't going to be small talk.

Jen's hands trembled as she gripped her mug, her knuckles white. She drew in a shaky breath and finally let it out, her voice breaking.

"It's about Fritz," she began, her words heavy with guilt. "I've been carrying this for so long, but it's too painful to say out loud. The night of his accident.

It was my fault."

Carrie and Tori exchanged uneasy glances, but neither interrupted.

Jen stared down into her coffee as if it held the courage she needed. "We were at one of his friends' parties. There was a lot of drinking—shots, beers, you name it. Fritz was throwing them back like water. When it was time to leave, I told him not to drive. I begged him. He was so drunk, but he wouldn't listen. He kept saying he was fine, that he could handle it."

Her voice cracked, and she paused, blinking back tears. "I should've fought harder, but I was drunk too. I wasn't thinking straight, so I got in the car with him."

Jen's grip on the mug tightened, her words rushing out now. "We were on this dark road when a deer ran out in front of us. He swerved, and we hit the ditch. Hard. He wasn't wearing a seatbelt, and he," Jen paused. "He went through the windshield."

Carrie gasped softly, her hand covering her mouth.

"There was blood everywhere," Jen whispered, her voice barely audible. "I'll never forget it. He was unconscious for I don't even know how long. I thought he was dead. But I had my seatbelt on, so I was fine. Physically, at least."

She finally looked up, her eyes shimmering with unshed tears. "That's why Fritz is the way he is now. Slow. That's why he has seizures. Because of me."

Tori reached out, placing a comforting hand on Jen's arm, but Jen pulled away, shaking her head.

"And then... I broke up with him," Jen added, her voice choked with shame. "I couldn't handle it anymore. Seeing him like that, knowing it was my fault—it was too much. How selfish of me. I left him when he needed me most."

Carrie and Tori exchanged a look before rising to their feet to embrace Jen. Their arms wrapped around her, a quiet solidarity forming as Jen's shoulders shook under the weight of her tears.

"It's not your fault, Jen," Tori said gently, her voice steady and soothing. "You tried to stop him. You can't control what someone else does, no matter how much you want to."

Carrie squeezed Jen's hand. "And leaving him doesn't make you a bad person. You were dealing with so much yourself, Jen. You didn't mean to abandon him. You just—" she hesitated, choosing her words carefully, "you needed to survive."

Jen sniffled, her tears now flowing freely. She looked between her friends, her voice trembling with a mix of pain and release. "I don't even care about the fire anymore," she muttered, almost as if the words surprised her. "I don't want this trailer. I don't want any of it. There are too many memories. Too much pain."

Her voice cracked on the last word, and she dropped her head into her hands. Tori rubbed her back in slow circles, while Carrie knelt in front of her, meeting her eyes.

"Then let it go," Carrie said softly. "If it's too much, let it go, Jen. We'll help you."

Jen let out a shaky breath, her tears subsiding as a glimmer of relief began to pierce through the storm of emotions. The three of them stayed like that, the quiet morning sun warming the deck around them as they silently reaffirmed their bond.

"Thanks, guys," Jen replied, her voice steadier, though her eyes were still red. She took a deep breath and managed a small smile. "Well, let's get ready. There's bound to be some fallout from last night's confrontation."

With a shared sense of resolve, they headed inside to start breakfast. The scent of coffee lingered in the air as the morning sunlight filtered through the trailer windows.

Dylan was awake, sitting on the couch, rubbing his eyes. He looked up when they entered and immediately noticed the tension hanging over them. Rising to his feet, he looked at Jen.

"What's wrong, Jen?" he asked softly, placing a reassuring hand on her back.

Her composure cracked as she let out a shaky wail. "It's all a mess, Dylan," she cried, her voice thick with emotion. "Bobby will be here soon, and all hell's going to break loose—the fire, last night— everything. I can't handle it anymore. I don't even want this place anymore!"

Dylan gently squeezed her shoulder and calmly told her, "Hey, it's okay, Jen. We're here for you."

Tori came over and handed Jen a fresh cup of coffee. "We'll face Bobby together. You're not alone in this."

Just then, Benny walked into the room, awoken by the conversation, looking disheveled. "That's right, Jen, we'll face Bobby together!"

Jen nodded, her lips trembling as she tried to hold back tears. Carrie joined them, a spatula in hand, and gestured toward the stove. "Breakfast first," she said with a gentle smile. "Let's face one mess at a time."

~ ~ ~

They all sat on the deck, enjoying a Bloody Mary that Jen and Carrie had concocted, when Bobby drove up in his golf cart, with Marcy at his side. His face flushed with anger, eyes darting sharply toward Carrie and Jen.

"Care to explain what the hell is going on?" Bobby demanded loudly. He got off the cart, edging toward the deck.

Jen stepped forward, crossing her arms. "We're talking about the fire, Bobby. About what Stacy and Marcy might have had to do with it."

Bobby's glare pinned her in place. "You're accusing Stacy? Are you serious? What gives you the right to drag her into this mess?"

Carrie, standing beside Jen, took a step forward. "We overheard Marcy talking. She admitted Stacy was there that night with Brandon, and they might have left a candle burning."

"You don't know what you're talking about," Bobby shot back, his voice rising. "Stacy's not reckless like that, and she sure as hell wouldn't do anything to hurt anyone!"

"Then why would Marcy tell Stacy that her secret was safe?" Dylan interjected from the side, his tone cutting.

Bobby whirled on Dylan, his hands balling into fists. "You're always sticking your nose where it doesn't belong, Dylan. You don't have the slightest clue about my family, so stay out of it."

Jen interjected, her voice sharp and unwavering. "Your family? Bobby, this isn't just about your family. This is about my trailer, my property, and the safety of everyone here. If there's something you know, now's the time to say it."

"Something I know?" Bobby scoffed. "I know that Carrie's been working her way around all weekend. First, with Conner, then Dylan, and now this. What's your game, Carrie? You have to have everyone's attention?"

Carrie's cheeks flushed, but she held her ground. "Don't make this about me, Bobby. We're trying to figure out what happened, and Marcy and Stacy aren't exactly innocent."

"Of course you'd say that," Bobby sneered. "Anything to deflect attention from you and Conner sneaking around. You think I didn't notice? Marcy told me everything."

The air grew heavier with the weight of his accusation. Carrie's mouth opened to respond, but Dylan stepped forward, his voice steady and low.

"Funny," Dylan said, his tone biting. "You're quick to act so righteous, Bobby. But you've got secrets of your own."

Bobby's head snapped toward Dylan, his face twisting in anger. "What the hell are you talking about?"

Dylan crossed his arms, his gaze steady. "How about the time I caught you in the bar basement with another guy? Should I remind everyone about that?"

The lawn seemed to hold its breath. Marcy's face drained of color, and a collective gasp rippled through the group. Bobby's jaw clenched, his hands curling into fists.

"You son of a—" Bobby lunged at Dylan, shoving him hard. The table between them tipped, spilling drinks and food onto the grass. People scrambled to their feet, chairs scraping against the ground.

"Stop it!" Marcy shrieked, grabbing at Bobby's arm. "Bobby, stop!"

Carrie darted forward, placing herself between the two men. "Enough!" she shouted, her voice trembling. "This isn't solving anything!"

Conner appeared out of nowhere at Bobby's side, gripping his arm firmly. "Back off," he said, his voice calm but unyielding. "You're out of control."

Bobby yanked his arm away, turning on Conner with a sneer. "Stay out of this, Conner. You're just here sniffing around Carrie like everyone else."

The crowd froze. Carrie's face turned bright red, but before she could respond, Jen's voice rang out, sharp and commanding.

"Everyone, stop! We're supposed to be adults!"

But Marcy wasn't finished. Her face was flushed with anger as she jabbed a finger toward the group. "How dare you accuse my husband of being gay? And then turn around and blame Stacy for the fire? You people are unbelievable!"

Before anyone could respond, Brandon and Stacy appeared from behind the crowd, tension hanging heavy in the air. Brandon cleared his throat, his voice surprisingly calm. "Hey, everyone. Look, I know you've heard that Stacy and I went to the trailer that night." His face filled with remorse as he pressed on. "Yeah, there was a candle, but we don't know if that's what caused the fire. It could have been something else."

All eyes turned to Stacy, who stood silently beside him. She avoided everyone's gaze, her shoulders hunched with guilt.

Carrie felt her anger boil over. She stepped forward, her voice trembling with a mix of rage and frustration. "It's not just about the fire. We've just discovered the truth about Bobby. He's gay, and you've been hiding it!"

The words hit like a thunderclap. Marcy's expression shifted from shock to fury in an instant. "You little slut!" she shrieked, and before anyone could react, Marcy lunged forward and struck Carrie across the face, full fist, the blow landing squarely on her eye.

Chaos erupted.

Tori surged forward, shoving Marcy back. "What the hell is wrong with you?" she yelled, her voice cutting through the noise.

Stacy's eyes narrowed and her jaw clenched as she stepped forward. Without hesitation, she swung her fist, landing a sharp punch to Tori's face that sent her staggering backward, her coffee spilling onto the deck.

Stacy's punch had Tori stumbling, and Benny's entire body tensed as he watched the scene unfold. "Oh, no. That's not happening," he muttered, his voice low and dangerous.

In one swift motion, he closed the distance between them. His hand shot out, gripping Stacy by the arm as she prepared to swing again. "Back off!" Benny barked, his tone sharp and unyielding. He yanked her away from Tori, spinning her around to face him.

Stacy struggled against his hold, her free hand

clawing at his shirt. "Let me go, Benny!" she snarled.

Benny didn't flinch. "You think you can just hit people and walk away?" he growled. With a firm push, he sent her reeling backward. Stacy stumbled, colliding with the edge of a table, a startled gasp escaping her lips.

His chest heaved as he stood between her and Tori, his protective stance clear. "Touch her again, and you'll have me to deal with," he warned her.

Tori straightened, fury blazing in her eyes, but before she could respond, Benny surged forward, his face dark with rage. "Oh, hell no!" he growled as Stacy went in for another hit, shoving her back with enough force to send her crashing into a nearby chair.

"Enough!" Dylan finally roared above the chaos. He stood between them, his hands raised. "This has gone too far! Everyone needs to calm the hell down before someone gets seriously hurt."

Marcy turned to Bobby with a look of rage in her eyes. "So our marriage was just a lie?!" She yelled with fury.

He smirked, brushing her hair back. "Come on, baby—you think a gay man could make you scream like that for ten years straight?"

She smiled through her tears as he took her arm and gently guided her away from the group. "Come on," he said, "let's get out of here." As they walked off, Bobby glanced back over his shoulder and shot Dylan a smug, almost sinister smirk.

Dylan looked at Carrie, Jen, and the rest and shrugged. They all thought the same thing-he must be bisexual.

~ ~ ~

An hour later, as the group packed up their belongings, the weight of the weekend's events hung heavy in the air. The trailer, once filled with laughter and chaos, now felt eerily quiet. Carrie folded a sweatshirt into her bag, glancing at Jen, who moved robotically, her expression distant.

A sharp knock on the door broke the silence. Jen froze, her hand hovering over a stack of dishes. Everyone exchanged wary glances before she sighed and walked to the door.

It was Dodger.

His usual demeanor was gone, replaced by something somber, almost hesitant. "I need to tell you something I just found out," he said, his voice low.

Jen stepped aside, gesturing for him to come in. The others watched cautiously as Dodger sat down at the kitchen table. His hands fidgeted in front of him, and for a moment, he stared at the surface as though gathering the courage to speak.

"Fritz told me something," Dodger began, his tone uneven. "Something about the night of the fire." Dodger swallowed hard as everyone stared at him. "Fritz said he came to your trailer that night. He was upset about you, Jen. He thought maybe he could find you here, and talk to you. He knew where you kept the spare key, so he let himself in."

Jen's hand flew to her mouth, her eyes wide.

Dodger continued. "He said the place smelled like someone had been there before him. He noticed a candle burning. Must've been after Stacy and Brandon were there."

The room crackled with unspoken tension—the weight of the words settled in the silence.

"He started looking around," Dodger went on, his voice strained. "Said he found a box of photos—pictures of other guys. He thought..." Dodger hesitated. "He thought you were moving on without him. It made him angry, so he kicked the candle, and the fire started."

The room fell silent.

Jen sank into a chair, her face pale as she processed the confession. "He started it," she whispered, more to herself than anyone else. "He really started it."

Dodger nodded, his expression heavy with guilt. "He didn't mean for it to get out of hand. He wasn't thinking."

Carrie reached out, placing a hand on Jen's shoulder. Tori, standing near the door, shook her head in disbelief.

"He should've come forward sooner," Tori responded bitterly.

Jen let out a shaky breath, her voice trembling. "Why now? Why is he telling you this now?"

Dodger sighed, rubbing the back of his neck. "I don't know. Maybe he's finally realizing he can't run from it. Maybe he thought you deserved to know."

"It doesn't matter. This place is gone for me. But I forgive him."

~ ~ ~

The late afternoon sun cast long, shimmering fingers across the river as Carrie and Tori stood on the pier, the roar of speedboats still echoing in the air. Riverbanks, a haven for thrill-seekers and weekend warriors, never truly slept, not even on Sundays.

Jen's trailer, a relic of countless summer escapades, sat nestled amongst other trailers. The rattling of boxes packed with treasures and memories filled the air.

"It's going to feel strange," Carrie sighed, the weight of nostalgia settling heavy in her chest. "So many memories here."

Tori, ever the cynic, couldn't resist a jab. "I'll miss the drama."

A truck rumbled to a stop, and Conner emerged, a look of melancholy across his face.

"I'll leave you alone. I have to head out anyway." Tori hugged Carrie and whispered in her ear, "Remember our conversation."

"Just wanted to say goodbye," he began, looking back at the trailers, "And… I'm sorry."

Carrie raised an eyebrow. "For what?"

"For everything. The chaos. Bobby, Marcy, Brandon. We were friends at one time, and they caused a lot of grief for you and everyone else."

She chuckled, a rueful sound. "You can't control other people's actions, Conner. You're a good guy."

"Thanks," he replied, a flicker of a smile gracing his lips. "Can I maybe call you sometime?"

Carrie hesitated, the image of Dylan waiting impatiently a short distance away flashing through her mind. "Sure," she finally agreed, the word barely a whisper.

Dylan appeared at the edge of the pier. "Ready to go, Carrie?"

"Yes," she replied, her gaze lingering on Conner for a moment longer. As she turned to leave, a strange sense of anticipation mingled with the sadness of farewell. The river, once a symbol of freedom and escape, now only carried memories of misunderstandings, turmoil, and sadness. Yet there was a flicker of hope that maybe saying goodbye was for the best.

EPILOGUE

The snow fell lightly and cracked under Carrie's boots as she walked downtown with grocery bags in hand. She had moved to a small apartment to experience more of the city's hustle and bustle. It provided inspiration for her writing. She still ran her cleaning business but had scaled it down, giving her more time to write.

Carrie had recently redecorated her apartment with thrift store finds, giving it a boho look. She put her groceries away and made herself a cup of tea. As she sat in her favorite chair, sipping her steaming cup, she opened her laptop to work on her memoir.

A buzz on the counter distracted her as she glanced at it. A text from Jen:

Jen: My new creation. The collection is growing! Call me when you can. A photo of a gorgeous beaded necklace accompanied the text.

Carrie smiled. Her heart warmed at the thought of Jen's resilience. Despite everything, Jen had sold the trailer as she'd promised, and was settling into a new life herself. She was expanding her jewelry stores with the proceeds from selling the trailer and had even begun designing her own pieces. They spoke often, their friendship one of the few threads Carrie had chosen to hold onto.

Her phone buzzed again.

Tori: I read your article. It's fantastic! Keep up the good work. See you this weekend.

Tori was accompanying her to an open mic book reading in the art district, and she hoped Jen would make it too.

Carrie scrolled down and peered at an older message that she had not responded to.

Stacy: I hope we can still be friends. I miss you

She was not ready to go there. Too much had happened, and although she apologized many times and swore nothing had happened between her and Dodger. Carrie believed her, but couldn't shake the sense of recklessness and her disregard for others' feelings.

Another buzz followed—a name she hadn't seen in weeks.

Conner: Just thinking about you. Hope you're happy.

Carrie stared at the message for a moment before setting the phone down. She wasn't ready to answer that one, either.

She turned back to the window, exhaling deeply. For the first time in a long time, she felt free of the constant desire to be wanted or needed. This was her time. Time to figure out who she was, without Tom's mental and physical abuse, without Dylan's easy charm, Dodger's ability to please her and make her feel young, or Conner's steady intensity and mystery.

She pondered for a moment and sent off a text.

Still planning on coming to New York with me?

Dots appeared instantly, showing he was responding.

Dylan: Absolutely! You have to see it before you move, although I don't want to let you :(

Carrie and Dylan remained friends, but who knew what the future held?

The snow continued falling, blanketing the town in a peaceful silence. Carrie stared out the window, reflecting on the past and how it brought her to this point of contentment. A smile formed on her face as she found solace in the stillness.

She didn't know what the future held, but for now, that was okay. She chose herself.

ABOUT THE AUTHOR

Jacqueline Miller is a debut novelist born and raised in Milwaukee, Wisconsin. Her lifelong love affair with books, which began in childhood, ultimately inspired her to write her first novel, Secrets Revealed.

This book is drawn from the carefree yet chaotic summers she spent as an adult along the Wolf River. The river's powerful currents and the vibrant, often unpredictable life on its banks provided the perfect, energetic setting for her debut novel.

When she's not immersed in her writing, Jacqueline embraces her love for the outdoors. She can often be found kayaking the rivers that inspired her work, taking long rides on her bicycle, perfecting her swing on the golf course, or simply reading books sitting outside and enjoying the Wisconsin air.